Cattle Kate

Books by Jana Bommersbach

The Trunk Murderess: Winnie Ruth Judd
Cattle Kate
Bones in the Desert
A Squirrel's Story: A True Tale

Cattle Kate

A Novel

Jana Bommersbach

Poisoned Pen Press

Copyright © 2014 by Jana Bommersbach

First Edition 2014

10 9 8 7 6 5 4 3 2 1

Library of Congress Catalog Card Number: 2014938562

ISBN: 9781464203022   Hardcover
      9781464203046   Trade Paperback

Poisoned Pen Press
6962 E. First Ave., Ste. 103
Scottsdale, AZ 85251
www.poisonedpenpress.com
info@poisonedpenpress.com

Printed in the United States of America

I dedicate this book to Bob Boze Bell
and *True West* magazine—

I'm still dancin' with the guy who brung me.

Acknowledgments

I don't know where I most loved writing this book:

On my mother's garden patio in Hankinson, North Dakota; at Maxine Beckstrom-Atkin's tropical apartment in Fargo, North Dakota; on Gail Adams and Jay Goodfarb's high-rise balcony in Coronado Island, California; on Mary and Denis Perret's veranda in Ocean Beach, California; on Mary Margaret and John Sather's porch overlooking Sedona, Arizona; in the guest apartment at Mary Wills and Sally Dryer's home in Jerome, Arizona; in the back seat of Marge Injasoulian and Barb Hanson's Explorer to and from New Orleans, or in my messy home office in Phoenix. But I loved writing this book.

My friend, Gail Adams, instantly recognized the importance of this book and gave me the boot now and then to keep me going. Barbara Peters of Poisoned Pen Press was a strong voice encouraging me to expand into fiction. Bob Boze Bell and Meghan Saar of *True West* magazine were unwavering in their support. My first cousins Jerry Tomayer and Debby Davidson were fabulous hosts as I researched in Rawlins, and their son's family—Josh, Sara, and Allysa Tomayer—gave me shelter and encouragement during my research in Laramie.

Kevin Anderson at the Western History Center at Casper College was terrific. Wyoming historian Tom Rea was invaluable help, as was Rans Baker from the Carbon County Museum. Carbon County Clerk Lindy Glode and Deputy Clerk Mary

Oaks uncovered long-lost records that delighted us all. Gregory Kocken at the American Heritage Center in Laramie went out of his way to help me—and this center is a must for anyone researching the American West. At the Wyoming State Archives, Carl Hallberg and Jim Allison were great. I found insightful research material at the Fort Caspar Museum and help from Michelle Bahe, curator of collections. Kristi Baxley turned me on to the Rawlins Main Street Project and the public mural on the lynching. The staff members of the Kansas Historical Society were very helpful. And I'm forever indebted to all the historians and writers who spent years of their lives trying to correct history.

Thanks for the excellent and thoughtful editing and constant encouragement of my longest Arizona friend, Athia Hardt. My thanks are boundless to Kristian "Magic" Nordhaugen for saving this book when my computer crashed. Thanks to the encouragement from my writing students at Phoenix College, the Board of Directors of The Friends of the Phoenix Public Library, my friends at Taliesin, the Southwest Authors Association and the 2013 senior class of Phoenix Country Day School.

Thanks to my friends for always being there, especially Tommy Martinez; Nan, Dave, and Tina Robb; Estelle MacDonald; Cathy Eden; Jim and Linda Ballinger; Adrienne and Charles Schiffner; Stella Pope Duarte; Ide Flores; Marge Rice; Ann and Tim Cothron; Mary Lou Shreves; Mary Anne Grimes; Richard Stahl; Mel Reese; Bob Hegyi; Bill Sheppard; Range Shaw; Cousin Ann Claudio; Brady, Shaun, and Oliver Breese; Katie Moore; Rose Prince; Perri Krom; Carole Weitzel; Sharon Austerman; Gayle Gerard; Anne and Tony Sammons; the late Kenny Smith; and the guidance from fellow writers Pam Hait and Shelia Grinell.

A most special thanks to my mother, Willetta "Willie" Bommersbach, who has always been my best critic and my best cheerleader; to my sister Judy; my brother Gary and his wife Susan; and my brother Duane and his wife Jeanette. Having a supportive family makes all the difference in the world.

How do you thank the fabulous crew at Poisoned Pen Press who lovingly and diligently made this book better than I ever dreamed? Founders Robert Rosenwald and Barbara Peters have set a very high bar for the books they publish, and it was a dream come true when they chose *Cattle Kate*. Thanks to Jessica Tribble and Pete Zrioka, who cared for this book like it was their own. And to my editor, Annette Rogers—where have you been all my life? Every writer should be blessed with an editor this fine and this talented. She made this novel sing.

Part One

My Surprising Life

Chapter One

I Can't Believe This

I never thought I'd die like this.

There's a bucketful of ways I could go. Snake bite. Thrown by Goldie. Shot by a cowboy. Trampled by a steer. Freeze to death. Drown in the river. Come down sick. Maybe an Indian attack, but this is already 1889 and I think the fight has been beat out of them.

I never thought I'd be hanging here at the end of a rope.

Not strung up like a side of beef. Not twisting and bucking and bumping into my Jimmy as he hangs by his own rope. His sad eyes begging forgiveness, like this was his fault.

Not lynched in a lonely canyon in Wyoming Territory on a pretty Saturday afternoon when I should be getting supper ready.

I'm still not believing it. This can't be happening. This can't be the end already. I know they'll come to their senses and cut us down. They have to!

No, I am not going to die like this. Not after I just turned twenty-nine.

I'm going to die proper. An old lady, tucked under a quilt in bed with my people all around me. Jimmy's wrinkled hand holding mine. Years and years of happy memories. My feet tired from all the dancing I did.

I intend to have a full life. I've worked hard for it. I've risked so much for it. I have too many plans. All my dreams!

I'm going to have children.

I'm going to be a happy grandma.

I'm going to reveal I'm Jimmy's wife.

I'm going to prove up my claim.

I'm going to become a citizen.

I'm going to celebrate when we're finally a state.

I'm going to see Gene grow up.

I'm going to dance at the fandango.

I haven't even been to the Opera House yet. I saved the beautiful hair comb Jimmy gave me, and a woman can't have something so dear and never get to wear it.

I will die listening to my cattle bellowin', like they had a complaint, which is the way a cow always sounds. I will die with the feel of their wirehair hides. I will die smelling their musty scent that town folks can't stand. I will die satisfied, because to me that is the sound and feel and smell of freedom.

When I die, our Homestead Certificates will be proudly framed on the living room wall, telling the world this land is ours and we worked five long, hard years to earn it.

Ma and Pa will be buried back in Kansas by the time I die. I'll fill in Ma's Bible with their dates, just like I've done with all our losses over my lifetime. *Oh God, I can't die before my Ma. She already lost seven children. It would kill her to lose me, too.*

They say that when you die, your life flashes before you in an instant, but I had it going into the future instead. I thought about all those things the seconds after that man finally got a rope around my neck.

And that's when it got through my thick skull: Ella Watson, you might really die out here today.

Oh, my God, I'm being strangled by a cowboy's rope!

If I had ever imagined this, the rope would come from some deranged bandito or dirty lowlife—someone who'd take my life like he was stealin' eggs from the henhouse. Who could imagine it would be these men?

That man sat at my roadhouse dinner table braggin' about my pies. *That* one got his mail from Jimmy every week. *That* one had me sign a petition for a new county. *That* one praised my sturdy corral.

Now here they are, these pillars of the community—liquored up, hootin'—pretending they're going to let me and Jimmy die. They're trying to scare us—alright, I'm scared. And mad. And more than done with this nonsense.

Sure, they're cattlemen and we're homesteaders and that's like oil and water. But somebody has to stand up to them. My Jimmy and me are standuppers.

But now it's getting us killed!

If they think I'll go peaceful-like, they're getting the surprise of their lives. I'm kicking and swirling and jumping and scream-ing like the Texas Rangers will hear me and ride in any minute.

I'm kicking so hard, I just kicked off the beautiful beaded moccasins I got this morning—they went flying, and now my feet are in their stockings and I'm kicking still.

"This is what cattle rustlers get in Wyoming Territory."

Just heard those words, but this isn't about rustling. We all know what's really going on here. And any second now, some-body is going to get his head on straight and put an end to this.

I'm certain we'll be saved.

By the end of this day, I'll be back in my kitchen. I'm making an extra special supper tonight. You bet I am! I've got to make up for all the pain and suffering we've been through this afternoon.

My Jimmy deserves a great big, juicy steak. I've got fresh peas from the garden and I'll stew them in real cream. I'll make his favorite pie. Rhubarb.

I'm going to eat like a pig until I bust my skirt button. I deserve it.

It's not every day a woman has to fight off a lynch mob that doesn't have the sense God gave a goose.

No, I didn't live this life to end up lynched by a vigilante mob. So STOP IT, RIGHT NOW!

Chapter Two

They First Called Me Franny

I took to the henhouse like I was a fox.

Even when my legs were chubby little stumps that waddled more than walked, I headed for the henhouse whenever I had a chance.

They called me Franny, just like my mother before me and my grandmother before that. If you went back to Ireland, you'd find people who'd tell you that great-great-great-Grandma had carried the family's favorite nickname, too.

"Franny, Franny, Franny, answer Mother, ELLEN LIDDY. Where. Are. You?" I loved the sound of my mother's voice, even when she was yelling. But I was busy with the hens and the eggs and when you're still in diapers, you can't focus on more than one thing at a time. Ma found me in the chicken coop, and I was surprised she was crying. So I held up the speckled egg as a present, but my pudgy fingers held too tight and before I knew it, yellow yolk and slimy white squished through my fingers. That, of course made me cry, and Ma's cry turned into a laugh.

"Oh, wee one, you'll be the death of me yet." She kissed me all over my face.

From then on, Ma said she knew to always check the henhouse first when she couldn't find me. So of course, that's where Uncle Andrew came looking the day my parents went off to get married.

"Your Ma said I'd find you here." He gathered me up in his lumberjack arms. My little arms couldn't even reach around his thick neck, but I loved being held by my Uncle Andrew. He was my first special friend. I was the only baby in the house and I got all his attention. I just loved that he was mine. And it was that way the seventeen years I lived in Canada.

Eventually, I'd piece it together—I had to figure it out myself because nobody wanted to tell me. I'd hear little things here and there. A snide comment or a sentence that was supposed to be secret. One day, I was about ten, it finally started to make sense.

What telling there was came from Uncle Andrew. Usually with hesitation, usually with a positive spin on everything. But he never could deny me anything. So over the years, I coaxed the secrets out of him. He always made me promise not to tell my Ma, and he didn't have to worry, because this wasn't the kind of news you want to confront your Ma with.

My birth was a family scandal. I can just imagine my Grandma wailing and my Grandpa swearing and my uncles threatening revenge when it turned out that my fifteen-year-old Ma was "in the family way" without a wedding band on her hand. It wasn't even a good Irish boy, but the Scottish farmer down the way. Boy, that really made it awful. I don't know why my Irish grandparents couldn't stand Scottish people—or why my Scottish father's people detested the Irish. Uncle Andrew said it went back to the Old Country.

"I've never had much use for that kind of hatred," Andrew told me one day when we were out in the field and nobody could hear him telling me family secrets. "Your Pa wanted to marry Frances right away, you got to know that. Yes, he did. But his Pa wouldn't hear of it. He threatened to disown Thomas and ban him from the family. I thought your Pa would…well, it's a terrible thing to lose your family, so they didn't get married right away." It was the only time I ever heard disappointment in my uncle's voice when he talked about my father.

"I was the logical one to take Frances in while she waited for you to be born." He answered the first part of my question. "It wouldn't look right for her to stay with Da and Ma, not being in the family way," was the answer to part two. "I already had my small farm, the one you first remember. Frances and I have always been real close, and I wouldn't let anything hurt her."

"So she was hiding at your place?" My uncle winced and said I shouldn't think of it that way. It was just best. But I knew I was right.

"Remember the day I found you in the henhouse and we spent the whole day, just us?" Of course, I remembered it. Because at the end of the day, my Ma and Pa came riding up in a carriage and they hugged me for a very long time. "That's the day they went off and got married. And your Pa was real proud to take his family home to his house that night."

I cried when I had to leave Uncle Andrew. But the new house had a nice crib Pa said he made for me, and a stone fireplace where I could play and always be warm, and that's where we lived for the next few years.

"I love Uncle Andrew," I announced one day when Ma was sewing and I was playing with my doll.

"So do I. He's my special big brother."

I'd never have a big brother, and I felt cheated. When I got older and asked questions every day, I asked Ma why Uncle Andrew was so special.

The stories she told me only made me yearn even more for a big brother of my own. I wondered if I'd ever find anyone who'd take care of me like Andrew took care of my Ma.

"It was Andrew who took the blame when I set the barn on fire," Mother confided. "He still carries the scars on his arms. Da whipped him good for the fire, and I cried all the time, knowing it should be me. But he told me to stay quiet, and he took all the blame on himself. I was about eleven then, and he was fifteen, and I knew right then that I could count on him for anything."

Almighty! To have somebody take blame for you. I had no idea how that felt.

"But even the fire wasn't as big as how he saved me when I was thirteen." Ma lowered her voice and leaned toward me to share a secret that only women should know. "I got my first time of the month when I was in school. I didn't know that I'd leaked through my dress, but Andrew saw it and he pulled me out of school, carefully walking behind me so no one could see. I would have died if anyone had seen my soiled dress. I was even embarrassed that Andrew knew, but he said to me 'that's what a big brother is for.' I was so grateful to him."

I cringed at the shame of bleeding through your dress, but my Uncle Andrew grew even higher in my esteem for knowing how painful that would have been for Ma.

"And he was the first one to know Pa, wasn't he?" I could see my question bothered Ma.

"Yes he was," was all she wanted to say about it.

But Andrew told me how he saw them talking together at the Mercantile one day when they'd gone into town for supplies. "Oh, the way your Pa looked at your Ma. They say sometime there's love at first sight, and this was one of those times." Then Andrew saw Pa's buggy down by the stream near the home place, and he added it up real quick.

"Did you like my Pa?" I asked Andrew.

"Oh sure. I liked him right off. But I knew they'd have problems, this Irish and Scot thing, you know. I just didn't know it would get that bad. I told her, 'Himself will never permit it, and I hear Old Man Watson is a hardass,' but of course, they were in love and none of that mattered to them. I thought it might help that we aren't even Catholic, but it didn't. The only thing your grandfathers had in common was that they hated the British even more than they hated each other. But that didn't do your folks one bit of good."

"So you tried to talk them out of it?" I wasn't sure how I felt about that.

"Franny, remember this. When you come from people who have nothing but each other, family means everything. That's what held people together in the Old Country, where nobody had anything because the Queen and her lords owned all the land. Our people could only rent, we couldn't call any land our own. So when the Queen offered free land in Canada for homesteaders, everyone jumped at the chance—well, everyone who could afford the fare over on the ship. It took years to save up. And sometimes families were split up because there wasn't enough to cover the fares for everyone. I bet every family in this county has folks back home still waiting to come over. So the importance of family becomes even more important when you've gone to a new country to start over. You see how all your uncles have farms around Da and Ma's. Well, your Pa's people are like that, too. People want to stay with their own. That's why me and Molly are right here, close to the home place."

"Molly is an Irish girl, isn't she?"

My uncle nodded. "I wouldn't have married anyone but an Irish lass."

I could see why. But I also knew I had two parents from different backgrounds and they loved each other and they loved us kids, and I wouldn't want to trade either one of them.

I never, ever knew my Grandpa Watson. Or Grandma Watson, either. I didn't know my Pa's brothers and sisters. I didn't know my cousins on his side. Those people wanted nothing to do with me or my parents, and I guess as far as they were concerned, we didn't exist. It was the opposite with my Ma's people. I loved my Grandpa and Grandma Close. There were lots of cousins and uncles and aunts.

I don't know much about Scottish people, but Irish people are a lot of fun. They love to dance and sing and play jokes on each other. They love big suppers and delicious food. They like to sit around the table and talk. They treat their children like gold.

That's how I felt growing up. I never told anybody I knew the secret. And I never once, in all my years, felt that anybody ever treated me different because my birth had been a scandal.

My Uncle Andrew was my special friend—"'Tiss me, woman," he'd croon as he gathered me up in his arms for a kiss.

But Grandma Close was the most precious to me.

Grandma was the best chicken-killer in all of Canada.

She wasn't a very big woman, either in height or weight, but she could swing an ax like she was a lumberman. With such grace and ease, it could have been an Irish jig.

I have lots of other fond memories of my mother's mother. She always cut her bread against her titty. And she never cut herself, either. She was a sort-of-singer. She sort-of remembered the melody. She sort-of remembered the lyrics. When it became hopeless, she'd just hum like she was singing the right words to the right tune. And while everyone else laughed at her, I thought it was wonderful that you could go through life singing your own song.

But mostly I remember how Grandma Close killed a chicken.

First, of course, she had to catch a chicken. Now, chickens are pretty dumb—not as dumb as turkeys, but close cousins—and Grandma was convinced a hen could tell if you'd walked into the coop to pick her eggs or to pick her for your Sunday dinner. And if you had the chopping block on your mind, she'd run around that coop like she was already a chicken with her head cut off.

Grandma could snatch a chicken quicker than you could blink, and she just ignored the squawking and jerking as she carried it out of the hen house feet first. As she walked to the chopping block marked with dark stains, she picked up the ax with her free hand. And then in a move that could have been set to music, she flung that hen's head down on the block while she swung the ax in an arc that cut it clean off.

She'd throw the chicken on the lawn. It always amazed me how that headless hen kept jumping around, spraying blood everywhere.

"Stand back, Franny," she'd yell so I wouldn't get all bloody.

She never knew, but I had no interest in touching a headless chicken that didn't know it was dead.

Grandma got a big pot of water on the boil, and after that chicken finally gave up, she grabbed it and dunked it into the scalding water. She swished it around so the feathers got all soaked. Wet feathers have a smell of their own. Nothing in the world smells like it. I could be blindfolded in a cave somewhere and I'd know if someone was scalding a chicken. Anybody who's ever smelled it knows what I mean. Anybody who hasn't, can't imagine.

Grandma Close's hands had to be like iron because chicken feathers straight from the pot are very hot, but she hardly waited before plucking those feathers. She'd leave a few on to cool off so I could pluck too, but really my job came after all the big white feathers were off and I picked out the pinfeathers.

"Be very careful, Franny, because nobody wants a pinfeather in their fried chicken."

"I'll be careful, Grandma."

She always double-checked that I hadn't missed any.

Since then, I have always killed my chickens exactly like she did. And I never cleaned a single chicken in my life without remembering that precious woman.

◇◇◇

The first time I ever heard my parents fight was the day we learned that President Lincoln had been shot.

I was almost five and when I saw Mother crying, I thought something bad had happened to somebody in our family.

"No, no. It's the president who freed the slaves."

My mother wasn't making much sense. But her grief over a man she never knew made her pick a fight with my Pa.

"See, I told you you were wrong to think of moving to the States. Imagine if I hadn't stopped you. Taking your family to a country in the middle of a civil war? What were you thinking? That wasn't a war. It was a slaughter of young boys. How many mothers are grieving their boys so old men can play war? I want no part of a country like that. They throw their sons away like they don't count, and then they kill a fine man like Mr. Lincoln. I'll not have my babies growing up in a country that could do that. Shoot him. In front of his wife. A southern man, probably had slaves—they'll never get over that war, you know. Never. No, I want no part of it. And the Indians…" but she never could go on with that thought out loud.

My Pa just listened and hung his head, like he'd done something wrong. He'd suggested moving to another country to get away from his awful family, who treated Ma like dirt whenever they saw her. She wouldn't hear of it then, and now when she cried over President Lincoln, she let him know she'd never hear of it.

"We have a good life here, Father, and I don't want you thinking about anything else. Our boys will take over this farm one day and our girls will marry nice Irish boys from here." I saw my father smart at her declaration that his sons-in-laws would all be Irish.

It took me a long time, and some good lessons in school, before I realized all my mother was saying.

I don't know how they taught it in the States, but in Canada, the American Civil War was taught as a lesson to never do that again.

"America went to war with itself over slavery," our teacher told us as she began our history lesson about our neighbor to the south. "When President Lincoln was elected, southern senators feared he would interfere with their slaves, and so they threatened to leave the union. They wanted to keep their slaves. They said they needed them to harvest their cotton and keep the plantations working. Northern senators said it was wrong to hold another human being in bondage."

I thought the northern senators were right.

"But nobody could see how bad that war would be. The North was strong and the South was weak. They thought the North would win so fast, that after the first shots in April, they predicted the war would be over by Christmas. But they were very wrong. The Civil War dragged on for four years. And it killed so many soldiers. Most of them were young men."

Ma's rant about the senselessness of it all made sense to me now.

"But some say it was worth it because President Lincoln freed the slaves. The war had just ended when President Lincoln was shot while he was watching a play in a theater in Washington."

"What did the Indians have to do with the Civil War?" I asked Teacher one day, remembering how Ma was so afraid of them.

"Nothing that I know. Why?"

"Well, my Ma was so sad when President Lincoln died, and she and Pa had words that day and she ended with talking about Indians, so I always wondered what they had to do with it."

Teacher promised to look into it, and came back a couple weeks later with news that showed me exactly why my Ma didn't like Indians.

"I'm sure your Ma was upset over the Sioux Uprising in Minnesota. That happened during the Civil War. The Indians went on the warpath and killed a lot of settlers who never did them any harm. It was horrible. They hanged a whole bunch of the Indians."

It sounded awful to me. I was a grown woman in Wyoming Territory before I learned there was another side of the story. The Indians fought back because a horrible Indian Agent was starving them. His famous words were "Let them eat grass." They wanted to hang about every Indian man they could find, but President Lincoln stepped in. Still, they hanged thirty-eight Sioux. I wished Ma had known the whole story, but I bet even if she had, she'd have said that was no excuse to kill and scalp innocent people. And I have to agree.

◇◇◇

My first brother was born in November of 1861, and even though my Pa had been thrown out of his family, he followed tradition and named his son after his father. Grandpa Watson never saw his namesake. I've often wondered if his heart would have been softened by a boy when it hadn't been by a girl. But we'll never know because Grandpa Watson died in 1872. Like he'd promised, he made no mention of my Pa in his will. It was like my Pa had never been born. That was the first time I ever saw Pa cry.

By the time little Johnny was three, I had fallen in love with Darby.

I called him "my pony," even though he was already an old horse. But he was a new horse to me and for my entire life, every new horse has been "my pony." Even my beloved Goldie, years later in Wyoming Territory.

As far as workhorses went, Darby was just fine. He was short and stout, gray with patches of brown. He had a skinny tail, one blotch of black on his right leg and a nick out of his left ear. He was no beauty to anybody but me. I liked the way he smelled and how his tail flicked back and forth and up and down. I liked how his nose felt so smooth. I liked how his hide tickled my little fingers. I heard my Pa brag, "She's a farm girl, alright. You'll be hard pressed, Mother, to keep her in the house."

My Ma was as good at hitching Darby as Pa was, and she was often in the barn helping out, and I thought of her as a farm girl, too. That didn't stop her from showing off in the kitchen and the garden and at the quilting frame. My Pa was a strong man who was a good farmer. But if you put him in the kitchen, he would have burned the house down. No, my Ma could do just about anything, anywhere on this farm. I wanted to be exactly like her.

◇◇◇

Mondays were wash days for Ma. She always said that after a Sunday of rest, it was best to get the worst job of the week out of the way. First, of course, she had to build a fire in the backyard, where she stored the tin tub for rinsing and her black iron kettle for washing (it did double-duty for making lye soap). Pa hauled wood for the fire—when Johnny got old enough, this was his first real chore. Thankfully, Ma had a well. Some women had to haul water from a stream, but we had it so much better. Ma taught me to use a fourth-cake of soap for each batch—eventually the family would be so big, we'd need a whole cake for each—and she washed the whites first, the coloreds second, the work britches and rags last. After stirring and scrubbing on the washboard, Ma would rinse everything out and hang the wash on the line that stretched from the house to the big oak tree. It was under this tree that Johnny and I played to stay out of the way.

Ma used the rinse water on the garden, with a special splash on the roses she was trying to grow. Soapy water cleaned the porch. By the time all this was done, so was most of the day, and I remember my Ma was more tired on Mondays than any other day of the week.

It's no wonder she lost track of me one day when I was supposed to be watching Johnny under the tree. But when I saw she was busy, I snuck off to the barn to see Darby. I was just going to pet him, but once I got there, he was standing by the stall wall and well…if I climbed up on the hay bale, I could reach the first log of the wall, and then I could climb up to the top log and get on top of Darby.

Usually, Pa lifted me up and led Darby around so I could have a ride. But Pa was out in the field and Ma was busy with her wash and Darby looked like he wanted to take me for a ride. It never occurred to me that once I got up on him, there wasn't much to keep me there. I could hold onto the mane, but my little legs couldn't even stretch to both sides of his back, so I just slid around on him as he moved. This didn't frighten me. It was a jolt of joy!

The first Ma knew what I was up to was when she saw me and Darby come out of the barn. If she hadn't screamed, we'd have probably just walked around the yard. But her scream scared us both. I turned to look. Darby took off.

Ma said later that she saw me flying off the horse and breaking my neck. She saw a small coffin and me all laid out in the white pinafore she was still sewing. She saw Uncle Andrew destroyed by grief. She saw Pa and Grandma Close and Grandpa Close and all her sisters and all her brothers and everyone in the world screaming, "Why weren't you watching her?"

But that didn't happened.

I realized right away that I had to hold on—HOLD ON— and snug my legs as best I could to stay on top. Darby didn't buck or anything, he just ran for all he was worth and it was a smooth, loping ride once you got the hang of it. I got the hang pretty quick. But then there was that little gully that Pa had built over with a wooden bridge—just four planks, really, with one length of board doing the trick. Darby dashed toward that gully and ignored the bridge like it wasn't even there and when he jumped—JUMPED—he did it in one fluid motion that made my tummy flutter. I'd never felt that before. I liked it. Darby and I landed solid on the other side of the gully and then—they don't call it horse sense for nothing—the animal realized it was time to tone it down. He slowed his gait considerably, ending up in a slow walk as I continued the laughing wail that started with the first leap forward.

"Darby, oh Darby, that was so much fun." I was giggling and patting my pony in pride and it took a second for me to hear the screams coming at me from two sides. From the house, Mother was running and tumbling over herself, her skirts hiked up to let her run. From the field, Father was running like a sprinter, his hat blown off by the wind he was creating. Back under the oak tree, little Johnny was crying and wetting his pants.

Pa reached me first and pulled me off the horse in his sun-burned arms. Ma was there a second later, crying and scolding and laughing and crying and scolding and telling Pa, "I just turned my back for a minute." Darby looked at the family with his big, brown eyes, and if he could have talked, I know he would have said, "I wasn't going to hurt her."

Pa patted him on the side of his neck and said, "It's all right, Darby. It's all right." Then he gave me a big swat across my behind. Then Ma spanked me too. I started to cry.

Ma picked me up to carry me back to the house. "Don't you ever do that again. Do you hear me? You could have been killed. You can't ride off on Darby by yourself. Do you hear me?"

I heard her. But Pa came home the next week with a little saddle. "You're just going to encourage her," Ma protested. "The girl had no idea she was in danger. I don't want her to be a scaredy cat, but I don't want her to be reckless, either. She's got to learn you can't take off without understanding the consequences."

But my Pa knew there'd be a repeat performance someday, and it was safer for me to ride on a saddle. That was the best gift he ever gave me. Until later, when he gave me the gun for my homestead in Wyoming.

◇◇◇

If Ma ever needed proof I was her tintype, it was when her labor came early.

I was in charge of two brothers now. John was four and James was one, and they were a handful. John always wanted to climb and James had just discovered he could follow his brother on his shaky legs. I was forever chasing after them. I was rounding them up, once again, the morning Mother came out on the stoop and shot off the rifle into the air. Twice. All three of us stopped in our tracks and stared at Mother. She was doubled over, holding herself up by the arm of the rocker. It scared me. It made little Jimmy cry.

I ran to Mother, my brothers following. "Mama, Mama, what's wrong? Should I get Pa?"

"Pa is in town, but Mrs. O'Malley will be here soon."

"Should I run get her?"

"No, she'll come. She knows the signal."

"Ma, what's wrong?" I was crying now and more scared than I'd ever been because it seemed like Ma couldn't stand up and certainly couldn't walk.

"My water broke. Our baby is coming. Help me to the bed."

I had been so happy knowing a baby was growing in Mother's stomach, but now that happiness turned to fear and I changed my mind and decided I didn't want a new baby at all.

"It's going to be all right, Ellen."

Mother only used my given name when she wanted to be serious.

"By tonight, we'll forget all this and we'll be laughing with our new baby. Just like when we got Jimmy. Now, you be my big girl and help me get ready."

I couldn't remember anything like this happening when Jimmy was born, but then Pa and Mrs. O'Malley were both there, and maybe that made the difference.

Katie O'Malley was twice in age and size of my Ma, but she knew everything there was about birthing a baby. Sure enough, the two-shot signal brought her hightailin' it into our yard.

I'd later learn she had been trained as a midwife by her own Ma back home in Ireland. She liked to say "us rural girls learned birthing and baking while town girls learned linen and lace."

"Now, there's nothin' to cry about," she clucked at my brothers who were crying on the front porch. "Your Mama's gonna have a baby, that's all. And while you wait, look what I brought you. It's a molasses cookie and I heard those Watson boys just love molasses cookies."

They did, and the cookies shut them up.

"Franny, I need your help," Mrs. O'Malley said over her shoulder as she marched right into the bedroom to check on Ma. "Get me all the towels you have and pile them on the table."

Mrs. O'Malley came out and grabbed the biggest pot she could find—it was more a bucket than a pot—and ladled water from the crock next to the sink. She stoked up the fire in the cast iron stove and put the pot on to boil. She used one smooth motion, like she'd done it every day of her life. As the pot was cooking, with all the towels stacked on the table, Mrs. O'Malley took the last cookie out of her pocket and handed it to me.

"Now child, you did real good getting me those towels, but now I need you to go out and watch your brothers."

"But Ma might need me…"

"Yes, your Ma needs you to mind your brothers. She's gonna be busy having this baby."

"I hope it's a girl, I already have brothers."

"I hope so too, but right now she wouldn't want anything to happen to her other children, would she?

"No, ma'am."

"Fine. Now, you might hear your Ma yell, but that's just part of bringing a baby into the world and it's nothin' to worry about, so don't get upset if you hear her yell some. And when you hear a baby cry, you'll know you have a little brother or sister."

"I don't want another brother. I want a sister."

"Sure you do. Now outside with you and watch those boys."

It seemed like we sat there forever before I hear Ma's first cries of pain. I closed my eyes, hoping the pain wasn't bad. More cries. More. I was holding my breath, praying for the cries to end. And then I heard a new noise. A little cry. My new sister!! I wanted to run in, but thought better of that and knew Mother would send Mrs. O'Malley to get me. And then, there was a second cry—a very different cry. It didn't sound like it came from the same baby at all. I was very confused now—the boys were busy with the last crumbs of their cookies and they weren't paying any attention at all. I couldn't wait any longer.

"You stay here and don't you move from this stoop," I barked at them and ran into the house. Outside the bedroom door, I called out to Ma, and Mrs. O'Malley yelled back, "Just a second, honey, just wait outside a second."

The minute Katie O'Malley opened the door, I flew into the room, stopped short, and stared. There in Mother's arms were two babies. They were so red, I thought somebody had smeared them with raspberry jam. And they were so small—half the size I remembered Jimmy being.

"We have twins," mother announced. "That means two babies born at the same time. They're both girls."

I could hardly contain my glee—not one, but two sisters all at once! I slowly walked toward the bed, smiling at the little red girls and gently touching one tiny hand and then another. It amazed me that you could have two babies at one time. Even Bessie in the barn only had one calf at a time. But here were two new sisters. I was crying with joy.

"What will we name them, Ma?"

"We'll wait on Pa for that."

"Come on, now, lass, let's let your mother rest. She's had a busy day. We'll go outside and let her sleep. You can tell your brothers."

The unnamed babies died within a few hours. One after another. Pa wasn't even home from town yet when it was all over. My heart was broken. I had two baby sisters. And now I had none.

By the next morning, the house was filled with neighbors who brought hot dishes and biscuits and cookies for us children. Ma was so heartbroken she could barely get out of bed. Pa was upright, but he spent most of his time in the barn. He was making the coffins.

I took charge of the boys and the house, because I had to take my mother's place.

"Thank you for the cake, Mrs. Adams."

"Thank you for the stew, Mrs. Hardt."

"This is beautiful jam, Mrs. Ballinger."

"Thank you for the bread, Mrs. Beckstrom.'

"Fresh eggs, how nice, Mrs. Hanson."

"Mother is asleep."

"Mother will see you now."

Now and then, I would go off to the corner of the living room and stare into the fireplace and cry for my dead sisters. I had wanted a sister so badly. I had hoped we'd name her Judith Ann, because I thought that was such a sweet name for a first little sister. A sister would even up the odds with the boys. They already had their own little club with their own little secrets, and I didn't like being left out. And then for a split second, I had *two* sisters and that meant there were more girls than boys! It was like having two living dolls of my own, because I was going to be right there at Mother's side to help every day. But then they were taken away and I had never felt a hole inside me like that.

But most of the time, I was busy doing what Mother would want. I was puzzled by the people who kept coming, always with something in hand. We'd been to a church picnic and seen most of these people, but few had ever been inside our home until now. I was glad they were here, but I wasn't sure why they'd come.

I asked Mother as we curled up together one morning.

"They're being good neighbors," Mother explained. "If one of them had trouble like this, you and I would be there helping them. Remember when we went to the Lehnis' house when Julie was so ill? That's what it means to be a neighbor. You're there to help. Remember the birthday party we had at Mrs. Cother's? And the christening for that darling Christina? We were there to celebrate. That's being a good neighbor, too. You're there in good times and bad. Especially bad."

I would never forget that.

◇◇◇

I prayed for a girl again when Mother got pregnant the next time, but Andrew came instead in January of 1868. By then, John and I were in school two miles away, a one-room schoolhouse that would eventually enroll six of us Watson kids. Father helped build the wooden structure—how fun the roof-raising party was!—and then had built most of the desks. Mr. Specht showed off his fine woodworking skills with the teacher's table, and someone donated the potbellied stove that kept us warm in the winter. For many years, I thought all schools looked like this.

I was a good student, better at reading than math, better at history than geography. I helped my brothers with their homework and even tried, unsuccessfully, to teach my parents to read. "That's why we have children we send to school," Father joked.

"Ellen, read us a story." Pa often requested that after he put down his fiddle after dinner. I always reached for the one book I was allowed to carry home, a history book that told the proud stories of how Canada came to be. And then Pa would tell us children how his family and Ma's family had come here on big boats, looking for a better life. Some nights he'd tell how terrible the passage over was, being stuck down below, where it was hot and stinky and where you couldn't get a breath of fresh air. But on those occasions, Ma would shush him and say that was just the price they paid for this new life.

Now and then, Ma would hand me the family Bible to read out loud—the only book the family ever owned. It was in this book that I recorded the dates and memories of my family. Mother would recite the dates and I would inscribe them with a neat hand.

There was only one time I paused, the pen already dipped, wondering if Ma really wanted me to write it down. That was when she recited her wedding date as May 15, 1861. My own birthday was July 2, 1860.

I looked up at Ma and she looked away.

"You can't lie in the family Bible," she said.

Neither one of us ever spoke of it again.

In that Bible, I recorded John's birthday on November 5, 1861. Jimmy's on October 10, 1864. Andrew's on January 6, 1868. Frances' on October 9, 1869—this girl now wore the family nickname of Franny, which I was more than ready to give up because it is a little girl's name. Annie's on September 20, 1872. Mary's on May 12, 1874.

The only dates that weren't recorded with certainty were the deaths. "Just put down 1865 for the twins, that's enough," Mother said. So in 1873 when another set of twins—this time a boy and a girl—also died, I didn't even wait for Ma to instruct me on the Bible notation. Nor did I wait in 1875 when two of the triplets died instantly, although I left a space to put in the exact date—June 12—in hopes Elizabeth would survive.

All six babies were buried, side by side, near a tree by the pasture, with plain crosses standing vigil.

Ma spread wildflower seeds around the graves and in the spring, they bloomed in profusion.

Chapter Three

I Agreed with Pa

We hardly ever got a letter, nobody did, so every one was a big occasion.

When one came from the Old Country, women carried it around in their apron pockets and read it aloud to everyone around them—or had me read it, if they couldn't, which was most of the time. It didn't matter that their neighbors didn't know the people in the letter, news from back home was news, and it was shared.

I wish I could say those letters were filled with joyful news of relatives who might someday come here and join their kin—the dream of them all, for all those left behind—and sometimes, it was. But more often, it was a letter of sorrow because someone they already missed and would never see again had died. By the time I was seventeen, I'd read more death letters than I'd ever thought I'd read in my entire life.

"With great sorrow, I must tell you Mother Rose has gone to her eternal reward."

"It is with a sad heart I write that Father Leo died in May."

"Our precious Grandma Peterschick passed away."

But sometimes there was happy news: "Mr. and Mrs. Shaheen had a beautiful baby girl they named Megan."

"Our Gracie is engaged to the nicest Stahl boy from the next village."

"The crops were so good, cousin Jay took on another section for next year."

"Everyone here is fine, thank the Lord."

I had to read the whole letter real quick to know which kind it was, so I'd know what voice to use as I read it out loud. And I was as overjoyed as they were when I could announce, "Oh, this is a happy one!"

They say it's the women who treasure letters from home, but that isn't true. I think the men cherish them even more. Those pieces of paper would be in tatters before a man would retire it to the family Bible or the keepsake box or wherever their family kept their precious things. I've seen grown men who couldn't read a word, just sitting there staring at a piece of paper from someone back home they loved. Here in Bruce County, Ontario, everyone shared every word of every letter.

But the letter from Bruce MacDonald was different. I saw the anxious faces of my parents when I opened the envelope and told them there was both a letter and a story cut out of the newspaper. "From who, from who?" Pa asked anxiously, and then their faces lit up when I looked for a signature and told them it was from Mr. MacDonald.

"He's a real good friend," Pa explained, and Ma added, "His wife was in my quilting circle."

"Dear Tom and Frances," it began, and I wondered when you were old enough to call adults by just their first names. "Estelle and I are settled. The trip was trying but we made it in one piece. There is good land here."

My father leaned back on his chair as he listened to those words and my mother's hand cuffed her mouth. Pa looked up at her. "There's good land," is all he said.

She shook her head. "Ellen, read what else."

"Somebody must be writing this for him," I told them, as the next words made that clear, and they both shrugged because they knew their friend couldn't read or write so they'd already figured that part out.

"Read, read," Pa pushed, and I knew that if he could read himself, he'd have already devoured the words that came in this envelope.

"Mr. MacDonald wants me to tell you that if you come, he will scout out a claim for your family. He says that is all I need to write and you will understand, but Mrs. MacDonald wants a few words, too," it read.

Pa laughed then, "Just like Bruce," and Ma smiled in agreement.

"Frances, this is a good place," the message from Mrs. MacDonald began. "Very different from home. People are nice. All kinds. I had a boy in February."

Ma exclaimed with delight, "After five girls, she has a boy! Oh, I know how happy she must be." Pa was smiling, too, and guessed correctly that the child would carry his father's name.

Mr. and Mrs. MacDonald might be people of few words, but the letter-writer wasn't, and so she added her own message:

"We have been happy to welcome the MacDonald family into our community in Pawnee Township, Smith County, Kansas. I can report everyone is in good health and prospering. I believe you will like Kansas, and don't listen to the bad stories about us, because all that is far away from here. This part of Kansas is already Dry. We are God Fearing people. From what they tell of your family, we would be proud to have you in our community, which is growing. I am a neighbor and can read any letter you return." Then she signed it "Mrs. Duane Heytens on behalf of the MacDonald family."

Pa was on his feet by now and he reached out to Ma like he was asking her to dance and she scoffed, "Oh, Pa," but she was laughing. For a second, I actually thought she would dance with him right then and there. It made me want to laugh myself. I'd watched my folks at barn dances and they could really raise the dust, but here, in our kitchen? Not the right place for a dance, and that's what Ma decided as she shooed Pa away. But they kept looking at each other like there was a message trying to get through, and then they remembered the newspaper.

"What does the paper say?" Pa asked, and I unfolded the gray paper and read to them the stack of headlines that spread halfway down the page: "Homestead Act of 1862. Free Land a Rousing Success. 160-acre Promise a Magnet. From Here and Abroad. Flocking to the West."

The news was finally getting through to me, and I looked up at my parents and thought, "They can't possibly…" but the wonderment on my father's face told me they could.

"Read it all, read it all," they said, and so I read them the article that changed all our lives.

During the Civil War, when the southern congressmen went home, northern congressmen finally passed a bill that had been blocked for a long time. It did for America just what Queen Victoria had done for Canada. And that wonderful President Lincoln had signed it into law.

"The Homestead Acts provides that any adult citizen, or intended citizen, who has never borne arms against the United States government, can claim one hundred sixty acres of surveyed government land," the article said. "Claimants are required to improve the plot by building a dwelling and cultivating the land. After 5 years on the land, the original filer is entitled to the property, free and clear, except for a small registration fee. Title can also be acquired after a 6-month residency, provided the claimant pays the government $1.25 an acre."

"How much is that?" Pa asked, although if he hadn't been flustered he would have worked out the numbers in his head himself.

My brother John, who was always looking for Pa's favor, chimed in real quick: "That's two hundred dollars, Pa."

Pa looked at Ma. She shook her head as if saying, that's-too-bad, and Pa returned with, "Five years is not so long."

I knew right then that no matter what objections my Ma could find, Pa would find an answer and we were going to Kansas.

She started right off. "That law came in years ago. By now, all the good land is gone."

Pa was right there to remind her that Mr. and Mrs. Mac-Donald had only moved on three years ago, "and he says there's still good land and he'll help us with the claim."

"We've got a nice life here, with good people around us."

Pa reminded her the lady who wrote that letter had gone out of her way—"out of her way, Mother"—to say how welcomed we'd be by new friends.

"Don't they call it 'Bleeding Kansas'?" Obviously, some busybody neighbor lady was feeding my Ma information. Pa didn't have an answer.

I did, because we had a lesson on the big, powerful country we bordered. "That was a long time ago, before the Civil War," I told them. "Before I was born. When Kansas was still a Territory. But it's been a state for years now." Even Ma had to admit that ancient-history bleeding didn't count anymore.

"My family is here," Ma argued, but she knew that wouldn't carry much weight. Uncle Andrew and Aunt Molly visited regular, but most of the others were only on holidays or funerals.

"What if the Indians go back on the warpath?" Ma declared one day. In unison, Pa and I assured her that would not happen. I don't know if he crossed his fingers behind his back, but I sure did.

That letter arrived in January of 1877, and Ma kept up her objections for two months.

It was a strange time in our family because we weren't used to seeing Ma and Pa on different sides. They always seemed a team to us kids—if one of them disciplined us for something, there was no use seeking refuge from the other. If one of them decided we were changing our regular schedule, the other never contradicted.

The time I most remember that teamwork was after our first day of school when Miss Theede came to teach us. She was the third woman we'd had in our schoolhouse by then. I was twelve and already reading pretty good, but I'd learn more from her than all the others combined.

Miss Theede had a big blackboard at the front of the room behind her table, and when we walked in, she'd already drawn on it a big map that showed Canada and the northern part of America. Then she'd swiped the chalk across the board to signify the Atlantic Ocean and on its far side, she had some strange shapes.

"This is a map of the world and today we'll get to know one another by learning where we all came from," she told us in her melodic voice. I liked her right away. But I was most fascinated by the map. Nobody had ever shown me a map before and even blank as it was, it looked like a lot to know.

"Let's start with you." She pointed to the overgrown boy who was new to the school and sat in the very back, because if he sat any farther up, he'd have blocked the view. "Tell us your name and your father and mother's names and where they originally came from."

The boy looked scared and when he opened his mouth, I knew why. "M-m-m-m-my name is Olaf Lar-lar-larson," he stuttered and there were snickers throughout the room. "M-m-m-my Far is Sven Lar-lar-larson." Some laughs now. "M-m-m-m-my Mor is L-l-l-lena." And now we all were laughing at the strange words he used and the way he said them. He quickly sat down as Miss Theede reminded him, "and where are you from?" and that's when he finally said his people came from "N-n-n-n-norway."

Marguerite Brumbach sneered, "He's a Norskie." Miss Theede silenced her—and our chuckles—with an upraised hand and a stern look, and then turned to the board and filled in a space that said Norway.

After telling us a little about Norway, she called on the next child, and it went that way until she came to me. "My parents came from Scotland-Ireland," I said.

"Those are two separate countries," Miss Theede said, and put their names on the map and honestly, that's the first time I realized they were different places.

"Your Pa's people wear skirts," Marguerite taunted, and Miss Theede gave her that look again.

I turned full in my seat to stare her down. Marguerite Brumbach was a big girl, with arms like tree stumps, and a hint of hair on her upper lip. She wore her hair in braids and was dressed in the same kind of broadcloth as the rest of us, so I didn't know why she thought she was so special. Oh, did she brag when it turned out that Germany, the country she came from was the largest place on Miss Theede's map. Taking her on was an invitation to failure—for the boys as well as the girls. But I wasn't about to have her bad-mouthing my Pa.

"Do not," I spat at her.

"Do too," she sneered back.

"Do not." That's when I felt Miss Theede's disapproving stare and turned back to face the front.

But at recess, I couldn't help myself. I walked up behind Marguerite and gave her a shove, and she looked like a windmill trying to keep her balance. She stayed upright and turned to rush me when Miss Theede stepped in and stopped it.

"I'll get you," Marguerite whispered as we went back into the schoolhouse.

To John and James, I was a hero, and they couldn't wait to get home to tell Ma and Pa how I'd fought the biggest girl in school because she said something bad about our Pa. The whole story came out over supper that night.

John did most of the telling, giving the punch line about the skirt right away. Pa wanted the story from the beginning and, unfortunately, the beginning was the stuttering Norskie who still used old-fashioned words from the Old Country. As John told it, Jimmy reenacted the funny scene and we three laughed. Pa stopped the story right there. Ma put down the spoon that was dishing out stew.

"You laughed at the boy?" he asked, and the tone of his voice was a strong clue that we were about to give the wrong answer. "Ellen, did you laugh, too?"

I frantically searched for a way to deny it, but since I was already smirking as the story had begun, I knew I couldn't. "Just a little, Pa," I said to make the best case I could. "But that's not the important part...." I heard my mother's disgusted cluck and Pa's eyes started burning through me.

"Not the important part?" he returned. "Laughing at a poor boy with a speech problem is not the important part? Laughing at a boy who still speaks his father's tongue, that's not the important part?"

"Let her tell how she fought that fat Marguerite because she said your people wore skirts," Jimmy chimed in, oblivious to what was happening. But Pa didn't want to hear any of that now. Neither did Ma. Eventually, I'd learn the difference between a skirt and a kilt, but it wasn't that night. That night the three of us were sent to bed without any supper.

"Ellen," my father commanded as I reluctantly climbed the loft with a hungry stomach, "did you like it when that girl made fun of your Pa?"

"No, sir, "I answered.

"Do you think that boy liked it when you made fun of him?"

"No, sir," I answered again, hoping the lesson was over and we'd be called back for supper. But we weren't. We went to bed with the disappointed voices of our parents ringing in our ears: "Our children do not laugh at people with problems. You will not shame us that way."

So, after seeing the wall of unity my parents represented, it was strange to see them on opposite sides of the fence about going to America.

At night, I'd lie in the loft with my sisters under our feather tick, and I'd hear the murmurings from their bedroom downstairs—never enough to make out words, but enough to know the arguing didn't stop at the bedroom door.

I could see Ma's side, looking around the nice cabin it had taken a whole summer to build, back when I was just a girl. We'd added on since then, of course, as the children came—raising that roof for the loft had been a job for Pa and the boys and all our neighbors—and you could easily see how much love and muscle was in this home. I think my Ma had about the best kitchen you'd find in all Ontario, laid out in an "L" so she could do several things at one time. She could be canning tomatoes off the cast iron stove while someone else was shucking corn by the sinkwell and there was still room to roll out a pie crust. Of course, I knew it was one thing to have a grand kitchen and another to know what to do with it, and my Ma knew what to do. Pa joked that the bachelor boys down the road could smell my Ma's baking bread better than their own smelly selves, and that's why they always showed up just when a loaf was cooling on the sideboard.

Randall and Gregory would sit down at the big table that took up most of the room—Pa had traded Mr. Specht an old plow for that beautiful table—and act like they just happened to be in the neighborhood. I could see why Ma wouldn't want to give this house up. I loved the place too. I don't remember living anywhere else, and until now, I thought I'd be coming here with my own children someday from my own farm not far away.

Of course, I didn't know yet who I'd be settlin' down with. It wasn't like I wasn't lookin'. I looked plenty, but nobody really seemed to be the right one and when I asked Ma if I should be worried—after all, she already had two children when she was my age—she looked me in the eye and said, "There's no hurry. What's important is to find the right one."

"I want a man like Pa," I told her and she smiled because she already knew that. Here's what I knew: I knew that Mickey Larkin wasn't the right one. I knew Adam Jennings wasn't the right one. I knew Joey Phalin wasn't the right one. And pickings got slim after them. Maybe I'd never find the right one, I worried at night in my bed. Maybe I'd end up an Old Maid. There was a shame in that I didn't want to feel, but I didn't want the wrong man, either.

But for all my sympathizing with Ma's side of things, there was something else pulling on me.

I saw a burning in my Father that would not be squelched. He wasn't a man who made quick decisions or foolish choices that put his family in harm's way. He was a thoughtful, hard-working, determined man. In all my years, I had never once worried about going hungry or not having a roof over my head. This was a man you could be proud of. I know my brothers,

John and James, shared the feeling. For the rest of the children, I don't think they ever thought about those kind of things. But we were old enough to pay attention to the decisions our parents made, and this time, all three of us were completely on Pa's side.

The barn's loft was where we nurtured our conspiracy, trying to think of things to help Pa sell the case. Poor Jimmy didn't know much about salesmanship. I started calling him "Stu-pid" whenever he came up with another idea that I knew would push Ma in the opposite direction.

It was after I discovered he got most of his information from Beadle's Dime Novels that I understood what I was up against. "You know, when the Cavalry fights the Indians, the Cavalry always wins," Jimmy told us one day.

John and I looked at each other and laughed out loud. "For a thirteen-year-old boy, you are pretty stu-pid," I hissed at him. "How about Custer? He sure didn't win. And, young man, you bring up fighting Indians with Ma and we will *never* get to Kansas."

He had to allow as how that was right. I vowed to find his secret stash of those ten-cent novels and throw them away. You'd think a pamphlet with orange wrapper paper would be easy to find on a farm in Canada, but James hid his dime novels so well, I never did find them.

Then one day he came home all excited, telling almost-ten Andrew that they were going to live with cowboys. The boys at school knew all about Kansas and there was this place called Dodge and there were gunfights in the streets, but the sheriff was strong and wise and....well, you can imagine how well that went over with Mrs. Tom Watson.

"You want me to move my family to a place where they have shoot-outs in the streets?" and she stopped Pa short for a moment there. "And I bet they have a drinking establishment every ten feet and that brings those women, and no, I want none of that for my family. You boys ever drink and play cards and I'll tan your hides, I don't care how old or tall you get. I had no idea Kansas was so *uncivilized!*" Pa reminded her that the letter-writing lady said our part of Kansas—I was already thinking of it as "our part"—was Dry, but Ma said she didn't believe that a place that would allow gunfights in the streets would ban liquor.

I wanted to tan Jimmy's hide myself and got him to lie and tell her the boys were wrong and they weren't talking about Kansas, but my Ma is no dummy, and she knew he was just trying to put the horse back in the barn.

Years later, a cowboy passing through our roadhouse in Wyoming Territory entertained us over my best stew with tales about Doc Holliday. He knew the man long before the Tombstone shoot-out and all the trouble in Arizona Territory. Knew him back in the days when he dealt faro in Dodge at night and was the town dentist by day. I almost spit out my mouthful of coffee.

"Doc Holliday used to live in Kansas?" I asked him in amazement, and because of my tone, he asked if I knew the man. "No, never knew him, just heard stories about him. Had no idea he once lived in Kansas."

The cowboy laughed and said most of the stories were dime novel inventions and Doc wasn't the killer everyone claimed. I had to laugh to myself. I sure was glad Doc Holliday wasn't yet famous when we were thinking of moving to Kansas, because if he had been, and Ma knew he lived within the boundaries, we'd never have moved there.

It took Pa a couple months to wear her down. I never knew if it was the strength of his arguments or just that she loved him so much she couldn't stand the disappointment of not letting him get all that land.

We learned on a Sunday in April in the glorious year of the Lord of 1877. Ma kept us inside for our praying circle because the Canadian spring doesn't come that early, and this day even Pa stayed to give thanks to the Lord. (He preferred the barn at moments like this.) Ma always said that it didn't take a church to make a Sunday service, but it did take clean children, so the boys came with their hair combed and the girls with fresh aprons.

While she was praying for all the good things in our lives, she simply said: "And please give us a safe journey to our new home in Kansas."

Well, I don't care if it was Sunday service, most of us jumped up and shouted in glee. We were laughing and yelling and hugging each other and Pa was beaming and Ma still looked hesitant, but she'd said the prayer, so it was settled.

"Your Pa wants to go this fall, so we have a lot to do to get ready." It was just like Ma to focus on the work ahead, rather than the journey.

We turned to Pa because we figured he was thinking like us at that moment. "How will we go, what can we take, when will we leave?"

Jimmy was beside himself to think he was going to live with real cowboys and breathlessly asked Pa, "Are we going in a *wagon train?*"

Pa laughed and tousled Jimmy's hair: "We're not going *that* far west, son. We're going to Kansas and they don't have wagon trains to Kansas anymore—probably did at one time, but Kansas is far more *civilized* than that now," and we knew Pa used that word for Ma's sake.

Jimmy was clearly disappointed, because he knew a lot about wagon trains from his dime novels, but when Pa said we'd build a covered wagon and go in that, it seemed a second-best that Jimmy could brag about to the boys at school.

"Can we take Bessie Number 4?" came a little voice from almost-ten Andrew, who was so fixated on his next birthday, he regularly reminded us, "I'm almost ten."

When that magic day finally arrived we were already in Kansas and had a special birthday pie for him. I told him: "I suppose now you'll want us to call you almost-eleven Andrew," but we never did, and that became one of our lasting family jokes.

Pa assured us that the fourth cow we named Bessie was going with us and we'd buy two ox to haul the wagon. Somewhere in the revelry he mentioned that we'd have to walk most of the way, but we were too excited to hear that just then.

"Ellen, you need to write me a letter," Pa told me that afternoon, and I didn't hesitate to get the paper and pen and ink. I sat next to him at our dinner table with everyone else hanging around—the little ones kneeled on their chairs with their elbows on the table. "Write to Bruce…Mr. MacDonald. Tell him we're coming and to start the search for my claim. Tell him we can be there before the snow. Tell him Ma sends her best to his missus."

We had a sale to get rid of what we couldn't take, which was almost everything. That beautiful table Mr. Specht made went to Gary Golder's family, and before they hauled it off, I saw Ma sneak a loving rub along one edge, her thumb sweeping over the top like it was memorizing every moment her family had sat there. I watched as she handed over her best linen cloth to her friend, Ann, and she whispered, "Please take good care of it and think of us when you use it."

Pa sold off the few acres he owned and our house. The Goss family was the new owner, and they were ready to move in. Their missus—a beautiful young woman who insisted I call her Lisa, instead of Mrs. Goss—was so happy that Pa threw in the stove and the pie safe. He did so only after swearing to Ma that he'd replace them when we landed in Kansas. He sold his favorite rocker to our uncle Mel, and the bachelor boys came and bought the washing cauldron. Ma insisted on keeping the rinsing tub, but to give it a reason to go along, she filled it full of blankets that cradled the fine dishes her Ma had given her over the years.

Pa's fiddle came with us, of course, and our clothing and bedding. Ma's butter churn was fitted with a strap so it could attach to the bottom of the wagon. Each morning on the trip, I'd milk Bessie Number 4 and the cream would go in the churn and by the end of the day, after all that jostling, we'd have supper butter.

There was no question the big coffeepot was coming along, with the box mill (although it ground more barley than real coffee over the years, but you get used to weak coffee that's stretched as far as its taste will go). Ma's favorite iron skillets were coming for sure—she was forced to limit them to three—and her kettles—four of them—and, God-forbid she should leave behind her rolling pin. The candle molds didn't take up much space, and the washboard was lashed onto the side of the wagon.

Of course, the family Bible was safely tucked away for travel. When we started making the list of what we wanted to take—then pared it down to what we should take; then cut it again to what we could take—the family Bible stayed Number One on every list.

What broke our hearts were the things impossible to take, and the top of that list was the graveyard. For awhile, I was certain we wouldn't go because Ma couldn't leave her six babies out there under that tree. At times, I wondered if I could bear that myself.

The graveyard was the last stop before we left for the State of Kansas in late September of 1877. Our family held hands and circled the last resting place of those precious little babies. Ma was so choked up she could barely speak, but she led us in a prayer. Little Elizabeth cried the whole time and her wailing spoke for the entire family.

As we walked away, I put my arm around Ma's shoulder and whispered, "We'll never forget them."

She sobbed back, "Never."

I know for the rest of our lives, my Ma and I shared this: We never looked back at Canada and put our minds on the ten of us who set off in a covered wagon with Bessie Number 4 tied onto the back. We only remembered Canada as the place we left six behind.

Chapter Four

We Found a New Life

The second before I heard almost-ten Andrew scream, I was mixing up biscuits and thinking how well this trip was going. Sure, my feet were sore, but I didn't mind because every step was taking us closer to our new home and our new life. We were already in the western hills of Iowa.

The kids had been wonderful. I couldn't believe how well the boys had been about doing all their chores—without anyone ragging on them. We'd stop for the day and they'd instantly run out to find us firewood. Or cow pies if wood wasn't available, and it seemed less and less was available the farther west we went. Ma said they were hungry and knew without a fire there was so supper, but I know she was proud they were doing their part.

I had expected the girls to be a problem and to whine about the trip, but even Baby Elizabeth was always cheerful—she liked to sing and that two-year-old entertained us many a long day. She often had a fancy-dancer enacting her songs, as three-year-old Mary was the dancingist child I ever saw. Franny at eight and Annie at five were each given duties, and they never shirked. They set out the dinner dishes and always washed them after.

I scooped out the butter each night and helped Ma with supper. Franny decided to bring out the blankets for us to sit on for supper, and then shook them out so they'd be ready for bedtime. That was a nice thought.

It didn't take a second to know the scream wasn't a prank his brothers were playing on him or a minor injury like a scraped knee or a fright that he'd seen something fearful. Almost-ten Andrew's scream was the sound you make only when you think you're going to die. I don't remember taking a breath before I saw my Pa dash in the direction of the scream.

"Get my knife, get my knife," Pa shouted over his shoulder, and that could mean only one thing. I prayed it was just a small snake. Pa came running into camp with almost-ten Andrew in his arms. The boy's eyes were as big as dinner plates. His face was red. His right arm was already swelling. He was still screaming.

Pa laid him down on the ground and growled, "Don't move. Don't move." But even a command that couldn't be misunderstood didn't get through my terrified brother.

"James, Franny, hold his shoulders so he can't move." I was barking myself. "Stay still, Andrew, you *have* to stay still or the poison will go all through you."

John ran up with Pa's bowie knife, and Ma was already on her knees, ready to suck out the poison. "Ellen, get me the salt box," and I ran as fast as I could to the wagon and back again.

Pa made an "x" over the fang marks, cutting so deep you couldn't even tell it was a bite anymore, and pressing his knife blade over the wound to get out as much poison as he could. Then Ma took over, spitting the poison out as she sucked. Twice. Three times. Four. Five. When all she could taste was blood, she grabbed the salt box and poured it into the wound. Andrew would later say he thought that hurt more than the bite itself, and he renewed his screams.

I sent Annie to the wagon for a towel, and Ma tore it into a strip that she wound around his arm, tucking in the end to keep the bandage in place. She wrapped her arms around the son she'd named after her favorite brother and let him cry as she assured him he was going to be alright.

"How big was it?" she whispered up to Pa, and he shook his head, like she didn't want to know.

We were all praying that almost-ten Andrew wouldn't die here, on our way to our new life.

Our neighbors in Canada had been filled with advice before this journey began, some of it useful, some of it absurd: "Never look an Indian in the eye," someone had said, but nobody knew why not. "Keep your girls hidden at night so cowboys can't steal them," someone else had offered, and little Annie kept bringing it up the whole trip. "Watch out for the Mormons," another said, although we had no idea what a Mormon even looked like. But there was one piece of advice that was worth all the nonsense, and that was from the old fur trader who told us what to do with a rattlesnake bite.

A week later, almost-ten Andrew was bragging that he'd been bitten by a rattlesnake on the trail to Kansas. It became his honor badge.

I never did think the snakebite was funny. Everything about it repulsed me. The snake. The wound. The poison that could kill. Every time I replayed the scene in my mind, I felt the same fear I'd felt at the time. It made my skin cold. What was wrong with me? I'm a strong girl. I can do almost anything in the house or the barn. My Ma says I soak up doings like a kitchen rag. My Pa says I'm like a third hand. My folks rely on me to be calm in an emergency. But almost-ten Andrew's fright kept me awake at night and fear was no longer a stranger. It took a couple weeks before I could finally admit what I'd never say out loud. What if the day came when I had to suck out the poison and I just couldn't? *Please don't let me ever have to. Please.*

◇◇◇

The road wasn't so rough, it was just so long. We'd left home with the good wishes of neighbors in our ears and caught the Kincardine Ferry to Detroit.

All that was brand new—none of us had ever been on a ferry and us kids had never seen that much water. Then off we went, across Indiana, Illinois, Iowa. When we reached Red Cloud,

Nebraska, we knew we were almost there. Our claim was near Lebanon, Kansas. That was about as far west as a decent person wanted to go. Farther west was a scary, dangerous, lawless place, filled with territories and Indians. I know more geography than most in my family, so I was real glad we turned south to an established state, rather than north into rough Dakota Territory.

It took a month and a half to cover the thousand miles, and even I had to admit it was hard to keep up the excitement of immigrating when you're walking ten hours a day. There weren't just holes in my shoes, but in my stockings. Clean clothes were a dream and the thought of a real bed almost made me dizzy. All week we looked forward to Sunday for a day of rest.

And then we were there.

I was walking with father as we came to the post Mr. Mac-Donald had staked into the ground to alert Pa he was finally home. He caressed that post like it was the Holy Grail. Then he stood real still, looking over the land with a face filled with joy and hope. I wanted to cry. To anyone else, it was just a hunk of flat prairie covered with chest-high grass and weeds and not a single tree, but to us, it was the Garden of Eden.

Pa reached over for my hand and gave it a squeeze. "It looks like good land," he told me.

"Yes, Pa, it looks like good land."

And then he did something we would never forget. "Mother," he bellowed (scaring the beejesus out of little Elizabeth) "it looks like good land!" And he ran like a boy after a kite, jumping and skipping and hollering his head off. John ran after him—almost a man himself at sixteen and already a half head taller than Pa. Which of course meant James would follow because he always did everything his big brother did, and then like a shadow ran almost-ten Andrew.

I glanced back to see Ma hand off Elizabeth to Franny and she started to run, too, and that was everyone's cue to join the race.

"Oh, Father, it's wonderful land," I heard Mother, puffing as she flew by me, her skirts whipping and her hair slipping out of its bun. She ran right into my father's outstretched arms. We had seen a loving pat here and a peck there, but we'd never seen our folks in a full hug until that morning when we first saw the one hundred sixty acres of land that held all our dreams. Pa lifted her up and swung her around like they were dancing to a smoking fiddle and they were both laughing and crying at the same time.

"You can thank Abe Lincoln for this," he yelled and the boys took up the chant, "Thank you Abe Lincoln, thank you Abe Lincoln."

I finally remembered my little sisters and looked back to see them hanging behind, kind of puzzled—startled?—at the pandemonium they were seeing. They couldn't be expected to understand. They were young and girls, and land wouldn't mean the same to them. Oh, someday they'd find a man, and his land would be important, but right now they were just relieved that they were finally someplace where they didn't have to walk beside the wagon anymore. But I didn't share those thoughts. My heart was up there, running on this precious land. My heart was with my Pa—and my brothers—with the pride of land ownership. I was jealous I'd never own my own land, but I was overjoyed that we would someday own this.

"Come on," I shouted to my sisters. "Come see your new home."

Franny led the way, carrying Baby Elizabeth. When Mary got to me, she threw her little arms around my legs and clung to my skirt.

"Where's our house?"

"We have to build one. We'll dig up this grass here, in big hunks, and we'll stack them up and make a house."

Pa had tried to explain a sod house to his youngest children while we were on the trail, but he didn't get any farther than I was getting now.

"I don't want to live in the dirt," Mary cried, and I assured her a soddie was just a temporary place to live until we could build a proper wood cabin. But when you're three, the only time that counts is right now and right now Mary was certain she didn't want to live in a soddie.

I finally shushed her and took the girls to meet up with the rest of the family. In the middle of the land, Mother quieted everyone down with a prayer. "Oh Lord, thank you for all you've given us. Thank you for our children (and here I heard the catch in Mother's voice). Thank you for saving almost-ten Andrew from the snake. Thank you for our safe travel and our ox, and that Bessie Number 4 is still milkin'. Thank you for bringing us here to this new land. Please watch over us and keep us safe." And just when everyone thought she was done and we were raising our bowed heads, she threw in, "And please, Lord, bring Mr. Watson to Sunday services."

Nobody dared giggle out loud, but we all smiled at the dig and Pa was so happy he just laughed, "Oh, Mother."

Our next joy was hearing a wagon coming over the prairie, and there was Mr. and Mrs. MacDonald and their children and a basket full of goodies. Oh, what a reunion that was. Hugs and back slaps and children mingling and the first thing Ma said was, "Where is that Baby Bruce?" and Mrs. MacDonald handed him over with pride. She had brought a basket of biscuits and ham and jams and we decided this was the best lunch we'd ever had.

Everyone let lunch linger a little that day, with everyone so happy. But a celebration on the day you end a long trip can't go on forever. The little kids were playing, becoming instant friends, of course, and Ma did allow that they should be given that treat.

"They were so good on the trail," she told Mrs. MacDonald, who completely agreed the little ones could get out of chores.

"We can unload the wagon ourselves," Ma declared, and I agreed.

First, I helped my brothers remove the wood arches and canvas that had transformed our buckboard into a covered wagon. John suggested we use the canvas for a tent until we had a soddie done, but it took just one word from Mrs. MacDonald to convince Ma the canvas needed to go on the ground instead. That word was "snakes."

The men started right away, cutting prairie sod into rect-angles. As soon as the buckboard was unloaded, I ran to help.

John was already an old-hand at cutting through the tough grass with a sharp blade. But I was better at stacking them precisely to make a wall. I saw Pa and Mr. MacDonald wink at one another as they watched John and me work, and I had to smile that we were doing our folks proud.

Mr. MacDonald put out the word and over the next week, homesteaders from all over Smith County came to help our family get settled.

"They did it for us when we got here, so now we do it for the newcomers," I was told by two nice sisters who became dear friends.

"We like any excuse to get together," Jessica said.

"Even building a soddie. We don't care. We just like seeing somebody besides our own. You know, it can get pretty lonely out here." That was Nancy, who seemed to know everything about everything.

"We really like wedding dances," Jessica said, like a woman who knew how to cut a rug.

"Or chivarees," Nancy added, and I had to admit I didn't know what that was. "On the wedding night, we show up at their house late, with pots and pans and we serenade them until they feed us to make us go away. It's really fun." I couldn't wait.

I was very pleased at how respectful everyone was to my Ma and Pa. What decent folks we'd have as neighbors. And I know it pleased my folks that they said such nice things about us kids.

"Your oldest boy is always the first to step up," I heard a man tell Pa one day. "He's going to grow into a fine man." Pa nodded and smiled at the truth of it. I wished that John had overheard that one because they weren't the kind of words Pa would ever say.

And I know Ma got an earful about me.

"That Ellen is such a hard worker."

"She's going to be a good farm wife someday."

"She's so pleasant looking. Those pretty blue eyes and that nice smile.

"I bet she's going to be snatched up lickety-split."

"Maybe I should start saving sugar for a wedding cake."

That last one came from Mrs. Kline.

"Oh, I think you're jumping the gun," Ma piped up, but the busybody wouldn't stop.

"This is important. We want our young people settled down and you know, a woman isn't happy until she has a man to care for. Besides, there's only two ways to see Kansas grow. Either we import people or we birth them." Nobody knew who'd named Mrs. John Kline the president of the Kansas Booster Society, but she had accepted the post.

So mine wasn't the only head that turned the day a handsome bachelor with a ready smile rode over to help with the soddie.

And that's how William Pickell came into my life.

Chapter Five

My First Big Mistake

The first time he hit me came as a complete surprise.

"Will…iam…you're…dr…drunk," I sputtered, like I was explaining it to myself as well as to him.

The punch had been so hard I reeled against the dinner table, lost my balance and ended up on the floor. I'd never been sprawled down here before and now I saw the crack under the door was more than I expected and I told myself, "Ellen, you need to get a bigger rag to keep out the skeeters," and then I thought, "What kind of goose are you to be thinking of that at a time like this?" and I finally heard my husband screaming at me.

"Shut up, bitch, or I'll hit you again. Don't you ever talk back to me and don't you ever ask me my business. Do you hear me?"

For a second I was hoping this man just *looked* like my William and wasn't him at all, but it was just a second and that passed. He stood over me and I knew he was waiting for me to cry, but I wasn't givin' him any reward, so I just picked myself up and pretended to be tending to the rising Sunday bread.

William staggered off to the bedroom and I heard him flop on the straw mattress and it wasn't until I heard a snore that I let my tears come. Don't know if I was crying' from pain or shame, but I think it was both.

Nobody had ever struck me before—oh my Pa once, on my behind, when I was a little girl and had my joyride on Darby— but never in my twenty-two years had anyone struck me in anger and that's the worst kind of hit. And nobody—NObody—had ever spoken to me like that. I'm betting my Ma had never in all her years been called that name and I sure never thought I would be. It's not a word you use around decent folk.

Until that slap, I was a married woman nearing her third anniversary with a husband and a decent cabin on a claim near my folks' home place outside Lebanon, Kansas. For the most part, I was a happy woman with a cupboard full of canning from my garden and a barn full of wheat from a good harvest and a new quilt ready to piece. But that all changed the instant his fist hit me that October 23, 1882.

Oh, was he a sweetie when he woke up and smelled the roasting chicken. He was all lovey and kissy and he acted like it never happened and we were still the happy couple that got married on November 24, 1879, just before Thanksgiving. He was just like he was when he courted me, when I thought I was the happiest girl in all of Kansas.

I'm not saying there hadn't been problems in our marriage, but the problems we had were ones I could overlook or, after fuming for awhile, forget. As my Ma always said, "In a marriage, you've got to make the best of it." And until that moment, I thought I was doing a pretty good job of living that advice.

The worst disappointment was the kind of thing a decent woman never discussed with anyone, so I always wondered if other women disliked how rough a man can be when he's claiming his husband rights. I don't know what I expected. Nobody ever explained anything. Ma just said to do what my husband wanted and to act like I enjoyed it. But I didn't enjoy it. Not from our wedding night when the sweet man who'd been courting me acted more like a routing pig. I guessed that was normal, because Ma said a man had needs we didn't understand. But our stolen kisses had been so sweet, and our secret hand-holding had been so tender, and I thought that was what the wedding bed would be like. I was so very disappointed. But I figured every woman had the same disappointment and, of course, I didn't complain. Besides, this is how we got babies and so I just closed my eyes and thought about the sweet children we'd have and hoped it would be over soon. But my time came every month and there was no baby. It became a monthly torture to get out the pail with the old rags that I'd need, and every one I washed was a stab to my soul that this was another month I wasn't growing a child.

William didn't like it either, and when he saw the rag pail, he'd turn away in disgust. Sometimes he'd yell over his shoulder, "Woman, we're gonna need children to help us with this farm," as though I were deliberately not getting pregnant. Ma told me not to worry, but I knew she was wondering why I wasn't having my babies, especially because she was still having hers. My baby sister Jane came in October of 1880; beautiful Thomas in '82, and just holding them punched a hole in my heart.

And then there was the drinking. I didn't notice right away because, looking back, I don't think it was too bad at first. I never smelled a single spirit on William's breath the whole time we were courting. I knew the men were outside after the wedding having a nip or two—even Ma, who was as Dry as any woman in the country, turned her head at that, saying it was just for a celebration. I thought that would be the end of it.

Oh, I was so happy the next year when Governor St. John forced through a vote to prohibit alcohol. Kansas voters went along with him and we became the first state to go completely Dry. That wouldn't have happened if my William had his say. He talked against the vote day and night, said it wasn't right for a bunch of do-gooders to take away one of the few pleasures a working man had. But when I asked him if he was going to vote in the election, he said he was too busy for stuff like that.

Of course, this discussion only took place in our own home, because in my Ma's, the story was completely different. When she'd start in on how wonderful it would be for Kansas to go Dry and show the nation, William stayed silent. So did Pa, who couldn't vote anyway because he wasn't a citizen yet. I had to laugh the day Annie forced the issue and asked him, "Pa, if you could vote, how would you vote?"

Ma stopped drying the kettle, as Pa carefully said, not looking her way, "Why, Annie, of course I'd vote to go Dry. I bet the whole country will go Dry someday and, Mother, won't that be a happy moment?"

I saw her smile as she turned away because she knew he was only saying that to keep peace and she was smart enough to know that's not how Pa really felt. I bet she guessed that William lied about his support, too.

Of course, I overlooked his drunk when President Garfield got shot. I almost wanted a drink myself because he was shot on my twenty-first birthday. Ma always made a big deal of our birthdays—no matter what was going on, she made sure the day was celebrated somehow. We were lucky that July 2 in 1881 was on a Saturday, so after chores, we gathered at my folks' place for a nice supper. Little did we know that a horrible man who had been denied a job shot our president.

We got the word the next day—why does bad news always spread so fast while good news is still trying to get some attention? I cried to hear such an awful thing. William went off by himself and when he came home Sunday night, he reeked of liquor. But I took it for grieving. Everyone was grieving and maybe this was just the way my husband handled such bad news. Then he tied one on when President Garfield finally died on September 19. That was a Monday and we had just been in church the day before praying for him. Then that fast bad news came again and while I dropped all my Tuesday chores and went back to church with Ma, William went drinking somewhere and he was so drunk he stumbled into the house and into bed.

It's easy to explain away moments like that—far better than the dark thoughts that creep into your mind, so I overlooked it. I see now, looking back, that I was a scared girl whistling in the dark to pretend she was all right.

And then things got worse and worse and I couldn't believe this was the same William Pickell who had come around to help us build the soddie.

◇◇◇

My brothers had started teasing me that very first day. "Ellen likes a pickle, yes she does, oh, she's so sweet for her pickle," Andrew sang while his older brothers snickered.

"You shouldn't make fun of a man's name," I shot back, but that didn't stop them.

"Ellen's in a pickle," John would whisper when he went by me.

"What's Ellen's favorite drink?" James would yell out, like it was a real question and then he'd sing, "pickle juice." Ma and Pa tried to hush them, too, but they were unmerciful.

William Pickell was a charming, good-looking man, I have to say that about him. He always wore his best manners when he was around my folks. He couldn't "yes ma'am" or "yes sir" enough and he wasn't pushy either (not like Mickey Larkin back in Ontario who must have thought I was desperate, because he came courting once and asked me to marry him, like I would marry a man so old and desperate himself).

William courted me for two years with buggy rides and polite conversation around our supper table. He told me about his dreams of a big family and those were the very words I was happy to hear. He had a nice spread not far away, with a three-room wooden house and a big barn. Nancy and Jessica figured he was the most eligible bachelor around. And I heard Mrs. Kline blessed our courting, like that was her right.

The first time William held me was when we lost Elizabeth. I cried into his shirt for a half hour, and he held me the whole time. Dear Elizabeth. The last of the triplets. We lost all three. All. Three. Ma and Pa were beyond consolation. Even the boys had the helpless look of grief, and I was certain my sisters would never get over this loss.

"Promise me, William, that when we have a girl, we'll name her Elizabeth for the angel that just went to heaven." He promised.

I put her in the Bible with the other two, with a birthday of June 12, 1875. I wrote "died, 1878."

William helped build the casket and dig the grave and he listened to all our stories about the dear child. He even rocked my little sisters, who were already seeing him as my man. That really tied him to my family, and that wasn't the only way.

To impress Ma, he went to Sunday services one time, but that backfired with Pa, because it gave Ma new ammunition to prod him in the same direction. He brought presents for my sisters—a piece of cloth for Franny, a hair ribbon for Annie, a rag doll for Mary. He let my brothers ride his fine horse and gave Pa a hand with breaking up the sod for our first crop. He gave me an embroidered handkerchief that had been his Ma's, and he never arrived without something for my Ma's kitchen.

"I have some fine corn this year," he'd say, as he laid down a sack filled with sweet, juicy ears. "I have some extra sugar I don't need and thought you could use it." Or, "I found an extra can of coffee and I'll never get to it."

But the day he snagged my Ma's heart for good was the day he brought her something still rare in the West—a cat! It was just a kitten and Mary claimed it for her own immediately, but Ma saw it was the mouser she needed in the house and the barn and she even gave him a big hug for the extravagant gift.

He cemented my Pa's love when he offered leftover wood from his own cabin for our first real house in Kansas. Then he helped build the cabin that started out with five big rooms! Mrs. MacDonald said it was the finest first cabin she'd ever seen in these parts. And little Mary, who never did warm up to living "in the dirt" thought the man walked on water for helping us get a real home. She liked that even more than her rag doll.

Was it any wonder that every single member of my family agreed I had a great catch? I was so pleased my people liked him, because I liked him so. It was time for me to get hitched and start my own family and I'd finally found the right man.

I spent the last six months of courting making a fine wedding outfit.

I saw a dress I loved in the Monkey Ward catalog and of course, I couldn't afford a store-bought dress and there was no need for that since I know my way around a sewing machine like nobody's business. I'd been making my own clothes for a couple years now, and even made Pa a shirt one time (although my Ma is better at men's shirts than I could ever be). I made dresses for my sisters and aprons for presents and so it was nothing for me to look at a pretty dress in a catalog and make it up for myself.

My Ma's wedding present was a piece of blue satin for my dress. I draped it across the front of the skirt and gathered in the back to resemble a bustle—the first almost-bustle I ever wore. I embroidered the dark blue waistcoat, put lace at the sleeves and covered nineteen buttons for down the front. On my wedding day, I wore ear bobs, a locket, and a bracelet from Ma, with my two favorite rings on my right hand. William said someday he'd get me a wedding band for the left, but right then he thought that money would best be spent to get us started.

We were married on a cool November day, not cold, no snow yet. Ma cleared out the big room of our cabin and filled it with tables to sit his kin and mine and neighbors.

Ma and Mrs. MacDonald cooked for days and there were big platters of fried chicken and potato salad and corn mush and pickles, of course, since this had been a really good year for cucumbers and we had canned up jar after jar. Mrs. MacDonald made the most wonderful white cake—that was her wedding present to us—and everyone was thankful for that because there was nobody in Lebanon, Kansas, who could make a more tasty cake than Estelle MacDonald.

My sisters wore ribbons in their hair and I know I wasn't the only one who imagined how pretty little Elizabeth would have looked. Nancy and Jessica came in dresses they made special for the occasion, and Mrs. Kline came decked in a new hat with a giant feather—the men all snickered, but us women coveted that fancy hat. People came with best wishes and presents to help us get started. I got some beautiful linens and dish towels and seeds and a pretty pot to plant with flowers. Ma made me a lovely nightgown with lace at the collar.

Before I went outside where William and the judge were waiting, I told my Ma, "I hope William is as good to me as Pa is to you." She hugged me real tight and whispered, "I hope so too." This is the honest truth: I thought I was marrying a man like my Pa.

We rode to his cabin in his buggy at the end of a joyous day. Ma packed us a basket of leftovers so we could start out with food in the house. I carefully took off my precious wedding dress and put on the new nightgown from Ma. Out of nowhere, came this horrible noise of pots and pans being banged with spoons and sticks.

William squealed. "We're being chivareed!"

He grabbed my hand to take me to the front porch, but I protested. "William, I'm in my nightgown."

"Throw a shawl over it." I followed his instructions and we met our neighbors outside. They were hooting and hollering and striking on those pots and pans like they were beating the tar our of the bobcat. Nancy and Jessica where there, of course, and my brothers, and Mr. MacDonald, and a few others.

"We don't have anything for you," William pretended, and they beat those pots even more. "How about our leftovers?" he offered, and I tried to hush him because that was all we had to eat.

"Don't worry. Just put a couple things in a basket and they'll go away. This is all for show." William knew more about this chivaree business than I did. I followed his lead and gave them a couple sandwiches and one of the jars of pickles. And indeed, they ended their "serenade" and rode off.

Thanksgiving came three days later and our whole family— including Pa—celebrated at our country church, just like the president asked us to do.

I always smile to myself when I remember how Annie made Pa going to church a national issue! Annie was becoming our official messenger—she gathered information as easily as picking flowers and was always anxious to share her knowledge. So when she got an old newspaper from a family down the way—it was already a month old, but was still news to us—Annie read every word and then came to Pa (without any prompting from Ma, I'd learn later) and declared, "President Hayes wants you to go to church on Thanksgiving."

Pa looked at her suspiciously and so Annie read directly from the Omaha paper about the president's proclamation.

"I earnestly recommend that, withdrawing themselves from secular cares and labors, the people of the United States do meet together on that day in their respective places of worship, there to give thanks and praise to Almighty God for His mercies and to devoutly beseech their continuance."

We all waited for Pa's response—Ma was chuckling into her apron—and he smiled to announce that he thought that was a very good idea.

Later I'd learn Pa had already planned to attend, because we all gathered for a potluck Thanksgiving dinner after services. But we didn't know that then and everyone thought it was our Annie who finally brought Pa to God.

William and I arrived in our fine buggy to a flurry of congratulations, and Thanksgiving dinner that year turned into a second celebration for us. When someone pushed William to speak after dinner, everyone could see the charming man I'd chosen when he told them: "Ellen and I thank you for this fine feast and you're welcome to throw us a dinner like this every year!" Oh, the laughter! And how proud I was.

Mrs. Eden brought a fruit cake in my honor and whispered, "An Irish girl should have a fruit cake for her wedding." There was a special smile on Ma's face.

That was the best dinner I'd ever had, and it wasn't just because I was a new bride.

"Look at the size of that wild turkey. I've never seen one so big. Be sure you roast it until it's golden brown."

"There's so much food here I think this holding table is going to break!"

"Those platters look like a garden. We've got corn and peas,

potatoes and rutabagas and squash. Who brought kohlrabies?
I love them!"

"Do you need any more pickles? I brought two jars."

"I brought a cabbage dish."

"So did I."

"So did I."

"I'm saving myself for rhubarb pie," Mary whispered to me,
and I had to agree. I wanted space left because I hadn't had any
rhubarb pie since the spring.

The church lawn was filled with long tables, and we knew
they'd fill up like usual—the men would all cluster at one table,
the women at another, the children at a third. But Nancy and
Jessica and Annie said that just wouldn't do on a Thanksgiving
celebration decreed by our president.

"In honor of William and Ellen's wedding, we want all married couples to sit together," Nancy announced. Everyone looked
at each other like this was a truly novel idea.

Jessica chimed in, "Yes, our president would want families
together today." And then Annie jumped in, "Ma and Pa, why
don't you sit right here? And William and Ellen, we'll put you
here."

Like sheep following the bell, we all sat down together, and
what a fun dinner that was. As pie was being served, Annie stood
in front of our table and announced, "I believe our president would
like our celebration." That ended the day with happy chuckles.

I didn't get a wedding ring, but I did get a wedding picture.
We went to Red Cloud, a couple weeks after the wedding. William needed supplies and he said we could kill two birds with
one stone. So I went along and took my wedding dress.

William sat on a velvet chair and I stood behind him with
one hand on his arm. We both had a hint of a smile, because
that's the fashion now. I'm glad, because I don't like that stern
look so many had for so many years. It never looked like those
people liked one another, and a portrait should show more than
just faces. We had a little smile because we'd had such a nice
wedding. And then the Thanksgiving celebration.

The next Thanksgiving all of my prayers were for children. The year after, they were *pleas* for children. By the fourth Thanksgiving of my married life, all my prayers begged for help to get me away from William.

I never did learn where he went to drink, all those Saturday nights he left our home to go off, never offering a word to explain himself, but coming home reeking so much he didn't have to. My Pa had never gone off to drink somewhere, leaving Ma and us at home. I'd never heard any other wife complain of such things, and I stayed quiet because I didn't want the embarrassment of our friends knowing I was failing somehow.

I can't even remember how many times I sat in my rocker, waiting for him to come home, worried he'd fall off his horse or get lost in the dark and die out there and leave me a widow. When I'd hear him finally come home, I'd rush into our bedroom and pretend to be asleep so he wouldn't know I'd waited up. Until that night in October when I decided it was time to stop this nonsense. It was when I confronted him that he knocked me to the floor.

How I prayed it would be the only time. I woke up the next morning to a sweet husband. He promised it would never happen again, and I wanted to believe him so much, I just put that fist out of my mind and promised to be an even better wife so he'd have no reason to go off to drink.

I wish I could say it was the only time, but it wasn't. I wish I could say I hit him back the second and third time, but I didn't. I was too ashamed to say or do anything but cower like a coward when he came home drunk. Now I rushed to bed, pretending sleep to kept me out of harm's way. And it usually worked. But not all the time.

I couldn't tell anyone. I was afraid if I told Ma, she'd tell Pa and he'd tell the boys and who knows what they'd do to William. Besides, I didn't want anyone to know, and I worried that even if I said something, people wouldn't believe me. They knew William as this sweet, charming man. Who would imagine he was so evil at home?

But mostly, I couldn't figure out why. I'm not a beauty, but I'm a good lookin' woman and I keep myself clean and pleasant. You won't find an untidy house when you come to mine, and God knows I'm a hard worker. William was always ready to sing my praises for how much I helped him on the farm. I knew for sure I pleased William with my cookin' because he gained about ten pounds the first years we were married and he always smiled at whatever I put on the table. It wasn't humbug. I'm a good cook, even a better baker, and so I knew it wasn't his home or his dinner table that wasn't up to his standards and that left only me not measuring up.

It's a hard thing for a woman to admit she doesn't please her man.

That thought slapped me in the face the first time I smelled sweet perfume on William's shirt. It had to be a mistake, I convinced myself. If I didn't know better, I'd think this was the smell of a saloon girl, but there were no saloons in Dry Kansas, at least none that were legal. And even if there was a secret saloon, certainly he'd have nothing to do with a saloon girl. Maybe he was playing poker and some girl was hanging around the table and her smell got on him and that was all it was. I remember I washed that shirt as fast as I could. But then there was the second time and the third and a woman can only ignore the truth for so long before she has to admit her husband is two-timing her.

I'll never forget Sunday morning, April 22, 1883.

I'd decided it was time to put my foot down when he finally rode up on Sterling, leaving him hitched outside. He staggered in, smellin' of that cheap perfume. I stood up from my rocker and with all my courage, I spit out the speech I'd been practicing for hours.

"William Pickell, that's enough. I won't have you coming home drunk and smellin' of another woman and I want this to stop right now."

In my mind, I thought he'd hang his head and promise it would never happen again. I saw him ashamed of how he'd done me wrong. Then it would be over and we'd live the happy life I wanted to be ahead of us.

But he didn't hang his head and he promised nothing. Instead he grabbed his horsewhip and tried to hit me. I don't know what got into me, but this was one Sunday I wasn't going to be hit. I pushed him back and wrenched the whip out of his hands. The tussle got him off balance and he fell to the floor.

"You hit me for the last time, William Pickell," I spat down at him. "I've been a good wife to you and it isn't enough for you. But I've had all I can take of you."

He grabbed up for the whip, but I was faster, being sober and upright. He snickered when he missed it, and I thought it was the ugliest laugh I'd ever heard. "Drop my horsewhip right now, do you hear me, bitch?" he screamed. Pretty haughty words for a man sprawled on my clean kitchen floor. It wasn't his demand that made me react. It was the use of that awful b-word again. I looked at him a second, thinking how foolish he was if he thought I'd drop the whip so he could pick it up and use it on me.

That's when I pulled my arm straight back. With all the might I had, I let that whip slap his shoulder. I am ashamed to admit how good it felt.

I don't remember coiling my arm up again, but I did it almost automatically, and this time the leather strap raised a red mark on his cheek. When he cried out in pain, I thought it was about time he felt the hurt I'd been feeling all this time. And then I snapped the whip one more time as he threw his arms over his head and I said in a strong, clear voice, "That's for calling me that name."

I turned and walked out of our cabin, grabbing my shawl, taking the whip with me. I was still clutching it when I rode up on Sterling to my Ma and Pa's cabin. Ma was just getting her Sunday fire going and she took one look at me and pulled me into her arms. I knew I had to tell her and Pa everything, but the first thing was, "I'm not going back. I know it's not our way, but I'm divorcing William Pickell."

Ma closed her eyes as I told the story, as though she could shut out such shocking news. Pa looked at me with a fire that said he wanted to horsewhip William himself. But I also saw the disapproving look they shared when I announced the divorce. This wasn't a word you heard very often, almost never, actually, because that wasn't our way. You married carefully because you were married for life, and I had believed that until this morning. But I sure didn't believe it anymore.

By now, my brothers and sisters had gathered and Pa didn't even have to turn around to tell his sons, "I want you boys to leave this alone." I could see John was already whipping up his anger. "I mean it," Pa added, and made the boys promise they wouldn't go over and beat the hell out of William Pickell. The girls were all crying, especially little Mary, and Annie had this look like this was the worst news she had ever heard.

Ma insisted I go up to my old bed in the loft, and although I protested that I should help her make breakfast, she wouldn't hear of it. I was awful glad because I'd been up all night and I was so tired I could hardly see. I slept through that whole day and when I woke up it was laundry day and everyone was busy.

Ma asked if I'd make the soda bread. I took down the green crock she always used and was kneading when she came in and stood next to me. "How bad was it?" she asked, and all I could choke out was that it was real bad.

I stayed at Ma and Pa's the next year, like I'd never left.

William came by again and again, demanding I come home, but my Pa or one of my brothers always stood in the doorway and sent him away. The boys and Annie went out to our cabin to get my things—William stood there to be sure they took nothing but my clothes and bonnet. I don't know what ever happened to the quilt I'd started piecing, but it didn't come back with them and it wasn't worth a second trip because I can always start a new quilt.

I knew Ma understood why I'd never go back, but I think Pa hoped this would blow over and things would go back to normal.

The day I burned my wedding dress put an end to all the fantasies that I'd go back to William.

I did all the preparations up in the loft at night, so nobody could try to stop me. I cut off the nineteen buttons—buttons are too precious to waste under any circumstance, so I saved them for my sisters. I ripped the dress into pieces. That pretty dress was nothing but a mound of fraying ripped cloth by the time I was done. One Tuesday, a month after I'd come home, I carried the pieces down in my apron and threw them on the burning trash pile. At first Ma didn't realize what I was burning, and when she saw, she wailed, "Oh Ellen, that's such a waste!"

I gave her a look. "There is no chance a woman will ever go back to a bad husband after she's burned her wedding dress." And I bet that's exactly what she told Pa, because he never mentioned me going back again.

Most of our neighbors weren't too happy with me, and I overheard more than one person scolding my Ma.

"She made her bed and she's got to lie in it."

"If girls could just leave their husbands because there's a bad patch, where would we be?"

"It isn't right for a woman to divorce a man. That doesn't happen in these parts, you know."

I was real proud of Ma when she stood up for me: "Ellen is a good girl and she has good reasons." Ma said those words in a voice that was sharp enough to stop the busybodies in their tracks. But still, when we went to church, I could feel them looking at me and whispering behind my back like I wasn't a good wife that didn't honor her vows. I wondered if some of those women weren't wishing they could escape like I did.

That next New Year's Eve, Pa gathered us to celebrate Hogmanay, like he always did. This was the one custom he kept from his people—he said his Ma always favored it. She told her boys she hoped they'd sing it in their own homes and to always remember it came from a Scotsman's poem long ago.

Pa told us that you'd normally celebrate at midnight as the new year came in, but that wasn't for us. "Farmers are never up at midnight unless a cow's in trouble with a new calf," he joked, so we did it after supper. We stood in a circle, holding hands and sang the song from the Old Country that Pa taught us. *"Should auld acquaintance be forgot, And never brought to mind? Should auld acquaintance be forgot, And auld lang syne?"*

The girls favored the chorus: *"For auld lang syne, my dear, For auld lang syne. We'll take a cup o' kindness yet, For auld lang syne.*

The boys liked the last verse best because it was about friends having a good-will drink together and that sounded manly to them. *And there's a hand, my trusty fiere! And gie's a hand o' thine! And we'll tak a right guide-willy waught, For auld lang syne."*

Pa always choked up when he got to the verse about being so far away from a friend, and I suspected he sang this one for the family that had turned their backs on him and Ma. *"We twa hae paid'd i' the burn, frae morning sun till dine; But seas between us braid hae roar'd sin auld lang syne."*

◇◇◇

It was a Thursday in February when John was sent to Red Cloud for supplies and I insisted on going along. I quickly filled Ma's order from the Mercantile, and while my brother was still at the feed lot, I ran over to the courthouse.

A very sturdy-looking woman was sitting at a desk, her spectacles perched on the top of her head. "I want a divorce," I told her, and she just looked at me like I was speaking a foreign language. "Is there something I have to fill out?" That brought her back to the moment.

"Yes, there's a dissolution of marriage form," she said, "but I've never handed one out before. I'm not even sure we have one." She still sat there, looking at me curiously, and I wasn't moving and finally, she said, "But I could go look," and I thanked her and she went into a big cabinet at the back of the room. It took her a couple minutes of digging until she finally announced, "Here it is!" like she'd found a missing treasure. And for me, it was. Here was the first legal paper I'd ever sign on my own and it was a paper most women in the entire country would never consider signing.

I filled it out and the whole time this clerk kept looking at me, but when I met her eyes, I didn't see a harsh judgment. I saw the kind of woman who'd never allow a man a second hit, and when I smiled at her, she smiled back like a loving sister.

"And I need to see the judge," I told her after the paper was signed and stamped so it was officially entered. She didn't even question me, but went to the door and knocked gently. She walked into the judge's fine-looking office and laid the form on his desk and told him someone wanted to see him. I was lucky he was in and even luckier that he was my Pa's friend who had married us.

There was a shocked look on his face as he read the form and then looked at me with eyes that said, "Ellen, this just can't be."

I ignored the look and went straight to my point: "I have to ask you something special that isn't on the form. I want my maiden name back. I don't want to be Ellen Pickell anymore. I want to be Ellen Watson again."

I could just tell he was primed to give me a lecture against divorce, but my request stopped him in his tracks. "But Ellen, your legal name is Pickell now and even if you divorce him, it's still Pickell."

I straightened up my back for courage and told it to him straight: "Judge, he wasn't a good man. I thought I was marrying a man like my Pa, but he wasn't. I can't honor a bad man by carrying his name. I want to honor a good man by carrying his." By his reaction, I knew it was a powerful argument.

"Did he mistreat you?"

"Yes."

I knew he wanted more but that was all I cared to share.

"There's no way you two can fix this?"

"No. No sir."

He took a minute to consider all this and then added in his own handwriting that upon the dissolution of marriage, I would resume the Watson name.

I walked out of that courthouse a happy woman for the first time in a long time. I pressed my hands against my heart and beamed, like I'd just gotten the best Valentine's present ever.

It was February 14, 1884.

Chapter Six

My Train to a New Life

I kept looking at the ticket as my brother, John, paced the platform. "Miss E. Watson. One-way. Cheyenne, Wyoming Territory."

"Don't lose that," my brother yelled over, as if I'd be careless with my ticket to a new life.

It was March 17, 1885.

"You know, these tracks aren't even twenty years old." He was reading a story about the railroad tacked on the wall. "But they say the cars are borrowed from the East. Bet they're old."

Those cars could have come from a Red Cloud shed and been nothing but two boards nailed together and I would have thought them beautiful. As it was, they were real rail cars—not the fancy ones toward the front—but just fine, as far as I was concerned.

John helped me to my seat.

"The floor is dirty and it has cracks so big, you can see the ground underneath," he complained, but I didn't care.

"The windows are grimy, you can hardly see out of them." But I saw that he was wrong. I could see out just fine.

"Do these cars jostle a lot?" he asked the couple in the seats across from mine.

The woman with the big hat said, "Well, let me just say, when we're underway, if you try to hold a tin cup full of water, it will all slosh out."

John gave me the I-told-you-so look. "I'm not going to hold a tin cup full of water," I told him. He had to smile at that.

"There's not a bit of upholstery on your seat. You're going to have a rough ride."

I hadn't expected a plush couch for my trip. Seat No. 19 was a wooden bench and it was a fine wooden bench.

From the moment we'd arrived at the Union Pacific station in Red Cloud for the 10:12 a.m. train, John had been trying to convince me to turn back. But there was no way. I was moving on. I was on an adventure. I was wearing my Pa's name and there'd be nobody to know any difference.

My trunk was safely stowed in the freight car and I carried a valise of gray and pink velvet that Ma had traded for making two men's shirts—perhaps her finest shirts ever. It was the prettiest valise I have ever seen.

It was a fine new thing for my fine new life. And my new name.

"I want to be called Ella from now on," I announced to my family soon after I came back from the courthouse. Mother understood instantly and agreed Ella was a fitting nickname for her grown daughter, just as Franny had so fit me when I was a child. "I know I'll sign legal with Ellen, but I like the sound of Ella," I explained to Pa. And then I told him the judge had agreed I could have my maiden name back. I think that pleased my Pa.

So now I was Ella Watson, except when Ma or Pa had something very important to say and then, as always, they reverted to my Christian name.

"Ellen, you can't be serious." That was Pa when I first mentioned my plans to go west.

"Women don't go west alone, child. If your Ma and I were going, sure you could come along, or if you brothers were moving or…[I could tell he thought better of mentioning the prospect of following a husband]…but you can't just go yourself. Ellen, that's no place for a woman on her own."

My family was unanimous in trying to dissuade me.

"Ella, there's still savages out there," Franny cried, as though this were still the 1870s.

"Ella, what about train robbers? You don't want to be killed by train robbers," argued Andrew, as though Jesse James were still alive.

"Ella, most of those places aren't even states," John scolded, as though Kansas hadn't once been a territory itself.

"Ellen, it isn't proper," Pa kept repeating, as though nothing was proper for a woman but staying home and clinging to a man.

But I held firm. None of them knew this plan had been in the works for months. Ever since Old Man Stone came home from his trip to Denver with that railroad brochure.

Not long after I filed for divorce, I knew it was time to move on. But moving on in Kansas didn't offer much. I wasn't from a family that owned a business that would give me a job and I wasn't educated enough to teach school, which was about the only other work women were allowed. But I did know everything about cooking and cleaning and so when Jacob Stone put out the word he was looking for a housekeeper, I jumped at the opportunity.

It was an easy job, taking care of a three-room house and one old farmer. With no children underfoot, once you cleaned, it stayed clean. Mr. Stone liked the same meals day in and out— flapjacks and fried ham with buttermilk biscuits for breakfast; beef stew and leftover biscuits for dinner; steak and boiled potatoes for supper. I never needed to slaughter and pluck chickens because, as Mr. Stone told me the first day, "I'm no friend to chicken."

I broke up the culinary boredom with my wonderful pies and he loved every kind I made. Since the cooking and housework were easy, I joined Mr. Stone in the barn and the fields and he was impressed I already knew so much. He bragged in town that in Ella Watson, he not only got a good housekeeper, but a good handyman, too.

I'd been with him two months when he took the train to Denver to visit his ailing sister, and in the ten days he was gone,

I realized something important—I was caring for this house and that barn and those fields all on my own. I had the strength and stamina to do it, since I've always been on friendly terms with hard work. I realized there was a joy to this work as though it were your own home and your own land. When my bone-tired body climbed into bed at night, there was a satisfaction to knowing a good day's work had been done and tomorrow was another day.

Until then, I had never been alone a day in my life. I'd never slept alone in a cabin without my mother or a sister next door. I'd never watered the stock or worked a field without my father or brother nearby. I'd never cooked a meal with no one but myself to eat it. I'd gone from my father's home to my husband's home and now to Mr. Stone's home. Years later, it would strike me that if he hadn't gone on that trip, I'd never have realized the possibility of a home of my own.

"I brought you this," Mr. Stone said sheepishly when he returned from his trip with a package wrapped in brown paper and held together, not with plain string, but with ribbons. "My sister said she thought you'd favor this soap—it's her favorite." I was moved that he'd think to bring me anything, and I loved the lavender smell of the cake that came in such a pretty package.

He also had a new cast iron muffin tin and sugar and vinegar. "Never can have enough sugar and vinegar," he said, as though he had to explain provisions for his own kitchen. "And oh, yeah, I thought you'd get a kick out of this." He threw down on the table a brochure from the Union Pacific entitled: "Wonderful Opportunities for Homesteader or Investor." It included a poem: "Mary had a little farm, she kept it neat and tidy. It gave her crops and chicks and cows and she loved it mighty."

Mr. Stone thought it was funny that the railroad was trying to get women to go west and claim land and he laughed about it, thinking I'd would laugh, too. But that silly little poem kept running through my mind and it wasn't long before I dared to think: "Ella had a little farm…."

The next time we went into Red Cloud for supplies, I stopped by the railroad office and asked about claims farther west. They were all too happy to give me brochures and articles from *Collier's* magazine. I read them all so often, I almost memorized the stories they told. They all painted such a rosy picture of life on a homestead. I took them at their word.

Mr. Stone provided room and board and I already had three good work dresses and a Sunday outfit, so I didn't need any more and could save almost every cent Mr. Stone paid. Within six months, I was able to save forty-six dollars. My grubstake.

That's when I told my family about the new life I saw for myself in Wyoming Territory.

"There's no land left to claim here." I didn't have to tell them, but I did anyway. They already knew that. My brothers already knew their dreams of their own claims were being crushed because there was no longer any land left to claim in Kansas.

"Pa, I want to own my own land, like you and Grandpapa. I want my own cabin and my own crops and my own herd. There's not many places a woman could have all that for herself, but Wyoming Territory is one of them. Women can even vote out there, Pa. Imagine that."

"You couldn't vote anyway cause you're not even a citizen," he shot back.

"But I will be. Like you, Pa. I'll file for citizenship and study and take my test, just like you're doing."

He jumped on that right away, insisting I couldn't even think of going until I'd helped him pass his citizenship test, but I had an answer waiting for that objection. "Annie is more up on her American history than I am. She can help you. She'll be better at it than me."

I swatted away every concern like I was at a field picnic, keeping skeeters off the cornbread.

If there had been any plea that gave me pause, it was from my little sisters. "Ella, you'd leave us?" Little Jane held onto my skirts while she cried out her disbelief. "How can you leave us?"

Annie wondered if I was going away forever and wailed, "I couldn't stand it if I never saw you again." I knew I couldn't stand that either. I had to admit that if I'd had my way, I'd have a sister old enough to go with me—the two of us would be company for one another, and it would be so much easier to go with someone else than stalk off on my own. But Franny was my only hope and at seventeen, she was already being courted and had no interest in moving away.

Whatever soft spot my sisters punched in my spine, William Pickell hardened back up. He refused to answer my petition for divorce—not once, not twice, but three times—and to pile on the agony, he filed his own decree claiming I abandoned him! He claimed to be blameless for the breakup.

He got darn right obstinate about it all. He kept showing up wherever I was. Mr. Stone threw him off the farm, but I saw him lurking more than once. I hated to admit how much that scared me. To be honest, sometimes I wasn't sure what was pushing my fantasies about a new life—the challenge of it, or the fear of what William Pickell would do if he ever caught me alone.

I pushed all those thoughts out of my mind as I settled into Seat No. 19 with my mother's blessings in my ears: "You're goin' on Saint Paddy's Day and that's a good sign." There weren't many Irish customs that clung to Ma—Irish potato soup, of course, and soda bread, and always saying if a fork fell off the table, "Oh, a woman is coming to visit." But St. Patrick's Day was always special in the Watson home, no matter what day of the week it fell.

"The Catholics aren't the only ones to claim him," Ma told us. "All the Irish honor St. Patrick because he drove the snakes out of Ireland." That's all I knew about it, but that's all I needed. Anybody who could drive the snakes out of a country was a saint in my mind.

"Saint Paddy himself is looking out for you as you start this journey. Don't you forget that. Be a good girl. Be careful. And come home to us someday." Ma turned away from me then, sending me off. I knew she was crying. I was too.

Pa waved to me from the barn and when I started to go toward him, John held me back. "Best let it be. He's taking this real hard." I knew my brother was right.

◇◇◇

"One way to Cheyenne?" the conductor asked as he punched my ticket.

"Yes, sir," I smiled at him. To my surprise, he returned a real smile to me.

I'd been watching him punch tickets along the way, and I saw the phony smile he gave to most of the passengers. Especially the painted ladies three rows up.

One wore a red silk dress and a hat full of feathers. Another had checks so red, I wondered at first if she was sick, but then I smiled to myself when I realized it had to be rouge. One had a snappy poodle and I thought it was queer that you'd bring a dog on a trip like this. Every one them had painted nails and hands full of flashy rings.

I had to look like a church mouse next to them. The conductor smiled at me again like he was looking at a sister after Sunday services.

"You have business in Cheyenne, ma'am?"

"I'm going to Cheyenne to start a new life."

"Your husband meeting you there?"

"No, I'm on my own. I'm going to be a homesteader one day."

I saw him flinch, like this was an amazing thing. I passed it off as just another man who thought I was a woman who didn't know my place.

"I wish you the best of luck. And you be careful, Cheyenne can be a rough place."

"I can take care of myself, but thank you, sir."

I snuggled into my seat and looked out the window. There was the familiar landscape of the prairie that I knew so well. Nearly flat land covered with crops or grasses, trees here and there standing guard, or lining a creek like cows at a trough. I'd seen this same picture every day for years, but now I was seeing so much at once—the train was going so fast, mile after mile was running by the window. I bet I saw more in the first half hour of my first train ride than I'd seen in all my twenty-four years.

I decided I was due a treat in honor of my new life, so I turned away from the window and pulled my valise up onto the empty seat beside me. Oh, I was thankful I didn't have to share this bench with another passenger, but could spread out for more comfort.

I took out a piece of cake carefully wrapped in cloth that Ma had packed. Truth be known, if I unpacked all the food Ma insisted I take, the valise would have been half empty. It was an extra generous piece of Ma's famous chocolate cake—a treat hardly ever made because cocoa was rare in our home. But Ma traditionally made it for St. Patrick's Day and this year, it not only honored him, but honored my trip. I was glad Ma had been so generous in her cut, and it looked to me like I'd be nibbling on this cake most of the way west. That's what I was thinking when I took my first bite of that delicious dark sweetness.

"My, does that look like a fine piece of chocolate cake."

I jumped at the surprise of a loud voice, only to find it belonged to the woman across the aisle in Seat No. 21.

"Ma'am?"

"I was just admiring that fine piece of chocolate cake. Someone sure loves you to send you off with something so delicious-looking."

Well, what was I supposed to do? My Ma taught me better than to stuff the cake in my mouth and ignore the woman who was salivating across the aisle. Yes, it pained me, but I did the only decent thing. I broke off a hunk and offered it to her.

"Oh, I couldn't." But her hand was already reaching while her mouth was protesting.

"How very sweet of you." She ate that hunk in two bites. Wouldn't you think you'd take it slow? Not this woman. I massaged my regret at losing a piece of my cake with the thought that it was a good omen to share something sweet when you're starting a new life.

"I'm Sally Wills. He's my husband." She cocked her head to note the man in window Seat No. 22. "He's Horace."

I noted that Sally Wills was busy licking her fingers of the last remnants of the cake and had not once offered to share with

Horace. He didn't appear to notice or mind. I bet it wasn't the first time his wife hadn't shared.

"Where you goin', sweetie?"

All I had to say was "Cheyenne" and that started a travelogue lecture that went on all afternoon. My contribution was nothing but "is that so"; "oh, that's nice"; "glad to hear it."

Sally Wills is one talker!

"You're gonna love Cheyenne, why it's one of the prettiest cities in all the West—not that I've been to them all, but it's so beautiful I just know it measures up. And they're going to build a grand Capitol building as soon as we're a state—everyone says that won't be long. I mean, Colorado was let in and if they took Colorado, they surely want Wyoming. Horace says all the territories will be states someday, well, maybe not Arizona, who wants them? There's just Indians and Mexicans and Mormons down there and Horace doesn't believe they'll *ever* catch Geronimo." I nodded, at least agreeing with the Geronimo part.

"We just love W.T.—that's what we call it, you know, because your jaws would be tuckered out if you had to say 'Wyoming Territory' every time, don't you think?" I had to agree it was a mouthful.

"My husband is a cobbler and you probably couldn't be in a better profession in W.T., because, believe me, those men go through boots and shoes like they're tryin' to wear them out. He has some very fancy customers—those cattlemen from Scotland and England like fancy things and they have the money to pay and my Horace said fine footwear is like a badge to them. My Horace is a real good provider. Do you have a husband?" I said I didn't and left it at that.

"We have four children—their aunt is taking care for them for us—and they're a handful, but I still have time for my temperance work. Did I mention I'm a member of the Woman's Christian Temperance Union?" I shook my head no and smiled at this crucial news.

"You know, I'm not a bloomer like some of those radical women, but I do believe we have to address the problem of too many spirits." Mrs. Wills lowered her voice, leaned across the aisle and confided: "Do you know, some men come home drunk and beat their wives?" I pretended I didn't know.

"Yes, it's true, and if we just had some sensible laws on all those saloons, it certainly would help. We're a growing group in W.T.—they said the WCTU could never happen here in the West because the saloons are so important. My own brother-in-law told me: 'Sally, there were saloons here before there was a single decent woman and so don't go gettin' all high and mighty on us', and I told him back, 'But there wasn't anything else here then and it wasn't until decent women and children came that this place was worth anything.' Well, I think I cocked his hat because he just turned and walked away and I took that as a win for our side. You know, our W.T. Chapter is getting so big, we think we can get Frances Willard out here to speak to us. Wouldn't that be something?"

I knew it would be and for a second, I considered doing a little bragging of my own by telling how I'd already heard "Saint Frances" speak at a temperance rally in Kansas—the top woman herself, convincing people all over the country to support Dry laws. But I thought better of it so I wouldn't have to explain anything.

"You should think about joining the Temperance Union. We're always looking for fine young women. Next meeting our topic is 'Intemperance causes more sorrow than war,' and I think it does, don't you?" I had to agree. I promised to look into joining.

"But women in Wyoming Territory can vote, can't they? Couldn't you just vote temperance in?" I thought it was a logical question.

"Oh yes, women in W.T. have FULL VOTING RIGHTS." She said the words like they were all in capital letters.

"But my dear, we don't have near enough women in W.T. to vote something like that in. You know, that's why they did it. Gave us the vote. To bring women here. I guess loneliness hurts worst than pride." Sally Wills chuckled at her joke. "They thought women would come if they gave them the vote and yes, many did, but it's still a man's world out here and don't ever forget that. At first, of course, the polling places were in the saloons, and no decent woman would go into a saloon, even to vote. But we got the voting out of there—at least we got that much—and into schools and churches and now women can vote in a decent place. But it just fluffs my feathers that the women who are here aren't good at voting. We work on them all the time, the WCTU does, and we always hear, 'oh, my husband makes those kind of decisions—I don't understand politics,' and I'd just like to swat them with my rug beater because that attitude is not going to get us anywhere. Can you imagine, if I let Horace make all those decisions [and by now, Mrs. Wills' voice was low and conspiratorial]. Well, I vote and I tell Horace how to vote in each election, and when he walks into that polling place, that's how he votes."

I had to look away so she couldn't see me smile—she foolishly thinks her vote counts twice because her husband does her bidding. Does she really believe that, or is she just saying it? Well, I decided right then that as soon as I could, I would vote—even if I had to go into a saloon.

The day went on like that until it was obviously time for a late lunch and my stomach was anxious for a piece of the chicken in the valise. Mrs. Wills finally succumbed to her husband's tugs and excused herself to open their own food-laden satchel. But not before she announced: "We didn't want to take our meals in the dining car this trip, not when my sister-in-law in Wichita— that's where we were visiting—is such a fabulous cook and just *forced* all this food on us. I told Horace, 'Horace, it would be a sin to waste this food by going to the dining car like we usually do' and of course, he agreed."

I rolled my eyes and hoped I'd never see the day when I'd wear such fake airs. Yes, I knew that elsewhere on this train, people were sitting at white-clothed tables and served hot meals by Negro waiters. There was wine and plenty of chocolate desserts. Then the women and children would retire to sitting rooms with more velvet and stuffed cushions than existed in all of Kansas and the men would go to the smoking car for their cigars. But I could never afford that fare—over ten times more than my ticket—and even if I could, it wasn't something I hankered for.

My chicken tasted all the better for the peace that came with it, because I learned Mrs. Wills would rather eat than talk and after she ate, she liked her nap.

I was watching the landscape—more trees than normal—when I nodded off myself. The jostling train was like being rocked, even if it wouldn't let you hold a tin of water. I have to write that to John in a letter! When I woke up, the scene out my window was something I'd never seen before. There were trees everywhere and rock walls that had been cut away to make room for the tracks. I cracked the window, and the smell of the air was totally different than the smells in Kansas. Even through the smoke from the engine, I could smell pines.

"Where you going to work?" I was startled again and doubted I'd ever get used to Mrs. Wills' trait of making no introductory remarks before resuming a conversation.

"I don't know. I'm going to see if there's a good boardinghouse that needs help." And then I prayed Mrs. Wills had not failed to mention she owned a boardinghouse that needed help.

"Oh, we have many nice places where a clean girl can get honest work. Maybe you could get on with the Inter-Ocean Hotel, oh, that's a fine place, the city's finest hotel. They do allow spirits, but you wouldn't be in the saloon part—they have a beautiful dining room. But of course, they require real waitress training? Do you have waitress training?"

I allowed that I didn't, but that didn't stop Sally Wills.

"Oh no, better yet. You should try at the Simmons Hotel—it's owned by a nice man from Norway and that's where the actors like to stay when they come for our Opera House. Have I told you about our Opera House? Oh my, you have to go there imme- diately when you get settled. It's on Hill Street. You know, it was the first Opera House west of the Mississippi, and it brings in the very best talent and the plays are always suitable for decent folk, and the actors like to stay at the Simmons Hotel and they have a big dining room and I bet they always need help."

I was only half listening because I never expected I'd work in a fancy hotel, but surely, there must be more modest places that could use a good, strong woman. Or maybe there was a farmer like Mr. Stone who needed a housekeeper. Or a rancher. I'm betting the wages out here are better than in Kansas. I should be able to save up pretty quick. But the blabbering kept on and when I focused again, Mrs. Wills was bragging about Cheyenne.

"Don't know if you realize what a fine city we have in Cheyenne. What's so remarkable is that it isn't even twenty years old yet—came in with the railroad, and oh, those days they tell me it was called 'Hell on Wheels,' but that didn't last the minute decent women arrived." By now, I had heard that term so often, I was sure I understand the western distinction between women and decent women.

"We already have a city park down by Lake Minnehaha, but stay away in the heat of summer because there's a terrible odor then. But otherwise, it's a very pretty place for a buggy ride. We're working on getting a library—won't that be wonderful?—our temperance group has been one of the big supporters and I can't tell you the hours I've put in. I'll tell you a secret, we already have 200 books collected. We just need an appropriate building and there's a committee working on that. I'm on the collection part and some of the books are in crates in my parlor—oh, it will be such a wonderful day when we can open a library and anyone can come and borrow our books."

I had never been inside a library. I had never borrowed a book, except for the Canadian history book back in school, but I could clearly see how wonderful that would be, and I smiled appropriately for Mrs. Wills.

"Even though Cheyenne is pretty new, my Horace says it already rivals Chicago or New York," and this time, I was sure Mrs. Wills was stretching the tale too far. "Horace says we have more millionaires in Cheyenne than they do back in the States and I wouldn't doubt him for a minute." I sure did.

"And wait till you see the club the cattlemen just built! Why, it's right in the center of town and has the first Mansard roof Cheyenne ever saw—oh, that was the talk all right." I had no idea what a Mansard roof was, but it didn't seem right to ask.

"It has this grand veranda and they sit up there, looking down at the city and knowing they're bringing millions, I mean, millions to W.T. because of all their wonderful cattle. Horace says their club is more highfalutin than anything else in the whole country. They only allow men who are rich ranchers and members of the Wyoming Stock Growers Association. They have to wear black tie or, or, or—Horace, what's that funny name they call the white tie and tails the men at the Cheyenne Club have to wear?"—Horace filled in the blank with "Herefords"—"Yes, that's it, the men have to wear black tie or Herefords."

I really didn't care much about a fancy place with strange clothes, but Mrs. Wills was sure I wanted to know every detail.

"And the women they invite to dinner! They wear the most beautiful jeweled evening gowns—some ladies send away to Paris for their gowns for the Cheyenne Club. I told Horace to save up, because I'm going to want a fabulous gown when we're invited. And they serve the most fantastic food: fresh oysters on the half shell and duck and veal and puffy French desserts. Horace says they spend more on champagne at the Cheyenne Club in one night than a ranch hand earns in a year. Can you imagine that?"

I couldn't imagine any of it.

It was a welcome treat when the train finally stopped at a station and the conductor yelled, "Ten minutes. Ten minutes at this stop."

"Oh, let's get some hot coffee." Sally Wills sounded like she was about to drink the finest wine in the world. Well, I knew the feeling because I was more than ready for a nice cup of coffee. But when we finally got inside the station, we found everybody on the train had the same hankering. The one waitress was handing out cups of boiling coffee as fast as she could. Boiling coffee!! I looked at my cup and knew it would never cool down enough for me to drink it.

"Not used to western coffee, ma'am?" The cowboy at the counter was looking at me with a smile in his eyes. In front of him was his own cup, sitting beside a saucer that was served to those who had more than a ten-minute stop.

"We like it real hot out here. Here, mine is already saucered and blowed." He handed me his saucer.

That night I wrote in my journal: "Today I learned about boiling coffee in the West and I drank a cowboy's coffee from the saucer. Oh my, I am in a new land."

◇◇◇

Sally Wills wasn't exaggerating about Cheyenne. My eyes got their first hint the minute I climbed down from the train and looked at more of a city than I'd ever seen. Two-, three-, and four-story brick buildings lined up like soldiers ready for inspection, and already, there was a grand street stretching out from the depot. There were fancy wagons and three-wheeled bicycles everywhere, and the streets were so crowded, I wondered at first if we'd arrived on a special holiday. My first real lesson in city living was to discover this was just an ordinary day in the territorial capital of Cheyenne.

Mrs. Wills was kind enough to take me under her wing that first day, barking at Horace to help with my trunk and load it onto their carriage. She took me to a reasonable boardinghouse where she knew the proprietor and thankfully, there was a room to let. We parted with promises to stay in touch and for me to come to a temperance meeting, but none of that ever happened.

The next morning, I set out to find work in the new city that was now my home, and I saw nothing that resembled the life I'd left. I went by the Inter-Ocean Hotel, but didn't even bother going in, for this was not a place where I would ever expect employment. The Simmons Hotel was just as imposing and I ended my tour concluding I'd be far more at home at Frank A. Meanea's Saddle Shop—"If it can be made of leather, we do it"—than anyplace else in town.

But my landlady knew a landlady with a large boardinghouse who needed help, and so by my third day, I was employed as a cook and waitress in a sturdy three-story home that catered to traveling cattlemen—the kind praying for the day they'd get beyond the waiting list for the Cheyenne Club.

Being the new girl, I was up at five a.m. to get the fire started, the coffee boiling, and the biscuits ready. I had to make sure the closing girl had done her job and put fresh linens on the tables, rearranged the wooden chairs and swept the floor, and more often than not, she hadn't so I did that, too. By the time the first men came down for breakfast at six a.m., it was my job to be sure everything was ready. It was a steady stream of customers all the way to nine-thirty a.m. and then the room had to be refreshed and dinner had to already be underway. By three p.m., I was making pies for supper and when I got done with that, I was finally done for the day. It wasn't difficult work, just long hours, but I soon found there were benefits I'd hadn't considered.

I had never lived anywhere there was a daily newspaper—well, not on Mondays, but that didn't count. Cheyenne didn't just have one, it had three dailies and a handful of weeklies and all of them were chocked full of news! I could just imagine how ecstatic Annie would be at this treasure trove, and it pleased me too, because I was anxious to learn about this territory. Of course, I never would have squandered the five cents to buy a paper, but luckily, many who came to the boardinghouse did, and they'd read it over breakfast and then leave it behind. I snatched up the discarded papers and folded them into my shawl that hung in the pantry, and after work, I'd read news that was already a day or week old, but that didn't matter.

I was surprised to find the Cheyenne dailies put mostly national news on their first pages—column after column of small type that needed a good lamp to read at night. Most of that was Greek to me, because I knew neither the place nor the names, and I skipped over most of the stories about the Panama Canal and the scandals in places like New Bedford. What caught my eye were the kinds of stories I wished I'd never read, like the one in May when a woman in New York—Lucy Gilebrist was her name—chopped off her baby's head. The woman was drunk. I thought that must go on the list of reasons women should never drink.

The June 23 paper gave me a real scare when a page one headline read: "Bad Day for Indians" and told how whites had killed six Utes near Denver. "The chief of the tribe is very much enraged," the story read, "and demands satisfaction. If the rumor proves true there will probably be trouble in southern Colorado with the Utes." When I brought this up to my landlady, she assured me there were no Utes in Wyoming Territory.

The local news went on page 2 of the dailies and often focused on the struggles of rural areas to get going—bond issues and plans for a school and irrigation conflicts. Of course, there were constant stories exalting the cattlemen of W.T. and how much money they were bringing in and how the price of cattle fluctuated wildly. I sure didn't find the same kind of stories about homesteaders. The only stories about homesteaders were about how they were ruining the "open range" and endangering the cattlemen and were probably bad people who shouldn't be in W.T. The first time I read a story like that, I shook my head like it had to be a mistake. Kansas had been so grateful that people moved there and homesteaded. Homesteaders in Kansas were respected people. It never occurred to me that it wasn't like that everywhere, and this new attitude was an unpleasant surprise.

I didn't even look for stories about women homesteaders. I was sure there had to be some out there—the railroad brochure said there were—but they never earned a mention in the Cheyenne newspapers.

Truth be known, some days I spent more time with the advertising than with the news stories. "SPRING HAS COME!" one ad in the *Cheyenne Daily Sun* declared soon after I arrived. "The grandest display of spring and summer dry and fancy goods at Kellner Bos." I thought I might just walk down to Kellners' one day and look over these fancy goods with prices so cheap, "they are the lowest this side of Chicago." One of the other girls told me not to bother, because cheap in W.T. wasn't cheap enough for our wages.

I never missed the society news on page 3, as I read about the grand happenings in Cheyenne. Each new opening at the Opera House demanded a great show of wealth and fancy dresses and carriages lined up with the richest folks in town showing themselves off. The papers always made a point of describing the "feathered chapeaus" worn by the town's society women, and I figured you couldn't go to the opera in W.T. if you didn't have a feathered hat. I always watched for the comings and goings of Horace and Sally Wills, but never found any of their activities worthy of mention in a Cheyenne daily newspaper.

The chatter was another benefit. The men who ate their meals here talked freely about their businesses and the price of cattle. They gossiped what they'd heard out of the Cheyenne Club and cost of good horseflesh. They harped on what territorial governor Francis Warren was up to—some days he was a hero, others a villain. They talked about who was in the political hot seat—it alternated between the "GD Democrats" and the "GD Republicans." I could listen all I wanted because they paid no attention to the kitchen help filling their china plates. The chatter was how I filled in the questions left from the papers I was reading. I especially listened to anything about homesteading, but these men didn't seem at all interested in homesteading. Except to swear at the "GD homesteaders" who were in the way.

The best benefit of all was my day off every week. It was really a half-day on Sunday afternoon and a half-day on Tuesday afternoon, but that was fine. I would put on my best dress and wrap myself in my shawl and walk down Seventeenth Street.

There it was, the grand Cheyenne Club that was always such a focus of the chatter. I knew the power in W.T. wasn't down the street at the territorial capital, but here at a club for members of *the* most powerful group in the territory—men so rich, they could buy anything they wanted. I wondered if they let their wives and daughters buy anything they wanted, too, or if they were misers who kept their money to themselves.

It was clear to see these were men who knew how to spend money on themselves. The club was about the grandest building

I had ever seen. Three stories. A veranda wrapping around three sides. That strange roof that looked so elegant. High-backed wooden rockers lining the veranda for men to sit and look out, just as Mrs. Wills had said. I never saw anyone sitting there on my half-days off, but I could imagine.

The other girls I worked with talked about this building like they'd had a private tour, which of course, they hadn't. But they talked like they did. I stood there looking at it and remembered what they'd told me. Not one, but two grand staircases. Rooms bigger than most homes. They say there's one room just for smoking. Another just for reading. Another just for billiards. A dining table for fifty. A wine vault filled with a fortune in fermented grapes. Floor-to-ceiling red velvet drapes and brocade satin settees. Tooled leather chairs and plush carpets. Silk wallpaper, stained-glass windows and glass-etched transoms. Full length diamond-shaped mirrors to reflect walls filled with oil paintings of ranch scenes. White china edged in gold and engraved with the CC logo. Sterling silver forks and spoons. They say they have a fork just for fish. A spoon just for berries. Cut-glass crystal wineglasses and matching goblets. And that was just the first floor.

Upstairs were the private apartments, the girls had said, each with their hand-carved beds and dressers and a large fireplace with white marble mantles. Behind the building were the tennis courts. I didn't even know people played tennis.

But as grand as the Cheyenne Club was, it wasn't my favorite place. That honor was held by 300 E. Seventeenth Street. I would stand across the street from the Victorian mansion and wonder what it would be like to live in such a beautiful home. Everyone in town knew this was the Whipple House. It was only two years old, but from the chatter at the boardinghouse, people were still marveling at what Ithamar C. Whipple had spent to build the finest home in all of Cheyenne. It wasn't its three-story height that so impressed me. What got me most were the beautiful windows that graced the front. It was almost as if there weren't any walls facing the street, just grand bay windows covered with lace curtains.

I thought it was one thing for a group of millionaire cattlemen to build a great building for their club, and quite another for just one millionaire to build a great home for his family. I found out I.C. Whipple was a banker and a founder of the Wyoming Stock Growers Association and a leader of the First Baptist Church. I guess I had my answer—men like him let their wives and daughters buy anything they wanted, too.

One day when I was admiring the Whipple House, I saw a little girl I bet was his daughter climb down the front steps. She was with her nanny. She was wearing a white layered dress that gathered at the waist by a pink sash. There was lace at the collar and the cuffs, and little pink roses were tucked into the lace. The nanny scowled, but the little girl smiled at me as she skipped down the street to a house that would have been considered grand itself, if it hadn't sat next to the Whipple House. I imagined the girl was going to a party and her nanny was carrying the gift, and I wondered what was inside the box. But what I'd always remember was the sweet smile on the girl's face. It was the kind of smile Elizabeth would have had if she had lived.

Other times on my half-day off, I devoted myself to long letters home to a family I missed more than I'd ever imagined. Of course, I reassured my parents that I had found decent employment in a clean house, and that I was well and happy—I fudged on that some weeks when the loneliness got fierce, but I never told them that. I gave glowing reports on how prosperous and pretty Cheyenne was and how I was saving money. "There are fine people here in Wyoming Territory," I wrote to them and just didn't mention those who weren't.

Like the cowboys with their fresh hands. The girls who served meals here were ignored except for one thing—a pat on the fanny or a pinch through work dresses and petticoats. The first time it happened, I was startled. Men in Kansas didn't do things like this, but here was this ranch foreman acting like he was in a saloon and had a fancy girl at his disposal. But my impression that it was just the hired help who acted like oafs was shattered a week later, when one of the big ranch owners did the same thing. I watched the other girls for clues and saw how they weaved and swayed to keep themselves away from prying hands, and I became an expert at the dodge.

But I never wrote home of such things. I just had to stay out of their way and they were harmless. That's what the other girls told me. I believed them. A few bad apples shouldn't spoil the whole barrel.

I held on to that thought for almost six months, until the day in September I learned about the Chinese massacre. I first overheard one of the regulars: "Did you hear they killed some Chinks out in Rock Springs?"

"Yeah, heard Governor Warren is waiting for a fast train comin' in from Omaha."

"Bet those Union Pacific guys have their balls in their throats—it's their coal mines, you know."

"Well, if the railroads hadn't brought the Chinese here in the first place, we wouldn't be having these problems. Can't expect a white man to stand by while a Chink takes his job!"

All of this was startling news. I had never seen a Chinese person. I knew nothing about them. But these men sure thought they did.

"They smoke opium."

"They live like rats, ten or twelve to a room."

"They eat strange food."

"They never cut their hair. They wear it in pigtails down their backs."

"They dress in pajamas."

"They're ruthless. They'd cheat you in a second."

"They aren't Christians."

None of those things made me want to meet a Chinese person, but that didn't stop me from feeling sick over the Rock Springs Massacre.

I read all the stories, even the ones that left me with a sour stomach. And while the stories never blamed the railroads, I saw right away that this was all their fault. Those railroad men knew how to squeeze money out of a stone. They forced their workers to live in company houses and to shop at company stores and from what I heard, the prices they charged were really high. But the workers didn't have a choice. Years ago, white men fought back, striking for better wages. So the railroad brought in strike-breakers who'd work cheaper. First they got Scandinavians, who didn't demand a white man's pay. But when even their cheap wages weren't low enough, they brought in Chinese who worked for almost nothing. By now, the Scandinavians were the "white men" whose jobs were being taken by "yellow devils."

I was horrified to read that as many as 150 armed white men attacked "Chinatown," where only the Chinese miners lived. The mob beat to death twenty-eight men. Wounded another fifteen. They burned down all of Chinatown's seventy-nine buildings. And I couldn't believe this—some white women had helped with the killings.

It got harder every day to listen to the chatter in the dining room. Because I didn't hear people sorry about what happened. I heard people make fun of it.

"'Did you hear how they snookered the Chinks? All of them that ran away were rounded up by the railroad and put in a boxcar and sent out of town and those heathens thought they were going to San Francisco. They were gone a week. But the railroad just ran them in a circle and brought them back to Rock Springs." Then that man almost bust a gut laughing at what the railroad had done.

"The railroad needs them to work, don't you know!" He said it like that excused everything.

The *Cheyenne Leader* told the rest of the gruesome story, and I couldn't believe anyone could be so cruel. The survivors returned to find everything they owned had been burned to the ground, not only their homes, but all their clothes and possessions, and most importantly, all their savings that were left behind as they escaped. But that wasn't the worst of it. A full week after the massacre, nobody had had the decency to bury the twenty-eight dead men, so the survivors came home to find their fathers and sons and brothers and cousins still lying where they were killed. Their bodies were mangled, bloated, and decaying.

I had to put down the paper in horror when I read they saw some of the bodies being eaten by dogs and hogs.

What kind of place had I come to that would tolerate such things?

But to the men in the dining room, those dead men had brought this on themselves. Because they came here to work. And nobody ever said they weren't good workers, either. Still, I heard lots of curses that they shouldn't be allowed in this country in the first place and they should all be deported.

I heard very few words criticizing the railroads, but then, it was already clear to me that next to big cattlemen, there was no one more important in W.T. than the railroads, so it wouldn't do to bad-mouth them. But it was safe to say bad things about a Chinese person.

The stories coming out of Rock Springs made me so sad. Those men were strangers to this land and would never fit in.

I was a stranger here too. Would I ever fit in?

I kept those thoughts to myself, of course, since nobody wanted to hear what a woman had to say anyway.

I was used to being invisible to my customers, useful only when they wanted a refill or a feel, so I felt very strange when I noticed a scar-faced man staring at me. A thick scar ran down his cheek and I wondered where he'd met the knife that marked him. But I wondered more why he would ever notice me, and I wished he hadn't. I was relieved when his stay was over, but a month later, he was back, and he stared all the more.

The man made me nervous and a little clumsy. It was a Thursday when I was serving dinner and dropped a knife. As it bounced on to the floor, I forgot myself and said out loud, "As my Ma would say, if a knife falls, a man's coming to visit." The scar-faced man jumped in, "My Ma used to say that too. And if a fork falls, a woman's coming to call." It seemed strange that we would have something in common, and I just turned around and left the dining room.

After dinner, I was taking the garbage out to the alley when someone grabbed me from behind and put a gloved hand over my mouth. I couldn't see my attacker, but I just knew it was the scar-faced man. I struggled to free myself from his grip, but he was far stronger and taller. I cried out when he ripped my dress and even through his glove, you could hear it.

Oh my God, please don't let him rape me. Give me strength, I prayed.

I tried tripping him by shoving my left leg back, like my brothers liked to do when they wrestled. But I was off balance and couldn't. I tried throwing myself to the side to pull him off, but he was too centered to fall.

I'm going to be raped right here in this dirty alley. And then that ugly man is going to kill me.

That big scar on his face came into my mind and I could just see him plunging the knife that made that scar into my chest.

I'm going to bleed to death in this alley and my Ma will weep over my grave. Our Father, who art in heaven… and that's when his hold gave away.

I fell to the ground, gasping for air, and saw four legs wrestling in the dirt. Smack. Smack. I heard fists hitting flesh and howls of pain. I crawled as fast as I could backwards to get out of the way, and it was only when I backed up to the coal bin that I saw what was happening in front of me. The scar-faced man was fighting with that nice, well-tailored man who just came in a couple days ago—the one who always said, "Thank you very much," when I served him. They were on the ground and the scar-faced man was on top. He kept hitting until the gentleman stopped moving.

I scrambled to my feet and grabbed a lump of coal as the only weapon I could find. I started to raise my arm when the scar-faced man stood up and asked me, "Are you alright, ma'am?"

But by then, I'd let loose and the piece of coal hit him in the chest.

"Hey. Slow down, Bessie. It's over." He held up his hands in surrender, and then said in a gentle voice, "He can't hurt you anymore."

I just looked at him, trying to comprehend what was going on, and in the time it took me to realize the difference between my attacker and my savior, I learned a valuable life lesson.

"Go in and tell your landlady to send for the police," the scar-faced man told me as he kicked the unconscious man aside so I could freely move past them.

My hands were still shaking when the policeman took away my attacker. The scar-faced man had to tell the whole story because I was too upset to speak. My nice housekeeper kept a protective arm around my shoulders as the tale was told and more than once said, "Thank the Lord you were there, Mr. Shaw. Thank the Lord."

I finally got my wits about me. "Sir, thank you very much for saving me." I held out my hand to shake his.

"You're very welcome, ma'am," he said, and he noticed I was having a hard time not staring at his scar.

"I got this saving another young lady from an Indian attack," he said, as he ran his hand over his face. "It was my sister, Mary, and darned if you aren't the spittin' image of her."

He smiled at me like a sister and I saw that, except for that scar, he had a nice face. He didn't linger once the policeman left. I sat there a moment, too ashamed of myself for all the bad things I'd thought about him.

That night in bed, I had a heart-to-heart talk with myself. I had suspected for some time now that a city like Cheyenne was no place for a woman like me, but now I knew for sure. I couldn't stay here. I needed to move on to a smaller place, a kinder place, a place where men didn't try to rape you in dirty alleys, a place closer to the land.

At that moment, I wasn't sure where that place was. I knew it wasn't Salt Lake City, because I'm not Mormon. I knew it wasn't San Francisco, because I didn't have the money to travel that far. I only knew it was farther west. And as far west as my money would take me was the county seat of Carbon County. It was the growing town of Rawlins, Wyoming Territory.

Chapter Seven

The Man I Love

I don't even remember noticing James at first—he says he'd been having dinners at Rawlins House for three days before I ever paid him any mind.

I suppose there are lots of reasons he went overlooked. Men who get my attention are at least six feet so my five feet eight can look up, but Jim wasn't like that. He cleared my bosom, but not my nose. Men I notice have a weight to them, not fat, but sturdy. They're men who can handle a horse and a cow and a hammer, like I can. I have a weight to me, too, but if I have to say it myself, my one hundred seventy pounds are nicely distributed. Jim wasn't that kind of man. I bet I had twenty-five pounds on him. But mostly I didn't notice him because at that point, I was still lookin' out for men. I sure wasn't lookin' for one.

So I didn't pay any attention to this man who kept coming in for dinner and seemed particularly taken with my pies.

Mrs. Hayes hired me the second day I was in town when I used an old trick my Ma taught me back in Kansas. I arrived at her doorstep tellin' her I was a clean, hardworking woman and my Ma was Irish, too—I knew that would get me points because the first thing anyone ever told me about Mrs. Hayes was that she was as Irish as a pig in Dublin. The second thing I'd been told was that she was strict, but fair. She and her husband were among the first real business folks in Rawlins and her boarding-house and restaurant were the pride of the town.

I knew I could tell her I'd worked for nearly seven months at a boardinghouse in Cheyenne, but I wasn't sure if that would help or not, so I used Ma's trick to make me more valuable. I told Mrs. Hayes I made the best pie you ever tasted and if she just let me use her kitchen, I brought along some canned apples and I would prove it. She smiled at my pluck and called to Brenda, who already was in her employ, that they were about to get a free apple pie. Well, I wasn't lyin' and she knew it from the first bite and hired me on the spot and I thanked my Ma for helpin' me get in the door.

"Ella, I have strict rules for the girls who work for me and if you think you can't handle them, you tell me right now so neither of us wastes our time," she told me. "I won't tolerate you messin' with the customers. I don't allow men in your room upstairs, and I don't want to hear any talk on the street that you're not a decent girl. I don't demand you go to services, but until we get a church built, if you want to attend I'll tell you where we're gathering each Sunday. No matter to me which group you go with. Myself, of course, is Catholic and we'd be glad to have you come with us, but I'm not like some of them that turn down their nose at somebody else's religion. Standin' in a church doesn't make you any more a Christian than standin' in a barn makes you a horse. As long as you believe in the Lord, you're all right in my book."

I promised I could follow the rules and thanked her for the offer of worship services and told her my Ma would be particu-larly happy to know the people of Rawlins didn't need a church to hold to their religions. I never mentioned that even with three churches to choose from around Lebanon, my Pa could not muster up the will to get to any of them on Sunday. Nor did I mention that my Ma didn't go off to a Catholic church as Mrs. Hayes presumed.

I have to tell this story because it always makes me smile, but when I started at Rawlins House in October of 1885, they were selling pieces from four pies a day. That's what Mrs. Hayes said I'd be makin', along with helping cook and serve dinner. I was already used to all that. But by the second week, after folks tasted the fine pies I made, we were selling eight pies a day and Mrs. Hayes joked she could make her rent just from the 15 cents apiece from my pies.

Besides apple, I used whatever fruit was put up or available and when that got skimpy, I even sold pieces of vinegar pie, although Mrs. Hayes said that was a pie of last resort when there was nothing else and she didn't think anyone would pay good money for it. But they did.

The first time I really noticed Jim was in January when he ordered his second piece of pie after a full dinner and was the only one left in the dining room. I remember wondering where a little guy like that put it all.

And then the next night he did it again. I wondered if this man had a tapeworm he needed to feed. There he was, the only one left in the dining room with only crumbs left on his plate and while I was still wonderin' about his queer appetite, he politely said, "Ma'am, excuse me, but this is the most delicious pie I have ever eaten and I believe you're responsible."

"Yes, sir," I said, pleased with myself. "I'm glad you're enjoyin' it and you seem to enjoy it more than most." Then I gave a little laugh and he laughed back.

"I'm making a pig of myself, aren't I?" he asked with a smile, and I noticed for the first time he had a pretty handsome face. Blue-green eyes, neat mustache, nice smile. "Well, it's worth it," he added to put a fine point on it.

Then he stood up and extended his hand and said, "I'm James Averell, but my friends call me Jimmy, and I'm glad to meet you."

I had a coffeepot in one hand and used that as the excuse not to reach back—and for a second I contemplated what a good weapon it would be if I needed it—and he withdrew his hand and said, "Of course, I'm being too forward. Give my regards to Mrs. Hayes. Tell her Jimmy Averell was in and really loves your pies."

He picked up his hat and laid a silver dollar on the table and nodded as he walked out the door. I looked at the dollar and realized he'd left two-bits too much to cover the dinner and the pies, and it took me a minute to realize the rest was a tip. I had never had such a tip before—most men left a penny or two, maybe a nickel, if they left anything at all—and I suspected then that he must be a rich man.

"I wouldn't call him rich, but he is a hard worker, that Jimmy Averell," Mrs. Hayes said the next day when I delivered the message. "He just opened a roadhouse out on the road to Casper, put it right where the roads cross so he gets the traffic from both ways, and I think he's doing okay for himself. He's a widower, you know."

The next night he was back and quietly said, "Good evening," when I brought him a plate of chicken and string beans and cornbread. "Good evening, Mr. Averell," I said, and retreated to the kitchen.

Mrs. Hayes went into the dining room and the two of them had a laugh over something and she called me out. "Ella, I want to introduce you to James Averell," she said, and then told him my name and he smiled and said it was nice to meet me.

It was no surprise when he ordered a piece of the rhubarb pie we had that night. But instead of ordering a second, he just ate the first one real slow, and I filled his coffee cup twice over that pie and he still ended up the only one in the dining room.

By now, Brenda's shift was over and Mrs. Hayes was long gone and it was my job to finish up, so I was glad to clear his plate and put an end to my long day. I'll never forget exactly what happened next.

"Miss Watson, I was wondering if I could walk you home tonight, after you finish?" Jim said, with all the politeness in the world.

"Sir, I just live upstairs, and I think I can get myself home, but thank you."

"Then I guess it would be short walk home," he persisted, and I laughed a little at that because most men would have been so embarrassed they'd have just turned and walked away. But he didn't. He stood there, looking determined to walk me home, even if it was just a few steps, and I let the thought creep into my head that this was a sweet thing for a man to do.

"You know, Mrs. Hayes doesn't like us getting friendly with the customers."

He jumped right in, "Mrs. Hayes knows I have only the most honorable of intentions. Otherwise she wouldn't have introduced us."

I'm not used to a man with such a quick tongue, but I liked what he said and how he said it and I thought his logic was right, so I'd take a chance. "Mr. Averell, if you wait outside while I finish cleaning up, I'd be happy to let you walk me home."

I felt a little flushed when I got back to the kitchen. I was wearing my kitchen dress, covered with a white apron and even when you took the apron off, it was still just a kitchen dress. Not a nice button or piece of lace on it—a working dress that seemed way too plain to be walked home in, even if it was just around the corner of the building. My one good broach was upstairs in its velvet box and my hair comb was on the dresser, and after fretting about all this a minute or two I realized this man had never seen me in anything but my kitchen dress and white apron, and he still asked to walk me home.

I messed a little with my hair to be sure it was neat and any flying strands were tucked in and I went out to meet him. He was sitting on the bench by the front windows and he stood up the minute he saw me.

"Perhaps you could sit for a moment," he suggested. That helped prove his honorable intentions because there we were, on Main Street in Rawlins, Wyoming Territory, and anybody who wanted to walk by or drive by or hitch their horse to the rail would see us big as day, and if you were intending something else, that's not where you'd be.

So I sat down and had the most pleasant conversation I'd ever had with a man.

I'm not saying my Jimmy bragged that first night, but he was intent on letting me know he was an upstanding man and not some roustabout.

"I fought in the Indian Wars in the U.S. Army. Thankfully, I never had any horrible battles, but I came close a couple times. But mainly, I learned the trade of surveying from the first man who surveyed Wyoming back when it was still part of Dakota Territory."

I imagined Jimmy in a uniform, even more handsome than now.

"We surveyed land out in the Sweetwater Valley and I found this land along Horse Creek. I told Billy—that was his name, Billy Owen—I told him that when these Indian Wars were over, I was coming back here. He said that would be a fine decision, and I always valued his counsel. And that's what I did. I filed a claim along Horse Creek and started a roadhouse sixty miles out of town by the old Oregon Trail."

I found all this acceptable, and it showed the man had gumption and drive.

He then worked backwards, explaining his wife died in childbirth, and his son didn't survive, either. I offered my condolences. He thanked me and pushed forward, saying he came from a good family of Scottish heritage and was born in Canada and wanted to become a citizen of the United States of America. It was right then that my interest got most peaked because I, too, had been born in Canada and like him, had a Scottish heritage.

"Excuse me, but do you know where Bruce County is in Ontario?" I asked.

He smiled with the assurance that he had the right answer. "Of course, I do. It's not far from where I was born in Renfrew County. How do you know Bruce County?"

"Because that's where I was born," I told him, and we both laughed.

"You're Canadian, too?" he asked me, like this was the best coincidence he ever heard.

"My Pa is Scot, and my Ma is Irish," I nodded in agreement. And then I told that I, too, had high hopes of following my Pa and becoming a citizen.

To be sure all this was real, I gave him a little test: "Do you know the words to 'Auld Lang Syne'?" He broke into the song right there and as we sang, we realized we had a whole lot in common.

"I'd like to hear more about your family," he said, and sounded like he meant it. So I started to tell it all, because this was the easiest man I'd ever talked to. He looked you straight in the eye as he talked and he paid attention to what you said—he really did. It was real dark by the time I'd told him about my Ma losing so many of her babies—and how Elizabeth was the hardest on me—and my family immigrating to Kansas and helping build a soddie and then coming West alone. I left out the part about my first husband because that wasn't the kind of story you told the first night you're getting to know a man.

As I'd find out later, James didn't tell his whole story that night, either, and I'd certainly come to understand why and, even when I found out, it didn't change the pull on my heartstrings I felt that first night.

"Ella, I do want to tell you, so we're straight from the start. I'm a lot older than you. I'll be thirty-five in March. But I'm healthy as an ox. I just wanted you to know that."

I thought that said a lot from a man doing his first Main Street visiting with a woman, so I knew his heartstrings were singing, too.

"Well, I'll be twenty-six in July," is all I said to show it wasn't a problem.

By the next morning, Mrs. Hayes knew all about my sitting in front of her hostelry with James Averell. "Everybody likes Jimmy," she told me, "and I haven't heard anything untoward, but I know your Ma would expect me to warn you," she said in her best motherly voice. "You've got to be careful because folks' tongues can be cruel. There's not much to do around here for recreation so folks like to sit on their porch and think about their neighbors and any little thing that's out of line becomes a big thing after it's told a time or two, so be careful. Now Ella, everybody knows I wouldn't employ you if you were not a clean, upstanding girl and you haven't shown anything but that to me. But I am worried that you might be naive when it comes to men, and you're new to these parts and don't know our ways. You might not understand how easy it is to lose a good reputation when people start talking."

I knew she was speaking to me like I was her own kin, and she had nothing but my welfare on her mind. But even Mrs. Hayes had to admit, when I protested, that it's hard to do bad things when you're sitting plain as day on Main Street.

Jimmy came back the next night for supper and pie and again, he waited for me to close up and we sat and talked. Oh, we had so much in common. Not just our ancestral blood and Canada, but how our families immigrated to the United States because this was a new country with lots of opportunities and free land if you had the mind and strong back to make good of it. His people stopped in Wisconsin, while mine went farther west to Kansas, but we were after the same thing. And then we both ended up in W.T. I came here, I confided, because W.T. was one of the few places I could have the kind of freedom women didn't have anywhere else, and one of those freedoms was to own my own land. I didn't need a big spread, just enough to raise a few head of cattle and have a good garden and a chicken coop and a log house with a little porch. I'm not a fancy woman and I don't need fancy things, I told him. I've been working on a farm most of my life, and I know how to do everything. The only thing I don't have is brute strength, but I figure there's lots of cowboys around with that and they're cheap labor. I don't want to live in a boardinghouse all my life, making pies for sale and serving dinners.

He said he could tell that about me from the very first time we talked and it was one of the things he most liked about me.

I don't know which of us blushed more when he talked about liking me, but we both sat silent a few minutes. Then he reached out and took my hand, real gentle like, and tucked it between us so only we would know and nobody had to say anything.

I must admit, I felt something I never thought I'd feel again. I felt safe with a man.

James Averell might not be a big man in size, but right then, I knew he was a big man in my eyes. I had to turn my head away when I smiled at the thought that if he tried, I'd let this man kiss me. But he didn't try. That night.

Instead, he said the most romantic thing a man could say to me at that moment of my life: "Ella, if you want to be a landowner in Wyoming Territory, I'll help you."

I had to hold myself back that I didn't leap over and kiss him. I just looked at him in awe. I saw a handsome, kind, smart man who was promising me more than a sack of gold or a mansion on Seventeenth Street in Cheyenne.

"You'll help me?" I could barely breathe.

"Yes, I'll help you with the paperwork and I can survey the site for you and in five years you can be the proud owner of one hundred sixty acres of choice Wyoming land."

He squeezed my hand and it was better than a kiss. I was all warm thinking about what this man was offering. "That's the same size as my Pa's homestead in Kansas," I told him, to show I knew something about such things.

He surprised me with his answer. "That's the problem. Those men back in Congress don't know anything about Wyoming or ranching—to them, one hundred sixty acres is a lot of land. They'd kill for that much land to call their own back there. But out here, it's a spit in the bucket. But try to talk some sense to them and you might as well be addressing a stump. They won't listen. That's one reason there's so much trouble out here—a man can't make it on just one hundred sixty acres."

I remember he paused a minute before he rushed back in to erase the frown on my face: "But that's a fine place to start Ella, and for you, it will be fine." Jimmy Averell could sound real convincing when he wanted to be.

The next night he was at his usual place for supper and he seemed to notice right away that under my white apron was a Sunday dress. Mrs. Hayes had spied it immediately and gotten a sly smile on her face. "I think somebody's sparkin' somebody," she almost sang and Brenda giggled. I just ignored them, but I am sure I was blushing.

It didn't escape my notice that Mrs. Hayes put an extra chicken wing on Jimmy's plate that night. He winked at me when I put it down in front of him, thinkin' it was my doing. I couldn't wait to tell him Mrs. Hayes was his benefactor and that it was a powerful sign of her approval.

We sat on our bench that night and right away, Jimmy whispered, "I found something for you." He pulled out a velvet bag tied with a red cord from his pocket and gently handed it to me.

My life hasn't been full of presents you can hold in your hand. From Ma and Pa, sure, but that's where it started and ended. I never got the ring I'd been promised at marriage and now that I think of it, I was the one giving presents in those years I was with him. I don't even like to say his name, but just now I'm adding to my list of grievances that he was so cheap he never gave me a present. And here was a man I'd known only days and he was holding out a pretty green velvet bag and it took my breath away.

"Mr. Averell, I wasn't expecting a gift," I said, not sure what you're supposed to say at a time like this.

"I hope you'll accept it," he answered, as though there were a question.

I took the bag and inside was an ivory hair comb inlaid with mother of pearl, and I had never seen anything so beautiful in my life. I gasped in delight, but it made Jimmy nervous: "You don't think it's too fancy," he started blabbering. "It's a proper comb, and I thought it would look beautiful in your hair, but if you don't like it, I can take it…"

"Oh no, I love it," I gushed. "It's just beautiful. I guess I'll have to go to church now so I have somewhere to wear it—it's not too fancy for church, do you think?"

"No, no, it would be fine in church. I was thinking maybe someday we could go to the Opera House and take in a musical—we have a beautiful Opera House in Rawlins—and you could wear it then, too."

"I've never been to a musical, outside my Pa and his fiddle, but I'd love to go sometime." I checked myself because I was startin' to use the world 'love' a lot tonight. "I would like very much to go to a musical with you."

I don't know much about men—I've already proven that—but I hoped my feelings were true that a man who'd eat that much pie to wait for you and then give you a hair comb this precious was not the kind of man who'd stomp on your heart.

"Thank you so much, Jimmy." I smiled at him and he smiled back, pleased with himself, and we sat like that awhile, just enjoying the moment.

He finally broke the quiet with a question even more precious than the comb. "Ella, would you like a little stream by your claim?" It wasn't really a question because the answer was so obvious, and I knew he was playing with me.

"Now, let me think," I acted all coquettish, "would I like a stream by my one hundred sixty acres? Well, I do believe I would!" And by then, we were both laughing.

"What if I told you there's some land next to mine by Horse Creek that could be claimed?" he got real serious.

"There is?" I was astonished.

"Yes, and it's good land—good pastureland, good farmland. Horse Creek isn't real big—it's a tributary of the Sweetwater, but it runs most of the year and there's plenty of water for stock and crops. Now, there's no trees, but you know enough about W.T. already to know that trees are few and far between out here. But we can plant some around your cabin. "

In my mind I saw a glorious place—rich land, a cabin with trees that would be big by the time I was an old lady; a little, tinkling creek edged by bushes, because there's always at least bushes by a creek. I asked a pretty dumb question for someone who should have been satisfied with water for stock and crops: "Are there berries by the creek?"

Jimmy grinned and nodded, "I believe there are," like that was the final selling point.

"I want you to think on it." He informed me he had to go back to his roadhouse now that his business in town was done. But he'd be back in a couple weeks and hoped I'd have thought it all through by then. I didn't dare tell him there was nothing more to think about because that would have sounded too eager to be proper, and so I stayed quiet and let him think this would take some powerful pondering on my part. "I hope you won't forget me," he said, as we parted that night.

I turned to him, and in the truest thing I ever said to a man, I promised, "Of course I won't forget you, Mr. Averell. You come back safe and sound."

I was real glad when he walked through the front door of Rawlins House again two weeks later, and I gave him a piece of pie for free. By then, I had figured out that if I worked here another year, I could save enough for the filing fee on a homestead and the first supplies I'd need to start a house. I figured James would help me with the loggin', and there's always cowboys out of work in the off-season who would help build a cabin for cheap wages.

As we sat on the front bench, I started spellin' out the plans I'd made as I'd laid in my bed every night for the last two weeks going over each detail I could imagine. He let me speak and at times, the words tumbled over one another because I was so excited to get everything out.

"There's a lot I could get done in a year as I save up," I started. "I could buy a horse and wagon now, I've got enough saved already, and I saw in the paper that there are auctions and these things can go real cheap. If you let me rent a place in your corral for my horse, I could go logging in the mountains and pile up the wood until I can lay a claim. I'm real good with an ax. I just want a small cabin, nothing fancy."

I didn't think I had to say anything about him helping me with the logging because I couldn't imagine him not. I thought he'd be impressed that I intended to use my own horse and my own wagon, rather than borrowing his, and I hoped his rent would be cheap. I sure didn't want this man concerned that he'd be saddled with a soft woman if he helped me get a claim.

Jimmy smiled as I was telling all this and later laughed that he liked how I was provin' myself up to him.

When I finally took a breath and let him speak, he said all that sounded very fine, but he had another route we could go.

"What if I told you that you wouldn't have to wait a year?" he began. "What if I told you that you could file on land now?" He let the words hang there and hang they did, because they didn't make any sense to me. I couldn't figure out how that could happen because right then, I had saved but fifty-three dollars since coming to W.T. I could pay the filing fee, but I sure didn't have enough to get started and it wasn't smart to file until you were ready to build a cabin and improve the land. After paying for the filing, the thirty-five dollars I'd have left sure wouldn't stretch far enough.

James laid out his plan and I will admit, at first I thought it sounded all wrong.

He told me if I came and cooked at his roadhouse, I could earn my homestead money. It would be good for his business if he offered a hot meal. Cowboys out there didn't have anything but the chuck wagons, and when they were fed and watered (although I knew it wasn't water he was talkin' about) they were free spending on other supplies in the store. The way he saw it, we'd both make good money on the deal. He said he'd buy all the groceries, but I could keep the fifty cents-a-plate dinner charge and it wouldn't take me long to save up. He'd even front me the money I needed to get going, and I could pay him back from my earnings. And he'd see I had a house up by summer.

I could hardly believe my ears. A payin' job and a chance to own my own land right now. That sounded so good, except for one thing. I don't care if this was the Wild West and they did things differently out here, a woman couldn't go off to a lonely ranch with a man and not be his wife, not even in Wyoming

Territory. He could tell from the questions in my eyes that this is what I was thinking.

"Ella, as much as I want to, I can't ask you to marry me right off in public because that would mean you couldn't get your own homestead," he said, lowering his voice and moving a little closer to my ear. "Married folks can only get one claim and since I already have a claim, if you became my bride, that would cheat you out."

Not since my first husband called me that ugly name can I remember words stinging so much. I had not thought that part through, and for a minute I thought that queered everything.

I sat for a second and then a clever idea hit me: "But what if I file and then we get married, and we could do that right away and everything would be alright..."

Jim started shaking his head after the first couple words, and I didn't feel so clever anymore. "Ella, the law says a claim is filed by the head of the household, and if you file and then marry, the land would revert to me as head. It wouldn't be your land, it would be mine."

I started thinking, well, it actually would be ours, but I knew I was foolin' myself because I knew of no law that saw an "us" in a marriage. If I hadn't known that, Mr. Pickell sure let me know how iron clad that was and that he was doin' me a big favor by even letting me have my own clothes. No, "us" wasn't real and I already knew how badly a marriage could turn out, and while I didn't think there was a chance Jim would be like that, I also knew what it felt to get burned, and I didn't want to feel that again.

Jim was already talking as I was thinking of all this, and I had to have him repeat himself because I wasn't sure I understood what he was trying to say. He made himself clear when I paid attention. "You can only file for yourself if you're a single woman, and besides, if the law saw us both as singles, we could both file two, three claims under different acts and get ourselves a healthy spread that would support the big family I hope we have one day." Now he was sounding like a man who had spent considerable time thinking this through, and I especially liked the part about the big family. But I'd heard that promise before, and for a second, I worried it could be a lie again. When I looked into those pretty eyes, they didn't look lyin' to me.

I dropped my eyes and wrung my hands and dared to say in a low voice, "So you do intend to ask for my hand."

He almost jumped—he reached over and took my hands in his and said, "Of course I want to marry you. I want us to be together forever. I love you, Ella."

His words made my heart sing.

"I just don't want that to ruin your chances to own the land you want so much. I don't want it to ruin our chances of building a decent life. Ella, I said I couldn't *publicly* marry you, but we could go off to another county and get married and keep it a secret. You and I would know the truth, but the law would still let us file claims and when they were proved up, we could tell everyone the truth, and nobody could do anything about it. I know this isn't the normal way to go, but it is a way for us to get everything we want."

I still had to say, "James, that's cheating, isn't it?"

He admitted it was. "But considering how the big cattlemen are cheating, this is small potatoes. Do you know what they do? They file fake claims and don't do a thing to till the land. The law says you've got to improve the land and build a cabin, so they put a rickety old building on wooden logs and haul it around like it's a real cabin and they claim they've met the law. When they've filed all the claims they can, they get their ranch hands to file some more for them—I know, I filed one for a man I worked for myself. They've thought of more ways of getting around the law than an honest man can imagine. Hell, oh, pardon my language, between the cattlemen and the railroad, it's a wonder there's any land left for an honest man. We're not cheating like that, Ella. It's not like we're trying to take all the land, we just want a decent share."

A lot of things bothered me about this plan, and the list in my mind kept growing as I imagined the faces of my family, but I also saw the chances it provided. I saw the dreams it made come true. I'd left my home and my family to come west so I could own land. In my own name. I saw myself on my land and my cows and my garden and that was just too big a plate to throw away. All my concerns went into second place as I saw all the chances Jim was offering and how this was the only way.

And that's how I presented it to Mary Hayes.

"Is he going to marry you?" she asked right off, sounding very sharp.

"We don't have plans to marry right away." I didn't want to go any further because this plan didn't work if people knew our secret. But as pleased as I was with how this would work, Mrs. Hayes was unpleased.

"Ella, you aren't the first of my girls to get her head turned by a man in these parts," she told me. "But you have to do it like Mary Agnes did it—she worked for me at the Union Pacific Hotel before we built this. She was smitten with that nice Tom Sun who has such a beautiful spread out by Devil's Gate. But they were married here in Rawlins before she ever went out on the range with him. That's the way it's done, Ella. That's the *only* way it can be done. You have no business being out there with him if you aren't married. People will talk, and they'll say bad things about you. Terrible things. Even if this is on the up-and-up, they'll label you and you don't want that, Ella. That's the last thing you want. I say, marry the man right here in Rawlins and then go off to his place, and everything will be alright. But if you just go, you're in for a lot of trouble."

I wouldn't believe her. I went and we followed our plan. On August 30, 1886, I paid my eighteen-dollar fee and that's how I ended up with Claim No. 2003 for one hundred sixty acres next to Mr. Averell's claim on Horse Creek.

But I've often wondered, considering how things worked out, how many times Mrs. Hayes said to herself or to her rosary beads, "Ella Watson, I told you so."

Chapter Eight

The Man I Hate

I was sweeping the porch of the roadhouse when A.J. Bothwell rode up. And oh my, you couldn't miss him if you tried.

He rode higher in the saddle than most men, with a back so ramrod straight it screamed, "I'm one helluva man with business to do." Yes, he was tall, and he wore that big black hat, but really, what I noticed first was that silly red vest he wore under his coat. Guess he wanted to be sure everyone knew he was coming, because that vest was the only spot of red you'd find out here in this dry countryside.

"What in the world?" I chuckled to myself.

Jimmy had already warned me about our neighbor, whose ranch was up the way from the roadhouse. Whenever I'd go to my claim, I passed right by his Broken Box Ranch and its big house and those awful wolves he kept. Jimmy told me to be careful with this man, because he thought was king of the Sweetwater Valley. Jimmy said he couldn't think of one decent thing to say about Bothwell, and that said it all.

I know more than most about swaggering, domineering men, so my mind was already set against him before my eyes ever confirmed the verdict.

I ignored him and kept sweeping.

"So what do we have here?" He said it in a very loud voice, like he was appraising a prized heifer. "I heard Jimmy got himself a cook and opened a dinner table, so am I right in guessing that's you?"

I turned full face on him. I will give him that he was right handsome behind that Van Dyke and mustache. I figured he was about Jimmy's age. His voice had that sneer of an arrogant man.

"That's me."

I could see he was waiting for more as his eyes traveled over me. I bet if I'd offered my left hip, he would have branded me.

"I'm Ella Watson." I announced myself like I was saying "I'm the Queen of England."

"I'm one of the finer cooks you'll ever encounter and I'm an even better baker, and your money spends as good here as anyone else's." I thought my speech was just snippy enough to show I could stand my own.

Bothwell threw back his head and laughed, like it was a joke that anyone could get the best of him. "Well, I'll be the judge of that. I'm Albert J. Bothwell, but you probably already knew that."

He marched into the roadhouse and sat himself at one of the four new tables. He took off his hat and laid it on the oilcloth and looked around like he'd never seen the place before.

"What ya got, lady? I got me a bear appetite."

"I can have the coffee boilin' in a minute and today I have fried prairie chicken, beans, and cornbread. I have apple and mince pie." That's just how I'd have told anybody the day's menu.

"Mince pie—my mother made mince pie so I guess I'll be able to tell from the first bite if you really are the baker you say you are." He barked at me like he was the territory's official pie eater. I smiled to myself because I knew I'd win this challenge.

By the time he finished his dinner and pie and coffee, Mr. A.J. Bothwell acted like a changed man. "Well, my dear, I must say, I haven't had a cut of pie like that since my mother's—I might just have to fall in love with you."

I couldn't tell by his tone if he was laughing at me or saying something true.

"That's fifty cents." He was getting nothing extra from me!

He laid down a silver dollar and walked out the door, and the extravagant tip was a nod toward something true.

I spent a few seconds congratulating myself on how I'd come out on top with a man Jimmy so despised, and decided I could handle Bothwell.

I was anxious to share my first encounter with Bothwell that night when Jimmy and his ranch hand came in for supper. Jimmy beamed, like I'd done him proud, and Fales was beside himself.

"I can't wait to tell the boys who work for that blowhard," John Fales announced in his Dakota drawl. "You know what his men call him behind his back? Robin Red Vest! He acts like he's some kind of European lord or something and everybody in the valley laughs at him. Behind his back, of course. Only behind his back. Oh, Miss Ella, the boys are going to love your story!"

I added another reason to love this strange man who constantly reminded me that first impressions can be deceiving.

John Fales was waiting on the porch when Jimmy and I arrived from Rawlins that first day. He jumped up and ran to the wagon to help me down.

"So this is the lady you speak so highly of," he yelled at Jim as he grabbed my velvet satchel. "Ma'am, I'm real glad to know you. I'm John Fales and I do about everything around here—don't I, Jimmy?—and I just know we're going to be real good friends. Call me Fales."

The man looked like a wreck. He didn't have a belly or a butt and his Levis were just waiting to fall off. His face always had stubble and his blue eyes looked like he was coming off a bender, but he never was. He smelled of smoke from his favorite pastime, and he had a face only a mother could love. But darned if he wasn't the most useful wreck I'd ever known. If Jimmy needed dinner tables, Fales could build them like he'd done it all his life. If he needed repairs on his house, they were fixed. If he needed someone to haul or load, Fales showed a strength you'd never guess. This was the man who'd build my cabin—it wouldn't be big, but I didn't need it to be big to start. All I needed was a place to establish my claim, and the two-room log cabin drawn on butcher paper looked like a palace. Besides, as Fales kept saying, I could always add on later.

I came to appreciate John Fales for far more than his skills with a saw and hammer. He constantly surprised me with how smart he was—a walking textbook on anything to do with W.T. or cattle ranching—and amazed me at how his ears were always primed for the latest news in the Sweetwater Valley. John Fales was the most gossipy man I would ever know.

And then there was John Fales the Entertainer. He was always ready with a joke or a sly observation—he saw the world as an amusement and thought everyone else should too. Some of his jokes were so bad they made me groan, but that was okay, because Fales would laugh and slap his leg like it was the most humorous thing he'd ever heard. His laugh was so infectious, I found myself laughing too, whether it was funny or not, and that was the effect Fales had on most people.

That first day, he'd immediately launched into his greeting joke. "Have you heard the one about the stranger who rode into town and stopped for a drink? Well, the locals always liked to pick on strangers so when he finished his drink he found his horse had been stolen. He went back in the bar and twirled his gun around his finger and tossed it behind his back from one hand to the other and then shot into the ceiling. 'Which one of you sidewinders stole my horse?' he yelled and when nobody answered he told them: 'Alright, I'm gonna have one more drink and if my horse ain't back, I'm gonna do what I dun in Texas. And I don't like to think about what I dun in Texas.' So he had his drink and when he went outside, his horse was tied up all nice and snug. He saddled up to ride out of town and the bartender couldn't stand it: 'Say, partner, before you go, just what did you do in Texas?' As he rode off, the cowboy yelled back over his shoulder, 'I walked home.'"

I stopped in my tracks, threw back my head and let out a belly laugh. "I sure didn't see that comin'." And I liked him right off.

Fales also thought himself a singer and there would be many nights when he'd entertain after supper with a voice that was rough around the edges, but pretty much on key. He sang about beautiful cows and beautiful sunsets. He sang about missing your Ma when you're out on the range. He sang about girls left behind and steaks yet to eat. I knew some of the songs he sang had been sung around campfires for years, but others, Fales was making up on his own.

And it turned out he was an expert on reading cattle brands. At first I thought it was funny that a man who never owned a cow in his life knew everything there was to know about the strange symbols that made up brands. But eventually I saw how it fit with his sense of humor. Fales not only could read brands, he knew all the secrets of changing them.

"Ma'am, if you want to run a joke on the high and mighty cattle barons, just mess with their brands. There's all kinds of ways to change a man's brand so nobody can tell the difference. You don't do it to little guys, mind you. Never them. But those cattle barons. Well, that's about the best joke in Wyoming Territory."

He also was an expert reader of men. After he snickered at how well I had bested Bothwell, Fales got serious a moment. "But you be careful, Miss Ella, because that man is dangerous. He acts like he's been here for years. He's a newcomer, but you'd never know it. He takes ownership of anything he wants, whether it's his due or not. He's got brothers that's just as bad and they've tried every trick in the book to make a buck—had an oil well that got no oil and a railroad that never saw a foot of track. Who knows what they'll come up with next. He's makin' a fortune on his cattle, lets them roam everywhere—the 'open range,' you know—and he's a big stick in the stock growers. But for all his high and mighty, he's really not much of anything. Don't know he's ever done an honest day's work. Won't get his hands dirty. I'll tell you what—that man's a snake and never forget it."

◇◇◇

The roadhouse was more than I had expected. The wooden building was large, with big windows looking onto the front porch.

The entrance room was a spacious grocery store. Behind it was a pretty good kitchen with a big pantry. There was a cozy room behind the cookstove, and I made a point of telling everyone that it was now my bedroom. I didn't want people thinking I was bedding down with Jimmy in his three-room cabin next door.

The first week at the roadhouse was a flurry of reorganizing the entrance room into a dining room. Fales built more shelves on the walls behind the counter, and his new tables fit just right. I got the kitchen rearranged to my liking and made a long list of supplies to fill up that pantry. By the time we were done, it looked like this roadhouse had sported a dining room for ages.

It wasn't until the next weekend that we finally found the time to go out to my claim. I had expected Jimmy promised more than he could deliver, but that wasn't the case at all. My land had a sweeping view of a beautiful valley with rolling hills and dramatic rock outcroppings. In the distance were hills that looked like mountains to me. The creek was even more perfect than I imagined. The water moved gently, but there was plenty for thirsty cattle and more than I'd ever need for a household. The best part was there were plenty of berry bushes. Oh, the jams I'd make!

I got out of the wagon and walked around on land that I would claim in my own name, and that does something to a person. I did a full circle to see everything I could see from here and everything I saw was beautiful. I loved the gray tint to the sagebrush. Even the dirt and the rocks looked like the best dirt and rocks anyone could ever want. The hills changed colors and shapes as the sun moved across the sky, and the hills at the end of the day were bathed in purples and golds. Off in the distance I saw a herd of antelopes and yelled at Jimmy to see.

"There's antelopes all over this valley. That will get old."

But I knew it never would. I hoped one day they'd come close enough so I could pet their bone-white hides.

"And you should know we've got mountain lions, so when you get your chicken coop up, you need to make sure they can't get in."

I knew I'd never want a mountain lion close enough to pet.

"Coyotes and gray wolves are everywhere. Their howling can keep you awake at night. And never leave a window open because they'll come right in, and you sure don't want that."

Jimmy had never mentioned any of these dangers when he was bragging about this land.

On my own, I discovered prairie chickens. Before I got my own gun, I borrowed Jimmy's, and my aim was pretty good. Had to be. Chicken was a mainstay on my menu, and although Fales liked to bring me ones he shot, I thought I should be carrying my own weight there.

I scared Fales one day when I told him I'd seen their courting dance and described it in great detail. Every sentence, his eyes kept getting bigger. At first, I thought he was enjoying my story.

"I went out this morning real early to get me some chickens and I heard the most startling sound. Everything had been quiet the moment before—just the usual birdcalls here and there—and then the prairie erupted with sound. I was so startled, I crouched down to stay clear of the sound. And that's when I heard their courting dance. It sounds like music. Like a chorus singing. The males boom and cluck and cackle and even hum. Each one had its own song and they sang over one another. They puffed up their cheeks into red balls and fluffed up their head feathers like an Indian chief and strutted—they actually strutted like they were the king of the walk. One would hop up high, facing another male as if to say 'you ain't much' and the other would hop even higher to answer the challenge. I must have sat there a good forty minutes before the dance ended and the chickens scattered. And that's when I realized I hadn't shot anything for dinner."

By now, Fales didn't look like he was enjoying this story at all, but that he didn't like a word I was saying.

"This ain't going to queer you on killin' prairie chickens for dinner, is it, Miss Ella?"

I burst out in an open mouth laugh.

"No, Fales, no worry of that." Boy, there was relief on that man's face.

Yes, this land and its critters suit me. I thanked the Lord every day that I'd had the guts to come west and He had given me Jimmy and all this.

Everything was all the more sweet because Jimmy felt the same way about me.

"After my Sophia died, I thought I'd never again find anyone to love. I thought I'd spend the rest of my life alone. So you're a lovely surprise. I haven't been so lucky since the Indian Wars."

That sounded peculiar to me because nothing sounded lucky about fighting Indians, but when Jimmy told me his story, I understood.

He just missed being in two of the biggest battles. As he was being discharged in 1876, his regiment in Wyoming got orders for Montana to join Custer. And we all know how Custer was wiped out at the Battle of the Little Bighorn. Then three days before he reenlisted, Chief Washakie of the Wyoming Shoshones saved General Crook and his men from an ambush by Crazy Horse. They called it the Battle of the Rosebud.

It made me feel really good that a man would see me as the luckiest thing to happen to him since he almost got himself killed by Indians.

There was only one thing standing between us. Jimmy wanted to go off and get married right away. I kept putting him off. For one month. For two. I never explained and he never pushed. I was biding my time.

And then the letter came. Fales handed me the official-looking envelope when he came back with supplies from town one day, and I stuffed it into my apron pocket. I couldn't wait to get away and hurried outside, away from the ice house, beyond the garden, and under a tree far away from the roadhouse. I wanted to read this letter without anyone else around.

"Oh God, please let this say what I need it to say." I hadn't prayed that hard since the night I thought I was going to get raped. I tore it open quickly, and burst into tears the second I saw the fancy lettering on top of the stamped and sealed paper: "Disillusion of Marriage." There it was. That horrible William

Pickell had finally agreed to the divorce and this paper from the courthouse said it was final. I wept into my apron, tears of joy and relief. That ugly part of my life was finally over. "Thank you, God. Thank you!" Now I could explain it all to Jim.

"Oh, please let him understand. Don't let this ruin things. Please let him understand."

That night after the supper dishes were done, I brought him a fresh cup of coffee. "Jim, I have something important to discuss with you." I sounded so serious he looked up, a little startled.

I held my cup so tight I feared it would break, but I finally told him the secret I'd carried all this time, saying it all in one burst so I would finally get it out in the open.

"Jimmy, I made a terrible mistake back in Kansas and that's one reason I came out here. I married a man I thought was like my Pa, but he wasn't. He was mean and he cheated on me and he hit me. I left him and I divorced him. At least I filed the papers for divorce. But the divorce wasn't final when I left Kansas. I couldn't sit around waiting, but he wouldn't answer the court summons and so I finally just left. But today I got this letter from the court and the divorce is finally done. He says I deserted him, but I don't care what he says. I just care that this paper says I'm a free woman and I can now marry you. I'm sorry I kept this from you, but everything is all right now."

Jim sat there looking at me like he had been hit by a stick.

"Why didn't you tell me before?" Oh, I dreaded that question. Would he resent that I cheated him, not owning up to a first marriage? Would he think I was damaged goods now? Would he still want me?

"I was afraid. I couldn't tell you I was married without telling you I was divorced, and I couldn't tell you I was divorced because I wasn't legally. I was free in my mind and my heart but not by the law. I was afraid this would queer you on me and I'd lose out on the man I love. I prayed that eventually this day would come and the court would say I was free and by then, you'd love me enough to excuse me for keeping this secret. It's been terrible keeping this from you, but I didn't want…."

Jim lowered his head and held up his hand to end my speech and my heart dropped. This was the conclusion I always feared. I just knew the next words out of his mouth would be 'get outta here.' I heard myself give out a little cry, and that brought Jim's head up. But his eyes weren't mean and hurt. They were kind and gentle.

"Ella, stop. I can't…I have to…please sit down because… please, sit…I have something I have to tell you, too."

And that's when Jimmy told me about how he had killed Charley Johnson.

It wasn't cold-blooded murder, like the indictment said; it was really self-defense, but that had never been resolved because there'd never been a trial. He said all that up front so I wouldn't spend any time believing the worst, and then he told me his side of the story.

Charley Johnson was a big bully who had been threatening Jim for months over some slight he couldn't even remember. Jim was in the army then and had gone to his commander to alert him to the threat and was advised to stay out of the man's way. Which, Jim stressed, he had done every time he came into Buffalo, but one day in May of 1880, Johnson cornered him in a saloon and came at him, demanding a fistfight. Jim knew he was too small to survive hand-to-hand combat with this large man. It happened so fast, it wasn't until it was all over that he realized he had shot three times as Johnson advanced on him— the first shot went into the ceiling, the second into Johnson's leg "and that spun him around and the third went into his back."

Jim emphasized that several witnesses were ready to speak on his behalf, "and there was only one man who took Johnson's side." Even so, he was indicted for murder and sent away, ending up in the Rawlins Jail.

"Some prominent friends posted my bail and I was very grateful to be out of there. The court finally dismissed the case, saying it should be handled in a military court. Of course, there never was a military court because everyone knew this man was out to get me and I had no choice."

When he was done, I took his hand and told him, "Jim, you had to protect yourself. Of course I understand. There's no reason you couldn't have told me this. This was unfortunate, but you didn't do anything wrong."

Jim started a smile. "That's exactly what I want to say to you. You made a mistake, but you corrected it by leaving that horrible man. I'm proud of you for that. I understand why you didn't tell me. But now I know. And you know what this means? It means you have no excuse not to run off with me and get married."

Jimmy and I had shared small kisses since we met. But tonight, when Jim took me in his arms, we kissed for a very long time.

◇◇◇

Within a month of the happy letter and the secret-sharing, we were bundled up in Jim's buggy on our way to Lander to get married.

Lander was 105 miles from the roadhouse and it took us five long days. We started out along the Oregon Trail that had been the highway for so many wagon trains over the years, and Jim told me stories about the immigrants.

The one that broke my heart was about the Mormon handcarts.

"You know, I'm not Mormon and I'm not like some who can't stand them, but even people who hate Mormons cry when they hear about the handcart disaster," Jimmy began, and he had that tone that let me know this was such a sad story, I'd probably cry, too. And I did, thinking about all those converts trying to get to the promised land in Salt Lake City, who froze to death in Wyoming instead.

"They say a thousand people started out and over two hundred died. They never even counted how many fingers or toes or limbs the frostbite took. Brigham Young tried to save them, but he didn't even know they were out there until it was too late."

I was quiet for a long time, trying to wrap my mind around the idea of putting everything I owned in a small handcart and then pushing it a thousand miles.

"Would you have done it?" I finally asked Jim.

He answered with a statement I adopted as my own thinking on the subject. "I've never believed in anything that much."

We rode along in silence for awhile, and I think it convinced
Jimmy that funny stories were more appropriate for a long trip
like this.

So he told me all about Big Nose George Parrott, the most
notorious outlaw W.T. ever knew.

"Now you can imagine how Big Nose George got his name
and I'm here to tell you, it was completely earned. I have never
seen a proboscis like that on another human being in my entire
life." Jim started out on a roll and never let up until the entire
story was told. "I met him when they threw me in the Rawlins
Jail for that mess in Buffalo, and you didn't have to say three
words to him to know he was nobody you wanted to know.

"Big Nose robbed stagecoaches for fun and killed people for
sport, and now he was in the hoosegow charged with killing two
Carbon County deputy sheriffs back in '78. They took three days
to try him and sentenced him to hang. They had him shackled,
but all day, you could hear him working those shackles. We
thought he was just wasting his time, but darned if he didn't
hack right through the bolt with a pocketknife. We didn't know
that then, not until we heard the commotion. Big Nose got out
of his cell and hid in the water closet. Sheriff Rankin's younger
brother, Bob, and his wife both worked at the jail—she cooked
some delicious meals, by the way. Anyway, Bob Rankin came
in and Big Nose beat him over the head and tried to get out
of jail. But Rosa, that's Bob's wife, she slammed the outer door
shut and the rest of us grabbed for Big Nose and kept him still.
I felt terrible for Bob. There was so much blood I thought he
was dead at first, but he wasn't. He just never was quite right in
the head after that.

"When word got out that Big Nose had almost escaped, the
men in town turned mean and formed a mob and attacked the
jail. For a minute there, we were afraid they'd take everybody
out, but they just came for Big Nose and they hung him from
a post on Main Street. Nobody ever was charged with anything

in Big Nose's lynching. If anybody ever had it coming, he did. Saved the county the cost of hanging him.

"The County Commissioners gave Rosa a gold watch to thank her for her bravery in stopping the escape. We never got anything, but then, nobody else in that jail was proud to be there in the first place, so it was just as well we didn't get any notice for what we did. I did hear that when the official execution day arrived, the sheriff informed the court that Big Nose could not be found in all of Carbon County. He had been six feet under for two months by then!"

By now, this outrageous story had wiped away my sadness and had me giggling.

"But that isn't the end of the story," Jimmy pushed on. "Big Nose was so hated that before they buried him, they cut off his head and they skinned him." I shuddered.

"No really. They skinned him and you know what happened to that skin? When Dr. John Osborne became governor, he wore shoes made from Big Nose's skin to his inauguration. Even bragged about it. And somebody still has the skull in a closet somewhere."

I slipped my arm under Jim's and cuddled closer. "Didn't know I had such a hero for a husband-to-be." He got a kick out of that.

The trip went fast as Jim told me stories like that. He promised that one day, we'd go even farther north and visit Yellowstone Park and watch the geysers. Jim was proud that W.T. had the first national park, and it flummoxed him that others saw it as foolish. Some said it would mean far more money to W.T. if developers could build up that pretty land, but Jimmy disagreed.

"There are just some things you have to protect for the good of everyone."

We stayed at the Rongis Stage Station one night, camped out the others, finally followed the Rawlins-Fort Washakie stage road into Lander on the Shoshone Reservation. I'd never been on an Indian reservation before, but while the surroundings were strange, I never felt any trepidation. I'd only seen pictures of teepees in books, but here they were along the road, and I couldn't help but stare.

One had a pile of brush in front of the opening flap and Jim explained that meant the owner was away for awhile but would return.

"So that's like their front door key?"

Jim had to admit, that was about it. He took a short detour off the main road to show me a grave. It was a mound of earth with stones covering the top.

"Why is there a washboard by those stones?"

Jim explained this was a woman's grave and that was her prized possession. "But couldn't somebody else use it?" My practical side. Jim said that's not how the Shoshones saw it.

"You know a band comes through by us now and then. They like the creek," he told me, and I hadn't known. Now that I did, I wasn't sure how I felt about a band of Indians in my backyard.

But I did know how I felt about this man next to me in the buggy. I felt safe with him. I felt sure with him. I could ride around an Indian reservation and not feel any fear. A soon-to-be new wife couldn't ask for much more.

Jim said it was necessary to go so far—and into the next county—so our marriage records wouldn't be detected. I totally agreed. Our plan from the start was to secretly marry so we could file a couple claims each. Our marriage wouldn't have been much of a secret if we'd just rode into Rawlins to get hitched. No, the long ride was necessary, even though my sore backside protested now and then.

I wore my Sunday dress and a hat to fill out our official marriage application. It was May 17, 1886. At the last minute, I decided not to use my given name, in case anyone ever checked if an Ella Watson had gotten married and was cheating the Homestead Act. Jimmy agreed it was smart to be cagey.

"After all, if this was ever discovered, it would be your claims at stake," he told me. I already knew that. So I used my first and second names, but made up a last name to cover my tracks. I signed "Ellen Liddy Andrews."

I carefully rolled up the piece of parchment and smiled at myself at what a good story this would be someday for our children. I tucked it away.

"I'm going to have this framed and we'll put it on the wall of the big cabin we'll build after we get all our claims. What a good story it will be for our children." Jim agreed that was a great plan.

John Fales was the only one who knew the truth. He'd hold our secret safe. He'd held down the fort while we were gone and his Ma had come over to cook the meals. But he took me aside to give a secret report:

"Now, I'm not sayin' my Ma isn't a good cook. She is, yes, ma'am, she is a very good cook. And she can sew better than the dress shops in Cheyenne. But I have to report, Miss Ella, that even though my Ma put a right good meal on the table, there were some very disappointed cowboys who come by for one of *your* dinners!"

He could have been a boot-licker, making points with the new Lady of the House, but this was another moment that endeared me to this skinny man.

Officially—and for anyone who came in for dinner—I was still living in the room behind the cookstove, but at night, after everyone had left, I'd join my husband in his home.

"It's *our* home now," he told me, and I liked the sound of that.

This time, marriage was a totally different thing. My man did not turn into a monster once he had me hitched. He wasn't a rough man. He never hit me. He didn't treat me with disrespect in our marriage bed. I never laid there with my eyes closed, hoping it would be over. There was no routing pig in my marriage bed now. There was a loving man who made me realize what it was about marriage that was so pleasant.

Chapter Nine

My Claim, No. 2003

Business was good at the roadhouse before I ever got there. It was strategically located at two major roads—one north and south, the other east and west—so there normally was healthy travel most days. Jim stocked up the kind of supplies travelers and cowboys needed—cans of Arbuckle's of course (his number one seller, but anyone could have predicted coffee would lead any shopping list); Greeley Snowflake Flour (cowboys said it was better than Nebraska Flour for biscuits); Kirk's soap, Fairbank's Lard, Michigan Salt, four kinds of canned beans.

Business got great when I started cooking. There was no place else to get a hot meal for miles—unless you had your own stove or campfire or a good woman at home. But not only cowboys came to have their noon meal at the roadhouse. So did neighbors, first the men and then they brought their wives, sometimes their children. Of course, never on Mondays, as that was the dreaded wash day that left women feeling "worse than a stewed witch." It was Mondays when I usually made Ma's Irish potato soup that hit a home spot with most cowboys. Whether their own Ma had made it or not, it tasted like something a loving Ma would make, and that was good enough for men who made their living punchin' cows.

If women came to join their husbands for dinner it was usually on Wednesday, and so that was the day I planned my best specials, for obvious reasons. It was one thing to please the belly of a cowboy; it was quite another to satisfy a cook whose own stove produced delicious delights. The kudos that really mattered to me came from my neighbor ladies.

I varied the menu so folks could taste it all after several visits: fried chicken, beef loaf, steaks, baked chicken and dumplings, beef stew, stewed chicken—the list went on, depending on what I had on hand or could kill. There were always corn muffins at every meal and I found folks were wild for my escalloped corn—my secret was the bits of real butter I put over the top that made the dish so good, grown men were seen licking their plates. I usually had a pot of soup on the back burner—I threw everything left over into the pot and it cooked up real nice—but my tomato soup with its secret teaspoon of soda was a favorite. And of course, nobody went away without a piece of pie. Once I decided to make cake instead of pie and while they ate every crumb, one cowboy after another politely asked if I could please have pie the next time they came. I scored big with my pig's foot jelly.

I got to know our neighbors through these dinners, although "neighbor" in these parts meant folks who lived miles and miles away. I was disheartened that the only exception to that rule was the big cabin on the Broken Box Ranch of one A.J. Bothwell which sat between the roadhouse and my claim. Darn, why did *he* have to be my only real neighbor?

It was at a Wednesday dinner that I first met Canzada Earnest, who became my favorite person on the Sweetwater. Mattie, as everyone called her, was older than me, but of the same sturdy stock. She always wore a sunbonnet and a smile on her face, and the stories she could tell! I could sit forever and listen to this woman tell about the adventures of her life. My favorite was the time she was traveling by stage from South Dakota to her sister's in Texas and ran into bandits. She had been warned the Indians were on the warpath and road agents were holding up stagecoaches left and right, but that hadn't stopped her. She sewed her fortune—three thousand dollars in gold!—into her petticoats and put two dollars in her purse. Sure enough, here came the road agents and they ordered everyone out and told them to hand over all their money. Mattie started to cry and asked if they'd take a poor girl's last two dollars, and danged if they not only gave her back her money, but five more dollars besides! Folks would cheer and chuckle for a half-hour over that story and Mattie would just smile like it was something any brave girl would do.

And then Boney Earnest would chime in with praise for his wife. How they'd hunted together and she'd fought Indians and herded cattle and they both knew a whole cast of colorful characters. "Like who?" somebody always asked, and that opened the door to stories about Calamity Jane and Wild Bill Hickok and Buffalo Bill.

One day, this stranger who was visiting one of the ranchers sat there with a pen and notebook all afternoon, writing down what Mattie said. When Boney called him on it, he introduced himself as Owen Wister and said he was a writer and found the West fascinating. Boney snickered and said it wasn't so fascinating when you were living it, and then everyone slapped their thighs in agreement. Yes, when the Earnests came to dinner, I knew to put on an extra pot of coffee and cut some more pie because it was going to be a full afternoon of stories.

I always hoped that Tom Sun would bring his nice missus to dinner so I could tell Mrs. Sun how we had the wonderful Mary Hayes in common, but he never did. The one time I brought it up to him, he screwed up his nose like he wouldn't want his wife to associate with me.

Things got even better at the end of June when Jim was appointed postmaster and the new Sweetwater Post Office opened in the roadhouse. Now folks came here to get their mail and darned if they didn't time it so they could have dinner, too.

At fifty cents a meal, my money box was filling up fast. Jimmy teased me about my growing wealth. "So you think you're rich now, do you?" he'd coo, and then tell me about the astonishing kinds of money some folks had.

"Well, you aren't exactly Andrew Carnegie," he told me one day as he shared the news from the local paper that the industrialist was on another spending spree. "He already gave a half million dollars to Pittsburgh to build a library—do they have gold desks or what?—and now he's giving one hundred twenty-five thousand dollars to Allegheny City for a library and music hall." Neither of us could fathom that kind of money, especially money that could be *given away!*

I came up with a great idea. "We should tell him about Rawlins. They could use some of that money. They don't have a library either."

Jimmy agreed. "I bet if he knew what a fine town we had, he'd really think about it. Just think, Rawlins is only eighteen years old and they already have an Opera House, and poor Allegheny City, which is probably a hundred years old, doesn't." Jimmy smiled at his fine point and I hoped that would remind him he'd promised we'd go to the Opera House one night so I could wear my beautiful hair comb.

Jimmy and I saw eye-to-eye on most things. But not on the Statue of Liberty. I was surprised that not only had Jimmy not contributed—Pa had proudly sent fifty cents—but he thought the effort was a waste of money. "You don't give somebody a statue and then tell them they have to build the pedestal for it—that isn't a gift," he argued, and I knew that logic held sway with a lot of Americans who still sat on their pocketbooks. "And a bronze woman—what does that mean?"

I thought it meant a lot. I was proud that the symbol of our country would be a woman holding a torch of light. I started to say so out loud and then thought better of it. But I'm convinced if France had given America a military man on a horse, there wouldn't be all this fuss about raising money for the pedestal to put it on.

The loan Jimmy gave me to get started was all paid up by the time the new post office opened, and now my money box was dedicated to the two-room cabin Fales and I would build. Every day after dinner, I'd ride over to my land and help until sundown. By the third trip, I vowed to get myself a western saddle, hang it if it wasn't lady-like, because this sidesaddle-riding was ridiculous out here. A new saddle went on the wish list.

I know I amazed Fales at how strong I was, and how I could work like a man. "Your Pa sure raised you right," he complimented one day. I'd spent most of my life working with Pa and my brothers, so I knew how to work with men to get things done. First thing, you can't be bossy. They don't like that. They'll do something the wrong way rather than take a bossy command from a woman.

"Fales, do you think we could do it this way?" That's the way to get a man to do it how you want it done.

My knowledge of men didn't work on Bothwell. I didn't know for a long time that he was harassing Fales, but finally it all came out when progress on the cabin seemed so painfully slow.

"Miss Ella, Bothwell has been around making trouble. He pulled up one day and sounded like he was the law. 'And what do you think you're doing'?" Fales could imitate Bothwell dead-on.

"I told him that I was building a house for that nice Ella Watson who was filing claim on this land under the Homestead Act. Well he huffed and puffed like he was going to have a stroke, right there on his horse, wearing his red vest.

"He spat at me, 'You know you're right in the middle of my grazing land.' I wanted to laugh out loud, but I've lived in these parts long enough to know that wasn't a smart thing to do.

"I did tell him, polite like, 'Mr. Bothwell, this ain't your land. This is homesteading land and Miss Ella is going to be our newest homesteader.' I thought he was going to pistol-whip me right there. He swore instead and said, 'We'll see about that. This has been my pasture for a long time and I intend to see it stay that way.' And then he galloped off."

"Oh, I can't stand that man."

I don't think Fales was even surprised the next day when he found everything he'd done had been torn apart. He only got things back together because he brought his friend, Frank Buchanan, to help out. Frank was always our fall-back guy when we had extra work, and Fales now knew he'd need to keep Frank on for awhile.

Frank was convinced the worst was over. "Bothwell has got to accept that when this cabin is up, the claim is real, and there's nothing he can do about it."

But everything was torn apart the next day, too, and so Fales decided to camp on the land at night to keep away the "critters" who liked to throw logs all over the place. He set up his sleeping rug beside a partial wall and sat there all night with his rifle resting across his lap.

I knew the men could use my help, so I hurried after the noon meal each day to get out to the claim. I was mixing mud the day four cowboys rode up and acted like ruffians. I didn't bother wondering who had sent them.

"So now you've got a woman mixin' mud for a house that's never gonna stand," one of the cowboys said, and the others screamed like it was funny.

"We're building my cabin," I told them, as though this were news.

"Lady, you're never gonna live here in the middle of Mr. Bothwell's pasture. This isn't a place for a lady on her own, is it men?" All four of them grunted agreement.

"I hear there's Injun pox in the soil," one of the cowboys said. "They liked to bury their dead around here and a lot of them had the pox and I'd be real scared to dig where I could get smallpox." I had never heard of such a thing, but the look on Fales' face said there could be some truth in that.

"If I were you, ma'am, I'd just move on or go back to Rawlins and forget this cabin out here and forget any claims. You know this is all Mr. Bothwell's land."

I knew it would do no good to talk back, so I kept working and wouldn't look at them and eventually their game got tiring and they rode off.

"Ignore 'em," was all Fales said about the visit that day.

The next day there was a skull left where my front door would be—Fales insisted it meant nothing, but I knew it was a death warning. Then there was a skull and crossbones. Then some more vandalism. If we went two days without a warning sign, we were lucky. I found myself having second helpings of second thoughts.

"Maybe my claim is in the wrong place," I offered to Jimmy one night in bed, and I thought he was going to go through the roof.

"Is Bothwell scaring you? You know he's all bluster. That isn't his pasture land. That land belongs to the government of the United States of America and they have offered it for home-steading. If you don't claim it, somebody else will. If Bothwell had any sense, he'd have filed a claim himself. But no, he thinks he's due the land because his cows like to graze there. Too bad. That's not the way it works anymore." Jimmy was so hopped up, I double-assured him I wasn't too scared. I swore I'd never give up my claim. I knew every word he said was true. And most of all, I sure didn't want my new husband thinking he'd married a coward who could be run off by a bully. But in my heart, I knew Bothwell was more dangerous than Jimmy wanted to allow.

There is a comfort in knowing you're on the right side of the law and your enemy is on the wrong side. In any decent society, being on the right side is exactly where you should be.

When Bothwell couldn't scare me out, he changed tactics. He showed up at the roadhouse one day, all nice and gentlemanly, ordered dinner, and then started up a friendly conversation.

"You know, Miss Watson, I run my cattle out there by that land where you're plannin' a claim, and I know it's a great inconvenience to move, so I'd like to offer you top dollar for that land—now I know it isn't rightly your land, but you have made an investment in getting those logs and hiring those men and I want to make it right by you. So I'll buy the land from you and you can find yourself another nice spot somewhere else and we'll all be happy."

"Mr. Bothwell, I'm very happy with the land I'm claiming," I spoke slowly and evenly. "But thank you for the nice offer." My heart was racing so hard, I feared he could hear it. But again, I was proud of myself for standing up to him.

He tried another day, this time coming at me like I was the object of his heart. "I have a beautiful ranch house up the way—I know you've admired it on the way to that land—and it needs a woman like you to make it a real home and I'm hoping you will consider that seriously, Miss Watson." I hardly knew what to say. It was nothing but an obscene offer. Jim walked in right after that speech and although he was a lot shorter and smaller than Al Bothwell, he looked like he wanted to punch his lights out.

The next time Bothwell broached the subject of the land, there was nothing nice or gentlemanly or romantic in his words.

"Listen here, little lady," he began, "if you think you're going to screw with my grazing rights, you're dumber than you look. If you value your health, you'll get the hell out of there and pull up stakes or I can't be held responsible for what happens to you."

Every single time I encountered him, the memory of my first husband came leaping into my head and the steel rod in my backbone hardened. I couldn't look at Bothwell without loathing and contempt. I couldn't see him without seeing William Pickell with a horsewhip in his hand. I had never been sure where men got their courage to face danger straight on. But I was learning a woman got her courage when she was tired of a man trying to beat her down.

Looking back, I'm amazed at how long I took his verbal abuse and his insults and stayed so calm. But that chapter came to an end.

The last straw was when he grabbed my arm to spit his threats right in my face. I yanked away from him so violently, it made him step back to keep his balance. My courage finally spoke: "Mr. Bothwell, you get out of my face and out of my way. I'm here. I'm staying. Do you hear me? I'm not going anywhere. That is going to be my land. I'm going to raise cattle there. I'm going to live there for the rest of my life. So get your filthy hands off me and stop this nonsense. You're nothing but a bully and I'm sick of it."

The look on his face was of absolute shock. That pleased me, but I didn't dare show it. Instead, I turned on him and marched away. I heard his horse whinny as he reined her hard to ride off. I held my breath. I prayed I wouldn't feel a bullet in my back.

Jim had been hardened like that for a long time, and he did more than tell Bothwell off. Our conflict was just one example of what was happening all over W.T. as homesteaders moved in and the cattle barons felt the pinch. To fight back, cattlemen scammed the land claims acts by filing phony claims. They might get away with it in some places, but Jim was determined not to let them get away with it in the Sweetwater Valley. He started writing letters to the editor to expose their fraud, and local papers like the *Carbon County Journal* supported him with editorials. Whenever an article came out, it was like a win for our side.

You could count on homesteaders to come into the roadhouse when Jimmy's letters were printed, to slap him on the back and tell him to keep up the good work. That should have been extra income for my kitchen, but Jimmy always gave them pie and coffee on the house. I didn't begrudge him, because it wasn't that often that our side got a win.

The point was driven home one day when four men were sitting around a table, and one of the real old-timers spoke up: "You know, I was a kid in Kansas when they were deciding if it would be a free state or a slave state. The slavers would never ask you directly where you stood, but one day one asked my Pa, 'Where are you on the goose question?' and my Pa lied and said he was 'fine on the goose question.' After they left, he told me that was their code to find out if you supported slavery, and if you weren't 'fine,' they were likely to shoot you on sight. It feels like that out here, now. Those ranchers hate the settlers so bad, but when they talk about us, they use their own code. They say they've got a 'rustler problem.'"

◇◇◇

I tried to avoid the political talk and convinced myself I just had to stay out of the way. Besides, Fales and I had plenty to do. I felt safe with Fales, safe enough to admit all the things I didn't know about this new land and the ways of Wyoming.

"Fales, can I ask you something and you won't tell Jimmy how ignorant I am?" and I didn't need an answer to know he wouldn't. "What's so important about a maverick?" Fales stopped hammering in mid-stroke.

"Well, Miss Ella, you gotta know about mavericks or you can't be a cowman—excuse me, ma'am, a cow lady—in W.T.," he said. Then began his tutorial that filled me in on how the big cattlemen had stacked the deck. By the end of the day, I clearly saw why Jimmy was so proud of every little win on the homesteader's side, and I realized he was a big voice in trying to knock over that stack.

Fales turned out to be a natural teacher and he started from the beginning: "Well, Miss Ella, as you know, a maverick is an unbranded calf. But that poor little thing has become the most despised critter in all of W.T., thanks to the Wyoming Stock Growers Association." He said the name like he was reciting Lucifer's title. I already knew the stock growers were the enemy, but now I was learning just how far they'd gone to shut out the likes of me and Jimmy, and I wished I'd paid more attention to the political chatter back in Cheyenne.

"Used to be, that in the spring roundups, those new calves were brought in with their mammas and whether you were a big cattleman or a small cattleman, they were yours. It worked out just fine and that's how guys grew their herds. But a few years ago, the stock growers got the legislature to pass a law they call the Maverick Act. Now all unbranded calves are branded with an M on their neck and that means they're the *exclusive* property of the stock growers association. So if a small cowman finds some calves with his cows, he no longer owns them like he should—they now belong to the association. Then the association auctions them off to the highest bidder and even in good times, you can imagine who's always the highest bidder. But it's even worse than that!" Fales sounded like a locomotive picking up steam, and you could hear the frustration and anger in every word he spoke.

"This year they made the act even more horrible by saying no one can brand calves except if they have a registered brand from the state, and to get a brand from the state you have to go through the Stock Growers Association. So the little guy doesn't have a chance. He can't get a brand, and without a brand, he can't get any calves. He can't even *bid* on mavericks without a brand. See, they shut out the little guy and the homesteader altogether. And they call it legal."

And just when I thought he was done, Fales rounded another corner with another outrage: "And listen to this, Miss Ella. There's this homesteader over the way named Larson and those cowboys stole his milk cow—his God-damned milk cow, oh, excuse me, ma'am—and they branded that cow as a maverick and sold it for the Stock Growers Association. Well, the paper in Rawlins went on a rampage and the stock growers were forced to give it back. Then they told the papers that giving it back shows they're a friend to the homesteader. Nobody could believe they would try to turn around their sins like that, but they did. And that's the kind of men they are."

I agreed none of this sounded fair, but I had been in W.T. long enough to know the cattlemen's side of the story was that they were being robbed blind. "They're always screaming about rustlers—that people are just taking their cattle and they're losing big money," I said, watching for Fales' reaction.

"Oh, they talk big about rustlin', but they stretch that whopper as far as it will go," he said, reaching his arms from the ground to the sky to demonstrate what a big lie it was. "Sure, some cows go missing now and then. Around here, we say they got caught by the longest rope. Or we call 'em 'slow elk.'"

Fales ha-ha-ha'd to himself for a couple seconds. "But the problem is nowhere near like they say and some of them are pullin' the same tricks, too. Some of those big outfits have investors back East or abroad and they say they've got hundreds more cattle than they ever had. It's their 'book count' and a lot of time, it bears little resemblance to the truth. So when the count comes up short, they scream they were rustled. Everybody knows it isn't a true count. And some of those big ranchers—know how they got to be big ranchers? By being rustlers themselves. And their men do it all the time to start their own herds. I'll tell you this, Miss Ella, if you took all the rustlin' goin' on in W.T., homesteaders would be doing this much." He spaced his thumb and first finger an inch apart. Then he spread his arms as wide as they would go: "And the cattlemen and their cowboys would be doin' this much."

Then Fales fell silent for a second, like he was mulling over something important and when he looked up, he looked right into my eyes. "But I won't lie to you, Miss Ella. If you call a man a thief and treat him like a thief and don't give him a chance to earn an honest living, odds are high he'll oblige you and become a thief." And I knew an honest thing when I heard it.

"So if I have cows…" I began, moving the subject along.

"If you don't have a brand there's no use to having cows," Fales said, "and good luck getting a brand."

"But if I had a brand," I pushed on.

"Then you'd better have yourself a corral to keep all your cows," Falls shot back, "because if one of your calves was found on the open prairie it would be called a maverick and you'd lose it."

"So it looks like we should build some corrals."

Fales slapped his leg: "I like how you think, young lady!"

On August 30, 1886, I was proudly riding into town next to Jim in his Bain freight wagon to file my "squatter's rights" claim on one hundred sixty acres along Horse Creek in the Sweetwater Valley. My claim number was 2003. To prove my intent, I noted I had already built a two-room log house and an irrigation ditch to bring water from the creek. There it was, an official paper with the seal of Carbon County, attesting to the fact that in five years, if I continued improving and using the land, I would own that property free and clear under the Homestead Act.

As soon as we left the courthouse, Jim and I marched into the Rawlins House and spread the document out on the table for Mary Hayes to see. She congratulated me and gave Jim a friendly pat.

"I hear you put out a nice dinner spread. And you're still making those wonderful pies! Good for you, Ella. And now, Jim, make me a happy woman and invite me to your wedding to this nice young lady." She gave him the eye of you-know-better-than-that-James-Averell. He smiled back and agreed that indeed would be a joyous day.

Jim took me on a side trip to see the Rawlins schoolhouse that was being built when we first met in January. They did an impressive job. It's a two-story brick building with a bell tower that makes it look like three stories. When Jimmy pronounced it "a real feather in Rawlins' hat," I couldn't agree more.

We stopped at J.W. Hugus & Co. for grocery supplies. I found a floral cotton fabric to make a new dress, and picked up old copies of the *Carbon County Journal* to catch up on the news. On the ride back to the roadhouse, I entertained Jim with the stories. The Panama Canal was under construction somewhere. A fourth of the United States Army was gathered in Arizona Territory to hunt down Geronimo—again.

I couldn't resist reading an item from my favorite column, "Home Happenings." We'd just left Dyer's where Jim had stocked up on whiskey to resell at the roadhouse, so I knew this would interest him.

"A character known as 'French Louey' became possessed of a desire to go into the wholesale liquor business and as a starter for his future stock he stole a case of 'Old Forrester' whiskey from Mr. J.C. Dyer. He was doomed to disappointment, however, as Marshall Finley nipped his scheme in the bud by taking Louey to jail. He was given a hearing and sentenced to do sixty days for the benefit of the city."

Jim hooted and said he'd never think of stealing from Dyer because if he did, he'd be out of luck the next time his own stock ran low.

"There are better reasons for not stealing, Mr. Averell."

"Yes, Mrs. Averell."

"Oh Jimmy, I wish we could go to Cheyenne in a couple weeks. They're having the first Wyoming Territorial Fair. It says the Union Pacific is offering half fare rates from all points of Wyoming. We could take the train and see the fair. We had great fairs in Kansas. My brothers showed their sheep one year and won a prize." My mind was dancing with the thought of such a grand trip in September—such a great month, with trees turning color and that ripe smell in the air.

But my dance stopped when Jim said, "We'll see," which meant we wouldn't.

We had a happy ride back to the roadhouse with my claim certificate in my pocketbook. This was a day I'd always remember with a smile. The hills shone purple and gold as we got home.

Chapter Ten

I Wanted a Nice Christmas

We didn't get much of a Christmas in '86.

I'd never seen a winter like that one, even back in Canada where winters are pretty fierce. Kansas wasn't like this, even on its worst day. A normal Wyoming winter is miserable, sure, and there are days I'd trade a winter here for almost anything anywhere else. The snow falls until you have to dig out of your cabin and then the wind howls and then it snows some more. By Thanksgiving, you're already getting tired of it, so you can imagine how you feel when it finally gives up to spring in April. I already knew that kind of winter, but that's not the winter we had in 1886. No, that year, I found out that a Wyoming winter can be Mother Nature's most unforgiving attack.

It started early and stayed late—it froze on top of ice and then froze again. It starved every critter that relied on the land, and it wasn't just cows that died of hunger and cold. A couple good men got lost in the storms. The only ones who got fat that winter were the wolves. Their nightly howls terrified me—their proud announcements of yet another feast on a beast that had died in its tracks. Their cries were so heartbreaking, I bet the Shoshones rethought their idea that a howling wolf at a full moon meant good luck. Because in 1886, it sure didn't.

No going into town because you couldn't stand to be in an open wagon that long, no matter how many layers you wore or how many blankets you tucked around you and pulled over your coat like an Indian blanket. Even inside the cabin, you had to break up the ice in the bucket before you could make coffee in the morning. And now you drank coffee, not because you loved it, but because you'd drink anything hot to fight off the cold that was sneaking into your bones.

I killed all my chickens rather than see them freeze and we needed that meat. I never ate so many beans in my whole life. There was a mountain of frozen cans out the back door. I ran out of flour and sugar before New Year's and it seemed like forever before we got more supplies.

So you did with what you had or you did without. Mainly without. I knew by December my wood wouldn't last. Every time I put on another log, I cursed the calluses I got in chopping all that wood, day after day, all spring and summer and fall. But I did it because the first thing you learn on the frontier is that if you don't chop wood every day when you can, you won't have wood when you can't.

Even following that rule wasn't enough for the winter of 1886-87, when every rule went out the door and every human hope died.

I wore almost everything I owned every day to keep my limbs from stiffening up with cold. I stayed in bed longer than usual because that was the only place I was warm—and that was only because I had all my pieced quilts stacked on top of me. The only thing I can say of a positive note is that I lost weight all that winter because you burn up fat just trying to stay warm and there wasn't that much to eat even when you wanted to.

And I knew if I was suffering this much—me, a young, sturdy, healthy woman who knew how to take care of herself—what was happening to those older and punier and weaker? Just thinking of that made me want to cry.

The winter would have been hard enough all by itself—eventually they'd called it The Great Die-Up—but it came after a miserable summer and fall. I'll never understand how you can have that much drought in the months when crops and gardens are supposed to grow, and then so much wet snow in the months they aren't. But that's the way it turned out.

Gunpowder isn't as dry as that summer. The grasslands that are normally full and lush were skimpy at best or not there at all. Poisonous weeds we normally didn't bother with because the healthy grass choked them out, now had a free reign and the poor cows didn't know any different—they were so hungry they ate anything and when they ate the poison weed, they died. Cowboys looked like ghosts when they rode to the roadhouse, covered with dust and dirt. They wore their neckerchiefs over their faces so they could breathe and always looked like dirty thieves when they showed up on your doorstep.

You could tell from their stories and their tone that they were sad for the poor, starving cows out there, fending for themselves on the open range, and they didn't even know about the winter that was coming yet. But they already knew there were problems.

The way it was supposed to work was simple—cows would roam wherever they wanted over the open range all summer and fall, eating their fill and then they'd survive by foraging whatever they could find under the snow during the winter. In the spring, a cowboy band would come round them up and take them home to be branded and sold off, especially happy to see all the mothers and their new calves. But the way things were supposed to happen and the way they truly happened in the winter of '86-87 were two different things.

My Jimmy was predicting bad things before we ever got one snowflake. "There's too many cattle out there on a range that can't feed that many in a good year, and this isn't a good year, my friends. This is the worst spring and summer I've seen." He used a word that you never saw in the newspaper and you only whispered. He said the land was "overstocked." And while he usually got a blasphemy back at him to scold that he was wrong, he sometimes got a nod that he was right.

But I wasn't worried about cattle on the open range. I was worried about my garden. I'd planted in the spring—planted way too much Jimmy kept saying, but I wanted to be sure my first garden on my first land was something to brag about. I never got a single bragging right out of that mess I called a garden. Bet I didn't get half the produce I should have—in fact, I know I didn't get half. My potato plants almost gave up altogether. When I'd pull up a plant and expect to find ten to twelve good-sized potatoes, I'd find one or two small ones. I expected enough tomatoes to can sauce for the winter, but I only got a few, and most got dry rot before they were even ripe. When I figured I could count on my squash, I saw the vines brown up and the yellow blossoms fall off in failure. And even what little grew, the grasshoppers got most of that. Never saw or heard so many of those terrible bugs in my life. Jim said they could eat as much as a cow—he's exaggerating of course—but there's so many of them that by the time they're done, they've stripped the land and the garden and that awful clicking sound they make has driven you crazy. It's the sound of someone eating you out of house and home.

If I remember anything of that summer, it's the sound of grasshoppers, and I bet even the cows knew they were their competition for the little grass there was.

I canned what I could, but by the time of the first snow, we'd already eaten most of what I grew that summer, and there was just a little to help us through the winter. Jimmy knew if I hadn't overplanted, we wouldn't have had anything, so at least I won a point there.

Even the berries down by the river didn't have their usual color and flavor, and they at least had water—not as much as usually flowed in Horse Creek, but still there was some. I tried to can them, like my Ma taught me, making clear, jewel-colored jars of sweet jam that anybody would love. I'd planned on making jam for my family and neighbors for Christmas, but what I got was dull, too-sour syrup I'd only serve to Jimmy if nobody else was around. The only time it tasted anything close to right was when it got soaked up in a flapjack. So the only good thing about not having much of a Christmas is that I didn't have much of anything to give as gifts anyway.

What got me most was how the land around me was screaming all summer and fall that it was hurting. This part of Wyoming Territory was one of the prettiest places you'll ever see. There's rolling hills here and there to give the land some personality, the sunrise streaks the sky with so much life you don't care that your day had to start early to get everything done. And the sunsets. Oh my, if I was a poet, how I could tell about the sunset. It is so golden you wanted to cry that you're lucky enough to see it. Not regular gold, but a color so deep and lush it's too good for a queen. And there's a blue in that sky that I've always wanted on a dress, but I can't imagine it on cloth.

That summer, you couldn't see those golds or blues anywhere. You saw faded out, washed out, dirty colors in a sky that looked so tired you felt sad. Little did we know then that the only color we'd see for month after month was either the white of new snow or the dirt of horses and wagon wheels trudging through it.

This would have been my first Christmas of my new life—a lovely home with Jim, as well as my own log cabin on my land. It would have been time for me to carry on my Ma's traditions and start my own. I'd watched my Ma carry her Christmas ideas from Canada to Kansas, so I knew it wasn't where you were in your body, but where you were in your heart. Even when we had nothin', Ma always made sure the holiday was special, and I wanted that to be part of life for Jimmy and me, too.

Before I knew none of this could happen, I planned on baking cookies and breads early, like Ma always did. I cut some pretty calico fabric so I could wrap cookies in the cloth to make a proper present. Ma always said that once a year you should honor the birth of the Christ Child by giving everyone you know a little something, and if it was sweet, all the better. I know people waited all year for those little cloth bundles to come to their door at Christmastime, which meant my Ma was thinking kindly of them again. That was one of my first real responsibilities—besides minding my brothers and sisters—delivering those bundles to our neighbors in the days leading up to Christmas. I figured I'd do the same thing here. I'd put all the pretty bundles in a basket and borrow Jimmy's buggy and go around to my neighbors and give them a Christmas treat. For the most special ones I'd add a jar of my jam, but we know how that turned out.

I'm not just sayin' this because it would make me look good, but I truly intended to drive all the way over to Tom Sun's place and give his pretty missus one of my bundles and then drive down the road to Bothwell's ranch house and give him one, too. Christian charity at this time of year was a tribute to the birthday we're celebrating, and even though I bet old Bothwell would throw anything I made away, that was his business, not mine. I had no idea how Mrs. Sun would react, but everything I hear, she's a good woman and I bet she would take it in the spirit it was given.

I wasn't sure what I'd use for a Christmas tree, as pine trees are scarce around here, but I knew I could make some kind of tree and once it was decorated, nobody would notice anyway. When I moved to W.T., I brought three tatted snowflakes my Ma had made and two paper cutouts from Grandma Close to put on my tree. They were small and easy to pack. I knew even as I left home that I wanted to take some pieces of home with me, so besides the Bible my Ma insisted I take along, these little ornaments were among the few things I brought. I kept looking all summer and fall for something here on my land to use for more decorations, thinking I'd find something that could be tied on my tree, but except for a jawbone of an antelope that was already bleached out, I didn't find anything. And I didn't think a jawbone was the right thing for a Christmas ornament. If worse came to worse, I could tie pretty ribbons on my tree, and I'd saved some for just that purpose. I wasn't sure I'd put candles on the branches, though, or maybe if I could find some, I'd put them on but not light them so as not to fear for fire.

I know they say a Christmas goose is the proper thing for dinner, but our family wasn't much on goose and I was bettin' Jimmy wasn't either, so I planned a wild turkey that I'd shoot and dress and fill with cornbread stuffing. It would be so big we'd have turkey for a week afterwards. But there were no wild turkeys this year. Don't know what happened to them, but my fear was they couldn't make it in our drought and my prayer was they'd come back again.

Before this awful winter, my neighbors and I had promised to get together at Christmastime to share our baking and our stories and I know someone would bring a fiddle and we'd all dance. For awhile this fall, I even had Jimmy helping me to make gifts for the children of our neighbors—I needed six things for girls and four things for boys. James was whittling sling shots, and I was making rag dolls. Of course, nobody could travel over the mountains of snowbanks, so all our dreams and plans were put aside. It wasn't until the spring thaw that we could deliver those presents and the children all liked them, but an after-Christmas present just wasn't the same thing.

I was making Jimmy a new shirt (he had no idea). For our new life together, I was piecing a special quilt that we'd use on our marriage bed when we could tell everyone we'd been hitched. It had the prettiest fabric, some even silk, and I would never have had piece goods like that, but I got lucky one day when a man came by the roadhouse for a hot meal. He looked so sad that I had to ask what was wrong and he told me he was movin' back East because his wife had died out here in W.T. and he couldn't stand it no more. I think he said he was from New Jersey, and he had hoped that leaving the West would help him forget his sorrow.

"You know, ma'am, you look kind of like my late wife and you're built like her," he told me, and I took that to be a right-nice compliment.

So I poured him another cup of coffee and I gave him a piece of my berry pie and I told him, "Here, nobody can stay too sad when they eat my berry pie, so have a piece on me and I hope it makes you feel better." Then I left him alone because a man should have his peace when he's eating the best berry pie he's ever tasted.

The man smiled at me when he came up to give me his fifty cents for dinner and he says, "Yes, indeed, Mrs. Averell [because strangers were the only ones I dared tell] that was the best pie I ever had besides my Margie's, and she'd have been pleased to know that another woman along the way understood how much I like pie." And we both laughed.

Then he put a suitcase on the table and told me, "I was taking these clothes of my Margie's with me home, but on better thought, I think you should have them. I think they'd fit you and you could maybe have use of them. Now, if this isn't proper…"

But he couldn't get the sentence done before I was saying how much I'd appreciate such a generous gift, and if he was sure he wanted to part with them, he could be certain I'd wear them in good health and care for them always.

Well, in grief, that man's eyes were lying to him because the dresses were all too small for me, but some were such beautiful fabrics that I knew right away they would be perfect for a splendid quilt, and that's what they became that winter of '86 when we didn't have much of a Christmas.

I ended up moving into the roadhouse that December because we thought we could make it if we combined the households and were certain we couldn't if we kept both places going. For appearance sake, I'd make a point of mentioning how cozy it was off the kitchen because the stove was lit all night. In truth, I spent most nights snuggled next to my husband in his cabin next door, and if you don't know how nice body heat can be on a cold night on the prairie, then you've missed out.

Christmas that year was another cold, stormy, ugly day, and even though I tried to bring some cheer—cooking up a jerky stew and using the last of my sugar for a pie with apples I had canned, it was pretty meager compared to the Christmas I wanted. Jimmy loved his new shirt—he didn't know Ma would have done a better job—and he thought the quilt was right handsome. He laughed when I told him the story of how I got the material.

He gave me a book of poetry printed years ago in England—it even has a royal seal, which looks very important. Jim is always trying to advance my learnin', and I thought this was the most handsome book I ever owned. He said he'd found it in Chicago years ago when he was there and knew he wanted it for something very special and that special was me. It had a black, soft cover with red silk thread holding the pages together and the prettiest drawings to illustrate the poem. We read it out loud on Christmas night as we sat by the fire. I thought it was kind of spooky and scary, but Jimmy just laughed and said he bet it was a poem people would read forever. It was written by a man named Edgar Allan Poe and is called "The Raven." I kept it on a shelf by the fireplace for all to see.

That Christmas night Jimmy took me in his arms and promised we'd have lots of wonderful Christmases in the years ahead—some with our own children under a decorated tree—and I believed with all my heart that he was right again.

The only thing that came close to what I'd imagined our first holidays to be was when I insisted we follow my Pa's tradition and sing "Auld Lang Syne" for New Year's. And even that didn't turn out. Jimmy was all for it, because, of course, his own Scottish people had done the same thing and we talked about it in bed at night and decided this would be one of our cherished traditions, too. In a good year, we'd invite our neighbors for a nice New Year's Eve supper and we'd all join hands in a circle and sing the song and it would be a fine way to honor our people and bring in the new year.

This year we were just going to do it ourselves, but Fales came by that day and we saw a chance to make a little party and so I made a nice dinner at noon—he'd have to get back to his Ma before it got dark—and after we ate, we told him we had a tradition and we'd like him to join in.

"We're going to hold hands and sing 'Auld Lang Syne,'" I announced, with a smile on my face, and Fales instantly began to laugh like a hyena.

"That's a good one," he finally got out through his cackling. "Sure, I'll sing 'Auld Lang Syne' with you. Just like the regimental band in Arizona Territory played it to Geronimo when they put him and his dirty Apaches on the train to Florida. That's a good one, Miss Ella. That's a real good one."

He only stopped when he saw the smile had disappeared from my face. "Did I say something wrong?" Fales searched our eyes, trying to figure out what was the matter.

"No Fales, that's alright," Jimmy said. "The song just means something different to us."

I never did understand why the United States Army would decide to make a joke of such an important song like that, and I hoped my Pa never heard they'd mocked Geronimo with a song he cherished.

My only consolation that winter was that when you're snowed in so long, you got lots of handwork done. I knitted twelve pair of warm socks and fifteen scarves. I even crocheted a shawl I later sent to Ma. Busy hands are one way to keep them warm when the house is so cold, and to keep your heart warm when it wants to weep.

But December wasn't even the worst of it. A new howling storm came in January, and then there was a terrible February storm. One snowstorm came on top of the last, and we'd later figure we had fifty-four days of constant storms. And it wasn't just snow, but ice, too. Jim figured the stage route to Rawlins was four feet of snow covering two feet of ice. Cowboys showed up on horses whose hoofs were bleeding from breaking through a layer of ice.

The stories they told were just as bloody. They said the cows on the open range—that's where all the cows were, of course—had worn off the hair and hide on their legs from trying to walk through this mess. "They're out there dyin'," the cowboys kept saying, and you could feel the hurt in their voices. These weren't their cows, but you can't be a cowman of any kind in W.T.—even a hired hand—and not hurt when you know those critters are dying like flies. Those poor cowboys weren't doin' much better themselves, out there in the storms trying to save the cows that couldn't be saved. I saw that they needed the socks and scarves I'd made and by the time the snow stopped falling, I'd given them all away.

You couldn't live through the winter of 1886-87 without knowin' it was bad, but we had no idea just how horrible it truly was until the spring came and the entire valley stunk of dead cattle. It was a stench you couldn't escape. You didn't need a breeze to bring the smell of rotting flesh to your nostrils, but any breeze from any direction just made it worse. Even inside a cabin with the door and window shut, the smell still invaded and left you with a constantly churning stomach. And if the smell wasn't enough, the taste made you want to puke. I never knew before then that a smell could be so powerful it made you *taste* it whenever you breathed through your mouth, but that's how it was that awful spring when I thought I might never want to put another piece of steak in my mouth for the rest of my life.

Jim came back from Casper one day after getting supplies and looked like somebody had hit him with a sledgehammer. "They're thinking the die-off is at least fifty percent and maybe as high as eighty," he said in a somber, frightened voice. "The rivers are full of carcasses, and wherever you find a fence, you find a pile of bodies. They're saying there hasn't been this kind of slaughter since the buffalo."

He went over to his house and stayed there awhile, like he was in mourning, and I guess everybody in W.T. was feeling the same way. We were seeing the end of something, when spring is usually a time to see the beginning.

Cattlemen had made fortunes for years on cattle that roamed the open land and ate the grass and got fat for slaughter and had calves that replenished the herd, and now all that was rotting out there. Some cowboys told me the saddest thing of all was finding a dead mother cow with her calf still inside her. A cowboy poet came through the roadhouse one night in the late spring and entertained us with poems for his supper, and he had one I'll never forget:

I may not see a hundred
Before I cross the Styx,
But coal of ember, I'll remember
Eighteen eighty-six.

The stiff heaps in the coulee,
The dead eyes in the camp,
And the wind about, blowing fortunes out,
As a woman blows out a lamp.

Roundups the summer of '87, if you can even call them that, were pitiful. The hungry East that had made the cattle "lords" into millionaires, decided they didn't want what little beef was offered from W.T. Prices fell down near to nothin' and there wasn't work for half the cowboys who needed work. When all those cattle died, they took so many living souls along with 'em.

By the end of '87, most of those giant cattle companies were gone. The Englishmen and Scotsmen and Irishmen went home or off to greener pastures somewhere else. I for one wasn't sad to see their likes go. I'd heard too many stories about what snobs they were to care much for them. They were men who'd never learned you had to earn respect—it didn't come with birth. They thought because of who they were and who their daddies were that they were high and mighty and everyone should just do as they say. They never understood they came to a new country that wanted to get away from all that. They were men who did little and looked down their noses at the cowboys who helped make them rich—they thought the cowboy so lowly they got downright mean with 'em.

Like Jimmy told me one night, it had been a rule since the first cowboy rode the range, that a hungry guy would be fed by any ranch wagon he came upon. During the off-season, when there was no work, he could survive on this generosity they called "riding the grub line."

But these high and mighty men from other countries decided that was too generous and cut it off, demanding their cooks not feed traveling cowboys. It liked to kill some cooks who couldn't stand turning away hungry men, and some risked their jobs to defy the new rule. Maybe that kind of cruelty was all right in England or Scotland, but it wasn't all right in the territories of this new nation—places that one day just knew they'd be states themselves. A man that can't respect a working man isn't much of a man at all. And to think those men were here, in a country not even their own, getting rich on land they didn't own but sucking off the federal land. It makes you downright mad that they were ever here. No, I'm not alone in knowing Wyoming was not sorry to see them go.

That didn't mean there still weren't big cattlemen in W.T., including some who wanted to put on the same airs. And of course, the almighty Wyoming Stock Growers Association was just as powerful as ever—soon to be even more powerful, we'd sadly discover—but the day of easy riches was a day in the past.

Jim kept saying after that horrible winter, "Things will never be the same. An era has passed. There's just a bunch of cattlemen who don't understand that yet." And some of those men were our neighbors.

But I could see the day when there'd be more little guys like us than big guys like them. And that day came racing faster when some cowboys realized there wasn't much work left and settled down to raise their own herds. I saw for myself that stories Fales told were true: Some of those cowhands just took a few cows from the men they used to wrangle for. I know that's rustlin', but it wasn't like they took one hundred or two hundred, they took a couple. Most took the unbranded mavericks that should have been shared in the first place, but the point is they took just enough to get started. Considering how long they'd worked for poor wages, that never seemed like a big sin to me.

I never pretended to see the big picture about what was happening in our territory or the country we wanted to join, but I did understand what Jimmy was saying. I didn't belong to the

old era that was passing. I was part of the new W.T. I had a piece
of land that would someday legally belong to me because I put
my sweat and heart into it. I was building a corral because one
day I wanted a little herd—I'd never be a big cattleman, but
I didn't need to be a big cattleman to earn a living off cows. I
would fence my land and keep my cattle nearby, and I'd feed
them during the winter, and if we had another winter like '86,
my cows wouldn't die alone and abandoned like all those this
year. My cows would get hay and they'd calf in the spring, and
that's the way it's supposed to be.

I held on to that thought as we thawed out from winter.
We finally had spring. I planted a new garden and bought new
chickens, and then I met the Indians.

It turned out so well that I can laugh about it now, but I have
to admit, I was hearing my heart in my ears when I first came
upon them, even though it was just a girl and an old lady. I'd
never been this close to an Indian before, and after all the stories
I'd heard, well, you just never know.

I was down at the creek, picking berries that were plump on
the spring bushes and thinking about how good they'd be in my
first jam of the year, and all of a sudden, there were these two
dark-skinned people looking at me like they were scared of being
this close to a white person. We both stopped in our tracks and
eyed one another for a minute or two. The old woman put her
arm out to guide the girl behind her, as though I would hurt
the girl, and I felt a twinge of sadness thinking she'd think that
of me, but then, I realized I'd had the same thought about her.

"Berries," I said, as though that were a proper greeting. "Are
you picking berries, too?"

They just looked at me, and I realized they probably didn't
understand English, so I took a berry from my bucket and put
it in my mouth and licked my lips like it was real good. That
brought a smile to the girl's face, but the old woman—she'd turn
out to be the grandmother—kept staring. I took another berry
and repeated my hand signals and smacked my lips real hard this

time like these were really, really good. And that's when the girl laughed and the old woman finally showed a kindness in her eyes.

The girl reached around her grandmother and took one of their berries to eat, and then Grandma followed, and we all stood there, eating berries together, and as I'd later write my Ma, that was a pretty unusual way to meet your first Indian.

We nodded to each other and then went back to our picking, and when I had enough, I turned to go back to the house and they were already gone. I wondered what they were going to do with their berries—I was making jam, but that certainly didn't seem like something that would happen in an Indian camp.

"I don't even know if Indians like jam," I said to myself out loud.

Well, I was right. The berries made the most beautiful and delicious jam, and I had four pints sitting out cooling the next day when there was a knock on my cabin door, and I found the Indian girl standing outside. She smiled at me shyly, and then held out her hand. In it was a piece of cloth, dyed red, and I realized this was what they did with their berries—they made colored cloth. She shoved the piece toward me and I understood it was a gift, and I thought, won't this look nice on my table.

I took the cloth and smiled at her and waved my arm to ask her inside, but she shook her head and started to leave.

"Wait," I yelled, and it made her stop, even if she didn't know the word. "Here, I hope you like jam." I handed her one of my pints. And the smile on her face convinced me that Indians like jam as much as we do.

"Ella," I patted my chest. "My name is Ella."

She looked at me a moment and then mimicked my motion, her hand patting her chest. "Shashas."

As she walked away, I knew this wasn't the last time I'd see her, and it struck me as queer that one of the first friends I made out here was an Indian girl.

When I told Jimmy about it, he reminded me that he'd told me a Shoshone band came through by the creek now and then, but I'd forgotten all about it. I wouldn't forget it again. Twice a year I'd find them there, and pretty cloth wasn't all they had to offer. The beadwork Shashas did—it was magnificent. Her grandma taught her and I saw the pride in the old woman's eyes when I admired Shashas' work.

The welcome spring of '87 went on and you know how life is, life goes on.

One of those life-goes-on things in W.T. those days was fighting the cattlemen for your claim. Jimmy was right—they have filed hundreds of claims on land they never touch, just to tie it up.

"Two or three men would control the entire Sweetwater Valley if we didn't stop them," he swore. My Jimmy was determined to stop them.

If you made a pecking list, Bothwell was at the top. Jimmy said he not only was greedy, but he was mean. He already owned miles along the Sweetwater River, and he kept trying to get more. Another hunk of river land was owned by John Durbin, who would be second on Jimmy's list, although some days he moved to the top. I never was clear exactly what had happened between Jim and Durbin, but whatever it was, it was nasty, and Durbin shared the disdain for my man. And just for good measure, Jimmy was fighting with a guy named Conner over a hayfield near Horse Creek. To be honest, I didn't know a big rancher in the valley that my Jimmy wasn't battling any way he could.

If you wanted one word to explain all this turmoil, it was water.

Water meant everything here in W.T. and controlling it was a full-time job. Some say a man values his water rights over the value of his children. I thought that was stretching it until I saw what men would do to get water.

Without a reliable source of plentiful water—or as plentiful as water got in these parts—your land was worthless. It couldn't be planted for crops. It couldn't grow hay. It couldn't feed a calf. It couldn't keep a family alive. So everybody tried to get land with water.

That's why Jimmy's and my claims were so valuable—we controlled a big hunk of Horse Creek. Now don't go thinking

this was like controlling a big hunk of the Sweetwater River. That
was a real river, with water all year round. Our creek had water
most of the year, but it was a skinny little thing that shouldn't
matter so much. But it did.

Jimmy sucker-punched Bothwell and all the others with our
claims—before they knew it, we were all snug and secure and
controlled a mile of Horse Creek. You should have seen Bothwell
when he realized he no longer had access to the little creek that
watered one of his hayfields! I thought the man was going to
shoot Jimmy on sight the day he stormed up to the roadhouse
and screamed that Jimmy was a low-down thief.

He yelled, "That water has been mine for years," and said
Jimmy had no right to block him. Oh, he went on and on and
Fales, who usually was quick with a laugh on any situation,
certainly wasn't laughing that day.

The only one who didn't seem upset was Jimmy, who stood
there looking smug. He told Bothwell he could certainly have
water from the creek—if he bought an easement from the claims
of James Averell and Ella Watson.

"An easement??" Bothwell screamed, as though he'd been
sentenced to hell. "You expect me to buy a fucking easement
for water from Horse Creek? Are you fucking nuts?"

"No," Jimmy said, real slow, "and watch your language around
the lady. We aren't nuts. We're just the rightful owners of the
land that fronts the creek, and if you want water from there,
you must buy an easement from us. I suggest all you need is one
about fifteen feet wide and about 3,300 feet long." Jimmy said
all this with a perfectly straight face, as though he were telling
A.J. that a good bottle of whiskey was only two bucks.

I wondered how Jimmy could recite something so absurd. I
knew settlers all over the Sweetwater Valley would instantly see
the humor in this, and I had an awful time hiding the smile on
my face as our neighbor turned purple in anger.

Bothwell was so shocked and so mad, he got on his horse
without a word and hightailed it out of there. But in the end,
he did buy that easement and, while I was right that it became

a big joke in the valley, Fales never once laughed about it. That should have told us something. But it didn't. Nor did Fales smile when I announced I wanted an irrigation ditch from the creek to my pasture—he dug that ditch in silence. At that moment, Jimmy and I were full of ourselves. Maybe if we hadn't been so arrogant, we'd have seen the omens.

What I saw was red. Because even with filed claims and improvements under way, those cattlemen were still trying to scam us. It made me so darn mad! One of Bothwell's pals came after me. Edgar Schoonmaker filed a timber claim on my land—imagine, a timber claim on land that has no trees—and I had to go to court to fight him. I did and I won. Jimmy helped me, but it wasn't hard to prove his claim was bogus and he hadn't done a thing on the land, while I'd built a house and corrals, so I just scooped him out of his boots.

I know it's un-Christian, but I gloated, knowing Bothwell and Schoonmaker were mad as hornets when they went to bed that night.

These men were used to writing the rules, not playing by them.

Like the rule on claims—the first rule was you have to improve the property with a cabin. I've got scars and scabs to prove how hard it is to build a cabin, but rather than put in all that hard work like I was doing, they hauled around their cabin-on-logs from one fake claim to another. The first time I saw it, I was insulted that they'd cheat so badly.

Like the rule on fences—you could only fence the land on your claim, but they'd run mile after mile of fence on land they didn't even own and then sit there smug, like they could do whatever they wanted.

Like the rule on being honest—those cattlemen hired "stock detectives" and paid a princely sum to catch "cattle rustlers," so of course, the detectives caught lots of "rustlers." Thankfully, our judges and juries aren't so stupid they can't see a setup when one is shoved in front of their faces, and they would turn those innocent folks free. Then the cattlemen screamed they couldn't get "justice." They never seemed to accept that the first rule of justice was you've got to be just—they didn't care. It was one more rule they wouldn't follow like decent folks.

Jimmy said it was justice he was after when he wrote his letters exposing their tactics and their land grabs and of course, they didn't like that one bit. But we didn't care.

In my book, the worst one of all was Bothwell. This wasn't on the first page, but it gave a good idea how awful he was—he killed a colt to feed those gray wolves he kept as pets. It's true because I heard it from a cowboy who saw him do it. Can you imagine, killing a wee horse to feed wolves? Made no sense to me, but then, hardly anything that man did made sense to me.

He had his men tear down my barbed-wire fences that were all legal, when he put up his own fence across a public road that he had no right to. The county commissioners finally made him take it down, but he tried to get away with it, and that told a lot about him.

Oh yes, the other horror story they told in these parts about A.J. Bothwell was that he once shot a horse out from under a man. Some have tried to say he was in his rights on that one, but I don't care—shooting a horse out from under a man is a real mean thing to do. I never thought about him without the word "mean" coming to mind.

But I wasn't thinking of any of that nastiness when the big day came. May 25, 1887. I wore my best dress and the shawl I'd eventually send my Ma. I pinned up my hair and put on my only bonnet, and Jimmy and I rode the sixty miles into Rawlins to the Carbon County Courthouse. I climbed the steps to the double front doors and then climbed up two flights to get to the clerk's office. I filed my Declaration of Citizenship. I got a fancy certificate, just like the one Jimmy got when he declared his intentions to become a full-fledged citizen.

Within five years, if I kept myself out of trouble, learned the laws of the land and the history of the country, and could pass the test, I would be a citizen. By then, we both hoped it wouldn't be a citizen of Wyoming Territory, but a citizen of the

State of Wyoming. Jimmy was certain we'd be a state by then and I believed him because I wanted it so bad.

On the way home Jim reminded me of something that made me so proud and happy—it took five years for our land to be proved up for ownership and five years to get citizenship. Those two monumental events would happen one after another. By 1892, we'd be land-owning citizens of this great new nation that promised a fair chance for everyone.

"We have so many happy years ahead." I snuggled up next to the man I loved and fantasized about the grand celebrations we'd throw.

I was in dreamland the whole way home.

Chapter Eleven

I Love Being a Homesteader

They were ugly cows, but I didn't care.

I was wearing a gray bonnet and a blue work dress, and I stood up straight so I looked like I was ready for business. I crossed my arms across my chest and walked around the small herd, looking like I knew what I was looking for and shaking my head in disapproval now and then to make it look like I didn't like what I saw.

It was a fine October morning in 1888 near Independence Rock, and I intended to relish every moment of this important step in my new life.

"Fales, these are some poor-looking critters," I said, as stern as I could sound. That was his cue to amble over, slow, like there was nothing to hurry about, and take over the lookin'. I went to stand next to the Nebraska wrangler who was trying to sell these straggling cattle on his way to the Territory of Washington. We watched my ranch hand look like these were the worst cows he'd ever seen.

Fales pulled on their ears, ran his hand over their hides, peered into their eyes, smelled them, and reached under to heft their balls. I bet no critter had ever been so inspected. Then Fales dropped down on his haunches—his favorite sitting spot, although I couldn't imagine it being comfortable and knew I'd never get up if I ever got down that far. He rolled himself one of his smokes and sat there like he was thinking the deepest thoughts in the territory.

"They're in pretty bad shape. Skinny as hell. Ain't worth much, to my way of thinkin'," he slowly drawled.

The wrangler jumped in. "I know they ain't the best, but they'll fatten up and there isn't a sore on 'em." There was a hint of desperation in his voice, because we figured he was counting on these cows for the last money he'd see out of W.T.

Fales came back with the obvious. "Thing is, they can't make it all the way to Washington, so if we don't take 'em off your hands, what you gonna do with 'em, shoot 'em?"

That was my clue that these cows could be bought for the lowest possible price. Fales had told me ahead of time the cheapest I could get these stragglers was three or four dollars a head.

"You wouldn't just shoot them and let them rot out here in W.T., would you?" I asked the wrangler in my best girly voice, betting he would mistake my concern for a sign of weakness.

Sometimes it's tiring, how predictable men can be because he bit like a trout on a fat worm. "I'll tell you what, little lady. I'll give 'em to you for five dollars a head—now that's a real bargain because your neighbor's been payin' as much as twenty dollars a head." To shine his point, he pulled out of his shirt pocket the stub of a pencil and a dirty piece of paper with the handwritten title: "Bill of Sale." He looked at me like he'd just caught the brass ring, all poised to fill it out with the little lady's name.

"Maybe," Fales said slowly, showing he thought the price tag had been gussied up. "Say you got that much. That was for good cows and we all know these ain't good cows." Fales stood up from his haunch without the least bit of trouble and flicked away his cigarette stub.

The wrangler screwed up his nose at this intrusion of reality and turned back to me with hope in his eyes that this "little lady" would understand what a great deal this was. I could see he was already counting up his money when I finally spoke.

"I'll give you fifty cents a head," I said in a strong, clear voice. I'd have to be blind to miss the shock on both men's faces. Fales looked at me like I didn't know the value of cows on the hoof, and the wrangler looked at me like I was a woman whose idea of a bargain was getting something for free.

"Fifty cents!!" he spit out like he'd just tasted rancid stew. "There's never been a cow sold in the territories for fifty cents. Ma'am, I know you're new to this, but you've got to be reasonable. Fifty cents isn't even a respectable offer. Okay, I'll go to four dollars a head."

"Seventy-five cents," I came back, just like I hadn't heard his scolding.

The wrangler spit on the ground and walked around like he was a dog lookin' for a place to lay down, pulled off his John B. and threw it on the dirt and acted like he was the most insulted man to ever see dawn in Wyoming Territory. I was finding all this very entertaining.

"Ma'am, with all due respect, I've got to remind you that full-grown cows can be worth sixty to seventy dollars apiece and it makes no economic sense—none whatsoever—to think you'd get that kind of return with an investment of seventy-five cents. Ma'am, that's just downright mortifying! The least I could possibly go is three dollars a head."

I didn't budge and I didn't open my mouth. Silence in a bargaining moment can be painful. This was one of those moments. After a minute or two, I even turned like I was going to mount Goldie and ride off without any cows.

"Two dollars," the wrangler almost screamed to stop me in my tracks and Fales had that pleading look like I'd better turn around because I was stretchin' the quilt too far. But I didn't. I took another step or two and the wrangler couldn't stand it: "Ma'am, if I don't get at least a dollar a head for these cows, I am going to shoot them, right here in front of your eyes."

"Sold," I yelled! I could hardly suppress the giggle building in my happy chest. I took three quick steps back, reached over and took the bill of sale. I filled in the date and signed my name, then folded the paper and put it in my dress pocket. "Fales, give the man twenty-eight dollars cash money, that's the dollar-a-head he says he wants."

That wrangler stood there with a mouth so open, flies thought they'd found themselves a hotel.

I turned and walked away. Nobody could see the smile plastered on my face. "Fales, thanks for helping out, and be sure you wave at Mr. Bothwell when you herd these cows past his ranch on the way to my corral."

And that's how I, Ella Watson, became a cattlewoman in Wyoming Territory.

Fales would retell that story a thousand times, regaling neighbors with my sheer pluck. I'd always blush a little and aw-shucks it, but I was real proud of myself.

◇◇◇

That night over supper, a happy and chortling Fales picked at his teeth and said in his drawl, "Now, Miss Ella, since you got yourself a herd, you'd better get yourself a brand. And aren't you in luck to have me?"

I sure was. True to his reputation, John Fales knew just about everything there was to know about what he called the "almighty brand."

"You make it sound like a religion," I joked.

He wasn't even grinning when he came back, "It pretty much is."

"Miss Ella, you gotta understand that to a cattleman, a brand is more important than his name. You've seen it yourself, those big outfits, they don't have the man's name on the gateposts to their ranches, they have their brand. Some of the rich ones have it etched into silver platters that they serve their steaks on."

A few days later, while we were working on the corral, Fales decided to start my formal lessons, and like he always did, he started at the beginning.

"Miss Ella, a brand is the way a cow says, 'that's who I belong to', and you want your cows to say that real loud. You want your brand simple but clear, but not so simple that it can be easily changed—if somebody wants to alter your brand, you've got to make it hard on 'em."

That's when I learned there are only three ways to read a brand—from left to right, from top to bottom, or from the outside to the inside. "You can tell a tenderfoot right off if he is looking at a 'Circle A' brand and he calls it 'A Circle'. It's a dumb mistake and I don't want you to ever say it wrong, because nobody will take you serious if you can't read a brand and you've got enough problems...."

He stopped then, short, but the message was real clear. I couldn't be a rancher—even as small as I was—without understanding brands. I especially couldn't be a woman rancher. If I ever said a brand wrong, the cowboys would laugh me out of the Sweetwater Valley. So I took my lessons seriously.

Fales wrote down two sets of numbers and letters and challenged me to read them. First he wrote down 2-X, and then he stacked a 2 over a line over an X. "That's the same brand, two different ways. What is it?"

I answered right away, "That's a two dash X brand."

He smiled like he had a promising student on his hands. "We don't say dash when we talk brands, we say bar," he explained. "So try again."

And that's how I learned what a Two Bar X brand looked like.

Of course, that was an easy one. I had so much more to learn.

There were "tumbling" brands where the letter was falling over and "lazy" brands where it's lying down and "crazy" brands where it's upside down. There were "flying" brands with little wings on the letter and "rocking brands" that had a half circle under the letter and "swinging brands" where the half circle was on top of the letter. I noticed that all the brands he printed out were in capital letters and when I mentioned it, Fales just said, "Well, sure." But that made him realize he also had to tell me that the letter "O" was always called a "circle." I was dizzy by the time that first lesson was over.

Fales insisted from the start that I shouldn't have a simple brand. I should do something interesting—both letters and numbers—and when it came to designing my brand, he'd help.

I started thinking about symbols. My initials? Would that be EW or EA? Neither one of them looked like a pretty brand—and Fales didn't laugh when I said that because he said a cattleman might not use the word "pretty," but that was one of the things we were after.

I decided to forget my initial, but to use a "W" in honor of Pa. "How about a crazy W, since my Pa thought I was crazy for coming out here in the first place," I suggested one day.

Fales came back, "A 'W' can't be a crazy, because you turn a W upside down and it becomes an M."

I never thought of that. "I could have a 'rocking W'," I offered next, where the W would have a half circle under it, but Fales said that would be the easiest brand in the world to alter if you just closed the circle and made it a Circle W.

"You've got enough problems without handing a rustler an easy way to steal your cattle," he reminded me and then launched into one of his stories to make his point.

"One spring somebody was stealin' fat calves and steers from the 'Bar S' ranch down in Texas and the owner complained to Judge Roy Bean," Fales began, writing out the brand as "-S."

"Well, Bean appointed himself a range detective and went out lookin'. Sure enough, six days later he came back with 20-some head of steers, all branded '48' and with a rancher tied-up behind 'em. A crowd gathered outside his saloon—that's where he held court under a sign that said 'Law West of the Pecos,' I know you heard of him. Now, this tied-up rancher insisted Judge Bean was nuts; that this was his own registered brand and these were his own cows and he had burned that brand on them himself.

"'You burned it, alright,' Bean said, 'but wait.'

"Right there, he shot one of the cows dead and when everyone started thinking he was nuts after all, he skinned back part of the hide. The crowd moved in to look and everyone could see the underside of the steer's skin showed a blackish '-S' brand real plain, but around and over it, was a reddish raw burn that made the '-S' into a '48'. They hanged that rustler within a half hour."

I got the point. I thought about it a long time and doodled as I cooked, and finally made a decision. My first choice was a TW brand in honor of Pa, Thomas Watson, but Fales knew immediately that wouldn't work because that was one of Bothwell's Broken Box Ranch brands!

I shrieked, "That's the last brand I'd ever want."

But my mistake sent Fales on a new mission. "Miss Ella, it's about time you know about your neighbors out here in the valley. I think I've told you all I know about Bothwell, and I know you hate the sound of that man's name, but I haven't told you about the other ranchers that you're gonna brush up against when you try and get a brand. I've gotta be honest, it's not going to be easy. I don't think a woman has ever had her own brand in W.T. You know Bothwell will be fighting any brand you want, but so will some of these others. I always think information about your enemies is good ammunition, so let me load you up."

That sounded logical to me, and besides, I loved Fales' stories and I completely agreed with him at how powerful information can be, so my new lessons began.

"Might as well start at the top," he said one morning as I rolled out a pie crust and he took a coffee break. "That would be John Durbin and his UT Ranch. You're not gonna find a bigger cattleman in these parts than Durbin. They say he's got a million head out on the range and I don't doubt it for a second."

I watched Fales take a long drink of boiling coffee—I never understood how he could drink it like that—and he settled in.

"He was a Civil War hero, you know, marched with Sherman to the sea and was at the Siege of Vicksburg, too. That was back East somewhere. Then he brought his whole family out to Cheyenne, his two brothers, his Ma and Pa. His family's real big in Cheyenne—they call his Pa 'Father John.' Those Durbin Brothers could do anything. They were carpenters and tinsmiths and paperhangers, and then they got in with Amos Peacock and his butcher shops."

Fales took two bites of pie and wouldn't say another word until he'd washed down the last bit. Then he pushed on.

"Anyone ever tell you most of Cheyenne burned down in '70? Well, it did and if it hadn't been for the railroad, that would have been the end of Cheyenne. After the fire, Peacock sold his butcher shops to the Durbin boys and they made a fortune. They ran their own cattle, so they had free meat to cut up and sell. Got government contracts, that was the big thing; supplyin' the forts. And of course, they shipped beef back East. Don't know anybody shipped more than them. That family has the Midas Touch—everything they touch turns to gold and I'm not just sayin' that."

Fales paused while I went to the storeroom for more cornstarch, then went on.

"The Durbin boys all went over to Deadwood during the Black Hills gold rush and bought themselves a little mine, and they made a fortune selling to that George Hearst who owns the paper up in San Francisco. Now it's called the Homestake Mine and they say it'll never play out and I wouldn't doubt that for a minute. Durbin took his millions and came out to the Sweetwater Valley before there were any real homesteaders here, and he's been makin' money every day of his life since. He got to be a big shot here real early. Helped form a group that became the Stock Growers Association—*that* kind of big. Don't know how many fortunes one man needs, but John Durbin is contendin' for the record."

I noticed Fales was helping himself to a second cut of pie, but I passed it off as the price for the fine story he was telling.

"You know, he's a hard man to figure out. In Rawlins, they'll sing his praises as a real generous man—one time he bought out the entire bond issue to help build a school. And another time he put up all twenty-five thousand dollars for the courthouse bond. Imagine that. Rawlins just falls all over itself wherever John Durbin is concerned. And I have to give it to him—that was a right decent thing to do. Then he turns around and hires Tom Collins, and a man who hires scum like that just isn't thinkin' right."

I needed no help understanding Fales' disgust, because like everyone else in the valley, I shared it. From the day Tom Collins came up from Texas, he'd been trouble. He always looked dirty to me, and he had those shifty eyes that couldn't meet yours square, and whenever he walked in the roadhouse, he acted like he owned the place. Officially, he was Durbin's foreman, but he was really a notorious cattle thief—the kind that would make Fales stretch his arms out as far as they would go. There was a big sigh of relief when his rustling became so blatant that even the stock growers blackballed him—they even publicly criticized John Durbin for looking the other way.

Fales said he knew why. "They say Durbin didn't dare turn Collins in or the foreman would have squealed on how Durbin's herds were full of other men's cattle. If I were you, I'd watch him like a dog at a rabbit hole."

Why a man that rich would resort to stealing, I'll never figure out, but I was learning that when it came to rich in W.T., it was never enough.

"And I hate to tell you this part, but you gotta know it all and the worst piece of news I can give you is that John Durbin and A.J. Bothwell have a special tie. They both first tried to ranch in Colorado, but homesteaders got in their way and they moved over here to the Sweetwater Valley. I hear both of them have sworn they'll never let a homesteader drive them out again. Miss Ella, did you hear that? Do you know what it means?"

"Of course I do," I shot back, like I wasn't a dunce. "So the two most powerful men in the valley hate homesteaders. Think I didn't already know that? John Durbin hasn't stuck his nose in my business, but Bothwell has certainly let me know I'm not wanted here. But you know what, my friend? I've got a legal claim, and I've got a cabin, and I've got cows, and I'm gonna get me a brand and I'm going to stay here in this beautiful valley for the rest of my life and there isn't a thing they can do about it."

I saw Fales drop his head and stuff his mouth with yet more pie.

He stayed quiet for a long time and I thought I'd made a powerful point he couldn't counteract. But there was a chill down my spine when he finally said, "I hope so, Miss Ella. I sure as hell hope so."

"Hey, do you know why Jimmy and Durbin hate each other?" I asked to move off the gloom Fales was spreading.

"Sure don't," but I knew he was lying.

"Fales, come on, if there's a problem between my man and Durbin, don't you think I should know? That might be just the piece of information that's most important. Come on, I know you know."

"You can't ever tell Jimmy I told you, because it makes Jimmy look bad. Believe me, Miss Ella, this was a long time ago and Jimmy was young and he wouldn't think of doing this now...."

I was getting impatient with all his stalling, and the more he hemmed and hawed, the more awful this story grew in my mind, until I just screamed at him, "Fales, just spit it out!"

He knew me well enough to know that when I scream I'm not kidding around, so he finally told me the awful secret that Jimmy had once filed a fake homestead claim for Durbin, and then snookered him out of it by selling the claim for himself. That's where Jimmy got his grubstake to file his own first claim. "And Durbin will never forgive him for it, and Miss Ella, John Durbin is the last man you want as an enemy."

I didn't say anything. Fales looked at me like he was trying to teach me something, and I guess he was, but I didn't really take in his last words—I was back at the revelation that my Jimmy had started out cheating, just like the people he was fighting against now. There's a word for somebody who says 'do as I say and not as I do' and it wasn't a word I wanted associated with my Jimmy. For a second I worried that Durbin would expose Jimmy for his cheating, but then I realized it had all begun with a cheat in the first place and Durbin would never expose himself. So the secret was safe. I hoped nobody besides Fales knew about it, and from the way folks around here admired my Jimmy, I bet that might be. I knew I'd never speak a word of this to anyone, because Fales was right, Jimmy was young then—he was a grown man now and he clearly knew right from wrong and so I passed it off as something to forget.

But my pondering left a big silence in the kitchen and it made Fales nervous, because he coughed real loud and said, "think we should move on because there's another man you need to know about." I was about to say it was time for his chores when thunderclouds moved in and fierce lightning lit up the sky. We both saw the weather as a good omen that chores were to wait and the stories were to continue.

"Now if you want one just as bad, you only have to go upstream a little to your neighbor Bob Conner." Fales rolled his eyes like this one was a doozie. "His brand is the Lazy UC, and by gosh, if that ain't fittin'. He's a rich man's son—well, stepson, I guess—and Daddy set him up out here and I don't know how much of a worker he is, but from what I hear, not much. He fancied himself a politician once and ran for office—he's a Republican, of course—but got his butt whipped and never tried that again. He's had some real characters for foremen, and everybody in these parts knows he thinks the longest rope belongs to him."

Fales cackled and mimicked twirling a rope over his head, and that's how I learned the cowboy term for rustling.

"We used to have all these snooty foreigners around here, acting like they were still lords in England or Scotland, and they didn't know one end of a cow from the other. They never did any real ranchin' and if you asked them how many cows they had, they'd say something stupid like 'a lot.' So of course, they were ripe for the longest rope, and Bob Conner built up his herds real good by goin' after those foreigners' cows. Word is he got a thousand cows before those foreigners pulled out and went away."

By now, Fales was in full hilarity, slapping his sides at how funny it was that Bob Conner stole so many cows. I will never understand the mind of a cowboy. One minute he was swearing about rustling, and the next minute, laughing about it.

It took him a couple minutes and three bites of pie to move on.

"Then there's Cap'n Galbraith—you know, the mercantile man who's in the legislature." I knew exactly who he meant, although the good captain had never been inside the roadhouse. "Of course, his claim to fame is that he helped inspire Thomas Edison's light bulb."

I chortled, "In a pig's eye."

Fales shot back, "No, he really did." So I shut up and listened.

"Cap'n Galbraith was a railroad man, guess he learned in the Civil War how to keep them going and after the war, Union Pacific hired him on. He kept those boxcars and engines in good workin' order. He came to Rawlins as the main guy, and on the side, he bought a dry goods place—Hugus, where you shop, that used to be his. He's been elected a couple times and he's a real friend to the cattlemen, even has his own place in the Sweetwater now. His brand is the T Bar T. But you want to know about Edison and that's a story they love to tell around here.

"Back in '78, there was a total eclipse of the sun and they said the very best place in the whole country to see it was at the Separation Stage Station right here in W.T. So astronomers and scientists and dignitaries all came out—they brought a newspaperman from New York with 'em—and one of those boys was Thomas Edison. I guess Cap'n was about as close to a local dignitary as we had, so he was their host and after the eclipse, he took them all fishing on Battle Lake and that's where Edison saw lighting or a fishing line or something and got the inspiration for his light bulb. They brag about that all the time in W.T."

Can you imagine? Turning a switch and having light? I don't think we'll ever have electricity in my cabin—maybe the roadhouse some day. Think of all the time I'd save not having to clean my kerosene lamps! But Fales was already moving on so I gave him my attention back.

"And I suppose you want to know about Tom Sun. Sure you do, because don't you have a tie to his missus?"

"We both worked for Mary Hayes in town—not at the same time, because Mrs. Sun was already married by the time I came around. I always hoped she'd come in to the roadhouse for dinner someday, but she hasn't. Guess she doesn't care we have a tie—maybe doesn't want to admit it!"

I expected Fales to lay out Tom Sun's sins and stealing, and it was a nice surprise when that's not the stories he told me at all.

"He's a real decent guy," Fales began and there was true admiration in his voice.

"He's French Canadian—hey, ain't you and Jimmy from Canada originally? He's known Jimmy for ages. Sun was an Indian scout when Jimmy was at Fort Steele in the army. And they both end up here, as neighbors. Sun is good friends with Buffalo Bill—they scouted together and now and then he comes through here."

Oh my, if that famous showman came here for dinner, I'd made him a special pie and have him carve his name in my counter!

"Sun's ranch over by Devil's Gate is the Hub and Spoke and he's been here longer than anybody. He filed the first claim on land in the valley and he respects the laws. You know, Jimmy made a mistake when he filed his claim last year, and he needed someone to vouch for him that it was only a clerical error and Sun stepped up for him. The man has a real feel for W.T. and the land. I'd be proud to work for him."

By now the rainstorm had passed—they come and go so quickly here—and we both knew Fales' chores wouldn't do themselves, so he excused himself for the day. I finished up my baking and started frying chicken. I had to laugh out loud, "I sure ended up in a nest of snakes."

◇◇◇

I was determined to honor Pa with my brand, so next I came up with WT for Watson, Thomas, like on official papers. But it also could stand for Wyoming Territory and that meant it did double duty. Fales agreed. So that went on my list. So did a Triangle W brand—a triangle with a W inside—because I liked the look of it and couldn't see how anyone could mess with it. Fales thought that would be a fine brand. But I threw in four or five more ideas, like a Circle W and a Box W and that kind of thing, hoping all the time nobody had taken the WT yet. I took all those brands to the Carbon County Brand Committee in December of 1888.

Fales came with me to the meeting, held at a ranch nearby where the men had just finished a fine steak dinner when we arrived. I tried to peek if the platters were etched with the ranch's brand, but they were too greasy to tell.

"So Miss Ella, I hear you've got yourself some cows and are settin' up a ranch," one of the men said to me, trying to sound friendly, but it came out like this was a ridiculous idea for a woman.

I smiled and ignored the tone. "I'm going to have a *little* spread," I said in my sweetest voice. I learned long ago that a woman should minimize because "big" meant something special to men. I didn't tell them the brand was in honor of my Pa, because Fales had advised against that—"none of their business why you choose a brand."

The men around the table pretended to be gentlemanly as I presented my brand ideas—Jimmy had taken care to write them out clear and clean, with no ink spots.

Their mouths curled up in an imitation of a smile when they told me that none of my brands would work and they were sorry but they had other business to take care of, dismissing me like I was the cleaning girl.

"But gentlemen…" That's as far as I got before Fales took my arm and pulled me out of the room.

"I know for a fact that some of those brands are available, so you didn't get rejected because of bad brands, but because of bad politics," Jimmy stewed when we got home. "The cattle growers control the brand committee and they don't want small ranchers and homesteaders having brands. I should know, because they turned down a dozen of my ideas. And I don't even have any cows yet—but I wanted a brand for someday."

They were doing the same to me, but I already had cows in my corral and now I had no way to mark them as my own.

Fales added his own two cents: "You knew to expect this. You're sittin' here in the middle of what Bothwell thinks is his pasture and you've got a legal claim and he had to buy an ease-ment from Jimmy to get water from the creek and you can bet all that went into their thinking—you're bestin' them, ma'am, and they sure don't like it."

I didn't feel much like a bester that day, but I had to admit the points were stacking up in Jimmy's and my corner.

◇◇◇

March 23, 1888, was about the most important day of my life so far. I took the train from Rawlins to Cheyenne to file the formal papers on Claim No. 2003. My squatter's claim had been enough at the start, but this formal claim in the territory's capital was demanded. On the form, I explained it took so long to complete the paperwork because of the time and expense of getting to Cheyenne from Rawlins.

My official homestead receipt came with a special gift from Jimmy: He bought me a round-trip train ticket to go home to visit my family in Kansas that summer, and I was so overjoyed, I thought I would burst.

Of course, I took my homestead papers home with me to show my folks. I only intended to stay the month of June, but then sister Franny decided to get married in the middle of July, so I stayed for that, too. It was the most wonderful visit, being in Ma's home and cooking with her and talking non-stop while we worked on a quilt for Franny. Of course, my brothers ribbed me every day.

"So I suppose you're a bloomer now, now that you've got your own homestead and everything," Andrew teased, and everyone laughed at the thought of their Ella wearing bloomers like some did.

"You know, you didn't have to go all the way to Wyoming to vote," John pointed out. "We've got women right here in Kansas taking over whole cities, they're so important now."

I thought he was foolin' until Pa told me that, indeed, the town of Oskaloosa was entirely run by women. I had never heard of such a thing and couldn't imagine it ever happening in Wyoming.

It was hard to leave my family again, and the good-byes were long and tearful, but I had a new life now and it was waiting for me in W.T.

I had no idea I was going home to a new family and a brand of my own.

Chapter Twelve

I Became a Substitute Ma

It was a cold day in February of 1889, when our neighbor John Crowder came racing into the roadhouse on his horse. "She's burnin' up, she's burnin' up," he sputtered, getting out that his wife had been sick three days already. "And she's coughing her lungs out. I tried nature's cure, but that didn't work."

I knew right then that things were bad. It's the first thing I would have done, made Catherine Rose fast for a day on water to flush out the sickness. But since nature's cure had already failed, this sounded like a pneumonia had set in.

Of course, there was no time to fetch a doctor—a fifty-mile ride there and fifty miles back and even if John tried, his horse would never last that kind of ride.

Jimmy and I jumped in our wagon to follow him home, knowing all we had was what we knew of nursing. Out here, you took care of these things yourself because there was no one else. If a neighbor was in trouble, you shared whatever knowledge you had. So I learned all I could about nursing the sick.

On the way out the door, I grabbed the best I had for medicines to help my neighbor. I had Jimmy put the pot of soup I was cooking into the wagon, knowing only a liquid diet would help right now. If Catherine Rose could get anything down at all. Besides, the rest of the family probably hadn't had a hot meal for days now. I grabbed my turpentine oil to massage into Catherine Rose's chest, hoping it would keep its promise to relieve the pain. I took two things for the cough: a bottle of carbolic acid for its fumes and the last of the lemon juice so I could make a drink with lukewarm water and salt. Of course, I took one of the poultices I made every spring. I gathered up fresh herbs and hops from the fields and balled them into little cotton sacks. Soaked them in water and broke open the sack to spread the herbs on their chest to help draw out the poisons. It was my fallback cure for everything.

The Crowder homestead was nothing to brag about—a shack of a house, a little better barn, a couple cows in the corral, a puny garden, a wagon on its last leg, three kids, and now a dying wife. By the time our wagon came thundering into the yard, John Crowder had already been inside the house to see that things had gone from bad to worse. He met me at the door, shaking his head, and I couldn't tell if his wife was already gone or just on death's doorstep.

I carried the pot of soup into the house and hugged the little girls curled together in a rocker. I figured they were five, six, years old. Then I walked to the bedroom door. I stood there a few minutes to catch my breath and used my apron to wipe away the perspiration of hurrying and worrying. My Ma had drilled into me that you never enter a sickroom when you're perspiring because the moment you cool down, your pores absorb what's in the air and that's the quickest way to get sick yourself.

Catherine Rose was barely alive. Every breath was a horrible wheeze and her eyes were the small slits of someone who doesn't have the strength left to open them full. Her whole bed was wet with sweat. I propped her up and pulled the nightgown over her head. Another one was hanging from a nail and I put that on her, soothing to her all the time that everything was going to be alright. I grabbed a towel and snugged it under her to get her off the wet straw bed and threw off the wet quilt. On a shelf at the back of the bedroom I found some tattered old quilts I supposed she was going to reuse someday, and put them on her to keep her warm.

I did all I could to make her last hours as comfortable as possible, but it was clear from the start that the poor woman wouldn't make it. I had the men take the children outside so they wouldn't see the end. I sat with this woman who would have become a friend if she'd lived long enough. I held her hand as she died.

John Crowder was like a walking ghost. He reminded me of a man who'd forgotten how to hear or see. He sat there staring as his little daughters clung to him, crying and begging for their Ma. Their older brother stood in the corner, his hands jammed into his pants pockets, his eyes wild, like he was searching for someone to hit. It just broke my heart to see a family so torn apart. I sent Jimmy home and stayed on to help get things ready for the funeral. Besides, somebody had to tend the children and wait for Catherine Rose's kin to arrive, and poor John Crowder wasn't up to any of it.

Eugene was the oldest at eleven and he knew most about what was going on. He acted mad at his Ma for dying and disgusted with his Pa for being so lost, and refused to let anyone see him cry. That attitude could mar a child for life, so I got him busy.

"Gene, you've got to help me and you've got to help with your sisters."

The boy's eyes said he was needy, too, but when I stepped toward him to offer comfort, he ran to the barn. I guess that was where he did his crying. A little while later, he stepped up to bring in firewood. He gathered the eggs for me, and when I nodded toward his sisters, he went over to put his arms around them.

I dished out hot soup and cut some bread from the cabinet, and those children ate like they'd never eaten before in their lives. The girls were asleep soon after. Gene went out to the barn and I fell asleep in the rocker.

Grief for very youngins is a momentary thing, I knew from my own family. It consumes them until the next distraction comes along. For Lisa and Kara, my distraction the next morning was rag dolls. The ache of losing their Ma would come back, but at least for now, I could redirect their attention.

"Now, how would you girls like new dolls?" Of course, my cheery offer stopped the crying and they were anxious for their presents. "We're going to make them." Their eyes got big, like saying five- and six-year-olds couldn't do such a thing. "Sure you can. Now you rip this old pillowcase into long strips, Lisa. Kara, you rip this one into small strips." I knew from watching my own sisters that ripping cloth was a joyful thing for a child to do.

I made Kara's small strips into one long braid and tied them off at each end with a little piece of twine. I took Lisa's long strips and doubled them over. Toward the top I gathered the fabric and tied a string around it to make a "head," then tucked Kara's braid into the fold for "arms." I tied the last string in the middle for a "waist." The girls had been so busy with their own tasks, they hadn't seen that while they were ripping, I took circles of fabric and gathered them to make hats. I tacked a hat on top of each doll and both girls let out an AHHHH.

"I love it," Lisa squealed." Of course Kara joined right in, "I love it, too." So off they went to play with their new dolls and I knew that would keep them busy for a little while.

John hardly left the barn where he was making the casket and the little he ate couldn't keep a mouse alive. Gene disappeared for hours, but he kept up his chores and I had plenty of firewood for the stove.

Without a Ma here, this wasn't a place that could last. By the second day, I was letting the thought creep in that this was a family looking for a Ma. And that could be me. I couldn't have my own children for five more years, until the claim was all set, and I'd be in my mid-thirties by then. But maybe I wouldn't have to wait. Gene was a strong boy and would be a great help on the homestead, and the girls weren't much trouble as long as you kept them occupied. By the end of the day, when their Aunt Mary Margaret arrived, I was set on the idea.

Mary Margaret was a small woman, but only in stature. Although she was less than half my size, she immediately took charge of her late sister's home. I put on the coffeepot but Mary Margaret—"call me MM"—said she preferred tea, so I put on the kettle and once the hellos and hugs were over, we sat down at the table.

I told the story of Catherine Rose's last days and John's dash for help and how I'd arrived with Mr. Averell—"I cook at his road-house and have a claim nearby," was all I said to explain Jimmy.

"You're a good neighbor to be here for my family," MM told me, as though those words needed to be said when, of course, they didn't. Being a good neighbor is a badge of honor on the frontier. It's a measure understood by all, and it doesn't take long to figure out who measures up and who doesn't.

Mary Margaret was a woman who'd lost some of her family to an Indian raid and some to misfortune and some to illness. She was used to being the survivor to take charge. She instantly saw her brother-in-law was shattered. She'd never thought he was much of a provider in good days, and these certainly weren't good days. He could never hold this family together. Her nephew was in better shape, but that wasn't really saying much. She tried to hug the boy, but he would have none of it. His surly attitude told her all she needed to know about his state of mind.

The girls were something else altogether. MM gathered them up and cooed at them and brushed their hair and talked to them like she was their own Ma. It came so naturally to her that I knew immediately these girls weren't coming home to my homestead.

It was time for me to move on, but MM held me back. "Ella, I need your help. I'm not sure what's going to become of this family. I'll take the girls, of course, but I can't take Gene, and John isn't in any shape to take care of him. Now, he's a big boy and a strong boy and he's ready to start earning his keep." She stopped there, as though it was my turn to end the story.

"He is a good boy," I began, to be sure his aunt realized that. "He's just so hurt at his Ma's passing. And he's smart. I can see that in him. And yes, he's strong and he's old enough now to be doing his share." I continued like that, reciting all his attributes. MM kept nodding her encouragement for me to continue. In the way that women read each other, I knew she was too proud to ask me to take Gene, but was praying with all her heart that I would.

"You know, I could just take him for awhile until John gets back on his feet," I offered, so I wouldn't sound too possessive.

MM jumped at that idea. "Oh, Ella, that would be so perfect. It would be good for the boy and for John. And you already know the boy and that always helps with kids his age. You're sure, are you, that nobody would object?"

I knew she wasn't clear about this Mr. Averell. "Oh, I'm sure." I'd have some explaining to do, but I could handle Jimmy.

MM went out to the barn to talk to John and tell him what had been decided. I never heard any objections coming from John Crowder, but I saw plenty of questions in Gene's eyes. Poor kid. I bet he felt lost right then. His sisters were going one place, him another. With a woman he barely knew. To a place he'd only been once before, when he and his Pa came to the roadhouse to buy beans. But you didn't have to be a mind reader to know this boy had no interest in staying here. I thought he might ask his aunt to go along with his sisters, but he didn't. He looked at me like I was a life raft, and pulled together two clean shirts and a pair of pants already too short. He climbed in our wagon and came home with me.

When we walked in and I told Jimmy what was happening, my eyes were so determined, he didn't dare make any protest. But then, I don't think he would have, anyway. Because he took to the boy right away.

Jimmy put him to work around the roadhouse, and Gene did whatever was asked. We had him sleep in the little room behind the kitchen. He didn't say much, but he ate like a grown man and if I ever needed a testimony to the wonderment of my pies, it was in the swooning eyes of Gene Crowder as he ate one piece after another. I bet he put away ten pies in his first week at the roadhouse. As he stuffed his face, I talked to him about anything I could think of. How I'd come to W.T. all by myself and my cabin and my cows, and how I got my cows cheap—that was the first time I heard him laugh.

After two weeks at the roadhouse, I asked Gene if he'd like to move to my cabin. "You know, I'm studying American history so I can take the citizenship test, and I could help you learn your alphabet and numbers. We could study together. My cabin is real nice and I'll put up a blanket to give you your own bedroom. You know my horse, Goldie, well, I could get you a pony of your own. How about it?"

"Guess so." He didn't have to say another word for me to get him ready to move to my cabin. Once we spent the nights there, I saw the boy blossom. He took to his lessons right away, and he knew more than I expected.

"My Ma helped me learn," he said one day, and I had a warm thought about Catherine Rose. He showed me right off that he really was smart, and curious about everything. His laughter was no longer a stranger, and every day, I loved that boy a little more.

He had me forever the day we were in the garden, tying up the tomatoes. All of a sudden, I felt the swish of the hoe behind me.

"Got him!" Gene yelled like he'd won a prize. I turned around to see him holding up a long rattlesnake. I tripped over myself running to the cabin. Gene got the hiccups, he laughed so hard.

"Ma, don't worry, I wouldn't let him get you!" he yelled at me, as he flung the snake away. That long, slender body sailed through the air, making wavy patterns in the sky, and it was the first time in my life that a snake ever looked beautiful to me. I guess that means anything can be precious the first time you're ever called Ma.

Gene had been at our place a month when his father finally showed up to inquire about his well-being. The boy ran to his dad, but stopped short, like he wasn't sure if he wanted to hug him or shake his hand or just say "hi."

John Crowder wasn't a hugging kind of man, so he patted the boy on the shoulder. "You doin' your chores, boy? "They treatin' you alright?"

Gene nodded. "Yeah."

"Good. Glad to hear that." John walked into the roadhouse and I brought him a cup of coffee. He said his pleasantries to me and Jimmy—you had to guess that's what they were because he was not a man who gave much. Gene followed after him like a puppy, and I brought him a sarsaparilla as a special treat.

John took a deep breath like he was going to give the Gettysburg Address, and talked toward the boy without looking at him. "I'm takin' off, boy. Gonna see if there's something for me in Laramie or maybe Casper. You know, that place is growing and there's bound to be jobs."

Gene opened his mouth and I held my breath, scared he was about to say he could have his pack together in ten minutes to go with.

His Dad saw it too. "Sorry, boy. I can't take you with me. Maybe later, when I get settled. Maybe I can come back for you. But for now, you should stay here."

I saw the breath leave Gene's lungs as he hung his head and slumped in his seat. "Yeah, fine," he finally said. He'd taken only one sip of his soda, but he left it there. He got up and walked outside to do whatever a boy does when he's got a plug in his gut because his Pa is leaving him behind.

"He can stay, can't he?"

I couldn't tell his Pa fast enough that of course he could.

I treated John to a nice dinner that day. Gene came in, but he didn't eat much and didn't linger. Jimmy and I tarried at the table so we could reassure John that he was doing the right thing.

"I bet the boy hates me," he said, and Jimmy told him not to think that and not to worry, we'd take good care of him.

"You know, I don't think I'll ever come back here," John finally admitted. "My claim's not proved up yet and I don't think I'm gonna bother. I don't have much to sell, so movin' on seems right."

We agreed it was right.

"But I do have one thing, Miss Ella." He hesitated as he said the words, like whatever he had was too puny to offer. "I'm wondering if you want to buy my brand."

I now know what they mean by a "deafening silence," because his sentence hung there in our roadhouse dining room and that was the only sound in the entire world.

He took the silence for rejection and continued rapidly: "I won't be needing it anymore and it's all registered and everything. I heard those stories about how the brand committee treated you. That's how they treat all us folks—I bought this brand off a guy who was movin' on himself, so I never had to face them. I just wondered...."

I realized I'd forgotten how to breathe.

Jimmy jumped up from his chair, so startled he was jabbering. "Of course, of course of course!" He clapped John on the back and shook his hand like he was pumping up water from the well. "Boy, that will show them!" Their laughter was like music. My eyes must have been as big as an owl's, because they pointed at me and hooted all the more.

On March 16, 1889, I, Ella Watson, bought the "LU" brand from John Crowder for $10. It just so happened there was a notary public standing right there and my very own James Averell notarized the sale. John had brought the branding iron along, just in case, and he ceremoniously handed it to me. I craddled it like a newborn.

"Can't wait to see this gray hot and planted on the left shank of your cows, Miss Ella," Fales said the next day when he came in and we shocked him with the news.

Four days later, on Jimmy's thirty-eighth birthday, we rode into town and filed the paperwork at the Carbon County Courthouse. The LU brand was legally registered to Ellen L. Watson.

Fales insisted this was the story I'd someday tell my grandchildren—how I showed those cattlemen what for. "I can just see you, Miss Ella, with that original iron hanging over a fireplace in your ranch house, and you'll tell your grandkids that the cattlemen of Wyoming Territory learned in the spring of '89 that they couldn't mess with you." And then he gave my brand a name. He said it stood for "Lucky Upstart."

I loved the name and the story, but I had my own ending. "When things get right around here and the cattlemen don't have their sway on everything, I'm going to retire this brand and get my WT brand for my Pa." Fales and Jimmy agreed that was a fine plan.

To everyone else, we kept this news pretty close. We didn't say much because nobody wanted to rile things up. We knew we had outdone the brand committee, but bragging about that in this country wasn't good—not when your neighbors were all ranchers in cahoots to keep a brand out of your hands. No, we didn't brag because we still had to live with these people.

Jimmy always said, "In a small community where everyone knows everyone, you either get along with your neighbors or shoot them on sight."

Chapter Thirteen

I'm Sorry I Haven't Written Sooner

I started on this letter to my folks the start of the month and I'm still not done. If I don't get it in the mail soon, it will never get to Kansas by their birthdays in August.

"Monday, July 1, 1889. Dear Ma and Pa. Here it is, almost my twenty-ninth birthday. Can you believe your oldest is that old? Ha. Ha. We're putting off our celebrating until the Fourth so we can go on a picnic and mark the nation's birthday and my birthday all on the same day.

"Everyone around here goes to Independence Rock. We bring our own lunch, but something extra to share, and folks go around visiting and it's the kind of gathering you'd really like, Ma. We're taking the boys. Yes, I say boys, because I've got THREE under my care now. Oh, I have so much to tell you!

"Jimmy says he'll tell them what the Old West was like and what this rock meant to all those wagon trains years ago. I can't wait to hear the stories myself."

That's as far as I got that first day and since then, I've added some now and then, but goodness, this July has been so busy. The poor letter has bacon grease and coffee splats and ink stains all over it, but if I started over every time something soiled the paper, like Jimmy does when he's writing one of his letters to the editor, I'd never get this sent. Last summer when I visited home, I promised I'd write more, and I'm doing a poor excuse of imitating that promise.

They got a nice letter before Christmas, and I told them about the barbed wire Fales and I put up at the end of summer. I'm one of the first homesteaders to use barbed wire out here, and oh, that created a stir! The cattlemen think it's a scourge from hell, and they tear it down whenever they can. Interferes with their "open range," as if there really was open range yet. They're just the last ones to get the news. Pa always wants to know about the cattlemen out here because he agrees that they're living in the old days.

In my Christmas letter, I told how they wouldn't give me a brand and about my first cows. I told about plans with the neighbors for a Christmas supper, which Old Man Winter ruined again, and how I was making extra by mending the clothes of cowboys who came by the roadhouse. Every little bit helps, as my Ma would say.

Then I got off another letter in March, right after I got my brand—couldn't wait to share that story—and told them about another horrible winter and how we never would have made it if I didn't have cows to slaughter, not just for us, but for some of the neighbors, too, who had nothing. But I haven't written a word since and I've gotten four letters from Ma and my sisters and I'm feeling real guilty.

It's not that I'm not thinking of what to write them, even when I'm busy at my place or the roadhouse. In my head, I compose all kinds of wonderful things to tell them. Just reciting our daily life is enough to make a letter worth reading. But actually getting it down on paper, well, that's a harder task.

I should make a list so I don't forget the important things. My Jimmy's new honor is at the top. My people already know he was appointed postmaster by President Cleveland that summer after I got here and then a notary public by Governor Moonlight the next year and now Carbon County has made him a justice of the peace! Every new honor speaks to the kind of fine man he is and every one brings new business to the roadhouse. There's even folks talking about running him for office. He shrugs them off, but I know he's pleased to be on people's minds. More than once I've heard him joke about how he got two votes for Sand Creek Constable back in '86. Here he was, a Democrat in a Republican precinct, and a newcomer at that, and he still got two votes!

From my visit home, I know that some of my life here amuses them, and so I throw those things in. Guess some of Fales is rubbing off on me because he's helped me see the humor in some of the nonsense around here.

Next time I sit down with pen and ink I'm going to tell them more about the snakes in W.T. Not that Kansas doesn't know snakes, but I don't remember them being so plentiful and so mean as they are here. And of course, Pa joins Jimmy in being amused that I am so afraid of them. But Ma understands and shares my feelings.

First off, they're everywhere. They're all through my garden and everywhere on the prairie and I never go without my snake hoe. I never reach down to pick a bean or dig a potato without checking there isn't one ready for me. I swear, they hide better than cucumbers.

Jimmy says I'm foolish—they're just snakes, there's just a lot of them. He tells me, if you stay out of their way they'll stay out of yours. According to James Averell, who claims to be an expert on these things, W.T.'s rattlesnakes are really scaredy cats who want nothing to do with people, and that's why God gave them rattles, so they can keep us away. But I think they've got rattles so they can brag that they're about to bite us.

I used to stand on my stoop and scream, "Snakes, I'm coming. Go away." Jimmy laughed so hard he choked when he heard me one day.

"Oh Ella, don't you know snakes are deaf? You can scream all you want and it won't do any good."

Of course I didn't know snakes are deaf. Bet most people don't. I did feel foolish, but even after I knew, sometimes I'd yell anyway, just hoping it did some good.

My Jimmy will not let my fear of snakes go and he taunts me all the time. He's even tried to get me on the snake's side. "Do you realize," he said one day in that voice he uses when he thinks he's a teacher, "that the rattlesnake was once considered for the national symbol of the United States of America?"

I called him on that right then. "You mean instead of the eagle?" I used the voice that tells him he's not as smart as he thinks he is.

"Don't go making up stories like that—not when we've got an eagles' nest not a mile from our land, and you know how excited the boys get whenever we see them."

"No, honestly," Jimmy came back. "There was a coiled rattler on the first flag in the Colonies. Remember, 'Don't Tread on Me'? The snake had thirteen rattles and the slogan had thirteen words and there were thirteen colonies. I always thought that was pretty clever. They thought of the snake as the national symbol to tell the English King to leave us alone or we'd bite like a timber rattlesnake."

"You're making that up," I told him, but he insisted it was true. Don't know if it is, but it never convinced me to look kindly at snakes. And when Gene got bit—well, all foolin' around ended right then. I had to save that boy and gal-danged, when the day came that I had to suck out the poison, I sucked out the poison! Gene always says I saved his life, and I thanked the Lord for giving me the stomach to do it.

Then again, maybe I shouldn't tell any more snake stories because it upsets Ma. She's got her own snake fears to worry about.

I know, I'll tell them about my campaign to get a western saddle. And my pony Goldie, of course, because they always love to hear about her. And I should tell about the ponies I bought for the boys. I know Goldie is considered an old horse now, but I still call her my pony in memory of Darby. I love riding her, even though I'm still riding sidesaddle, and I was sure by now I wouldn't be.

Even out here, ladies are expected to ride sidesaddle. Not that all women in W.T. ride, of course, but those who do loop their right leg over the leaping horn and snug their left leg under the grip and tuck their left shoe in the stirrup so they can arrange their skirts all dainty like. You know, it's actually a lot more sturdy than it looks. Since you can't see any of it under those skirts, you can't see how the rider is balanced. Instead it just looks like a silly woman perched on one half of a horse. I think it's ridiculous. I bet someday that's gonna change, because I think you're a lot safer straddling a horse, and I've decided I don't care. You can't herd cows sidesaddle. You can't gallop along at a speed that will get you someplace by the end of the day. And I don't see how ladylike has much to do with being a homesteader in W.T. You'd think the world would end if your skirts didn't hide all of your leg. My goodness, you're always wearing hosiery or stockings, so you can't see any skin anyway, but that's the way it is.

So I'm savin' up for a new western saddle. It's been moving up my wish list all year—oh, my people would laugh if they saw how that list started out. It began the first night I got my hands on Jimmy's Monkey Ward catalog—Ma hates that I call it by its nickname and says such a fine company deserves to be properly called "Montgomery Ward." Half the country sets its dreams by that catalog, and I certainly am no different. I first leveled my sights on some fancy dress goods that I just knew I'd buy with my earnings from the roadhouse suppers. It was a colored Alpaca in green, and I remember it cost 32 and 1/2 cents a yard and I figured six yards would be just right for a dress and a cape. Of course, fabric that fine would demand a pretty piece of lace and some nice buttons, but the bill was climbing pretty fast. And the funny part, of course, is that it didn't take me long to realize there was no need for a pretty Alpaca dress out here, and I had far better things to do with $1.95.

I've discovered that being a homesteader pushes out the wishing and punches up the practical in you. So now I look for necessary things when I get to studying the catalog.

Jimmy supports my plan for a saddle. He says if I scandalize everyone, so what, it's not their neck he's trying to save by having me safe and not getting thrown. Monkey Ward doesn't sell saddles. If I could, I'd get a fine leather one from Mr. Meanea in Cheyenne, but I don't ever hope to afford one of them. There's a livery in town, and I saw one there for $8.85. I'm saving up. I think I'll tell Ma and Pa how the saddle fund is building—Ma agrees, but Pa thinks I should stay in a buggy.

Pa has come around a little to my homesteading, especially since I've got Jimmy. They know the truth and although they don't cotton to lying, they understand what we're doing. Pa even sent back money for Jimmy to get me a twelve-gauge scattergun, and I thought that was a fine thing for a father to do for his homesteading daughter. When I tried to hug him in thanks, he waved me off like he does when he's embarrassed by affection. But I knew he was proud knowing he was helping keep me safe.

I'm a real good shot—Fales has helped me polish that point—and I'm never careless because I think it would be the most stupid thing in the world to die from shooting yourself. Now, somebody else shooting you is another matter. I have to admit, sometimes when those cowboys from the Stock Growers Association ride by, glaring at my corral and barbed wire, I just know they'd give anything to pull out their revolvers and shoot me deader than Santa Ana.

I sometimes take hold of my gun then, just to let them know I have the means to defend myself—Fales says most cowboys think a gun in a woman's hands is a right dangerous thing, and not in a good way. I'm hoping that's what they think, and so far, nobody has shot me. I wouldn't dare even joke about that in a letter to my folks or Ma would go crazy. But even with a gun, I hate it when those guys come around.

So does Jimmy. He calls them "cowboys" like he's saying "killers and scum." But then, they call us "homesteaders," like they're saying "rustlers and lowlifes."

I'll be sure to write all about the boy. I've had Gene for four months and already he feels like he's mine. He wore that harness around his heart and didn't say much for a couple months—that's how much he loved his Ma. But he's better now. I'm teaching him to read. His own Ma and Pa knew only a little, and there was no school for him. So he's starting out a little late at eleven, but he'll catch up quick.

I've gotta tell Ma about Gene and the pot holders. I guess his Ma never made them, because he was real curious the first time he saw me sewing mine.

"You makin' a leather sandwich?" he asked in all seriousness, and it took a moment to understand what he meant.

I started to say no, and then realized he was pretty close to right. A pot holder is just a piece of leather sandwiched between two squares of cotton.

"You know, that's just what I'm doin'," I told him. "And all this came from Fales' Ma. She sent over her late husband's leather shoes, and a pretty piece of calico fabric. They sew up real nice. I bet I get a dozen pot holders out of all that." My kitchen is full of them, I never have to reach far to get help with a hot pot. But I don't sew them anymore without chuckling at how I'm making leather sandwiches.

That Gene is a real smart boy, and I school him when I'm studying for my citizenship. He likes learning right along with me. For the life of me, I can't remember all twenty-two presidents, but one day the boy started reciting them backwards, like he'd been schooled all his life: "Cleveland, Arthur, Garfield, Hayes, Grant, Johnson, Lincoln…" I was really impressed.

"Don't get discouraged," he told me. "I bet by the time you take your citizenship test, you'll know a whole lot more about this country than those greedy ranchers around here who got to be citizens just because they were born here."

It was nice to know the boy was on my side, and I've got to be sure to tell Ma what he said.

She'll get a kick out of how Gene can't stand castor oil. Whenever he has a bellyache, I go for the green medicine bottle, and he begs, "Not the fish, not the fish." I have to laugh in spite of his discomfort. Was it almost-ten Andrew who had the same reaction to that fish-shaped bottle? I think it was. Gene hasn't let me hug him yet, but one day he slipped and called me Ma, and I have to be sure to tell that.

I'm proud to call Gene my boy and my last letter only had the first weeks he was with me, so I've got catching up to do. Ma asks about him in every letter. She's praying for grandchildren and knows I won't have my own for awhile yet, so this is a nice second.

And they don't even know about John and Ralph yet!

John is fourteen and strapping and is as natural on a ranch as a gopher. He showed up at the roadhouse a couple months ago, looking like he hadn't had a decent meal since Thanksgiving. He offered his labor for whatever was needed. I remember what a gentleman he was, standing there in shoes too tight and jeans too short and hands too dirty, but that didn't hinder his presentation.

"My name is John DeCorey, ma'am and I'm sixteen." He'd later admit he added a couple years to improve his circumstance.

"I'm the handiest boy you'll ever find. I can do anything and I'm strong as an ox, and in good trim and I hope you have need of me."

I liked him immediately because he gave his entire speech while his stomach was growling like a grizzly. First I fed him, and I thought he was going to eat the table cover, he was so hungry. In the short time it took me to fill up a plate for him, he'd already eaten all the Crosse & Blackwell Chow Chow I had on the table. Just ate that relish like it was the best thing he'd ever tasted. I agree it's real good—one cowboy joked that if I ever stopped putting bottles of chow chow on my tables, he'd have to find another place to have his supper. But Lordy, to just eat it like that?

After he finished his meal, I hired him to work at my place, and I'm sure glad I did because he's keepin' it up real nice. John doesn't have much book-learning, but he's smart and has a good memory. He's honest as the day is long. He's especially good for Gene.

And then Ralph arrived in April, and he's a wonderful story all on his own. Ralph Cole is Jimmy's sister's boy from Wisconsin. He's around twenty and he is one talker. Fales has named him "Windy Ralph," and that's really tumbling to his talents.

I'll have to start with when I first met him.

"Watson?" he asked, like it was a name he was hauling up from the well. "Are you related to the Watsons in Oklahoma?"

I hooted and said I didn't think so, that my people were the Kansas Watsons. Pa will get a kick out of that bit of fluff. Windy Ralph just kept right on because when he has something to tell, he says it all before he stops.

"They're saying it was a Watson who shot Belle Starr in the back. Shot her right on the road going to her ranch, and don't you think it's a scoundrel who'd shoot a woman in the back, even one like Belle Starr?"

I nodded, pretending I knew who Belle Starr was. Fales later told me what a tough character she was. They called her the Bandit Queen. We all agreed it wasn't much of a man who'd shoot a woman in the back. I hope he's no kin to me.

Ralph came out to work with his uncle. He's real dear to Jimmy, being his sister Sarah's first boy. Sarah and Able pretty much raised Jimmy, and gave him his first leg up and now he's returning the favor in giving the boy training. That boy is one hard worker, although all his talents live inside the roadhouse. He can sort mail and do books and keep inventory, and he made some changes that really spruced the place up.

But by the wildest stretch of the imagination, Nature never intended him for a ranch hand. His hands are too soft and he has no natural feeling for it, but that's alright. The other two boys are just the opposite and they can handle a ranch with their eyes closed.

Ralph already treats the boys like his little brothers, and they're always horsing around, trying to outdo one another. And that's what happened the day Gene thought he saw Buffalo Bill.

I'm gonna have to tell Ma and Pa this story because it's so funny. Gene came running into the roadhouse kitchen, one of his overall straps hanging down his back, and he was so out of wind that he couldn't talk. Then he got the hiccups and I had to hold his nose and force him to drink water, and when he finally came back to normal he almost screamed, "I just saw Buffalo Bill!"

"Did not," John yelled from the storeroom, where he was stacking cans for me.

"Did too," Gene yipped.

"Come on now," Ralph scolded, like the boy was fibbing through his socks.

"Did too," Gene shouted all the louder.

I shushed everyone and told Gene to tell what he had to tell—thinking like the boys that his eyes were deceiving him.

"I was on the road to Casper and these men came along on horseback. And there he was. He was in buckskins and had that white mustache and beard like on his poster, and when I yelled up, 'Hello, Buffalo Bill', he called back, 'Hello, young man', and they kept on goin' and I ran here as fast as I could."

"Did not," John said with disgust.

"Did too," Gene sneered in defiance.

"Did not, did not, did not."

"Did too, did too, did too."

Jimmy came in from outside and wanted to know what all the ruckus was. When Gene quickly repeated the entire story, Jimmy shocked us all by saying, "Could have been."

Gene puffed up as Jimmy explained, "He's friends with Tom Sun. They were Indian scouts together. I met him once at Fort Steele. He's in these parts now and then, when he isn't traveling around the world."

Gene was as happy as a coyote. "See," he spat at John. "See, see," he bragged to Ralph. And you could tell John and Ralph felt cheated that they hadn't seen the famous Buffalo Bill themselves. Then all three of them looked at Jimmy with new respect that he'd actually met the famous showman.

◇◇◇

"Thursday, July 11. Hi again. Well, we went on our picnic to Independence Rock and you would have had a good time because my Jimmy was as good a storyteller that day as any of those men who write books. I'm sure it helped that his audience was listening like a hawk. He starts telling boys about the Indian Wars and how he almost was at the Little Bighorn. He tells how he served under General Crook—THE General Crook who went after Geronimo. I tell you, those boys could have listened to stories like that forever

"Of course, our hired man couldn't help himself, so he got into telling his own stories, trying to one-up Jimmy. It was a battle of the stories. You would have laughed and cheered just like we did, and it was a very fun day."

I don't think I've ever had such a fine birthday in my entire life. First off, the weather was just beautiful, warm but not too hot, a little breeze. I'd cooked up chickens ahead of time and made biscuits fresh that morning so we could take off first thing and spend the entire day. I made molasses cookies to share and we didn't bring a crumb home. We saw so many of our neighbors, and everyone was in a grand mood. A man brought his fiddle and we sang campfire songs. A man in his Civil War uniform sang "The Battle Hymn of the Republic" and we all enjoyed that.

I wish my folks could see Independence Rock, and they'd understand why it is so precious. It stands by itself, like it was dropped on a flat piece of prairie by the Lord Himself. And it kind of resembles an old-fashioned haystack. It sits right along the Sweetwater River and from up there you can really see how the river meanders across the land. The rock's sides are gentle enough that you can climb all over, and that's what everyone does because the rewards are so great.

The boys went scrambling up the rock as soon as the buggy slowed down, and you could hear them shouting with the other kids who were exploring. We climbed up, too, because I hadn't done my own investigating yet. When I came upon the first name, I thought my heart stopped a second. Scratched into the rock was "Hiram Meck, July, 50."

"Jimmy," I whispered, "who do you suppose he was and what do you think happened to him?"

Jimmy said all we knew was that he'd gotten this far by 1850, and had celebrated the Fourth like we were doing. Then he smiled and encouraged me to look for more, and I found so many names, I couldn't even count them all.

As Jimmy later told the boys while we ate our chicken, the Conestogas and prairie schooners that brought so many people west on the Oregon Trail had to get to this rock by the Fourth of July so they could get through the mountains before the snows came. Getting here was a triumph all its own. And it meant they were about a third of the way to the West Coast.

Those pioneers named it Independence Rock, and then started carving or painting their names on it, like people do when they're pleased with themselves. Jimmy said sometimes people coming later would find the names of their kin and would rejoice knowing at least they got this far and it gave them hope to carry on.

"It took them months to get here, and remember, most of them were walking," he said. "The wagons were full of everything they owned, and there wasn't room left for passengers. So I'm betting their feet were pretty sore when they stepped on this rock. You can imagine how happy they had to be. And how strange all this had to look to them—they came from back East and to them, the West was St. Louis and Omaha. They were used to towns and cultivated fields and trees and none of that was here. Here you can see for miles, and mainly what you see is dirt. They were going where few people had ever gone before, and they knew there were hostiles waiting for them, but they came anyway." Jimmy paused.

"You know, when we moved here, we arrived in just a few days on a train," he said. "Well, it took them months to get here. But just like them, we're immigrants, too. And just like these folks, who risked everything to settle in a new land, that's just what we're doing. It's a lot more comfortable and safe now than in the old days, but the idea is still the same."

And I had to admit, I'd never thought of it like that before.

Gene begged Jimmy to tell about the buffalo because, of course, the boy had never seen one.

"The herds used to be so big, when they went by, it would take hours if not days for them all to pass," Jimmy began. "Do you know how the Indians found them when they wanted to go on a hunt? They'd get up real early and look over the horizon for a little cloud, and that's how they'd know where the buffalo were—their breath was creating a vapor cloud. That's how many there were! And the Indians used everything from that animal to survive. Meat, hides, horns, hoofs. They didn't waste anything."

"And they're all gone?" Ralph said like it couldn't possibly be true.

"Almost. It didn't take long either, to slaughter millions. Many of them rotted where they fell. Some people thought if they killed off the buffalo, they'd get rid of the Indians, too."

"Did you ever kill one, Uncle Jimmy?" Ralph asked, and I saw Fales give a little smile because he knew Jim never had. But Jim fudged and said he'd been on a couple hunts in his early days in the Army, and it was a tough thing to kill a buffalo because even your horse was scared of them.

"The Shoshones blinded the right eyes of their horses so they couldn't see when they got up close," he said. Then quickly added, "But Chief Washakie wouldn't do that—he loved his horse too much to blind him. At least, that's what he told me."

If you want to see admiration in the eyes of boys, tell them you know an Indian chief.

All three boys looked at Jim like he walked on water because he knew an Indian and survived. "There were good Indians and there were bad Indians, and I was lucky to know one of the good ones," Jim explained, and he started in telling his Indian stories.

"Chief Washakie was the main chief of the Shoshones here in W.T. and he didn't fight the white man like so many did. He wanted peace. You know, they named the fort after him because they so appreciated that he fought with them, not against them. I met him when I was serving with General Crook. He saved Crook at the Battle of Rosebud, you know—saved him from a fate just like the Little Bighorn. That's just what the Indians had planned for Crook out here in Wyoming—they were going to lure the soldiers into a ravine where they couldn't get out and then slaughter them. But Washakie knew their ways—Shoshones hate the Sioux—and he didn't let Crook get ambushed like Custer did in Montana. If Washakie had been with Custer, those men would still be getting their rations every day instead of dying at Little Bighorn."

From their reactions, I figured this was the first "good Indian" story these boys had ever heard.

"And you know what?" Jimmy went on. "Chief Washakie looks just like George Washington."

Well, the boys thought that was impossible, and Jimmy bet them each a nickel that when they met him they'd think he looked like our first president.

"We're gonna meet him?" John asked with astonishment, and Jimmy promised that one day he'd take us all over to the reservation and we could meet the old chief himself. That was a day I didn't want to miss.

I didn't see any reason to mention that I knew some Indians, too, because mine weren't chiefs. Boys don't care if you just know a girl and her grandma. So I stayed quiet.

All this time, good old Fales was sitting there ready to hop in with his own stories. He wasn't about to be outdone when it came to storytelling.

"That ain't nothin'," he finally cut in. "When I was just a little older than you boys, I met General Tom Thumb."

Well, I learned right then that nothing trumps an Indian chief like a world-famous midget.

The boys shifted their attention immediately, as Fales told them a story from the days when he was twelve years old.

"I was in school in Laramie and they were coming through town with P.T. Barnum's show," Fales began. "It was General Tom himself, Mrs. Tom Thumb, Commodore Nut, and Minnie Warren, so we had all the famous midgets the world had ever known. We got to skip school because Laramie declared a holiday, they were so happy the show was stopping there."

Fales puffed up his chest and shouted like he was a ringmaster: "P.T. Barnum's Grand Traveling Museum, Menagerie, Caravan and Hippodrome—that's what they called it. I don't think I was ever more excited than waiting for them to come to town. Of course we knew they'd be staying at the Union Pacific Railway Hotel, and us boys all lined up outside in case we'd catch a glimpse of them. Up comes a tiny carriage pulled by Shetland ponies that weren't as big as my friend Richie's hound. We couldn't believe our eyes. The ponies had gold harnesses and the carriage was silver—I tell you, I'd never seen anything like it in my life and haven't seen anything like it since. They say Queen Victoria herself gave them the carriage when they performed in London, and it looked like something a queen would have. Well, the little people came out—they were dressed so fancy. Their clothes were silk and velvet. They climbed in that little carriage and went all around our town, and us boys ran after them for awhile.

"That night was the performance, and I bet every school child in Laramie was there. The tent was so packed it would be safe to say there wasn't anybody in the entire town that wasn't there—I even saw Snaggletooth Johnny, the town drunk. My Ma and Pa came early to get good seats.

"I talked to Tom Thumb myself—he was a very nice man and was perfect in every way, except he was so small. They say he was only thirty-one inches tall! He asked us boys how we liked living way out here in Laramie, and if we had horses, and if we'd ever been attacked by Indians, and he seemed real interested in us. We asked him how the Queen was and he said she was a very nice woman, but he thought she should take off some pounds. Boy, we hooted at that, and the General laughed too, knowing he'd said something naughty.

"Mrs. Tom Thumb was like a fairy princess, and she sang in a childish voice. She sang 'In the Cottage by the Sea' and some of the ladies cried." Fales explained the song was about a woman who had just been widowed, and the boys screwed up their noses.

"I ate my first roasted peanuts that night, and I favor them to this day. And it's one of those things I'll remember to my grave—how I got to talk with the smallest man who ever walked the Earth."

Even Jim was hanging on his every word, because that would have been something to see. I'm betting Fales took his snooze thinking he'd won the storytelling contest.

But when it comes to winning, my Jimmy is No. 1 in my book and in a lot of other people's, too. I'm going to send my folks the newspaper clipping to show them his letter to the editor that has created such a fuss. That will help sweeten the pie when the letter finally gets off. I'm going to send the picture we had made of me on Goldie, too.

I worried a little when he first wrote the letter, because things are bad enough with Bothwell and some of our neighbors that this would surely fan the flames. But Jimmy said, "If I don't stand up, who will?"

I know I'm bragging, but Jimmy is about the most prominent settler in these parts. *The Journal* in Rawlins calls him "the gentlemanly Sweetwater postmaster." And now being the justice of the peace, well, he's right that he has a standing that nobody else has.

Some days I wish there was *something* we could agree on with the cattlemen, but they won't budge off a dime, and my Jimmy won't stampede for a penny. Jimmy says a lot of it is that they're all Republicans and he's a Democrat, but I think it's a more than just that. I've seen some Republicans I like and some Democrats I don't, but I keep my own counsel because Jimmy is pretty set on his views.

One of the Republicans I surely don't like is Bothwell. That man will not give up trying to get our claims on the creek. He thinks he's so clever and he must think I'm dumb. Like when he offered to loan me money to buy my claim—you'd have thought I stabbed him in the heart, he seemed so disappointed when I politely turned him down. And he acted so puzzled. I guess he thought I was dumb enough to be indebted to him. Then if I couldn't pay back the loan, he'd take my land. Lord, that man is sneaky. I'm hoping he's going to get tired of all this and give up, because he's tried about every trick in the book and Jimmy and I are still here.

I did think I'd found a mutual stand with the cattlemen when it came to the new county of Natrona. Last spring, they brought around a petition to split Carbon County in two, with Rawlins staying the head of ours, and growing Casper as the head of the new one. I must say, I was very pleased that they asked me to sign. There they were, some of my most prominent neighbors and some of the big cattlemen, right there on the same petition as me. Proved they don't realize we aren't citizens yet and, of course, neither Jimmy or I ever bring that up.

I signed big and bold, "E.L.Watson," and was glad to do it because Jimmy agreed the county was getting too big and the folks in Casper should have a chance, too. But then, those cattlemen changed horses and came back wanting to change the first petition to say we no longer wanted the split—just goes to show, there's nothing we agree on.

And that's how Jimmy started his letter:

"We find two distinct views on the matter; namely the settlers who have come here to live and make Wyoming their homes, and the land grabber who is only here as a speculator in land under the Desert Land Act. The former are in favor of dividing Carbon County, believing it to be for the welfare and proper development of the country, and the latter are opposed to the organization of Natrona County, or anything else that would settle and improve the country, or make it anything but a cow pasture for eastern speculators."

Jimmy's letter went on and on about the "land grabbers" and how we had to fight them and that it was the "honest settler" that was the future of Wyoming.

You know, for a while there, it seemed like my Jimmy was the only one who dared stand up and challenge these speculators, but now even the president is interested! President Cleveland had one of his men investigate desert claims and he found a whole lot of them were fake and they cancelled a whole bunch of claims. Guess who owned them? Only the man who runs the Wyoming Stock Growers Association, that's who! Oh, it created an uproar in W.T., and you can bet not one single cattleman was happy that the president stuck his nose in. But every single homesteader was pleased as punch.

And it was turning out that when homesteaders wanted a public voice, they looked to my Jimmy, so his letter was a big deal. He also used it to give Bothwell a poke in the eye.

Put all the ugly cats you can find in one sack, and that's A.J. Bothwell. The water and pasture problems aren't the whole of it. Now he's pretending he's developing a town—even calls it the Town of Bothwell. He claims a railroad will soon link it to Casper and—here's the best part—that this town will someday be the new capital of the new State of Wyoming. Wonder what the boys in Cheyenne think about that! He's trying to sell lots for up to four hundred dollars an acre—Lordy, you can buy homestead land outright for $1.25 an acre, if you don't want to work the five years to prove it up. So if I had an extra two hundred dollars in my pocket, I could have gotten all my homestead land. At Bothwell's prices, I'd have had to spend sixty-four thousand dollars!

I'm wondering if folks back East are that dumb, and Jimmy says some of them are, and so he included that in his letter, too:

"Do not be misled by the matter of the town of Bothwell. There is not one house in that town, and you can safely say, that the town of Bothwell is only a geographical expression."

Well, you can imagine how that went over. Bothwell and his pals brought in two men to start a newspaper in his "town," and they were publishing stories like there really were houses and churches and schools there, when the only thing there was the newspaper office and these two men. We heard that Bothwell was selling "houses" and "lots" for his town like crazy, and when people back East found out it was all a fraud, well, that would look bad for W.T. That's what we cared about. One paper called it "Mythical Bothwell," and another said it was "A Home for the Feeble Minded Populace of the East." But Bothwell didn't care about our reputation. He cared about his own pockets.

Fales, for one, read Jimmy's letter while drinking coffee and warned him, "Don't push Bothwell too far, Jimmy. That man won't take it." Jimmy flicked it off as balderdash, because he was having a hero's moment. Lots of men came to the roadhouse and gave him a slap on the back in thanks for that letter. But I heard more than one of them quietly tell him they thought it was a mistake to sign it. He didn't just sign it, he made a point of pointing out that he was signing it. He ended the letter "Not wishing to disguise myself in the matter, I remain yours truly, James Averell, February 7, 1889."

But while I was a little scared, I was also proud that he dared stand up to them, and it helped to prop up my own courage. And I think it gave courage to others, too, and that's just what Jimmy had wanted.

Well, we didn't have much time to dally after our picnic on the Fourth because we had to get the roadhouse ready for the election on July 8. They were choosing delegates to the Constitutional Convention—that's the big step toward statehood and even on that, there's disagreement. Although me and Jimmy are siding with those who want Wyoming to be a state, some of Jim's Democratic friends are hanging back, worried it will be too costly and we should wait. I think the Democrats are plumb wrong.

Jim himself was one of the three judges for the election, and his nephew, Ralph Cole, was one of the clerks. We expected a whole lot of folks in that day to vote, so I baked extra pies. I served stew for lunch, because I wanted to be sure to have enough and you can always stretch stew. And they sure came. But all of them were men. I'd have thought some women would have come to vote, too, since it was so important. When I get my citizenship, I'm going to vote every chance I get.

"Friday, July 19. I'm sorry to be away from this letter for so long but we have been real busy. We did our first branding—I have forty-one head now. Some of my cows calved, and I sometimes trade dinners for cows from cowboys. I might be a strong woman, but I'm sure glad to have men to brand for me. And I have to admit, I don't like the smell. Everyone here is fine, if not a little tired after all our activities. Gene is growing like a weed.

"Ma, I'm trying real hard to keep up with my quilting and am working on the Star Pattern now, and isn't it a doozie. But my sewing machine has been busy with mending—boys need lots of mending, as you know—and in my spare time (ha) I'm making a new dress for the barn dance after the cattle are shipped. They always have a dance at someone's farm. It's mainly new settlers, but some of the ranchers come, too. We're all praying for a nice fall and an easy winter.

"Speaking of praying, Ma, you'll be real glad to hear that a very nice man named Reverend Moore has visited us several times in the last couple months. He gets his mail at the roadhouse, and he gets a lot of mail because he heads up some missionary society for the Congregational Church. I know he'd like to get a church started around here, and Jim offered to let him have a religious meeting right here at the roadhouse, and Reverend Moore was grateful for the offer. Can you imagine that, the roadhouse might turn into a church on Sundays? I know that would please you, Ma.

"I have to tell you about the Indians. Now, Ma, don't get all excited. The Indians here are no danger to anyone, at least not the ones I know. They like to camp down by the creek and I met them by accident one day when we were all picking berries. Isn't that an interesting way to meet your first Indian! They're real poor and half-starved most of the time. I've got bread raising to take them some tomorrow, because I saw they came in last night. I know you've heard that Indians are beggars, but these aren't, and the only way they'll take anything from me is if they give something back, so we trade for all kinds of strange things. I have three eagle feathers, thanks to trading. Gene wants to wear them in his hair, but Jimmy put his foot down on that and said no white boy should be running around W.T. looking like an Indian. I always take something to eat because I know they're always hungry, but they won't eat it in front of me. Fales says by rights, they're supposed to stay on the reservation, but I see no harm in them coming to the creek. Bet their people came to this creek before any of us ever got here. The girl's name is Shashas and she's pretty, for an Indian.

"I have a new bonnet from Mrs. Fales. Her son is the hired man I told you about. She's poorly. I sent him home with sweets and jam, and I think the bonnet was her way of saying thanks."

I am so close to being done with this letter! I think they're going to be real pleased to get this one because it's so long and it has the picture and the article. I hope they forgive me for not writing more. I'll send it off on Monday.

Chapter Fourteen
The Last Day of My Life

I always loved 4:30 a.m. because it was my own time to spend.

The rest of the day there were boys and men and cattle and chickens, but nobody else wanted to be up now, when you could only see by lamplight, so this was how I purchased my only free moments.

Some mornings I read, my quilt still tucked around me. I hoarded any reading material that came my way. Newspapers, sometimes books, but mostly magazines. What a joy to have a new magazine. Of course, it was never new. Sometimes the cover was so tattered, it could hardly hold the pages. But like all the hands before me, I'd treat the pages with love and then pass them on to someone else.

Sometimes I'd get a magazine in trade for a meal. Jimmy never knew, but I never passed up that offer. I'd read anything. My sister Annie would be proud of me. I'm reading a most curious magazine now. It's called *The Century Illustrated Monthly Magazine* and it's four years old. But it has held up well. I have already read the real story about the planets and the moon. I'm about to tackle a made-up story by Henry James. Right on the cover it says this was the 225th Thousand, so I knew a lot of other people read this too. Wonder if other women stared at the Coraline Corset advertisement, and were happy it wasn't for them.

But this morning I didn't read. This Saturday—this July 20, 1889—I had plenty to do and there was no time to read.

Cowboys were at the roadhouse yesterday whooping and hollering that branding was over. They ate me out of house and pantry! They drank all Jimmy's beer, and most of his whiskey. He's going to Casper for supplies and last night in bed I remembered a couple other things for my list that I've got to tell him.

But that's not the most important part. The end of branding is a big deal in the valley, and it's not just the cowboys who want to celebrate. Next week or the week after, somebody is going to announce a barn dance. And I'm sewing a new dress. It's a pretty blue fabric—not as blue as our beautiful sky, but as close as I could find. I've started the handwork on the collar, and have buttons to cover. I'm copying a dress I saw in the catalogue. Can't wait for my neighbor ladies to see it. Oh, of course I want Jimmy to like it, but he'll never appreciate my clever copying and my fine hand sewing.

Do I love to dance! Come hell or high water, nobody in this valley misses a barn dance. All the settlers come and even some of the ranchers. Everyone brings food and the children bed down on the hay bales as the night goes on, and sometimes we dance until the sun comes up.

This morning I had a couple hours before the boys stirred. I made real progress on the collar.

Once the boys were up, I started a hearty breakfast because on Saturdays, we normally work through lunch and then have a great big supper. Today was one of those normal days. Jimmy would be up in Casper and would spend the night, so I'm taking the boys to the roadhouse for steaks.

I made oatmeal and we all gobbled it up like it was our last meal. I like mine with molasses and raisins. So does Gene. John prefers his with brown sugar and fresh berries.

"So who wants to go to the Indian camp with me this morning?"

The looks that went between the boys told me they'd privately had this conversation already.

"I'll go," John spoke up.

I thought to tease Gene about his silence, but checked myself. I was doing up the dishes when I remembered some of his Ma's family had been killed in an Indian raid. I was glad I'd kept my mouth shut, because obviously the boy had no interest in visiting Indians.

Gene's first job of the day was to weed the garden. He always complained, "These weeds grow far better than anything else in here." He wasn't that far off. "Killed three snakes today," he shouted through the door when he finished.

I'm sure he tells me because he knows how much I hate snakes. Ever since he got bit, he's taken it as his personal duty to kill as many snakes as possible. Payback.

John was cleaning up the corral and mending fences.

I baked bread and straightened up the cabin.

"John, let's go." About ten o'clock, we started off toward Horse Creek with the basket of fresh bread that had just come out of the oven. It was a clear, warm day with a gentle breeze.

I wore my new bonnet from Ma Fales and my Mother Hubbard dress.

I usually found the Indian family in about the same place on their regular trips through the valley. Today was no different.

"Hello!" I announced myself with a friendly shout. Shashas was already waiting. This year they were later than usual, and I worried Shasha's deerskin dress looked too hot for a July day.

The girl ran up to me. We smiled and nodded to one another. We didn't hug. We didn't touch. I saw John pull back like he was afraid we would.

"This is John," I patted his chest as I said his name. Shashas' eyes studied the ground. John took another step back, like he was hiding behind my skirts.

"Say hello, John."

"Hi." It was a mumble.

"Bread. I brought bread." That was a sure way to get over the awkwardness. I pronounced each word slowly because Shashas knew some English, but not a lot.

"Good," she said, and I could see how pleased she was with the offering.

Grandma came out one of the teepees and nodded her own approval at the bread. Some of Grandma's teeth are missing and when she smiled, I heard John titter. I turned and gave him the stop-that-right-now look. He stopped.

His eyes were big and wild and I knew he was scared, this being as close to an Indian as he'd ever been. I know he's going to take it all in and report everything to Gene. I wish I could make those boys see there's nothing to be afraid of.

There were three teepees at this campsite and a skinny dog. A very old man with long braids was sitting by the fire smoking a pipe.

"He doesn't look like George Washington," John whispered. "That's not Jimmy's chief."

"Where are the boys? There's only old people and girls and little kids here."

"Because these are grandparents taking their family on a camping trip."

"Really?" John sounded astonished. I knew he'd never once, in his whole life, considered such a thing.

I presented the basket of bread to the old man, who smiled at me, inspected the offering, and then handed it to the old woman. Then he motioned for everyone to sit around the fire. He said something to Shashas in their language and she went into the teepee. She came out with a pair of beaded moccasins, gave them to the old man, and he handed them to me. In the past, I got eagle feathers and a basket and a saddle blanket. It felt special to be offered beading.

But one close look at these moccasins and I realized these people were worse off than normal.

The deerskin moccasins were old and worn and already repaired. But they were decorated with gorgeous bead work. The tongues, which hung over the front, were mainly white beads with accents of blue and red. The shoes themselves had touches of blue and red—these had to be the precious colors—but were mainly white and green. I bet there were at least a thousand beads in each shoe.

Whoever had first worn these moccasins had walked crooked, because the sole of the right shoe was imprinted with toe marks that were completely different from the wear spots on the left. The back of the right shoe had a piece of deerskin added to make the shoe wider. Wonder what it's like to have two feet that didn't recognize one another.

Shashas was watching me look over the moccasins. I could feel her fear that they weren't a fair trade for the delicious bread. But of course, I'd never do that.

"I should put them on." I saw John's face turn to horror.

"You can't," he spit into my ear.

"Hush, John, be nice. This is all they have to offer. We're not going to insult them."

I took off my shoes and put on the moccasins and then walked around the fire to show them off. I smiled like they were a treasure and Shashas looked very relieved.

We sat around the fire a few moments. It was so quiet and peaceful down there. Horse Creek gurgled and a warm breeze cooled the morning. It was the kind of morning when you're happy to be alive.

But of course, we couldn't dawdle all day and so after some nods and smiles and good-byes, we started back. We were coming up the slope when I saw men at my cabin. They were on horseback, so it looked like they'd just arrived.

"What do *they* want?" I said out loud, and then had a worrying thought that they'd come with bad news. *Oh no, has something happened to Gene. To Jimmy?* But those thoughts disappeared when I saw one of my cows was running away. I expected one of those men to go after the cow, to bring it back to my corral, but none of them rode after it, and that just felt so wrong. I started to run. John was right beside me.

The most ridiculous scene was in front of my eyes.

Bothwell, obviously liquored up, was shouting orders like he was on a roundup. Durbin was ripping apart my corral. Ernie McLean, the one who stutters all the time, was racing around the yard. Cap'n Galbraith was stationed like he was a prison guard. Conner was slumped over his saddle like he was going to be sick. Tom Sun was sitting proud in his fancy buggy.

Cows were running everywhere. My just-branded cows that had been so much work.

"Stop that. Stop that right now. Get away from my corral. Get away from my cows. Stop that!"

John joined in the yelling and ran toward the corral to stop the fleeing cattle, but McLean cut him off. Bothwell shrieked at him to get inside the cabin. John looked back at me and I nodded for him to obey.

"Gene, Gene, "I screamed to find him.

He yelled out of the cabin. "Those men made me come in here."

At least he was safe.

Bothwell aimed his horse right at me and reared up. If he expected me to step backwards, he was disappointed.

"We caught you red-handed, rustlin' our cattle, and we're taking you to Rawlins to the law."

I thought he was joking and let out a sarcastic laugh.

"No, you aren't. You know perfectly well that those are my cows and I'm not going anywhere with you."

I maneuvered around his horse to head for my cabin—I wasn't sure what I was going to do, but that's where my gun was and that seemed the most important thing to reach right now. Bothwell cut me off.

"You get in that buggy right now and you're goin' to Rawlins," he spat at me.

I frantically looked to the other men for help and saw there was none to give.

"I'll go to Rawlins with you, alright. And we can go right to my bank, and you can see the receipt for these cows. You're going to be sorry about this, Mr. Bothwell." I spat out his name.

"I need to change into a decent dress. I'm in a work dress. I can't go to Rawlins in a work dress." I moved once more in the direction of the cabin, knowing now that I must get to my gun.

"You don't need a fancy dress where you're going," Bothwell sneered.

All of a sudden everyone's attention was drawn toward the cabin, when Gene made a mad dash to a pony in the corral. He reached the animal and jumped on in one fluid motion, and was poised to ride free when Durbin grabbed the reins and held them firm.

"Where you think you're goin?" Bothwell hollered at Gene. "You help Mr. Durbin get those cows out of there. Do what I say, boy." Poor little Gene could do nothing but obey.

Defiance was getting me nowhere so I changed tactics.

"Gentlemen, if you look at those cows, you'll see that they have my LU brand on them. You all know that is my legal brand, all registered." I was hoping I didn't sound too smug to these men I'd snookered.

"I bought those cows last fall, drove them right past Mr. Bothwell's ranch to get them here, and if he was a mind to, he could sit on his front porch and admire them any day of the week. I didn't rustle these cows."

"There's a lot of calves in there," Durbin came back, like my explanation was puny. "Some of them look like my calves."

If the situation wasn't so deteriorating, I would have belly-laughed at the absurdity of that statement.

"Sir, those aren't your calves. They're mine. I bought a couple calves from cowboys who wanted a hot meal—you men all know what a good cook I am. I bet you've all been up to our place for dinner. I didn't steal anything. I've only got about forty head, that's nothing to you gentlemen with your fine ranches...."

Galbraith broke in. "Forty head of rustled cows is forty cows too many."

"These ain't rustled," I bellowed. "I bought these cows. I've had them all winter. I fed them all winter. I don't take things that aren't mine. Now if you want to see the paper that proves

I bought them, then let's go to Rawlins to the bank and I'll show you."

I thought I had them there for a minute. I sounded pretty convincing, if I have to say so myself. I sounded sure of myself. Why would I offer to go to Rawlins if there wasn't a bill of sale in my safe deposit box at the bank? I could see them mulling all that over, and I thought, *Oh thank God. I've got so much to do, I don't have time for this nonsense. And now we've got to go after those cows!*

Bothwell pretended to soften. "Sure ma'am, we'll get you to Rawlins and you can show us your receipt, if you've really got one. Now get in that buggy."

I distrusted this new attitude and again pleaded for a chance to change my dress. Again I was refused.

Bothwell's patience ran out. He spit at me, "You get in that wagon or I'll rope you and drag you to death."

It was the first time the word "death" had been spoken this morning, and it had a sobering effect on everyone. Especially me. I climbed into the backseat of Tom Sun's buggy.

I only looked back once at my cabin and my busted corral.

◇◇◇

Jimmy was just pulling out of his gate when we arrived at the roadhouse fifteen minutes later. When I first spied him I saw he had a smile on his face, like a man going on a mission he enjoyed. I knew his wagon was filled with brown bottles he'd refill with beer at the brewery outside Casper, and he had my list of supplies in his pocket. He always loved his two-day trips to Casper—"July 20, off I go," he'd whistled all week—and these days he could leave Ralph in charge of the roadhouse and not worry about a thing.

I watched the smile disappear as he saw me in Sun's buggy.

"Is she hurt? Ella are you hurt?"

Oh, my dear husband thinks these men are bringing me for help.

But that notion disappeared as Bothwell pointed his gun and ordered Jimmy, "Throw up your hands. You're under arrest. We're taking you two to Rawlins to face the law."

"Just what are we being arrested for and where's your arrest warrant?" My defiant Jim refused to raise his hands.

Bothwell snickered, waving the gun and announcing, "You know why, and this is all the warrant we need."

By now Jimmy could see I looked both angry and worried. "Are you alright?" he yelled over to me, and I nodded. He turned to men he knew by their first names and started with the obvious. "Just what in the hell do you think you're doing? Tom, what's up here?"

But Tom Sun didn't say a word. It was obvious Bothwell was running this show, so Jim turned all his attention to him.

"Bothwell, put that gun away. I don't know who you think you are, but we're not going anywhere with you—Ella get out of that buggy—and you'll be lucky if I don't call the law myself and have you arrested for kidnapping...."

He would have said more, but he heard the click of a gun being cocked and that's a sound that can stop a grown man in his tracks.

"Get...in...the...wagon." Bothwell stretched each word.

"I've got a horse and wagon and I can drive myself into Rawlins. I'm not leaving them out here," Jim declared, as though this were the most obvious thing in the world. "John, you wouldn't want me to abandon my rig," but John Durbin offered no solace and the other men didn't show any sympathy either.

"I'm not saying it another time, Averell. Unhitch your horses and get in that wagon or I'll shoot you where you sit."

I knew Bothwell well enough to know the man needed little excuse, so I called over, "Come on Jimmy, come on. Let's go with them to Rawlins and I'll get my papers to prove we aren't rustling."

"Rustling? RUSTLING?? You think Ella is rustling? Are you out of your goddamn minds?" Jim's face got red and he was flinging his arms around. I coughed real loud to calm him down, and he took the cue.

He put on his politician's voice: "Gentlemen, you know better than that. She bought a small herd last fall and they calved in the spring and they've been in her corral, big as life and there for everyone to see. Bothwell, you can see them from your place, for God's sake. Tom, you must have seen them when you went looking for your own cows. John, you know damn well the last thing we would do is rustle cows."

He sounded like a man who believed common sense would kick in any second.

"How would it look to have your justice of the peace rustling?" He actually snorted at that one.

"It would look really, really bad. And you think anybody would let me keep the post office if they thought I associated with rustlers? Of course not. I wouldn't jeopardize my business and my appointments like that. And Ella sure wouldn't jeopardize her claim by becoming a common rustler. You've all seen how hard she's worked to build that cabin and those corrals. People all over this valley brag about what a tireless worker she is. She'd throw that away for a couple cows? Think about it—why would she ever do that? Gentlemen, this doesn't make any sense. So, stop this so I can get to Casper and this lady can go about her business."

I was real proud of my Jimmy for saying things so clear and honest. But the next second, it was clear Bothwell was doing all the thinking for this group. He laughed out loud at Jim's recitation and declared, "You homesteaders are all alike—you think you can take our cows and we can't do nothing about it. Well, that might be the way things were lately, but that's not the way things are today."

Not one of those men said another word. If this was a play, the only character was Bothwell and everyone else was just a prop. I couldn't believe men this powerful and this important to the valley could be this stupid.

Neither could Jimmy. His common-sense speech hadn't worked so now he launched a shame speech. "I cannot believe you gentlemen are letting this young hot-head lead you around like a bull with a ring in his nose! You're all in your forties—he's just in his thirties, and yet he's the one I see running this show. Every one of us has years on him. Since when do mature, seasoned men take orders from a young bully? You're going to look ridiculous when the newspapers…"

"SHUT UP!!" Bothwell screamed so loud, I saw birds fleeing the trees. It so startled me, I jumped. Jimmy did too, a little. Enough that it was clear his shame speech was over.

Bothwell waved his gun from Jimmy to the wagon. Jimmy unhitched his horses and climbed in next to me. Bothwell led the caravan north, away from the roadhouse and away from other ranches. He led us toward the hills where other eyes couldn't see what was happening.

"Hey, this isn't the way to Rawlins," Jimmy piped up, like he was the only one who knew the geography around here. That didn't even get a response. My stomach turned.

Jimmy held my hand and talked to me with his eyes.

"Don't worry, they're just trying to scare us."

I prayed he was right.

◇◇◇

Have you ever watched drunk men trying to make a decision? It's an ugly thing. Nobody is thinking straight. Some can't even talk straight. I don't think McLean ever got a decent sentence out all afternoon. Cap'n Galbraith tried to sound like the educated man he was, but alcohol has its own language and it isn't the one sober men speak.

Bothwell and Durbin rode side by side and they'd exchange words now and then, but I couldn't hear them.

What I did hear, all afternoon, was a barrage of commands that Jimmy and I give up and move away and forget our claims. "You can start over someplace else where you're wanted," Cap'n Galbraith instructed, like it was as easy as changing your shirt.

"You know damn well you're right in the middle of Bothwell's pasture. Now that just isn't fair." John Durbin had a perverted sense of fairness.

"You're just troublemakers and we don't like troublemakers in the Sweetwater Valley. You'll be happy someplace else." Conner wasn't much of a thinker on his best day, and this wasn't his best day.

"Don't worry," Jimmy whispered. "They got to sober up soon. And they're just bluffing." Jimmy sounded certain. I had to trust he was right.

Here's how stupid drunk men can be. Bothwell took the entire group into the Sweetwater River—it's real shallow there. He had us driving down the river for a good part of the afternoon. Was he trying to erase any tracks? Na, I decided that was far too complex a thought for a man in his condition. He was just being an idiot. I wasn't the only one who thought so.

"Bothwell, this is stupid." Tom Sun finally found his tongue. "We're not getting anywhere. This is getting out of hand." He argued to turn around and go back to the roadhouse.

"We delivered our message, loud and clear." That was Cap'n Galbraith, trying to sound like they'd just won.

"We should…should..should…" but nobody waited for the stuttering McLean to finish his thought.

Those men shouted at each other for a good half hour, while Jimmy and I sat there, seeing our prospects improving by the second.

Jimmy couldn't help himself. "Gentlemen, I think we've had enough for one day. I've got a helluva lot to do and so does Ella and our behinds are getting tired sitting in this buggy. Nice buggy, Tom. But enough is enough."

Bothwell exploded. "Close your trap or we'll drown you right here in the river."

And then I couldn't help myself. I started cackling and snorting and giggling and it grew into a full-throated laugh that spit out, "There's not enough water in this river to give a land hog a decent bath."

Jimmy hooted like that was the best joke he ever heard.

But we were the only ones laughing. Those men stared at us like we were from China.

Bothwell reined his horse around and started upstream. Everyone else followed. Nobody was saying anything now. We went on like that forever. Must have been two, three miles.

I figured they had to be sobering up and coming to their senses. I tried a nice approach.

"Gentlemen, I'm getting hungry. You know, it's almost supper time."

"Me, too," Jimmy then tried to take charge. "Hey, if you boys want a great steak dinner, my Ella will cook one up for you back at the roadhouse. How about it? No hard feelings. I don't have any beer, but I've got some good rye whiskey and tonight, it's all on the house."

"And I can whip up a great pie by the time supper is done. I'll make you a mince pie, Mr. Bothwell. Like your Ma used to make. Remember how you love that? I've got some berries. Plenty of pie for everyone."

Bothwell turned in his saddle and aimed his gun right at us and poured out his rage in a wrath that stunned everyone. "You think this is a joke? You think we're just gonna forget about all this? You think you can buy off your rustlin' with a steak dinner—probably a steak from one of our cows? You think this is funny? You don't see us laughing, do you. You fuckin' people are just disgusting, and I'm not standing for any more."

"*You're* not standing for any more!?" I exploded. Jimmy pulled on my sleeve, but he couldn't hush me. "Bothwell, you are a lyin' fool and I've had all of the nonsense I'm gonna take today. You men have had your fun, but that's enough. I've got things to do and boys to feed and I'm sick of being hauled around by a bunch of liquored up idiots who know damn well those cows are mine. Now turn this buggy around and *take me home!*"

It was about four o'clock. In that instant, everything changed. Bothwell whipped his horse, took us out of the river and headed for a rocky canyon. Nobody tried to stop him. They just followed along like sheep. He was in a real hurry now. Jimmy threw me a worried look.

We stumbled into a canyon where things got really bad. Bothwell climbed off his horse, charged over and yanked me out of the buggy. McLean pulled Jimmy down.

"Get me a rope. Get me two ropes." Bothwell screamed the words like they came to him naturally. Conner handed over the rope from his saddle. Durbin added his. Bothwell grabbed one and threw the other to McLean.

They dragged us over to a big, flat rock under a tree that didn't know where it wanted its limbs to go. One hung over the rock, others stuck out in every direction. It was an odd-looking tree.

"Just a minute, just a minute. This is going too far. Come on, Bothwell, you can't do this." Jimmy was yammering. "WE NEVER RUSTLED ANY CATTLE. We can prove it. Please stop. For Chrissake."

But nobody was listening to him.

Bothwell threw one lariat over the limb, then the other. He grabbed Jimmy and forced a noose around his neck.

McLean was trying to get his noose around my head, but my new bonnet was in the way. He ripped it off my head and stomped it in the dirt. In the dirt! I kicked him good in the gut. He rolled on the ground holding his belly like it was about to burst. Then the bastard got up and came at me with that rope again. I was bobbing and weaving so much, he kept missing his mark.

"Please, if you're going to kill us, please give me a chance to say a prayer, let me meet my maker with a prayer on my lips," I begged.

Bothwell taunted me, "You can deliver it in person." He was the only one doing any talking. Only McLean was helping him. The rest of the men stood back, like they were silent spectators at a ball game.

Bothwell was clearly enjoying himself. "Hey, Averell, if you're so brave, why don't you be game and jump off?" He chuckled, but he was the only one.

Suddenly there was a shot. I had no idea where it came from or who was coming to our aid, but I thanked the Lord for whoever it was! Durbin was hit in the hip and he screamed like he was mortally wounded. The men jumped down from their horses and grabbed their Winchesters and started shooting back. There was a lull—our savior had to be reloading, and it seemed he had a smaller gun, probably a handgun. Then the shooting started all over again. And then it stopped. I knew there were no more bullets to save us.

McLean finally settled the noose around my neck. He picked me up and forced me onto the rock. I screamed with every ounce of strength in my body. "No! No! If you have a mother—a sister—No!"

Bothwell rushed forward and pushed Jim off the rock. He didn't fall but two or three feet—not enough to break his neck. Jimmy kicked wildly, trying to pull himself up on the rope. But even when he gained an inch or two, he couldn't hold it.

I shrieked again as McLean pushed me off the rock. Now I was kicking. I couldn't get a toehold. In my jerking, I banged into Jimmy, and we both spun around. We grabbed for each other, but that failed. I was wrenching so frantically, I kicked off the moccasins. First one. Then the other.

Bothwell was laughing like a man being mightily entertained. Even as I choked, I could hear him jeer, "Look at the bitch—she's wearin' Indian moccasins! What kind of decent white woman puts on dirty Indian moccasins? Maybe she's sleepin' with 'em too. Wouldn't put it past her. What a lowlife."

Those words weren't important now. What was important was my prayer. "God, please make it break, PLEASE MAKE IT BREAK!"

But the limb held.

◇◇◇

And all the while, I could hear Bothwell's ridiculous laugh. I prayed it would so sicken the others, they'd rush over to rescue us. Cut the rope. Shoot it free. Take control.

But they turned away, like they didn't want to see what was happening. Like they weren't witnesses to their own crime. Like they couldn't be as guilty if they hung back and didn't join Bothwell's pushes. Like it had to be his sin alone, and not theirs, too. They stayed in the background, cowards until the very end. And I hope they never slept another night of their lives without seeing what they had done. Because they knew they were just as guilty as the monsters who actually pushed us off that rock.

But how will they explain to everyone in the Sweetwater Valley—and probably everyone in W.T.—that they went so low as to hang a woman? There's nothing to compare this to. Nobody hangs a woman in W.T. I've never heard of them hanging a woman anywhere—oh, that woman who they say helped the killers of Lincoln, but other than her, women don't end up on a vigilante's rope. What's the old saying, 'women and children get saved first'? That sounds good, even if it's a phony chivalry. They pretend they've got this respect for women and put us on a "pedestal," but really, they've put us under their thumb. Except for drunkards like my first husband, most stop short of physical harm. So women play along because we learned long ago that when you've got so little, you cling to whatever you got.

I didn't even get the benefit of fake chivalry to save me from the noose.

These men strung us up like we were a side of beef. They have some powerful answering to do for that. Justice can't abide that kind of vigilante lawlessness and belly-draggin' sin.

The only thing justice can really do is tit for tat. It can string up each and every one of these horrible men, just like they did us. Let them dangle with their toes not quite touching and slowly strangle to death, just like they killed us. But their execution wouldn't be done out in a private gully, where no one but God could see. Theirs would be done in broad daylight in the middle of town. I'd stage it on the front lawn of that new prison they're building in Rawlins. The whole town can come out and see that men who murder innocents are the worst men there are.

◇◇◇

No, I won't die like that. Until the very last second—the very, very last second, before it is mercifully over—I won't believe this is my death.

Not at the end of a plain rope, like you find on any saddle in the territory.

Rope I have at home by my corral. Rope tied to the water pail when I go down to the creek. Just a simple rope.

But it isn't a simple rope when it's thrown over your head and settles on your neck. It's so rough and so strong. It makes you think of a snake strangling you, and since I hate snakes so much, that makes the terror even worse. This is silly, but I am thankful the good dress I'm finishing has a high neck, so nobody at the summer dance will see the rope burns.

See, I still hope I'll be dancing at the summer fandango. My Jimmy will be doing his best jig, and all my good neighbors will share a night that nobody wants to end. I've dreamed about this night for so long, I refuse to give it up.

So I keep twisting and kicking, hoping to get a toehold on the rock.

Just got it! I'm standing on the rock! I steal a breath. I'm balancing and…My foot slips off.

Jimmy has his hands above his head, holding the rope and trying to pull himself up, but I can't reach up that far. Oh my Jimmy—seeing him like that breaks my heart, but crushes my soul. That good man, that good, decent man. I love him so. Is this the last time I ever touch the man I love, when we bang into each other in our ugly death jig?

Jimmy. Jimmy. Ma. Oh Ma. Pa. Gene. God help me.

◇◇◇

When that rope tightens, it cuts off any air getting to my lungs, so I last as long as the last breath I have. As that seeps out, it feels like my chest is on fire. I'll just start burning up, that's how hot it gets.

My eyes seem to blow up, like they're looking for their own air out there, outside my body.

My nose starts bleeding into my throat because there's this putrid taste in my mouth.

Most of all it hurts. It hurts so bad I can't believe a vicious pain like this exists.

It hurts so much it makes me blind, so the blackness comes first.

Then it closes my ears.

All I can hear is the sound of my heart beating like a whole bunch of Indians were banging on a drum, really hard and really fast.

Then they stop.

And that is the last beat my heart sings.

◇◇◇

I want to tell that Jimmy and I didn't die so rich cattlemen could have our land and water.

I want to tell that justice stepped up, like any decent citizen would demand.

I want to tell that our friends saw these men convicted of first-degree murder.

I want to tell that Pa and Ma got some peace, knowing justice was done.

I want to tell that our loved ones watched these men hanged by the neck until dead.

I want to tell all that.

But I can't.

Because none of that happened.

Part Two

What Happened Next

Chapter Fifteen

"Cattle Kate" is Born

Edwin Archibald Slack had a busy Sunday ahead of him that hot July 21st of 1889.

The publisher and editor of the *Cheyenne Sun* planned to accompany his family to the Presbyterian Church to hear the famous visiting contralto Madame D'Arona Dawson. Capitalizing on his one free day—the Sunday paper was already on the streets and there was no Monday paper—he intended to spend the afternoon at the baseball game at the fairgrounds where the Cheyenne Capitals would face off against the Sandens of Denver. To top off the day, he was taking his family to dinner at the Normandy, the restaurant his newspaper declared the "finest in the city."

But Slack did none of those things on that Sunday. He missed out on obligation and fun alike because he'd have had more important things to do. Stock Detective George Henderson showed up at the Slack residence and impatiently knocked on the front door.

"What the…" Slack muttered, as he hefted his six foot one, two hundred thirty-pound frame from the breakfast table. The minute he saw it was Henderson, he knew something big was up. It took only the whispered words "double fuckin' lynching" to tell him just how big.

Wyoming Territory was home to dozens of newspapers, but the only ones that really counted were the Cheyenne dailies. The rest were weekly publications in rural towns. What they said might matter at home, but they carried no weight in the capital city, or anywhere else in the nation.

In the capital city of the Territory of Wyoming, the pecking order started with Ed Slack and his *Sun*. His Republican daily was the most prominent and important western voice outside Denver.

Slack believed a frontier newspaper's role was to "boom the town," and he was an unapologetic booster. His paper bragged about Cheyenne's rapid growth and prosperity. He highlighted the cultural offerings that proved the town was "civilized." He touted new businesses and the natural resources of the territory. It goes without saying that he was the best friend of the cattle industry that dominated the entire economic picture of W.T. He'd championed them in the bonanza days when there were 100 times more cows than people in the territory. He hung with them now that the bonanza was waning and the cattle industry was just holding on.

He wasn't the only editor who understood that, like the Indian and buffalo, cattle could go away, too.

Slack's attitude made him a wealthy and prominent man. He bragged that the *Sun* had "the largest city and territorial circulation."

But Ed Slack didn't get all his prominence from his newspaper. He got some from his famous mother. Esther Hobart Morris had twice distinguished herself as a groundbreaking woman. First, she was instrumental in 1869 in convincing Wyoming Territory to defy every other government in the nation by giving women full voting rights. One year later, she became the first woman in the nation to hold a judicial position, serving as a justice of the peace. Slack's newspaper spread the word about this remarkable woman that Wyoming would always revere. He crowned her "the mother of woman suffrage in Wyoming."

Yes, Ed Slack had it good. His voice was strong. His word meant something.

Slack seldom looked over his shoulder, but when he did, it was to watch his biggest competitor and political opposite, the Democratic *Cheyenne Daily Leader,* whose own bragging rights were "the oldest daily in the territory."

For the rest of America, the only news ever telegraphed out of the territory came from one of these dailies. Their voice was the voice of the West for readers in New York and Boston and Chicago and Omaha. Slack had never been more aware of that than on Sunday, July 21, 1889.

He instantly knew this would be a national story. It was paramount to put the lynching in the right light. He hurriedly dressed and headed off to his newspaper office in the center of Cheyenne. On the way, he took note that the cattlemen's Cheyenne Club on Seventeenth Street—normally dead as a doornail on Sunday morning after a busy Saturday night—already showed signs of life.

"Archy" Slack had spent many a fine evening enjoying the Mums champagne and Roquefort cheese imported for this exclusive club some called "little Wall Street." He counted its members in the Wyoming Stock Growers Association as not only his friends, but his benefactors and major advertisers. If you asked him which side of the bread his butter was on, he'd tell you it was the side with the fine cattlemen of Wyoming Territory.

Knowing some of those fine cattlemen were involved in a double-fucking-lynching in the Sweetwater Valley made Ed Slack's heart race.

George Henderson knew it would. He knew hearts all over Cheyenne were beating at stroke level, ever since Durbin's telegram last night laid out the basics. The wire ended with four words that were often the marching orders for George Henderson: "Take care of it."

Henderson hadn't become the territory's richest stock detective by being unimaginative. His name didn't inspire fear or disgust because he was timid. He could read these cattlemen like a book, and no matter where the storyline wandered, the important part was that it ended up on their side.

Henderson couldn't count the nights he'd downed Bothwell's whiskey while listening to his wails about that "fucking Watson woman" and her "fucking partner, Averell." How many times had he eaten one of Durbin's steaks while the man preached his gospel of never being run out by settlers again? How many times had he ridden by the Watson claim on Horse Creek and wished he could burn down her stupid log cabin and tear out her silly corral?

Oh, he well knew the men who'd done the dirty deed last night—Sun's involvement was the only surprise—but he knew their victims, too. And that was the problem.

Averell was about the most prominent and respected settler in the Sweetwater—postmaster, J.P., all of it—and Ella Watson, well, if George Henderson were called to testify about that good-looking woman, the first words out of his mouth would be, "She makes the best pie I've ever tasted."

But he wouldn't tell Ed Slack any of those things. No siree. Not when he had to spread the word that they'd been hanged. That would never do. They couldn't be upstanding citizens. They *had* to be despicable lowlife rustlers. They couldn't be helpful neighbors who could be counted on in a pinch. They *had* to be ruthless criminals who'd terrorized the good cattle-raising families of the Sweetwater Valley. They couldn't be lynched in a lawless act. They *had* to be receiving their just rewards in a clear case of rangeland justice.

And there had to be something extra special for the woman—*they hanged a fucking woman!* She couldn't have a shred of decency, or the old code would kick in. It wasn't only the rule of the sea that women and children were saved above all others. It was the rule of the West, too. Only a coward or a cur would not step in front of a bullet or an arrow to protect women and children.

The only way to get everyone to forget chivalry, was to make the Watson woman contemptible. She *had* to be a female of the lowest order. She *had* to be doing the things no decent woman would do—living the life that women and men alike would turn their backs on. She *had* to be a filthy whore.

Nobody had to spell out this story to Henderson—his years of working for the stock growers had primed him. Now he needed to get the Cheyenne editors to see it his way. Either he did that, or he'd better hightail it out of the territory, because this wasn't an assignment that allowed for failure.

This assignment demanded Henderson at his best, and at his best—the man was proud of this—he could not only lead horses to water, he could made them drink.

"Ed, you know how bad the rustlin's been out there—the courts are worthless. They won't convict a rustler for anything, and these two were the leaders of the pack. You just could hear 'em laughin' at the cattlemen that they could steal all they wanted and nobody would do a fuckin' thing. I saw it myself plenty of times. And I did what I could to stop it—you know that—and these two were the worst. On top of that, they were such lowlifes. The Averell guy had a string of prostitutes at his place. She was one of 'em—his madam, if I'm not mistaken." Henderson's speech did not fall on deaf ears.

"So he ran a hog ranch?" Slack tsked, using the favorite slang for a house of prostitution. "How low can a man go?" Slack started scribbling notes as he sat behind his big oak desk in the *Sun* office. Henderson sat across from him, filling in any blanks.

"You know, those names sound familiar," Slack mused, and Henderson worried that maybe the *Sun* had reported on Averell's prestigious appointments. Boy, that could pose some real problems. He was already concocting a counter story—a face of respectability hiding a tawdry whorehouse—when Slack continued: "Averell. Averell. Wasn't he that Harvard man who came out here?"

Henderson had never heard of any Harvard in Averell's past— was quite certain no Ivy League college had ever seen him—but he didn't correct the publisher. He could see right away where Slack was going—from fine schools to a filthy end. It was exactly the kind of story they were looking for.

"And Ella Watson," Slack said slowly, letting the name slide off his tongue as he tried to remember. "Oh right. We've had her in the paper before. A bad character, I tell you."

Henderson had no idea why Ella Watson had ever been mentioned in the *Cheyenne Sun* before, but he didn't care. A "bad character" was all he had to hear. Whatever story Slack was thinking about, it was about a bad woman and that was perfect. It was imperative the Watson woman be mentioned in nothing but the worst possible light.

Slack was on a roll. "Nobody's gonna cry for her. She wasn't a decent woman. She was the kind of woman we don't want in W.T. So was he. We've got to get rid of these lowlifes. Once decent folks see they were bad rubbish, they're going to see how this happened. Now, who were the ranchmen that were driven to desperation?"

Henderson carefully unveiled the powerful names of the men who had been in attendance. Slack whistled through his lips as he stared at the stock detective.

"You can't be serious. This isn't even possible. Henderson, are you sure?"

Henderson nodded with certainty.

"I know these men," Slack said quietly, as the story sunk in. "My God, Bothwell and Sun are on the executive committee of the stock growers! Cap'n Galbraith represents that county in the legislature—isn't he running again? And Durbin. His family practically built W.T."

Slack sat quietly, doodling on his notepad. Henderson got nervous. Should he let the man develop his thoughts or should he push some more? Henderson decided to hold his tongue. You had to be careful with these newspapermen. They liked to think they were the ones who saw the truth in a story. They liked to think they were the smartest men in the room. Pushing now might insult him. Henderson's armpits were sweating through his shirt when Archy Slack finally made his pronouncement.

"Nobody's going to believe those good men would do something that wasn't justified."

Henderson was the happiest stock detective on Earth when he heard the words out of Slack's mouth: *Bad character. Lowlifes. Hog ranch. Good men. Justified.* Henderson could already taste the fine whiskey he'd be able to afford with the hefty bonus for this Sunday's work. He left the *Sun*'s office for the Cheyenne Club, anxious to report this was going even better than expected.

Of all the things Edwin Archibald Slack had planned for this Sunday, creating a western myth had not been on the agenda. But he started writing a story that would do just that—create an Old West legend that would last, unchallenged, for nearly a century.

Slack's words erased Ella Watson—homesteader, secret wife, foster mom, wannabe citizen—and replaced her with Cattle Kate—rustler and whore.

If he ever learned what really happened in the Sweetwater Valley that fateful Saturday, he didn't bother to print it.

Chapter Sixteen

How to Stage a Hanging

Albert John Bothwell had been waiting for this morning all winter. It had been a decent winter, as things go in Wyoming Territory. Nothing like the ones so vicious they killed the cows on the open range. No, last winter had been fine and those mama cows had pushed out a whole lot of new calves. Just yesterday, they'd finished the spring branding and now he could relax.

He and the boys were camped in one of his hay fields. Cookie had rustled up a fine breakfast of flapjacks and coffee and of course, steak.

They'd been at this since mid-May, the crew traveling throughout the Sweetwater Valley to brand the new calves of 1889. Bothwell was one of the commissioners overseeing this roundup for the Stock Growers Association. He was joined by Tom Sun and John Durbin—most of the cattle being branded were owned by these three and it was tradition that the main cattlemen supervised the branding. Some nights, all three men bedded down with their cowboys, but forty-seven-year-old Durbin had already decided that part of the ritual was reserved for younger men. At forty-five, Sun wasn't far behind in that thinking. Bothwell still found it invigorating, but his thirty-five-year-old bones weren't as brittle yet.

They were finishing up the strong coffee when Ernie McLean raced up, stammering that he'd found twenty cows recently shot and their calves nowhere around.

"Some...some...somebody's steal...steal...stealing mavericks," he stuttered.

Everybody instantly suspected it was the nesters who were ruining the valley for honest cattlemen. As Durbin liked to say, you see a settler and you're looking at "a thief or potential thief or sympathizer with thieves."

Bothwell grabbed at any opportunity that came along. Some crumbled like sand in his hands, but others left a nugget of gold. And on the morning of July 20, 1889, Bothwell knew he was reaching for the gold. He now saw the opportunity he'd been waiting for since he first spied that woman who dared defy him.

"Bet it's that whore over at Averell's." Some of the cowboys looked at him in surprise, because they knew he was talking about Miss Ella, and they knew she was no whore.

"Ernie, go check," Bothwell yelled, giving orders to the small-potatoes rancher who was always so eager to please. McLean jumped on his horse—grabbing a flapjack on the way—and headed off toward Ella's claim.

He got there and saw fresh brands on the small herd in her corral and knew this was exactly what Bothwell wanted to know. She must have stolen these cows and branded them as her own and that was the very definition of rustling. He raced back with the news.

"Goddamn, Holy hell, Christ Almighty, that's fuckin' enough," Bothwell swore, on hearing McLean's news. "I've had it with these rustlers," and he knew full well he wasn't the only one with that thought. "They think they can steal our cattle and nobody's going to do anything. The courts sure fucking aren't. We can't get a conviction if the guy has his arm up the cow's ass. They're laughin' at us. They think they've got a free fuckin' ride. And I tell you, that Watson woman is one of the worst. She and Averell have been making trouble in the valley for years, and now they're rustling. When are they going to be stopped?" His face was red with anger, and around the circle, other men felt their blood pressure rising.

"There's no fucking respect," Durbin declared.

Tom Sun agreed, "There's no respect."

"We have to stop them," Bothwell pronounced, and he didn't get any resistance. "I say we go get 'em and show them what for."

Somebody else suggested they "arrest" them and take them to Rawlins, but Bothwell snorted at that. "Yeah, like that would do any good. We've got to make an example of them or this rustling will never stop. I say we string 'em up as a warning that we're at the end of our rope. Hey, that's a joke!" But nobody else was laughing.

Tom Sun, who'd come over from his ranch this morning in his new buggy, protested immediately. "Al, stop talking like that." He argued—"vigorously," some of the cowboys would later report—that the most they could do was scare them, and that would put the fear of God in others.

"Okay, okay, okay," Bothwell backed off. "But we've got to scare them for good, because I want them out of this valley."

Bothwell jumped on his horse and yelled "follow me" as he took off. Durbin was just as hot—his Irish temper was always just under his skin—and that wannabe Ernie McLean would do anything Bothwell suggested, so he saddled up.

Just as they were leaving, Cap'n Robert Galbraith rode in and was quickly informed of the situation. "I'm in," he announced, and turned his horse around.

The group stopped at the offices of the *Sweetwater Chief,* the phony newspaper set up to sell lots in the "Town of Bothwell." The *Chief* was in a new flat-topped building that sat all alone on the prairie, but oh, the stories it printed to laud the wonderful "community" it pretended was all around it. Cowboys said you didn't need to know much more about Red Vest than that he could afford his own newspaper, and Bothwell had smiled when he overheard the remark.

The editor and his assistant—Henry Fetz and Isaac Speer— were there and so was Bob Conner, whose own ranch bordered Ella's claim.

"Bring out John Barleycorn," Bothwell yelled at the editors. Nobody thought it was too early to drink because when you're on the trail of rustlers, it was time to drink. One, two bottles of whiskey disappeared that morning as the cattlemen broadcast their complaints about all the nesters that had moved into their pastures and put up the hated barbed-wire fences.

"That Watson woman had the first barbed wire in this valley," Bothwell declared, as if that were reason enough to run her off. "God, I hate that stuff. Tears the hell out of a cowhide. Breaks up perfectly good pastures. Barbed wire is going to ruin the West. Mark my words. Ruin it!"

By the time the angry army left the *Chief*, more than one of the men stumbled to his horse. Sun followed along in his white-topped buggy with its tandem seats.

Along the way, they met Sam Johnson, a foreman who knew Ella better than most. He'd had to repair some of her fences when his own cattle invaded her corral. He'd been a gentleman about it and she'd been understanding—"cows have a mind of their own," she'd joked with him, as he weeded out his cattle from hers. Bothwell filled him in with a shorthand, "going to go show some rustlers they can't get away with it anymore." But when Sam discovered who the "rustler" was, he reigned his horse around and headed for home instead.

Fetz and Speer took their field glasses and climbed to the roof of their office to watch the procession. From that vantage point, they saw almost everything.

The men arrived at Ella's cabin, but she apparently wasn't there. Durbin wasted no time ripping apart her corral, and cows started running all over the place. A boy ran out of the cabin, waving his arms in protest.

"Oh kid, if you know what's good for you, you'll get out of there," Fetz said, as Speer demanded a turn with the glasses.

"Hey, that Watson woman just came running up," Speer reported.

They passed the glasses back and forth for the next fifteen minutes or so, as Ella fought with Bothwell about who was going where with whom.

"She's in the wagon!" Fetz had the glasses now. "Oh man, this is going to be bad."

"I already knew that," Speer now admitted. "Those men mean business. Bothwell told me when they were leaving that they were going to hang those two. I'm betting he'll get his way before the day is out."

Fetz nodded, having had the same conversation with the man somewhere between the second and third bottle of whiskey. "And they're liquored up," Fetz reminded, as though that absolved them of rational thought.

The men watched the procession stop Jim in his wagon.

"They're makin' him unhitch his horses!" Fetz yelled, and Speer grabbed the glasses.

"Man, they're making him leave his wagon out there. He just got in the buggy."

"Let me see, let me see," Fetz said, then whistled real slow as he watched the parade leave the wagon and freed horses behind.

The procession was getting too far away to see anything anymore, so the newspaper men climbed down from the roof and went back to work.

Under normal circumstances, they would have penned an "Eyewitness Account!" of what they'd seen. But this wasn't normal circumstances. They knew they wouldn't be writing about this strange Saturday, revealing what they'd heard and seen. Or what they knew was about to happen.

"Think they'll get away with it?" Speer asked gingerly, and Fetz didn't need any time to think it over: "Of course they'll get away with it. Ever heard of rangeland justice?"

But not writing about it and not talking about it were two different things. Maybe it was the real newspaper men in them coming out, or maybe they were just natural gossips. But that afternoon when a couple cowboys rode up, looking for a place to plant themselves for awhile—knowing there was always a supply of liquor to be had here—Fetz prematurely spilled the beans, "You boys know what happened this afternoon? Jim Averell and Ella Watson were hung!"

"You don't say," one of the cowboys said in wonderment.

◇◇◇

"They looked so mad. So mean."

Gene Crowder had never been as scared as when the armed men took Ella away. John DeCorey had to second his observations. The boys huddled together inside Ella's cabin, daring not disobey the last order to "Stay put!"

"They let all the cows out," Gene said in astonishment, and John started reciting all the reasons that rustling was a ridiculous indictment.

The boys paced inside the cabin, frantic that they couldn't help Ella. Disgusted that they couldn't stop those terrible men.

"I tried to help," Gene wailed, remembering the first moments the men had arrived.

"Me, too." John knew nobody could blame them when men with guns stopped them.

"Ella was worried about us," John declared.

"Do you think they'll hurt her? Oh, please don't let them hurt her." Gene started to cry. John told him to cut it out, they had to help.

They sneaked a look outside. When they saw the procession disappear around the mountain, they ran out and started to repair the damage. John discovered he could round up cows better than he'd imagined, and Gene wasn't too bad at it, either. They got most of the cows back in the corral and rigged up the fence as best they could and then ran for the roadhouse.

Ralph was behind the counter when Frank Buchanan rode up to the roadhouse that Saturday morning. Ralph had to smile because you always knew when Buchanan was coming—he wore a brightly colored bandanna that he knotted so it would stick out from his shirt. Ralph didn't know anybody else in the entire valley that wore their neckerchief that way.

"Your usual?" Ralph asked as he grabbed the coffeepot, and Frank grunted his thanks. He was the first customer since Jimmy left for Casper, and Ralph was ready.

Ella had made extra pies, knowing cowboys would be coming in, now that branding was over. Ralph figured he'd sell all the pies and most of the stew she left to be heated up, and by the time his uncle got back Sunday night, he would have a nice profit to show off. He was feeling very adult to be in charge.

The boys burst in, so out of breath they could barely speak, but finally blurted out what was happening. "Bothwell and a gang of men grabbed Miss Ella and Mr. Averell and said they were rustlers and they're going to show them what for."

Then they remembered to add: "And they made Mr. Averell unhitch his horses and they're running around out there."

Ralph ran to retrieve the most valuable possessions his uncle had—the boys helped. They found the horses hadn't decided to go far, and it wasn't hard to get them hitched up to the wagon again.

Frank Buchanan didn't spend one second worrying about the loose horses. He didn't need any translation to know what was going on. Not on the range. Not for a charge of rustling.

Frank was an all-around cowboy. He'd worked the round-up crews for many men in the Sweetwater Valley—Durbin, Sun, Conner, Galbraith—but he never would work for Bothwell. He thought the man was evil. "Pure evil," he'd say in the most ominous tone. He knew cowboys who worked for the man, and none of them ever had a nice thing to say—worked them hard; paid them little; showed cruelty whenever possible; filthy mouth and even dirtier mind.

Frank was having a bowl of beans at the roadhouse one day when Bothwell showed up, and the way he talked to Miss Ella, Frank bet the man was sweet on her. But she handled herself very well, polite but positive that she wanted none of it. Frank had smiled to himself that day, thinking that old Red Vest wasn't used to not getting his way, but he certainly was not getting his way with Miss Ella.

Now he had a bad churning in his gut at this news that Bothwell had Ella and Jimmy.

Frank Buchanan ran to his horse and headed out after the procession.

◇◇◇

Buchanan heard the caravan before he actually saw it. They were down in the Sweetwater River, men on horseback and the buggy with his friends, all sitting there in the water, like this was a swimming party or something. He hid behind a rock and watched the noisy scene.

He couldn't make out everything they were saying, but there was no mistaking that this was a heated argument. The ranchers were all yelling at each other, obviously in discord. The angry tone gave Frank his first ray of hope. He guessed the argument was over what to do next. He prayed that "next" was to take Ella and Jim home and let that be the end of it. At one point, Bothwell pointed his horse downstream and took a few steps before he realized nobody but Durbin and McLean were following. He went back to the group and yelled some more. Someone, Frank wasn't sure exactly who, was bellowing that they'd made their point and the law should take over now. Somebody else was barking they should "string 'em up."

And then he saw that Jim and Ella weren't being mute during all this, but offered their own two cents. Jim was talking with his hands, gesturing like this was the biggest mistake ever made in W.T. "Shut up," Bothwell screamed, "or we'll drown you right here in the river."

Then the most remarkable thing happened. Frank heard Ella Watson laugh. It wasn't a giggle, like something was funny, but a full-throated laugh like somebody was stupid. "There's not enough water in this river to give a land hog a decent bath," she spat at them, and then Jim laughed, too.

Frank immediately had mixed emotions. If they were laughing, maybe things weren't as serious as they seemed. Maybe everybody knew this was a game, and it was almost over and they'd laugh about it over supper. But if the laughter was a taunt, that was another kettle of worms altogether. Frank had seen too many men maimed or killed because they laughed at an armed man.

His fears were ratified when the group started moving, traveling up the streambed that would leave no tracks. He jumped back on his horse and followed along best he could, keeping undercover. He skulked after them all afternoon, watching their slow progress.

Frank shook his head at the futility of this. So much time had passed, he now clearly believed this was all a stall, and nobody was really going to hurt anybody. He figured Jimmy and Ella were thinking the same thing and he hoped with all his might that it would cool their attitude so they didn't provoke anything. "Shut up for once," he thought out loud.

About four o'clock, everything changed. Frank saw the group abruptly shift direction, leaving the river and heading for a rocky canyon. He was far enough off that he couldn't hear much, but he could see Ella trying to stand up in the wagon and gesturing wildly, and he heard enough to know she was a mad hen.

"Oh shit," he sadly said out loud. Frank Buchanan went to his grave wondering if things turned so bad because Ella had gotten too mouthy and pushed the men over the edge.

He jumped on his horse and followed almost in their exact path. When he reached the canyon, he slid off his horse and climbed a rock, dropping to his belly when he saw the group below.

He prayed his eyes were deceiving him because Jim and Ella were standing next to a flat rock under a tree whose limb was decorated with two lariats. One noose was already around Jim's neck. Bothwell was tying the loose end to a tree.

"We never rustled any cattle," Jim was screaming in a voice that already was hoarse. But nobody was listening.

McLean was trying to get his noose around Ella's head, but she was bobbing and weaving so much, he kept missing his mark. Her bonnet was in the way and she was like a wild woman trying to get free.

Bothwell was the man in charge. Only McLean was helping him. The rest of the men were standing back, some already turned away from the scene, others studying the ground.

Frank took aim with his six-shooter and started shooting, hitting Durbin in the hip. The men grabbed their Winchesters and shot back. Frank emptied his gun, quickly reloaded, and kept shooting. He was well aware he was outgunned. He didn't expect his shots to rule the day. He did hope that discovering an eyewitness would be the shot of reality these folks needed.

Instead, he heard Ella scream. He instantly poked his head up and saw Bothwell and McLean force his friends onto a boulder. Bothwell rushed forward and pushed Jim off. Frank watched in horror as Jim kicked wildly, trying to pull himself up on the rope.

Ella screamed again as McLean pushed her off the rock and her writhing and jerking began. She tried to get a toehold, but kept slipping off. Frank could see his friends were being strangled, and in their dance of death, they banged up against each other, spinning and grabbing and flailing unmercifully, trying everything they could to free themselves. Ella was kicking so frantically, she kicked off one moccasin, then another. Frank wondered why she was wearing moccasins in the first place, but it was a fleeting thought. Bothwell was laughing over something Buchanan couldn't make out.

Frank saw that his friends were both suspended from the same limb, and he yelled out loud, "God, please make it break!"

But God wasn't listening.

It seemed like it took forever for them to stop kicking. They were stronger than Frank ever dreamed, and for a second, he thought Jimmy might just make it. He saw that Ella was losing strength quickly, but Jimmy kept grabbing the rope above his head, trying to hoist himself up enough to give him another breath. Ella wasn't strong enough for that, and Frank started crying when he heard her gurgling sounds.

Frank kept ducking down behind the rock, not afraid of bullets now, since they'd stopped when he finally ran out of ammunition, but because he couldn't bear to watch what was happening. But even when he wasn't watching, he could hear the awful sounds of his friends in their last seconds and it made him vomit.

The last time he dared look, blood was coming from Ella's nose and mouth and her eyes were bulging out. Jim looked like he was trying to reach for her, but his arms were now too heavy. They were no longer kicking. Just twitching, their arms limp at their sides. Frank would forever be sorry he took that last look.

And then everything went silent.

No sound of thrashing as they lost the fight. No death rattle as the air in their lungs was spent. No creaking as the limb no longer held two struggling people. No scratching as the rope wasn't snapped by the twisting couple. They just hung there in empty silence.

Frank's efforts to save his friends had failed. They had left this Earth for, he hoped, a better place. He rushed down the hill and jammed his spurs into his horse to head back to the roadhouse with the gruesome news. He knew he would stop only a moment before he galloped to Casper to get the sheriff.

The men in the canyon made no move to follow him, but they weren't languishing. They had more important places to go—to homes and ranches and wives and children and, frankly, anywhere but here. Without a word, they mounted their horses while Tom Sun turned around his wagon. Nobody looked back at the two bodies hanging from the limb, their tongues swelling and dangling from their mouths.

The only sound in the canyon was horse hooves and wagon wheels on rock. The sound of leaving.

Nobody noticed, but not even the birds were singing.

◇◇◇

Frank Buchanan never made it all the way to Casper to alert the sheriff.

He collapsed from exhaustion by the time he reached "Tex" Healy's log cabin about three o'clock Sunday morning. He was still twenty-five miles from Casper, but it was clear he was in no shape to continue. Healy quickly dressed and saddled his own horse to carry the horrifying news to Deputy Sheriff Philip Watson.

"We've had a lynchin' out in the Sweetwater, and I'm lookin' for able-bodied men to form a posse," Sheriff Watson announced in the saloon, which was the only business open. "Have to have your own gear. Town will buy you dinner. Payin' $10 for any takers." There were several takers.

Sherriff Watson told the barkeep to get them some grub and put it on the town's tab, and went looking for the coroner. But Dr. A.P. Haynes wasn't to be found. It took several hours to get everybody gathered up, and still the coroner wasn't around. Sheriff Watson deputized Casper attorney B.F. Emery as the acting coroner.

"Can't wait all day," he said, as he led the posse out of town. It was almost three o'clock on Sunday afternoon. They rode all night and arrived in the dark, first hours of Monday. They were greeted by a dark roadhouse and two newly made caskets on the front porch. Sheriff Watson yelled out his identity as he knocked on the door. A sleepy Ralph Cole answered it, but not far behind, their eyes wild in fear, were the boys, John DeCovey and Gene Crowder.

It took only a second for Frank Buchanan to come out from the room off the kitchen.

"So glad to see you, Sheriff." He held out his hand. "Thanks Tex," he said to his friend, who'd carried on for him.

Buchanan had gotten back to Averell's place about four o'clock, in time to help the boys with the final preparations on the caskets.

"I'll take you out to the hanging at first light," Buchanan told the sheriff. "Hey, take the bed back there," he offered, and the sheriff didn't argue. Most of the posse had already stretched out their bedrolls wherever they found a space and it didn't take long before sleep visited. You sleep fast and good after more than a half-day in the saddle.

Buchanan led the caravan the next morning to the hanging site. It was a gut-wrenching scene.

Death, decomposition, and the sun had taken its toll. After two-and-a-half days of hanging there, neither one was recognizable. The only way you could tell a man from a woman was that the woman was wearing a dress. Their faces were so swollen, there was no evidence of a nose. Their exposed skin was black. Their tongues hung from their mouths, as hard as beef jerky. Their eyes bulged, smothered with flies. One of the posse threw up. Everyone else pulled their handkerchief over their mouth and nose, trying to keep out the stench.

Men in the posse cut the couple down, wrapped them in saddle blankets and took them back to the roadhouse. Over their bodies, acting coroner Emery conducted an official inquest, taking testimony from all the eyewitnesses: Frank Buchanan, Gene Crowder, John DeCorey, and Ralph Cole.

He charged that the couple had been hanged by Albert Bothwell, Robert Conner, Tom Sun, Earnest McLean, Robert Galbraith, and John Durbin.

Jimmy and Ella were each placed in a newly made casket and buried in a single grave.

"You boys need somethin' to eat," Buchanan told the posse, and those were very welcome words. Inside they found Frank, Gene, and Ralph trying to copy one of Ella's dinners, but everyone could tell right off that they didn't know what they were doing. A couple of the posse men took over and fried up bacon and ham and scrambled some eggs.

Everyone was eyeing the pies Ella had left—intended for cowboys, but served instead to the men who buried her. The sheriff got the first piece, of course, and the acting coroner the second, and it seemed only right that Buchanan should get one, and the posse drew straws for the rest.

Somebody said it was the best pie he'd ever eaten in his whole life and Gene started crying. That touched off John, who'd held his grief in all this time, and Ralph swore as tears filled his eyes.

Frank Buchanan put on his bravest face. "Miss Ella was known for her pies, boys, and for her good cookin' and for her kindness, and to think her hands made this pie and she's now out in that grave…" He wept like a woman.

Sheriff Watson and his posse set off for the Hub and Spoke Ranch to arrest Tom Sun. He was expecting them, and owned up to what had happened. He went peacefully with the sheriff.

Their second stop was the Broken Box Ranch to arrest A.J. Bothwell.

Chapter Seventeen

The Man with the Pen

The minute he got word that he was urgently wanted at the Cheyenne Club, Ed Towse grabbed a reporter's notebook and ran—not walked, ran—to the ritzy club that held all the power in Wyoming Territory.

The young city editor of the *Cheyenne Daily Leader* had only been summoned there once before, and that time he was told to come in the service entrance—a slight he found demeaning. But then, his paper wasn't always a handmaiden to the interests of this club like his horrible competitor, the *Sun*. This time, he was told to come up the front steps to the front door. He'd never walked in the front door of "little Wall Street" before.

He had no idea why he was wanted.

He didn't know this was about the Sweetwater Valley, which he knew well from his days as a reporter in Rawlins.

He didn't know this was about prominent ranchers from that area, some of whom he'd interviewed over the years.

He didn't know two people were still hanging from a limb in a lonely canyon in the Sweetwater Valley.

But he did know this—you aren't summoned to the Cheyenne Club at noon on a Sunday and told to come in the front door unless this is the story of your life.

Although he was slight and in good health, he was out of

breath when he reached the door and had to stop a second before he rang. A black butler in full regalia answered the door.

"Mr. Towse," the man said in a deep, southern voice, "they're waiting for you."

Ed Towse straightened himself up and put on his most professional face as he was led to a reading room off the main lobby. "Keep your eyes straight," he said to himself, but he couldn't help but gawk at the rich oak paneling and the chandelier that had to have a hundred bulbs. This was the first place in the city to get electric lights and at night, they turned so many on, the reflection lit up this entire section of Seventeenth Street. "Showin' off," some townspeople had said about the amazing amount of light that came out of this private club. Cattlemen laughed and countered, "Just showin' you the light, boys, just showin' you the light."

"Mr. Towse," the butler announced as they walked into the reading room, and Ed Towse straightened up even more, because never in his life had he been announced before.

Three men stood up, introduced themselves and shook the young editor's hand. The butler produced a silver tray with a crystal glass full of whiskey, and Ed Towse thought he'd died and gone to heaven.

"I think you know our stock detective, George Henderson," one of the cattlemen said, as he motioned to a man sitting outside the main circle.

"Oh yes, hi George," Towse said, and then wondered if this time he should have called him Mr. Henderson. But Towse had already interviewed George so many times, he let their familiarity slip.

It was Henderson who kept the editor informed about the awful—simply awful—situation with cattle rustling throughout W.T. Towse had already written several articles decrying the rampant lawlessness that had come as settlers moved in on the cattlemen. It wasn't a stretch for him to parrot the thoughts of the men in this room because he shared their disdain for the silly laws coming out of Washington.

Those idiots back East kept divvying up land these men needed for their vast herds—their laws had brought a whole new breed of poor settlers into the territory. Towse couldn't understand why anyone thought it was a good idea to displace men of wealth and power with people who'd never bring any real riches to the territory. If this were a ball game, he would root for the home team over the visitors, and the home team in W.T. was the cattlemen.

"Eddie, there's a story coming out of the Sweetwater Valley and we want to be sure you get it straight from the horse's mouth," the main man said, and Towse liked the fatherly tone.

Over the next hour, Ed Towse heard the most incredible story he'd ever heard. It had an impressive cast of characters who had been so pushed to the brink, they even hanged a thieving woman! A telegram had brought the news to Henderson, who said he'd been watching these maverickers for months, and someone had finally caught them red-handed.

"You know the law out there is on the side of the settlers, and a cattleman can't get a fair shake, no matter how obvious the crime," Henderson noted, and Towse nodded, because he well knew that story.

Henderson talked and talked. Towse scribbled notes. Other men in the room smoked their cigars and drank their whiskey, chiming in only when they murmured agreement to what was being said.

He guessed at the spelling of Averell's name—guessing wrong—and thought at one point of asking what the woman's name was, but that didn't seem very important, so he didn't ask.

Finally, Towse spoke, simply saying, "This sounds like self-defense to me—I mean, what were those men supposed to do? Lose all their cattle to rustlers?" At that, all the men in the room spoke at once to encourage this bottom-line thought.

As he rushed back to the *Cheyenne Daily Leader,* Ed Towse was already composing a headline and mentally writing sentences that would sing out a story he knew would go national.

Back at the newspaper office, he was alone except for the boy who came in on Sundays to clean the type. He had all the time he'd need to compose his story for the next edition on Tuesday. This was the story he wanted time to polish.

◇◇◇

Two stories were telegrammed out of Wyoming Territory on Monday night, July 22, 1889. They alerted papers throughout the land to the most explosive story to come out of these parts in a long time. These were the only versions of what happened in the Sweetwater Valley that most people would ever read.

Archy Slack and Eddie Towse did their jobs well.

Their mistakes, their fantasies, and their lies spread over the country like dirty dishwater thrown from the porch.

Slack's front-page story said it all:

DOUBLE LYNCHING

Two Notorious Characters Hanged
For Cattle Stealing.

James Averell and His Partner Ella Watson
Meet Their Fate at the Hands
of Outraged Stock Growers.

The story carried a "Special to the Sun" tag.

Slack made sure readers knew that hanging cattle thieves wasn't so unusual—even if in this case, they'd hanged a woman. He ran another Saturday night lynching story on Page One: "SUMMARY PUNISHMENT; Three Stock Thieves Disposed of in New Mexico; One Shot and Two are Taken from Jail and Hung."

For their five cents that day, readers of the *Cheyenne Sun* learned it had been a very deadly Saturday night in America for "cattle rustlers."

Ed Slack introduced the world to the late James Averell like this—"Averell kept a 'hog' ranch at a point where the Rawlins and Lander stage road crosses the Sweetwater."

He introduced the world to the late Ella Watson like this— "Ella Watson was a prostitute who lived with him and is the person who recently figured in dispatches as Cattle Kate, who held up a faro dealer at Bessemer and robbed him of the bankroll. Both, it is claimed, have born the reputation of being cattle rustlers...."

If Ella had been able to rebut that story, she would have given one of her belly laughs and told everyone: "I have never been to Bessemer in my life. I don't know how to deal faro. I've never robbed anyone of their bankroll, and nobody has ever called me 'Cattle Kate.' Other than that, he spelled my name right."

Her given name was indeed the only item in that sentence that was accurate. Ed Slack had mistaken Ella for someone else, but it was a mistake that would stand. He created "Cattle Kate" to explain away the lynching, and it sounded so good—so Wild West-like—that the legend of Cattle Kate lived on forever.

He wasn't any kinder, or accurate, about Jimmy—"Jim Averell has been keeping a low dive for several years and between the receipts of his bar and his women, and stealing stock, he has accumulated some property. While on one of his drunks not long ago he so abused one of the women that she tried to escape. Averell caught and tore her clothes from her body but she got away and ran from the place. Unable to catch her otherwise he got in a wagon and drove in pursuit. Upon capturing the woman he tied her up in the wagon and left her outside during the whole night. Averell evinced his right and title to be called a dangerous citizen by using his gun on several occasions and in one instance he killed his man.

"Jim Averell was not always thus. Few men in the West had better opportunities. He comes from an excellent family and received instructions in one of the best educational institutions of the east....

"The story of the man's descent into the vile avocation which he pursued when justice overtook him is not a marvelous one. It is the old tale. A few words will suffice. A passion for gambling, for liquor, and for lewd women carried him on to destruction."

Although he'd eat the words later, Slack thought he was doing his pals a big favor when he wrote, "The lynching is the outgrowth of a bitter feeling between big stockmen and those charged with cattle rustling. Every attempt on the part of the stockmen to convict thieves in the courts of that county for years has failed, no matter how strong the evidence might be against them and stockmen have long threatened to take the law into their own hands. This fact, together with the further one that Averell had had more or less trouble with every stockman in that section, probably accounts for the violent death of himself and the woman Watson."

If Jim had been able to rebut those words, he would have had plenty to say. How the reports of rustling were wildly exaggerated by an industry that was being squeezed off the land by new homesteads and barbed wire. How the powerful "stock detectives" were notorious for framing innocent ranchers as rustlers to collect the whopping two hundred fifty-dollar bounty they got for every arrest. How the courts were smart enough not to fall for the hogwash the detectives were serving. Or he could have simply used one of his favorite words, "Bullshit."

◇◇◇

Ed Towse's story in the *Cheyenne Daily Leader* carried the same message of "rangeland justice" for bad people, but he took it even farther into the realm of fantasy. Rural editors throughout the territory decried his stories as nothing but "dime novel literature"—the kind of fanciful fiction that romanticized the disappearing Old West. But those denouncements never got to the papers back East. Nobody east of the Rockies knew Towse made most of it up, so they ate up his very "polished" scenes.

A DOUBLE LYNCHING!

Postmaster Averill and His Wife
Hung for Cattle Stealing
They were Tireless Maverickers
Who Defied the Law
The Man Weakened But the Woman
Cursed to the Last

"A man and woman were lynched near historic Independence Rock on the Sweetwater River in Carbon County Sunday night," he began, getting even the day wrong. "They were Postmaster James Averill and a virago who had been living with him as his wife for some months. Their offense was cattle stealing, and they operated on a large scale, recruiting quite a bunch of young steers from the range of that section...."

Towse didn't know Ella's name—"The female was the equal of any man on the range. Of robust physique she was a daredevil in the saddle, handy with a six-shooter and adept with the lariat and branding iron. Where she came from no one seems to know, but that she was a holy terror all agreed. She rode straddle, always had a vicious bronco for a mount and seemed never to tire of dashing across the range."

He misspelled and slandered Jimmy's name—"Averill, always feared because he was a murderous coward, showed himself a cur. He begged and whined, and protested innocence, even saying the woman did all the stealing."

Towse wasn't content to charge them with stealing forty-one cows, as their lynchers had done. He upped the ante considerably. "Lately it has been rumored that the woman and Averill were engaged in a regular round up of mavericks and would gather several hundred for shipping this fall. The ugly story was partially verified by the stealthy visit of a cowboy to their place Saturday. He reported that their corral held no less than fifty head of newly branded steers, mostly yearlings, with a few nearly grown."

But where Towse got most creative was in reconstructing the scene of their capture and hanging. His version didn't have just six men, but "ten to twenty." His version didn't have an abduction in broad daylight and hours of wandering, but this fantastic scene:

"A few hundred yards from the cabin [the ten to twenty men] dismounted and approached cautiously. This movement was well advised for Averill had murdered two men and would not hesitate to shoot, while the woman was always full of fight.

"Within the little habitation sat the thieving pair before a crude fireplace. The room was clouded with cigarette smoke. A whiskey bottle with two glasses was on the deal table, and firearms were scattered around the interior so as to be within easy reach.

"The leader of the regulators stationed a man with a Winchester at each window and led a rush into the door. The sound of 'Hands up!' sounded above the crash of glass as the rifles were leveled at the strangely assorted pair of thieves. There was a struggle, but the lawless partners were quickly overpowered and their hands bound."

Towse portrayed the death scene with great vigor—"The female was made of sterner stuff. She exhausted a blasphemous vocabulary upon the visitors, who essayed to stop the vile flow by gagging her, but found the task too great. After applying every imaginable opprobrious epithet to the lynchers, she cursed everything and everybody, challenging the Deity to cheat her enemies by striking her dead if he dared. When preparations for the short trip to the scaffold were made she called for her own horse and vaulted to its back from the ground.

"Ropes were hung from the limb of a big cottonwood tree on the south bank of the Sweetwater. Nooses were adjusted to the necks of Averill and his wife and their horses led from under them. The woman died with curses on her foul lips."

Making it sound like he had visited the death scene, Towse wrote, "Yesterday morning the bodies were swayed to and fro by a gentle breeze which wafted the sweet odor of modest prairie flowers across the plain. The faces were discolored and shrunken tongues hung from between the swollen lips, while a film had gathered over the bulging eyes and the unnatural position of the limbs completed the frightful picture."

And then the young editor exonerated the lynchers.

"An inquest may be held over the remains of the thieves, but it is doubtful if any attempt will be made to punish the lynchers. They acted in self protection, feeling that the time to resort to violent measures had arrived."

He ended his story with the most understated sentence he'd ever write. "This is the first hanging of a woman in Wyoming."

Ed Towse might have wanted to leave the impression that other states and territories had already hung their share of rustling women, but he knew that wasn't true. He knew that hundreds had been lynched or legally hung for rustling, and until now, every single one of them had been a man.

◇◇◇

Ed Towse had his feet propped up on his desk and was smiling. He was rereading his story on the hanging when the newsboy finally delivered a copy of the competition. Towse handed over six cents—a nickel for the *Sun* and a penny for the kid—and the front page article on the hanging brought his boots hammering to the floor.

"Dammit," he swore. Slack had the story, too, but hadn't the cattlemen told Ed this was his scoop? That's the way he heard it. Obviously, that's not the way it turned out.

Towse didn't get past the first paragraph when he began swearing like a sailor. "Goddamnit, fuck you, Slacker." His blood pressure kept rising as he read. It incensed him that Ed Slack had out-scooped him on two big points: not only had he actually named the woman, but given her the most delicious title of "Cattle Kate."

Towse scrambled to search through his paper's archives, and it wasn't until he found something breathtaking that he stopped swearing.

The following day, Towse did Ed Slack one better: He declared his inept competition had completely misidentified the woman hanged in Carbon County. Her name wasn't Ella Watson at all. Her name was Kate Maxwell, and you'd be hard-pressed to find a more despicable woman in all of Wyoming Territory.

The July 24 edition of the *Cheyenne Leader* contained Ed Towse's lasting contribution to the legend:

"Cattle Kate Maxwell, the woman lynched with Postmaster Averell, has been a prominent figure since her advent in the Sweetwater country three years ago. She had been a Chicago variety actress…fond of horses, she imported a number of racers…It is said Kate poisoned her husband…a colored boy made away with Kate's diamonds…when the queen and Averell joined issue, Kate was but a poor tramp of the worst kind." Later, Towse would improve upon his title, and call her "Queen of the Sweetwater."

In the thousands of words that Ed Towse would write about the lynching, he never would correct his mistaken identity. And then he'd complicate it further with yet another mistake, reporting the hanged woman was the "Ellen Watson" arrested for drunkenness and prostitution in Cheyenne in June of 1888. There were two things wrong with that: there would have been no such arrest, because prostitution wasn't illegal in the territory. And in June of 1888, the real Ella Watson wasn't even in Wyoming Territory—she was home visiting her family in Kansas.

Her family read the horrible stories coming out of Wyoming in the *Omaha Bee*. Papa Watson wasn't sure, at first, that it was his daughter they were talking about. Sometimes there was no name. Sometimes the name was different. They said all kinds of things he knew weren't true. He had no idea who this Kate Maxwell was. Maybe there was something going on there that he didn't know and his girl was still safe in her cabin. He held on to that myth for a long time, until a letter finally came informing him of the truth he'd known all along. His oldest child had been lynched.

◇◇◇

Out in rural Douglas, W.T.—far from the powerhouse dailies of Cheyenne—reporters and editors at the weekly papers didn't get their information from the stock growers over crystal glasses of whiskey. They got their information the old-fashioned way— from eyewitnesses and people at the scene. And that's how the weekly *Bill Barlow's Budget* learned the truth about the lynching in the Sweetwater Valley.

Bill Barlow was thirty-two years old and a veteran of Wyoming Territory journalism. He worked in Laramie and Rawlins before he and his wife landed in Douglas and created a paper known for its progressive tone and its honest reporting.

Few realized that Bill Barlow was a pen name—the real name of this journalist was Merris C. Barrow—so even his closest friends called him Bill. He'd been a fixture in Douglas since he opened his weekly newspaper in June of 1886, just three months before the railroad came to Converse County.

By the time Bill Barlow read the first stories out of Cheyenne, he knew they all were bunk. It didn't surprise him in the least, because he was used to the kind of fanciful fiction that was often passed off as journalism from the capital.

Ed Towse particularly irked him, and Barlow bellowed about "Ed Towse's mythical compositions." After blasting one Towse story, Barlow wrote: "If there is one true statement therein, I am unable to find it." On another, he complained, "it reads like the third chapter of *Pop-Eyed Sam*."

For himself, he saw what had happened and wasn't afraid to say so: "Of course, the hanging of James Averell and Ella Watson was nothing but murder—and a murder of the coldblooded, premeditated order, also."

◇◇◇

Ed Slack was none too happy when he got a scathing telegram from his friend and fellow newspaperman, Bill Barlow. Barlow laid out the real story and took Slack to task for the lies that had filled the first *Sun* article.

As a booster for the cattlemen, Slack wanted to ignore it. As a newspaper man—"I've got printer's ink in my blood"—he couldn't. But he couldn't eat crow, either. So without comment, on July 25, he printed Barlow's entire telegram. It was the only moment in the entire annals of this story that a Cheyenne newspaper reported the truth.

THE TRUE STORY

Of the Lynching
of James Averell
and Ella Watson

Graphic Details of the Affair
Given by Eye Witnesses

The Coroner's Verdict
Implicates Some Very
Prominent Men

A Sheriff's Posse Arrests
Sun, Bothwell and Others

"The dime novel literature telegraphed from Cheyenne Monday night regarding the lynching of James Averell and Ella Watson Saturday last is the veriest bosh," Barlow had telegraphed. Even readers with a limited vocabulary knew you couldn't get any more false than "veriest bosh."

Barlow told everything, from Buchanan riding for help to the grave that held the bodies.

"Sheriff Watson and party then proceeded to the ranch of Tom Sun, who admitted he was one of the lynchers and readily gave the name of the others.

"Taking Sun into custody the party next proceeded to the ranch of A.J. Bothwell, who also readily admitted that he had assisted at the hanging. He told Buchanan and Healy that both would go over the range in the same way if they did not leave the country, and on being told he was under arrest and would be taken to Rawlins, he warned the sheriff to take a good look at every tree he came to on his way back to Casper for he would be likely to find six or eight more cattle rustlers hanging by the neck. The two men who furnished these facts left the party there and returned to Casper. Watson probably had no trouble in arresting the balance of the lynchers and should have reached Rawlins with them sometime today."

If the true version of what had happened embarrassed Ed Towse or his *Cheyenne Leader*, they never let on. Nor did they ever acknowledge this version of events. When Towse reported the arrests, he wrote it matter-of-factly. "A Rawlins telegraph says that all the men were arrested by Sheriff Hadsell of Carbon County and given a preliminary hearing…Bail was fixed at $5,000 each and surety promptly furnished."

If Towse knew, he didn't care that Wyoming law didn't allow bail for a capital offense, and a lynching definitely qualified as a capital offense. But the lynchers were charged with the lesser crime of "manslaughter," as though the hangings were an accident. Alarm bells should have gone off everywhere with the charge and the bail, even an astronomical $5,000, but they didn't to the *Leader* or the *Sun*. Nor did the papers notice the absurdity of what happened next—what "surety promptly furnished" meant: Each of the accused men wrote a $5,000 check to bail out each other.

Papers in Cheyenne didn't notice, but everyone else did. Papers in Casper and Rawlins and Douglas and Bessemer were outraged, calling it nothing but a "farce," to let accused murderers out on bail in the first place and then allow the accused to bail each other out.

Back in Cheyenne, Ed Slack proved he hadn't had a come-to-Jesus moment by printing the telegram. The very next day, on July 26, he editorialized. "The honest ranch men and stock growers were met only by threats and fresh depredations. Averell constantly threatened death to those who interfered with him and the wretched woman he kept was equally desperate and uncontrollable. Buchanan was known to be one of the gang. Bothwell, Sun, Durbin, and other prominent settlers had received intimations that their lives would be taken. Neither the property or the lives of these men were safe at any time. The worthless wretches who carried on these depredations completely controlled and terrorized the whole region and the conditions of life there became unbearable."

Bill Barlow sat in Douglas shaking his head that the truth didn't matter to Ed Slack, but he spent only a moment wondering why. It was clear the Cheyenne editor had been "shown the light" and was marching to the drummer of the Wyoming Stock Growers Association.

Slack proved it once again when he swallowed his words that the hangings were the result of a land conflict. Boy, was that the wrong message to send. So he just reversed himself: "It was not and is not a conflict between large stockmen and poor ranch men, but a question of life and death between honest men and cut-throat thieves. The heroic treatment must prevail and the gentlemen who have resorted to it are entitled to the support and sympathy of all good citizens."

But the controlling interests of Wyoming Territory had a problem on their hands. An inquest had named some of the most prominent ranchers of the area. It couldn't be allowed to stand. It took pulling just a few strings for someone to declare the first inquest—the one that not only named the men, but brought about their arrest and their release on the farcical bond—wasn't valid. A second inquest was staged.

Ed Slack crowed in the *Cheyenne Daily Sun* on July 27, "The verdict was that the parties came to their death by violence by persons unknown to the jury. This is more like it."

Outside Cheyenne in the territory, one newspaper after another reported a totally different story—all praised Jim Averell as a fine and honest man. "Did I know Jim Averell?" asked Jim Casebeer of the *Casper Weekly Mail*. "Well, I should say I did—knowed him as a pretty decent fellow, too. They talk about Averell stealing cattle. It is all bosh and buncombe. The writer was personally acquainted with him and knows that he expected there would be serious trouble over land affairs in the valley. As to the woman, she was never accused of using rope and branding iron by anyone near her." Casebeer surmised that a "legal hanging" seemed to be in order for those who had taken these lives.

Meanwhile, John Friend of the *Carbon County Journal* in Rawlins gave his testimonial: "Jim Averell was one of the biggest-hearted men in the country. No one ever went hungry from his door and his house was always open for all."

Most of the rural weeklies defended Ella against the rustling, but repeated the prostitution charge, not realizing that was a Cheyenne invention, too.

It didn't take long for the battlefield to be divided. As John Friend wrote in the *Carbon County Journal* on August 3, "The

Cheyenne papers are the only ones in the territory that condone the Sweetwater lynching!"

But none of this haggling ever got beyond the borders of the territory. As far as the rest of the nation—and papers in Europe—were concerned, two bad-ass rustlers had gotten their just rewards at the end of ropes held by honest, struggling cattlemen.

At home, nobody was paying much attention to what was being written elsewhere. They had a real murder case on their hands. And so the focus was on what the justice system would do. The next step was a grand jury hearing to issue a "true bill" that would bring the lynchers to trial.

But as the weeks passed, the writing was on the wall.

Everyone could see justice slipping away. Men who had admitted their guilt when Sheriff Watson came to arrest them, now used the guise of the "second" inquest to deny they had anything to do with it.

The only chance for justice was the eyewitness testimony of Frank Buchanan, Gene Crowder, and John DeCorey, but everyone worried about that.

"That settles it probably," Bill Barlow wrote with sarcasm dripping from the page. "Averell and Watson committed suicide, probably! Buchanan will disappear, probably, and that will be the end of the matter—probably!"

Sadly, Bill Barlow was a good predictor.

Chapter Eighteen

Pa Wept at Her Grave

By the time Thomas Watson arrived in Wyoming Territory a month after the lynching, the roadhouse was no longer home to anyone.

Ella's father had expected to stay there, learning face-to-face from Ralph and John and Gene every detail about her final hours.

He expected to slap Ralph on the back in gratitude.

He expected to praise John for being so brave.

He thought he might hug Gene. Mrs. Watson said that if he thought it was right, he should bring Gene home to them and they'd continue raising the boy. After all, he was the closest to a child that Ella ever had. And it was obvious she'd loved him.

He expected to shake hands with Frank Buchanan and thank him for doing all he could to save his daughter.

The Watson family learned about the boys from the letter Ella had been writing the whole month of July—the one she never got a chance to send. But thankfully, they'd finally gotten it. They almost didn't. That letter had told them about the real life being lived out here—one you'd never recognize if you read the stories coming out of the territory.

Once they got the letter, Tom Watson knew he had to come.

He arrived in Rawlins on the Union Pacific Railroad the

afternoon of August 26, 1889. He immediately went to the law office of George W. Durant.

"Mr. Watson, I'm so pleased to finally meet you," the tall attorney said as he did a two-handed shake in greeting. "I am so sorry for your loss. How was your trip?"

"Fine," Mr. Watson said, managing a weak smile.

George Durant was just what Tom Watson had imagined about the man who was Carbon County's official coroner and had been named the executor for the estates of James Averell and Ella Watson. His hair was neatly trimmed, his spectacles were perched on his nose, and his suit was well tailored. Right away, he seemed a nice man, and Tom Watson would never be dissuaded of that thought.

"I'm sorry it was so hard to find you," Durant began, as Watson settled into a leather arm chair on the client's side of the desk. "Nobody seemed to know who to contact."

"You'd think the sheriff would have figured that out," Watson said, and Durant agreed that would have been the decent thing to do. But if the sheriff had tried, he'd failed miserably.

It was Tom Watson himself, with his daughter Annie's help, who made the first contact. Annie read her family the horrifying stories from Cheyenne reprinted in the *Omaha Bee*. Surely, the woman described in the stories wasn't their Ella. Surely, there was some terrible mistake. When no word came, Annie wrote a letter seeking information, sending it to: "Post Office, Sweetwater, Wyoming."

What they didn't know, is that the letter was sent to one of Ella's killers. To add insult to injury, A.J. Bothwell inherited the postmaster job after Jimmy was lynched.

He'd come by the roadhouse a couple times a week to check on the mail and check on Ralph Cole, who was still living there. Ralph was scared of the man, but he felt an obligation to handle his uncle's estate, and that took some time, and so he was forced to coexist with Jimmy's killer.

The only moment he was glad for this arrangement was the day a letter arrived from the "Watson Family, Kansas." Ralph grabbed the letter and stuffed it in his pocket—he knew if Both-well saw it, it would never see the light of day. Ralph went to Jimmy's house, shut the door, and sat down to read the words from Ella's people. He immediately began a lengthy letter in return. He told the family not to believe the lies coming out of Cheyenne. He told how John had tried so bravely to get help. He told how Buchanan had tried with all his might to stop the hanging. He told of the burial and the arrests. He filled the family in on Bothwell and his new postmaster job. And he directed them to George Durant as the man officially in charge.

Ralph urged someone from the family to come to W.T. and said he would, of course, want to meet with them and tell them anything he could. "Of course, you'll stay here at the roadhouse. Uncle Jimmy has a very comfortable home and you are welcome here," he wrote.

"And I am enclosing a letter that Ella was writing to you, but never got a chance to send. I saw her many times, when she had a spare moment, writing on this letter. She often joked that she needed to make it a really good letter because she'd been so tardy in writing." He sent the picture of Ella on Goldie and a copy of the newspaper article with Jimmy's letter to the editor. "She wanted you to have all this, and I'm so sorry it has to come like this."

Annie read the letter slowly because she couldn't stop crying. Here was her real sister, with so many hopes and so many dreams. Here was the girl the whole family knew, filled with joy and a good sense of humor and so proud of her secret husband. By the time she finished the letter, everyone knew that the newspaper stories were all lies.

Ma Watson tucked the letter in the family Bible, expecting to keep it the rest of her life.

◇◇◇

"I'm just glad that nice Cole boy wrote to us," Tom Watson began, and noticed that George Durant's color seemed to fade before his eyes. "He says we can stay at the roadhouse in Jim's house…" and he couldn't continue because Durant was now clearly in distress.

"I'm so sorry to have to tell you this," Durant began. "You've already been through so much. But I'm afraid I have more bad news. We just got word that Ralph Cole died two days ago."

Tom Watson sucked in his breath, feeling anguish for a boy he'd never met. "How much more…" he said, before he put his head in his hands.

"I know, I know," Durant soothed. "The sheriff went out there today. There's fear that he was poisoned because he was an eye-witness…" and then Durant thought he ought to stop because this was an awful lot of heartbreak for a man already grieving.

"They think the boy was killed?" Watson shrieked in disbelief. "Because of my Ellen?"

"We don't know," Durant back stepped. "There's just rumors. The boy got sick and went to his neighbors—those editors at that newspaper in the phony town Bothwell is promoting. They took care of him for several days and he just got sicker and sicker and then he died. I'm told Bob Conner—he's one of the lynch-ers—was there a few days ago. Feelings are so raw here, that I think people jumped to conclusions. So we shouldn't do the same thing," he ended, hoping that final message came through.

"But they wouldn't poison him, would they?" Watson asked, incredulous at the thought.

"No, I don't think so," Durant lied.

"What about the other boys?" Watson anxiously asked. "Her last letter home said she was raisin' a boy named Gene and had a John working for her." Durant was already shaking his head before the sentence ended.

"They've both disappeared," he said, and let the sentence hang there.

"They're just boys," Watson said in a shocked voice. "What do you mean, they disappeared?" Durant explained that nobody knew where the two younger boys had gone, but within seventy-two hours of the lynching, they were nowhere to be found.

"People here think they were just afraid and ran away. Everyone hopes they're safe somewhere," Durant reported. He silently prayed nobody would share with Mr. Watson the rumor that eleven-year-old Gene had been fed to Bothwell's wolves. Durant himself didn't believe it, but then, things were so strange these days in these parts that he could understand such a ghastly rumor.

And he decided he'd better complete the lineup because Mr. Watson had a right to know everything: "And the man who tried to save your daughter, Frank Buchanan. He's on the run. He's the one who actually saw the lynching, and they'll need him to testify against the murderers, so folks are pretty concerned that he stay safe."

"Of course, without him…" Watson responded, and both men nodded as they imagined the murder charges falling apart. But neither man was ready to face that horrible possibility, so they agreed Buchanan was probably hiding out to keep himself out of harm's way. That just *had* to be it. There had to be *somebody* left to sit in a courtroom and identify the men who killed Ella and Jim.

In his mind's eye, Pa Watson had been inside that courtroom, watching Frank Buchanan point his finger, one after another, at each of the six lynchers. Even with this news, he refused to let that image fade.

"So there's nobody to tell me about that day," Watson concluded, and Durant finally had something positive to share: "No, but there are people in town who are anxious to talk with you. They want you to know what they knew of Ella." Watson finally had hope that there would be some comfort in this trip.

That night, a small group gathered at the Rawlins City Hall and one of the ladies brought cookies and a pitcher of lemonade. Everyone warmly greeted Tom Watson and as they sat in a makeshift circle on wooden chairs, they told nice stories about Ella and Jim and offered their sympathy.

The next day, Tom Watson took George Durant up on a generous offer. As Tom talked, Durant's male secretary wrote down the words so the family back home could know what was happening. He started the letter by reporting on the city hall gathering: "The chairman of the meeting said that the hanging of Ella Watson and James Averell was one of the most cold-blooded murders on record, and that something must be done to prevent such crimes. A fund was started to bring those criminals to justice, and there was $75 raised and $100 subscribed that evening."

Tom Watson had been very moved by the generosity and loving words of the group, and thanked them profusely—hiding the watering eyes that almost gave him away. He didn't add that to his missive, but asked the secretary to keep the letter so he could add more later.

Then he and Durant climbed aboard the mail stage to Sand Creek, riding several hours to get as close to the ranch house as the stage went. Durant hired a buggy to take them the last twenty miles and on the way, Durant had some sage advice: "I think outside Rawlins, you should travel incognito," he said, and Watson had already been in W.T. long enough to see the wisdom.

They arrived at the roadhouse as the sun was thinking of setting, finding two men on the property. One was picking through a stack of old wood. The other was picking the ripe tomatoes from Jimmy's garden. Whatever suspicions Watson had, disappeared when the men immediately greeted Durant warmly. "These men are friends," Durant whispered, and Watson could see they were and revealed himself.

"Oh, Mr. Watson, this was just terrible," said J.S. Sapp, who had been Bothwell's foreman. But Sapp had vigorously confronted his boss on the hanging and of course, Bothwell wouldn't stand for that and fired him on the spot.

"He fired me before I could quit," Sapp declared. "I couldn't work for that man after what he did."

Watson clasped his hands in gratitude and said it was a brave man who stood up for what was right. "Tell that to my missus and three kids," Sapp joked. "They're wondering where the next paycheck is coming from." The men laughed and Durant offered that Sapp was such a seasoned ranch foreman, he wouldn't have trouble finding work on another ranch. Nobody then knew that Bothwell would blackball Sapp so nobody in the Sweetwater Valley would hire him. He ended up moving his family to Rawlins, where the best he could get was odd jobs.

The other man was Joe Sharp, who had worked the roundup that ended the day of the lynching. "Mr. Watson, I am so sorry for you and your family," he said in a kind voice. "I couldn't believe it when I first heard it. I still find it hard to believe."

"How did you first hear?" Watson asked, and Sharp answered: "It was that boy Ella was raising."

Then he told how brave little Gene Crowder had run into Bothwell's pasture on Monday morning, where cowboys were getting their orders for the day, and sobbed out the story about the hanging and that the posse from Casper had just arrived. He named all six men who'd been involved. "I was saddled up right next to Al Bothwell and I turned to him and said 'Why, you didn't hang them, did you Bothwell?' and he never said a word. He just looked at the ground and cowboys all around me were grumbling and swearing and Bothwell reined his horse around and just rode off. We tried to comfort the boy, but he was really broken up. He bolted and ran back toward the ranch house."

"What happened to the boy?" Watson asked, hoping someone out here would know more than the people in town. Sharp took a secret look at Durant, as if asking for permission to tell the rumor, but Durant was shaking his head in rebuttal, and so Joe Sharp gave the same story everyone would tell Tom Watson: "He just disappeared. Nobody knows what happened to him."

Sharp was anxious to change the subject. "Mr. Watson, do you want to see your daughter's grave?"

He gently led the man to the place where Ella and Jim shared a common grave. Watson stood there silently for a long time, his hat in his hand, his head bowed. "I wish my little girl had listened to her mother," he finally said. "She told her not to leave home. If she had listened to her mother, she wouldn't be buried here today."

And then Tom Watson started to sob uncontrollably. Sharp wept his own tears as he watched the man and thought, "His poor little girl, his firstborn baby, lay murdered under all that soft, fresh dirt."

From the garden and the larder, there was enough to pull together a supper, and Watson was surprised to find he slept through the night. The next day, Durant drove him over to Ella's claim. He walked into her log cabin and ran his hands over her few belongings.

He found the eagle feathers and a nice saddle blanket. He found the dress she was sewing. He saw that she'd already started canning. He thought it looked like a nice home, but he was glad Ma wasn't here to see any of it.

In the corral, Goldie was eating hay—the other ponies were gone and nobody seemed to know where. He had brought Jim's western saddle along—he remembered that Ella didn't yet have one. He saddled up the old horse for a ride to find the place his daughter died. He had gotten a good description of the site from Sapp, and it didn't take long before he found the place.

A piece of rope was lying on the ground, and he could see how the limb had been rubbed clean from the lariat's scrapping. He sat there on Goldie for a very long time, and he never knew before that moment how broken a man's heart could be.

But Pa Watson wasn't in W.T. just to cry; he was here to settle Ella's estate and he acted as Durant's assistant at the auction on August 31.

Durant was an efficient and diligent executor for the estates. He had already held a chattel mortgage auction in Rawlins to settle Jim's big debts—and it turned out, the man who was supposed to be such a large-scale rustler was over his head in debt. On the courthouse steps in town—the courthouse that Durbin had helped build with his generosity—he sold off Jim's major property to repay $430.90 to Rawlins' leading merchant, J.W. Hugus and $323.80 to saloonkeeper J.C. Dyer. The debts were covered by selling the roadhouse site, the Bain Wagon, a breaking plow, furniture, two bedsteads, and one thousand pounds of oats. Joe Sharp bought Jim's Regulator clock, which forever would hang in his family's home.

Now auctions were scheduled at Ella's homestead and the roadhouse to sell off everything else. A dozen folks showed up to the auction and only a few realized who Tom Watson was.

Among the bidders who didn't know were the two editors of the *Sweetwater Chief*.

Durant's secretary was on hand to write out the sale. His notes showed that Fetz bought her "bed stead" for $3.50 and her wool mattress for $2.00, while Speer spent $3.00 for six chairs, 50 cents for a clock, 25 cents for a rug, and $21.50 for a cookstove. There also were some cows and a horse for sale, as well as furniture. In all, Ella's belongings brought $241.10.

Then they moved up to the roadhouse to sell off Jim's last things, making another $174.50.

From those sales, Durant paid the taxes: $6.76 for Ella; $18.68 for Jim. After he took out his fees and some court costs, he gave Tom Watson just over a hundred dollars as Ella's next of kin. Pa Watson gave Durant half of it back to go into the legal defense fund.

The only things that weren't for sale were the few things Thomas Watson took home with him—Ella's sewing machine, one breast pin and earrings, two finger rings, one chain, one pair of bracelets. He thought of taking home the few documents he found—her claim certificate, the application for citizenship, the marriage application—but decided against it.

"Do you need these?" he asked Durant. The attorney saw no need for them, so Pa Watson tore them up and threw them away.

He didn't recognize the pretty ivory hair comb inlaid with mother of pearl, so he let it go at the auction. He was surprised when a big German man bid the item up to twenty cents and took the ribbing of his neighbors: "Rudolph, isn't that a little fancy for your bald head," one yelled. He blushed a little as he took the joke. "You know this is for my Willetta," he said through his grin, and everyone agreed it would look nice on his missus.

Pa Watson came away from his visit and the auction with a special message for his family. "Our Ellen lived around people who killed her, but she lived around right decent folks, too."

He took home to his family the stories people told about what really happened, why Ella really died. He took home kind remembrances of his first child.

"See!" Annie insisted. "Those people wouldn't be so generous and donate to a defense fund if she was the bad woman they say."

Tom Watson agreed. The thought gave Frances Watson some comfort.

That made Pa Watson's pronouncement all the more startling.

"We're never going to speak of Ellen again," he said in his most authoritative voice. "I want you to burn all her letters, Mother. And nobody in this family will ever discuss this again. I never want to hear another word about Wyoming or lynching or Ellen. She's gone and that's the end of it."

His children were befuddled. "But Pa, you know those men murdered her and she wasn't guilty of anything," Franny argued.

"Please Pa, you know she was a good girl," Andrew said with certainty.

"Papa, you can't believe she'd ever do those things," Mary wailed.

"You can't erase Ellen, Pa. You can't expect us to forget her." John was beside himself.

But Pa Watson held firm. "Not one more word," he scolded, and stomped out of the house.

The only one who ever knew the reason was Ma Watson, who heard the chilling story in their bed late at night.

"He said they'd kill us all if we ever made a fuss," Pa Watson told her, and it was clear from his tone that the confrontation had been terrifying. "This big stock detective cornered me one day. He told me to go home and forget I ever had a homesteading daughter in Wyoming Territory. If I didn't, he said I'd be sorry. He said there was nowhere in the country our family could hide. He said they'd kill one child after another and make us watch. I believe him, Mother. I believe them."

At that moment, Ma Watson felt the first real terror of her life. She agreed that threatening her living family with questions about her dead daughter was too dangerous. So she upheld her husband's secret and seconded his demand that Ella be forgotten. If nobody talked about her, if nobody asked questions, then they'd be safe.

To prove her support, Ma Watson burned the last letter that had been so dear. But she hid the picture that had come with it.

She had only two images of the first child she'd brought into the world—the wedding picture with Pickell that Ella thought had been torn up, and the picture of Ella on Goldie that everyone thought had been burned.

Chapter Nineteen

A Man with Guts

George Durant felt sickly the September day he took Thomas Watson to the railroad station for his return to Kansas.

The lawyer had developed a real liking for this broken man whose daughter had been murdered and then slandered to cover it up. He was moved by the generous donation to the legal fund—he knew the man could have well used that money, and that made the gift all the more precious. He was so grateful the people of Rawlins had stepped up to share the truth and give the father some comfort. But all that can wear on a man, and Durant was feeling sickly.

That afternoon, instead of going back to the office he shared with George Smith, he went home and slumped into his armchair. He couldn't get the last few days out of his mind. Remembering Ella's pitiful belongings made him feel even more sickly.

George Durant had looked over the auction items and seen Ella Watson for exactly what she was—a homesteader and homemaker who had a new dress underway and an ordinary cabin. One table and six chairs. One lamp. A washbowl and pitcher. Three flat irons. A mismatched set of dishes. Fifteen chickens. Eight head of cattle.

He couldn't think of the auction without thinking of John Fales.

Fales spent most of the auction wiping his dripping nose on his sleeve, pretending it was a cold. Fales bought the dress that was nearly done, saying his Ma would finish it. But it was after the bidding, when he took Durant aside, that he branded himself on the man's mind forever.

Fales handed the attorney the LU branding iron. "I used this to brand forty-one of Ella's cattle," he said, with the sound of truth in his voice. "Bothwell and Durbin stole 'em. Ran them out of here after the lynching and put them on a train to Cheyenne the next day. I hear they rebranded them along the way. You want to know the real rustlers here? It's Bothwell and Durbin. Those were Ella's cattle. She never rustled. I was with her when she bought them. Saw her sign the receipt. Those cows were in this corral all winter and Bothwell could see them from his front porch. You're the man in charge of her estate now. What you gonna do about that?"

Durant couldn't get Fales' scraggly face out of his mind. He couldn't stop the man's words from replaying in his head. He sat there in his armchair, so saddened by all that had happened, and knew exactly why he was feeling sickly. By the end of that afternoon, George Durant determined not to let his conscience make him sick anymore.

He couldn't let all this go as though the truth didn't count. As though Ella Watson never counted.

But taking on Bothwell and Durbin? Two men still waiting to face the grand jury over the lynching?

How do you challenge the most powerful men in the Sweet-water Valley? Local icons? Territory leaders? Cattlemen with credentials?

How do you turn around and tell the world the very cattle they claimed were rustled legally belonged to Ella Watson? How do you announce the real rustlers in this story were these prominent men? How do you declare any alibi of rangeland justice was a bold-faced lie?

How do you buck the tide and the power of the Stock Growers Association?

George Durant sat there all afternoon, as the sun went down and a lamp was needed. By the end of the day, when his growling stomach finally told him it was past dinnertime, he didn't feel sickly anymore.

He made the most important decision of his life. He wouldn't ignore his conscience anymore.

He got up and selected leftovers from the icebox, and as he sat at the kitchen table, he mapped out one of the most courageous actions any attorney in Wyoming Territory would ever take.

On September 12, 1889, George Durant filed suit on behalf of Ellen L. Watson against A.J. Bothwell and John Durbin. He charged the prominent men "forcefully took possession" of forty-one head of cattle that were legally branded with her LU brand. He contended they drove the cattle from her corral and rebranded them—all against the laws of the Territory of Wyoming. The suit demanded repayment of $1,100. The total included $600 to cover the cost of the cattle, $250 for damages for the rebranding, and $250 for costs.

The lawsuit raised an uproar. The *Carbon County Journal* in Rawlins announced the suit with fanfare, driving home the central point: "It will be remembered that at the time of the lynching there were forty-one head of cattle in the Watson woman's corral. The coroner claims that he ought to have been allowed to take charge of these, but they were driven away by Bothwell and Durbin and sold as mavericks in this city in the name of the Wyoming Stock Growers Association and subsequently shipped to Cheyenne. It is to recover these cattle, which bear Ella Watson's brand, that the suit has been brought."

All over W.T., people shook their heads. "George Durant is either the bravest man in the territory or the most foolish," people said.

"He's got to have proof that those were her cows," everyone agreed.

"She had a legal brand?" many said in astonishment—wondering how she ever got that past the association.

Who would dare make such a charge without physical proof?

Proving she had a legal brand was easy. He had the actual branding iron from Fales, and it was in the Carbon County Courthouse that he found the records that she'd duly recorded her LU brand. He could foresee the day in a courtroom when he'd hold that branding iron over his head and get justice for Ella Watson.

But proving she bought the cattle was something else. He had Fales as an eyewitness to the purchase and found another man to back him up. But where was that dirty piece of paper that attested to the sale?

"I searched her cabin to find it right after the lynching," Fales told him. "Damn, I couldn't find it."

Durant knew Mr. Watson hadn't found it among the other documents she kept at home. He thought it was strange such an important piece of paper would go missing, but this one had.

Attorney Durant had no idea Ella herself had offered the proof to her lynchers, begging them to take her to Rawlins so she could show them the bill of sale in her safe deposit box at the bank. It never occurred to him that a woman with such a paltry estate—who kept important documents in her cabin—would also have a safe deposit box. So he never went looking for one.

But there were six others in the Sweetwater Valley who well remembered her constant pleas to go get the proof. And every single one of them was convinced she hadn't been bluffing. Every single one feared Durant had discovered the bill of sale in a safe deposit box at the bank in Rawlins.

Most convinced of all were the two men named in the suit. A.J. Bothwell and John Durbin both made frantic trips to the bank when they learned of the suit. That was the second thing they both did. The first thing was swear and pace like caged tigers.

Both inquired about a safe deposit box under the name of Ellen or Ella Watson. Although both were large depositors at this very bank, they were told that such items were confidential and couldn't be disclosed.

"Maybe there isn't a safe deposit box at all," Durbin offered, as a helpful suggestion to the bank president he'd known for years. "I have one, but I also have more than $50,000 in deposits here. It makes sense for me. It didn't much sense for a woman like her, who had so little."

"Nobody would ever know if there was a box or not, being as how these things are confidential," Bothwell offered as his own solution. "And I appreciate how careful you are about that. I know my $60,000 in deposits are safe in a bank with integrity like yours."

The banker—how many steaks had he eaten at Bothwell's? How much of Durbin's whiskey had he swilled?—thanked his wealthy depositors and told them not to worry themselves.

But worry they did. The stock growers gave them the best attorneys in the territory to fight the suit, and John W. Lacey proved himself a pit bull. His firm was already gearing up for the upcoming grand jury hearing on the lynching charges, but now he had to deal with this outrageous suit. What did that Durant guy think he was doing? Well, he'd show him.

It took months before he even got around to replying that the suit was too ridiculous to even answer. He simply refused a response.

The court said, no, you need to respond.

He took his own sweet time again. Then again said, no, this was stupid and he wouldn't dignify it with an answer.

Courts didn't work with any speed in those days—never would. It wasn't until March of 1891—seventeen months after the suit was filed—that the court gave Lacey a deadline, demanding an answer.

He now filed a flat denial of everything, claiming the suit was nothing but a "false clamor."

By then, George Durant was gone. After waiting a year to get a reply to his suit, an "opportunity in Salt Lake City" prompted him to move. He left town in January, 1891. Most knew his days in Rawlins were numbered anyway. Durant left the case in the hands of his associate, George Smith. He gave Smith twenty-five dollars to cover his legal fees to see the suit through.

"Good luck with this," he told his partner. They both knew this was a real long shot. But Smith agreed it was worth the effort to at least get some stab at justice.

On May 13, 1891, the court made its first decision in the case of *Ella Watson vs. A.J. Bothwell and John Durbin*. It granted Lacey's request to continue the case until the next term.

On October 12, 1891, the court again continued the case, thanks to Mr. Lacey.

On May 11, 1892, Lacey needed yet another delay and the court obliged.

Lacy was making good on his promise to his clients that they would never have to worry about a thing, because he could delay this suit forever.

On May 15, 1893, it was George Smith requesting a continuance.

Finally, on October 24, 1893, Smith gave up. He asked the court to dismiss the case.

It was dismissed without prejudice, meaning it could be refiled again later.

The court charged George Smith $12.80 to cover court costs.

Ella had already been in her grave fifty-one months by then.

And the wheels of justice had long ago fallen off.

◇◇◇

The writing was on the wall hours after Ella died.

Frank Buchanan didn't need telling twice that he was in the rifle sights of some vicious men, and if he'd had his way, he'd have rode out with the posse to safety. But what's a man to do, with little Gene so distraught, he wet the bed and wouldn't stop crying. Or with John pumping himself up like he was going to single-handedly avenge Ella and Jim. Or with Ralph destroyed at the loss of his uncle and haunted by his duty—"Oh, God, how am I going to tell Mother?"

Frank thought Fales would step up, but John Fales was reduced to a weeping old lady over this—Frank had never realized how close the handyman got to the couple. How much he loved them.

So for the first day after the posse left—after they'd buried his friends, after he'd told all at the inquest held over the grave, after he'd named names—Frank Buchanan did what he always did when he had some thinking to do. He sat on the porch and he whittled.

In all the Sweetwater Valley, there was hardly a better whittler. Frank could do magic with a piece of wood and the pocketknife he always carried, and he decided today would be a proper day to do his magic and make a cross for the grave. So he let the boys grieve—what could he possibly say to ease their pain?—and he started whittling.

The events of Saturday night replayed in his mind so vividly, it was like watching one scene after another all over again. He would never know of movies or television, but if he had, he'd have recognized them from his mind's movie of the hangings. Jim had struggled with more strength than he thought the man possessed, and Ella had refused to go easily. Did he remember it or was he imagining that her last words were a prayer? Some members of the posse had tried to console him, telling him he'd done all he could, but in his mind, if he'd done all he could, Ella and Jim would still be here, so there was no comfort.

Frank knew someday he'd forget some of the details of the lynching—the sounds and smells and how the breeze was so gentle. But he knew he'd never forget his final look at Ella as she hung from that rope. He'd never forget the taste of the vomit.

It wasn't until he nicked his finger that Frank Buchanan realized he had not whittled the wood into a cross, but had whittled it into nothing but a heap of shavings. That was when he understood just how devastated he was. And how scared.

He had almost convinced himself to walk into the roadhouse and tell the boys they were on their own when John Fales rode up and planted himself on the porch.

"You did all you could," Fales began in a strong voice, proving he had regained his composure. "All you could. More than most men would have done. More. I still can't believe they hanged them. Just can't believe it." There was a long silence as the men shared their grief and disbelief.

Then John Fales voiced the final verdict: "You know, it's your eyewitness account that's gonna convict those men. And they'll call the boys to back you up on who was there. Your lives ain't worth a plugged nickel in these parts. You gotta get out of here."

Buchanan left within the hour. Gene and John weren't far behind.

◇◇◇

There are many stories about what happened to Frank Buchanan in the three months before the grand jury convened to hear the case against the six lynchers. Some say he went to Cheyenne, but most think that would have been foolhardy—into the lion's den! Some say he took a train out of town, although he probably couldn't afford the fare. Some say he was paid off by the cattlemen and took his money to someplace more conducive to his health.

But most think he was murdered. Most think it was George Henderson who put a bullet in his back. Most think it was Bothwell's cowboys who buried him. Of course, what most think and what happened isn't always accurate. But this time, it probably is. That's what everyone said several years later when bones were found. The skeleton was about the right height for Frank. A bright bandanna around the neck—especially the way it was knotted—convinced everyone that good man had long ago gone to his last reward. And not because he wanted to.

"If he'd have lived, Frank Buchanan would have been inside that grand jury hearing and he would have named names," people in Rawlins long said.

"I can see him pointing to those men one at a time and calling out their names."

"You can't be so brave to try and stop a hanging and then run away."

"No sire, that's the move of a coward, and Frank Buchanan was no coward."

"When he didn't show up, I knew he was dead."

◇◇◇

The grand jury convened on October 14, 1889 in the case of *Territory of Wyoming vs. A.J. Bothwell, John Durbin, Robert Galbraith, Robert Conner, Tom Sun and Ernie McLean.* Judge Samuel T. Corn presided.

The prosecution was unable to produce a single witness to testify against the men.

Frank Buchanan wasn't the only one unavailable to testify.

Little Gene Crowder couldn't tell what he knew, either. He had disappeared, too, and except for the rumors about Bothwell's wolves, nobody had any idea what happened to him.

Everybody knew what had happened to Ralph Cole. Jim's nephew had mysteriously died under the care of the newspapermen in Bothwell's fake town. He was now buried in one of Bothwell's pastures. Suspicions that he'd been poisoned ran so high, his stomach was sent for testing. Nobody ever named the laboratory it supposedly went to. Everyone was told there was no sign of poison and that was the end of it.

John DeCovey ran all the way to Colorado, where he wrote back a long and passionate letter detailing what he knew about the hanging. But there was no sense calling him back for the grand jury hearing because he hadn't seen the lynching itself, only the abduction.

The judge had no choice. He set the six men free for lack of evidence.

In Rawlins and throughout rural W.T., the outrage that justice had been cheated was overwhelming.

In Cheyenne, the boys thought the outcome was just fine.

Chapter Twenty

And in the End

Everyone knew what happened to Ella Watson and Jim Averell. Everyone knew how Ralph Cole ended up. Everyone suspected the end of Frank Buchanan and the horrifying rumors of how little Gene's life was devoured.

But the years passed and people moved away or moved on, and the final stories of the lynchers got lost. Until now.

**Ernie McLean caught the last train out of Rawlins the night after the lynching. By then, his conscience had gotten the better of him and he'd blabbed the whole lynching story to a neighbor. John Durbin bought him the twenty-nine-dollar train ticket and ranch records show Durbin paid Ernie two hundred forty dollars in "wages." The man who pushed Ella off the rock was never heard from again.

**Robert Galbraith was re-elected to the Wyoming Territorial Legislature in November of 1889—less than four months after the lynching. He went from the lower house to the upper house that is now called the Senate. But he received so many threats about the lynching, he eventually left Wyoming and settled in Arkansas, where he became a prominent banker. He died in 1939 at the age of ninety-five.

**Robert Conner left Wyoming soon after the lynching, making millions on the sale of his ranch, and moved back to Pennsylvania. He died in 1921 at the age of seventy-two.

**John Durbin faced "relentless public humiliation" after the lynching and sold his holdings two years later, moving to Denver. He died in 1907 at the age of sixty-four.

**A.J. Bothwell continued ranching in the Sweetwater Valley for the next twenty-seven years, taking over Ella's and Jim's land claims, buildings, and frontage on Horse Creek. He remained on the executive committee of the Wyoming Stock Growers Association until 1902. He finally sold his holdings in 1916 and moved to Los Angeles, where he died in 1928 at the age of seventy-three. Those who knew him in his later years say he never voiced a bit of remorse over the hanging of Ella Watson and Jim Averell.

**Tom Sun's family still ranches in the Sweetwater Valley. A public mural in Rawlins exonerates Sun for his part in the lynching, saying "Tom Sun was against the affair." He died in 1909 in Denver at the age of sixty-five.

**Thirty-three months after the lynching of Ella Watson and James Averell, on April 9, 1892, fifty Wyoming cattlemen and Texas hired guns invaded Johnson County to free it of "rustlers," in one of the most outrageous events of the West—The Johnson County War. Some believe the cattlemen were emboldened because everyone got away with the murders of Ella and Jim.

**The legend of Cattle Kate as a rustler and a whore lives on to this day in dozens of magazine articles, books, movies, and websites. Zane Grey's version was titled *Maverick Queen*.

**On July 20, 1989, on the hundredth anniversary of the lynching, a group of Ellen Watson's nieces and nephews gathered in the Sweetwater Valley. She and Jim's grave now lay under the new Pathfinder Reservoir. A marker was erected in the vicinity. It reads: "These innocent homesteaders were hanged by cattle ranchers for their land and water rights."

Part Three

The Facts of the Matter

Author's Note

I'm afraid I was snookered about "Cattle Kate" just like every-body else. My ignorance lasted a few years. It took nearly a century for history to get wise.

I got serious about western history when I went to work for *True West* magazine in 2002, and two things soon became obvi-ous. First, women helped settle the Wild West, but you could read a hundred history books and never know it. And secondly, even if you read all those books, you'd be forgiven if you con-cluded the *only* women in the West were whores or "soiled doves."

While popular western history tells us all about the bandits and bad boys, the gunfighters and goons, we know almost noth-ing about the women who held it all together with grit and spit. They say history is written by the victors, and it was clear men thought they alone won the West. It doesn't take much digging to discover they're wrong. So I knew that women had never gotten their due.

True West Editor Bob Boze Bell—a real western man who isn't afraid of real western women—suggested I create a new series called Women of the West. Starting in January of 2004, I spent five years writing a monthly column that profiled courageous and outrageous women.

"Cattle Kate" wasn't on my original list of women to explore. I had the likes of Esther Hobart Morris and Sarah Winnemucca and Donaldina Cameron and Ann Eliza Young and Biddy Mason and Sharlot Hall. These are women whose names might not be familiar, but that makes my point. Each one of them has a fabulous story to tell. "Kate" just played into the stereotype of "bad, wanton women" that history had shoved down our throats, and that's not the kind of woman I was writing about.

But then I read an award-winning story by Lori Van Pelt in 2004 that questioned the official take on Cattle Kate—it didn't exonerate her, but raised some real questions. Then I was set on my heels by the assessment of Wyoming historian and State Librarian Agnes Wright Spring that the lynching of Cattle Kate was "the most revolting crime in the entire annals of the West."

So Kate wasn't a worthless footnote in history, but the victim of a "revolting crime"—so revolting that in some minds, it takes first place in a century of revolting crimes. The 2005 story I wrote for *True West* was headlined: "So-called Cattle Kate Rises from Rubbish: Evidence points toward Ella Watson's innocence."

I soon found I was only the latest to come to this horrifying story.

George W. Hufsmith spent twenty years digging into the truth for his 1993 book, *The Wyoming Lynching of Cattle Kate 1889*. Hufsmith wrote, "When I first began probing into the so-called 'Cattle Kate' affair, I had no idea that the whole story was pure fabrication….Not one shred of substantive evidence exists to show that those two settlers were anything but hard-working homesteaders, trying to eke out a living from a primitive and difficult environment."

The same assessment came from Daniel Y. Meschter, who spent twenty-five years pouring over legal documents to give an exhaustive history of the lynching he self-published in 1996 called *Sweetwater Sunset*. As he notes, "The fact is that Ella Watson was never called Cattle Kate or Kate Maxwell or even plain Kate in her own lifetime."

Then there were the words of John Fales, the neighbor and handyman who knew Ella and Jim well. "Neither of them ever stole a cow," he told the Wyoming Historical Society years later.

"And those who say that Ella Watson slept with the cowpunchers, are slandering a good woman's name."

Suspicions leapt when I realized Jim Averell had credentials that couldn't belong to a "pimp." Appointed postmaster for the Sweetwater Post Office by President Grover Cleveland; named a notary public by Wyoming Governor Thomas Moonlight; named a justice of the peace by the Carbon County Board of Commissioners. And only twelve days before he was strung up with Ella, he was an election judge when voters came to his roadhouse to chose delegates to the Wyoming Constitutional Convention—the same roadhouse the Cheyenne press would later brand a "hog ranch" full of prostitutes led by "Cattle Kate."

As Meschter discovered, "Whatever else anybody might have said about Jim Averell later that summer of 1889, he certainly was not the low scoundrel, murderous coward, mavericker, and cur the Cheyenne press chose to call him in defense of his lynchers."

I'm no stranger to knowing history can be dead wrong—my first book was about the infamous "Trunk Murderess" Winnie Ruth Judd and the 1930s murder in Phoenix that shocked the nation. By the time I finished researching that award-winning non-fiction book—and found the living Winnie Ruth Judd for extensive interviews—I knew history had told a false story about her. So when these doubts about Kate started rising, they didn't feel strange to me. They felt very familiar.

I had a long and startling telephone interview with Ella's great-nephew, Daniel Watson Brumbaugh, in October of 2008—me from my home in Phoenix, him at his home in Ohio. Since 1988, he had been traveling and searching to find the truth. He had found plenty of evidence to refute everything history said about his aunt, and plenty more to attest to who she really was. "She was a strong, Scottish woman who went West on her own because she wanted to own her own land, like her grandfather and father," he told me.

During the summer of 2009, I read Philippa Gregory's *The Other Boleyn Girl*—a historical novel that grabbed me from the start and took me back into the days of Henry VIII like no history book ever could. I loved how Gregory defined historical novels—"History is the skeleton; the fiction is the breath."

I was sitting on my mother's beautiful backyard patio in North Dakota reading that book, when I heard the words "I never thought I'd die like that."

I remember holding the book to my chest as I looked around—I'm not kidding, it sounded like someone had said it out loud—and I told the birds feeding in the backyard, "That's what Ella would have said."

This is how I came to write this historical novel that lets Ella Watson largely tell her own story.

By the end, I don't know what outraged me more—the lynching of Ella and Jim or the filthy way it was excused. My only comfort was that everyone who has come to this table has gone away with the same heartache. And the same heartburn.

Historian Hufsmith—the first to actually go back and read *all* the newspaper coverage of the case to get the real picture— ended his groundbreaking book like this:

"The evening shadows regularly and gradually throw a heavy, black veil across the now deserted site of Ella's and Jim's eager and desperate hope for the future. That hope was arrogantly and brutally smashed to pieces on the selfish, iron will of one man's insatiable greed. That terrible immolation sadly cannot be undone, but the twisting contortions of a Cheyenne reporter's pen, which has hoodwinked the whole world for a century, is finally exposed for what it was. May that luckless and guiltless couple find an ultimate vindication at last. *Requiescat in pace!*"

I couldn't have said it better myself.

Endnotes

This historical novel is a work of fiction based on the life, death, and times of Ellen "Ella" Watson. These Endnotes provide a blueprint to the real-life facts, dates, and events.

Chapter One—I Can't Believe This is the End

On Ellen "Ella" Watson: She was a twenty-nine-year-old immigrant homesteader the morning of July 20, 1889, when six of her neighbors—among them the most powerful cattlemen in Wyoming Territory—kidnapped her and her secret husband, James Averell. He was the thirty-eight-year-old postmaster of the Sweetwater Valley and had just been named a justice of the peace. He owned a roadhouse—a general store that also sold liquor—about sixty miles north of Rawlins, on the main road to growing Casper. Ella cooked hot meals for their customers. The vigilantes were A.J. Bothwell, John Durbin, Robert Conner, Cap'n Robert Galbraith, Tom Sun, and Ernie McLean. They claimed Ella and Jim were cattle rustlers.

On homesteading: President Abraham Lincoln signed the Homestead Act in 1862 to encourage development of the western territories. It provided one hundred sixty-acre homesteads for both men, single women, and female "head of households," provided they "proved up" the land by adding a home and improvements and lived on the property at least seven months a year for five years. Two million people sought patents on land through the Homestead Act, which ran from 1862 to 1976. Historians note the cherished Homestead Certificate was usually framed and proudly hung on the cabin wall. But the law was greatly misused. The National Archives reports that of the five hundred million acres dispersed under the Homestead Act, only eighty million went to homesteaders; the rest went to speculators, cattlemen, miners, lumbermen, and industrial interests.

Chapter Two—They First Called Me Franny

On Ellen Watson's family history: According to Ellen Watson's great-nephew, Daniel Watson Brumbaugh, who spent twenty years researching her life:

- Her father, Thomas Watson, was born in Stonehouse, Lanarkshire County, Scotland, on August 6, 1836, the son of John and Sarah Watson; the family immigrated to Canada around 1855; Tom established his own one hundred-acre farm and built a two-story farmhouse.

- Her mother, Frances Close, was born in Dromore, County Down, Ireland, on August 17, 1841. Her parents' names are unknown. The family immigrated to Canada around 1858. Their farm was two farms down from Tom Watson's.

- Their families immigrated to Canada when Queen Victoria opened up the country for homesteaders, giving these families their first opportunity to own land in their own right. In the old country, all land was owned by royalty, and people like the Watson and Close families could only rent land to farm.

- Tom and Frances (called "Franny") were forbidden to wed because his Scottish parents couldn't stand the thought of an Irish daughter-in-law, and her Irish parents couldn't stand the thought of a Scottish son-in-law.

- The couple got pregnant and Ellen Liddy Watson (who inherited the nickname "Franny") was born out of wedlock on July 2, 1860 in Bruce County, Ontario, Canada. Most biographers put her birth a year later, but Brumbaugh says his information comes from her family's Bible notations. Franny and her mother lived with her mother's brother Andrew Close until, on May 15, 1861, her parents married, defying their families.

- Because of pressure and resentment of his family, Thomas Watson moved away from his farm and found another farm on which to raise his growing family. Seventeen children were born to this couple: John in November 1861; James in October 1864; twins who both died in 1865; Andrew in January 1868; Frances in October 1869; Annie in September 1872; twins that did not live in 1873; Mary in May 1874; triplets in 1875—two died in Canada, the other, Elizabeth, died in Kansas in 1878. Three more children were later born in Kansas: Jane in 1880; Thomas Lewis in 1882, and Bertha in 1884. The author assigned specific days to these birth months and years.

- Thomas Watson's father held true to his promise to disinherit him.

On washday: In *Westering Women*, Sandra Myres notes there was no more detested day on the frontier than washing day. First, women had to make the lye soap; then they had to haul water, usually from some distance; and then began the eleven-step "receet" for washing clothes that she quotes with all its original spellings:

"1. bild fire in back yard to het kettle of rain water. 2. set tubs so smoke won't blow in eyes if wind is peart. 3. shave 1 hole cake lie sope in bilin water. 4. sort things. Make 3 piles. I pile white, I pile cullord, I pile work britches and rags. 5. stur flour in cold water to smooth then thin down with bilin water [for starch]. 6. Rub dirty spots on board, scrub hard, then bile. Rub cullord but don't bile just rench and starch. 7. take white things out of kettle with broom stick handel then rench, blew and starch. 8. pore rench water in flower bed. 9. scrub porch with hot sopy water. 10. turn tubs upside down. 11. go put on a cleen dress, smooth hair with side combs, brew cup of tee, set and rest and rock a spell and count blessings."

Chapter Three—I Agree with Pa

On the letter from Kansas: Although the precise wording no longer exists, Brumbaugh notes it was a letter from an old friend who had immigrated to Kansas that led Thomas Watson to move his family there. He established residency on one hundred sixty acres near Lebanon, Kansas, on November 18, 1877, and filed a homestead claim on August 10, 1880.

On Beadle's Dime Novels: These popular novels, printed originally on orange wrapper paper, told fanciful stories about the settling of the Old West.

On the Civil War: The North had a cavalier attitude as the Civil War began in April, 1861, with many thinking it would so quickly overpower the South that the war would be over by Christmas. That was just one of the delusions in the War Between the States, or the Civil War, or the War of Northern Aggression, or the Lost Cause. History tells us that in Washington, women in silk dresses and men in fancy shirts rode out in buggies with picnic baskets to watch the battles. On both sides, it wasn't so much an army as a gathering of young boys—always dirty, certainly exhausted, usually hungry, forever scared. It wasn't so much a war as a slaughter. The casualties became grotesque. Six hundred thousand dead. Over ten thousand battles. It remains, all these years later, America's deadliest war. The Watson family claims Tom Watson joined his Canadian neighbors and signed up with Company 1, 96th New York State Volunteers, but records to confirm that have never been found.

On Lincoln's assassination: President Abraham Lincoln was shot while attending a play at the Ford Theater the night of April 14,

1865. He died the next day. His assassin, John Wilkes Booth, was a Confederate sympathizer, angry that the South had lost the war. Among those punished for his murder was board house owner Mary Surrat, who was hanged on July 7, 1865—the first woman executed by the U.S. government. Modern historians question her guilt.

On "Bleeding Kansas": According to www.history.com, "Bleeding Kansas is the term used to describe the period of violence during the settling of the Kansas territory. In 1854 the Kansas-Nebraska Act overturned the Missouri Compromise's use of latitude as the boundary between slave and free territory, and instead, using the principle of popular sovereignty, decreed that the residents would determine whether the area became a free state or a slave state. Proslavery and free-state settlers flooded into Kansas to influence the decision. Violence soon erupted as both factions fought for control....During the Civil War, Kansas suffered the highest rate of fatal casualties of any Union state, largely because of its great internal divisions over the issue of slavery."

On the Sioux Uprising: Calling it "Minnesota's Other Civil War," Kenneth Carley writes a definitive account in *The Dakota War of 1862.* He notes the annual allotment of gold due through treaties to the Dakota Indians of Minnesota was delayed that August, while the annual ration of food was stored in a warehouse. The Indian agent didn't want to call the people into the agency headquarters twice, so he refused to release the food until the gold came, even though the Sioux were starving. His famous words were "Let them eat grass." The horrific, bloody uprising that followed saw "at least 450—and perhaps as many as 800—white settlers and soldiers killed, and considerable property was destroyed in southern Minnesota," Carley notes. Minnesota officials—it was then the newest state in the nation—rounded up and wanted to hang some 300 Indians, most of whom had not participated in the war. President Lincoln interceded. Still, thirty-eight Dakota hanged in Mankato on December 26, 1862, in the largest mass execution in U.S. history.

On Doc Holliday: In her excellent historical novel, *Doc*, Mary Doria Russell details Doc Holliday's days in Dodge City and his growing friendship with Wyatt Earp. He arrived in Dodge in 1878, a twenty-six-year-old dentist "who wanted nothing grander than to practice his profession in a prosperous Kansas cow town," she writes.

Chapter Four—We Found a New Life

On snakes: It is almost impossible to read any personal account of western settlement without reading about the plentiful snakes that made life miserable. Although later discredited, early thoughts were that the only remedy for snakebites was cutting the wound and sucking out the poison.

On the family's route west: Ella's great-nephew, Brumbaugh, spelled out the route of their immigration from family records.

On Lebanon, Kansas: Founded in 1873, this small town was about as far west as most wanted to go in those days—with nothing but the wild territories beyond until you got all the way to the Pacific Ocean and California. But in 1898, it was determined that Lebanon was the mid-point between America's boundaries on the Pacific and the Atlantic. For years, it called itself the "center" of the country—until the later annexation of Alaska and Hawaii. On June 29, 1941, civic leaders erected a stone marker that declared it the Historical Geographical Center of the original forty-eight states.

On soddies: According to *Sod Houses on the Great Plains,* written and illustrated by Glen Rounds, early pioneers cut two-feet thick "bricks of earth" from the prairie sod, then stacked them on one another to form walls for a small shelter—usually sixteen by twenty feet. They left a space for a door and a small window hole—before they had glass, homemakers rubbed bacon grease on paper to fill in the windows. The roof was made by spanning ridge poles from one sod wall to the other, then covered with four to six inches of dirt. It is said that after a rain, the roofs leaked for days. Field mice burrowed into the walls and snakes hunting mice overhead sometimes fell through the ceiling. Most soddies had dirt floors. They were meant to last a few years until lumber could be hauled in to build a cabin.

Chapter Five—My First Big Mistake

On Ellen's marriage: On November 24, 1879, eighteen-year-old Ellen Watson married twenty-one year-old William A. Pickell. A wedding portrait of the couple, printed in several books inspired the description of her wedding dress. The couple had no children and Ella's father would later tell the press that Pickell's "infidelity" caused a breakup, while family history uncovered by Brumbaugh says Pickell was also abusive and once beat Ellen with a horsewhip. Ellen left Pickell in 1883, lived with her family for a short time and filed for divorce, Brumbaugh reports. Records show Pickell ignored three notices of divorce.

On Kansas going Dry: Governor John St. John, with the backing of the national Woman's Christian Temperance Union, forced the legislature to pass a constitutional amendment for Prohibition. Kansas voters then approved it in 1880, leading the nation toward a ban on all manufacturing and sale of intoxicating liquors.

On President James Garfield: After only a few months in office, he was shot twice on July 2, 1881, by Charles Guiteau, who'd been turned down for a federal job. The wounds were not fatal, but poor and unsanitary medical practices were. Garfield died on September 19, 1881. Guiteau hanged, declaring: "Yes, I shot him, but his doctors killed him."

On Thanksgiving: It had been celebrated in America from the earliest days, but became an official national holiday in 1863, in the midst of the Civil War, by proclamation of President Abraham Lincoln. He finally responded to a forty-year campaign for a national, annual holiday led by Sarah Josepha Hale, editor of *Godey's Lady's Book* and author of "Mary Had a Little Lamb." It became tradition for each subsequent president to issue an annual proclamation naming the last Thursday in November as Thanksgiving Day. The 1879 proclamation, quoted verbatim, was issued by President Rutherford B. Hayes. In 1939, at the urging of merchants who wanted a longer Christmas shopping season, President Franklin D. Roosevelt changed the date to the second to last Thursday in November.

On the family's New Year's celebration: Hogmanay is a major holiday in Scottish tradition. The original words in "Auld Lang Syne" are from a website on the famous Scottish poem.

On Ella's divorce: Brumbaugh notes the ironic date of February 14, 1884, as her move to divorce Pickell. Divorce was extremely unusual—and highly objectionable—in those days, so it was a defining moment for Ella to demand a divorce, and then to demand her maiden name be restored.

On her family's history: Court records show Thomas Watson became a citizen of the United States on December 17, 1884, and his homestead was proved up on May 23, 1885. Printed obituaries say Thomas Watson died on May 29, 1921, and is buried in the Odessa Cemetery near Lebanon. Frances Close Watson died on April 3, 1924.

Chapter Six—My Train to a New Life

On Jacob Stone: Brumbaugh says the family history notes Ella went to work for Jacob Stone after filing for divorce.

On enticements to immigrate: Railroads issued brochures with titles like "Wonderful Opportunities for Homesteader or Investor" and one included a poem entitled "Mary Had a Little Farm." (The author has rewritten the ditty for Ella. The original portrayed it as an investment opportunity and Ella never intended it for anything but her own farm.)

- Brumbaugh told the author in a 2009 interview that Ella wanted to go west so she could own land like her father and grandfather.

On Jesse James: Jesse James was a notorious train robber—he and his gang held up seven trains in a sixteen-year crime spree. He was shot in the back of the head and killed by Bob Ford on April 3, 1882.

On women voting: On December 10, 1869, fifty-one years before national suffrage, Wyoming became the first government in the nation to give women full voting rights. One reason historians give for this momentous move is that men in the territory hoped it would attract unmarried women to move to Wyoming. But when it came to statehood, Congress demanded Wyoming rescind its woman suffrage. History gives us two versions of the strongly worded telegram that told Washington that wouldn't do: "We may stay out of the Union for 100 years but we will come in with our women," or "We will remain out of the Union a hundred years rather than come in without the women." Wyoming, known as the "Equality State," entered the union in 1890 with full suffrage for women. Wyoming again made history in 1924 when its voters elected Nellie Tayloe Ross, the nation's first female governor.

On poodles: According to Anne Seagraves' *Soiled Doves*, poodles were the preferred pet of western prostitutes. "These soft, cuddly little dogs were a favorite of the parlor ladies, so no 'decent' woman dared to own one," she wrote.

On Frances Willard: Called "Saint Frances," Willard led the Woman's Christian Temperance Union from 1879 until her death in 1898. In the first nine years of her leadership, she spoke in every American community of ten thousand people and many of five thousand, according to the PBS documentary *Prohibition* by Ken Burns. History now realizes Prohibition was the nation's first campaign against domestic violence. A popular

Literary Society topic in the 1880s was "Intemperance causes more sorrow than war."

On boiling coffee: This is taken from *The Old West Quiz & Fact Book* by Rod Grace, who recounts that an Eastern matron in a Western train station was dismayed by the boiling hot coffee, when a cowboy came to her rescue, offering her his coffee "that's already saucered and blowed."

On Cheyenne: Ella Watson had arrived in "The Magic City of the Plains." According to the *Cheyenne Centennial* report, in the decade of the 1880s, Cheyenne was the wealthiest per capita city in the world. It had the first municipal electric and telephone systems in North America. It would have the first library in the territory when it opened in 1886. The coming capital that the fictional Sally Wills bragged about would be as grand as anyone could imagine, built for the princely sum of one hundred fifty thousand dollars and dedicated on May 18, 1887, just in time for Wyoming to become the forty-fourth state on July 10, 1890. And yes, all the territories would become states—even Arizona, even though it would be the last one, not admitted until 1912 as the forty-eighth state.

On the Cheyenne Club: There wasn't a boast about the Cheyenne Club that was over-the-top. Sitting like a beacon on Seventeenth Street, it was about the most lush and exclusive club in the nation. You had to be a member of the Wyoming Stock Growers Association to join and there was always a waiting list. Its description is taken from Wyoming historical records, as is the description of Cheyenne's major attractions and the Whipple House. The club lost its luster in the early 1900s and the building was eventually used for the Cheyenne Chamber of Commerce until it fell into disrepair and was torn down in 1936.

On Herefords: Historical records of the Cheyenne Club show they called their white tie and tails "Herefords" in honor of the beloved sturdy beef cattle with white faces and chests. Tuxedos were not yet a common style in America. Herefords and Texas longhorns were the favorite cattle breeds in Wyoming Territory at the time.

On women homesteaders: In her article "Ella Watson. Rustler or Homesteader" for the *Annals of Wyoming* magazine, Sharon Leigh wrote in 1992: "The opportunities for women changed dramatically with the passage of the Homestead Law of 1862.... It enabled women to provide for themselves and their families by continuing, for the most part, the same kind of work they were used to doing. However, being able to homestead in their own names changed the power structure of the family as well as the roles of women."

In her book, *Staking Her Claim*, Marcia Hensley estimates as many as two hundred thousand women attempted to homestead and as many as 67,500 were successful. She quotes a study that found before 1900, single women made up twelve percent of homestead claims, and after 1900, about eighteen percent. Nowhere in her excellent book on women homesteaders does Hensley mention the name of Ella Watson, one of the first and few single women homesteaders in Wyoming Territory in the 1880s.

On the Rock Springs Massacre: By September 2, 1885, the Rock Springs coal mine employed almost six hundred Chinese workers and three hundred whites—all digging up coal to fuel the hungry engines of the Union Pacific Railroad. The portrayal of the massacre is based on the historical record, and an excellent article by Wyoming historian Tom Rea, published on his website.

Chapter Seven—The Man I Love

On Rawlins: Rawlins was founded in 1868 as a railroad settlement and incorporated as a city in 1886, according to its official website. It was named for General John A. Rawlins, a decorated Civil War veteran who was guarding a work crew building the Transcontinental Railroad in 1867 when he asked for a drink of fresh water. Scouts went out, bringing back what Rawlins declared as the best water he'd ever tasted. He said he hoped if anything were ever named for him, it would be a good spring. By 1870, Rawlins had 333 electors (mainly men who could vote—but there also were uncounted women and children); in 1884, it had 1,906, according to a report to the Secretary of the Interior. When Ella Watson arrived in Rawlins, in the fall of 1885, it was the second wealthiest area in the territory, with its grazing, mining, and railroads. It was and remains today the county seat of Carbon County.

On Ella Watson: She is described by her nephew and others as five-foot-eight inches tall and weighing about one hundred seventy pounds.

On Jim Averell: He is described as five feet six inches, with no weight specified, but his pictures show he was a slight man. Hufsmith's 1993 book *The Wyoming Lynching of Cattle Kate, 1889*—considered an authoritative source on the hanging—notes he was called "Jimmy." He was born March 20, 1851, in Renfrew County, Ontario. He was married in 1882 to Sophia Jaeger, but she died soon after giving birth to a son, who also died. On February 24, 1886, he filed Homestead Claim No.1227 on one hundred sixty acres on Horse Creek.

On Rawlins House: Mary Hayes and her husband, Larry, originally from Missouri, were among the first businesspeople in Rawlins, Wyoming Territory, arriving with the railroad in 1868, according to an article in the Rawlins *Daily Times*. They owned and operated the Union Pacific Hotel for a decade—then the city's "leading establishment," but moved "uptown" in 1880 when they bought and expanded a boardinghouse they named the Rawlins House, which became "the leading hotel" of the town. Mary Hayes was a strong Irish Catholic woman who demanded decency in the girls who worked for her. Wyoming historian Rans Baker told the author in an interview that Mary Hayes said of Ella Watson, "She was a very fine domestic." And he noted: "I guarantee you, if Mary Hayes felt Ella was immoral, she wouldn't have worked in Rawlins House." Mary Hayes operated Rawlins House until 1900. It was torn down in November,

1958 in the name of "progress" to make way for a parking lot, the *Times* reported.

On vinegar pie: *Heritage Recipes from Kansas* supplied the recipe for Vinegar Pie: "2 tablespoons butter; 1/2 cup sugar; 3 tablespoons flour; 2 teaspoons cinnamon; 1/2 teaspoon ground cloves; 1/2 teaspoon ground allspice; 1 egg, lightly beaten; 2 tablespoons cider vinegar; 1 cup water; 1 pie crust. Cream butter and sugar. Sift together flour and spices, then add to flour mixture, mix well. Beat in egg, vinegar, and water. Pour into double boiler and cook over boiling water until thick. Pour into pie shell and bake about 30 minutes at 350 degrees."

On territories: What is now Wyoming was originally part of Dakota Territory, as were North and South Dakota and most of Montana. Wyoming was established as its own territory on July 25, 1868.

On Ella missing out if she married: The ins and outs of homesteading that Jim tells Ella are based on the rules of the Homestead Act. According to *Staking Her Claim*, a single woman with a claim was no longer the required "head of household" if she married within the five years of "proving up," and her claim would revert to her husband. Jim complaining that one hundred sixty acres in Wyoming was way too skimpy was indeed the much-heard complaint about the Homestead Act.

On Billy Owen: William "Billy" Owen was one of Wyoming's earliest surveyors and became U.S. mineral surveyor for Wyoming. A partial autobiography—eighty-four typewritten pages, single-spaced, written in about 1930—is on file at the American Heritage Center at the University of Wyoming.

On Mary Agnes Hellihan: She married Tom Sun in Rawlins in 1883; their descendents still ranch in the Sweetwater Valley. Sun met Mary at the Union Pacific Hotel where she worked for Mary Hayes. They ranched near Devil's Gate, one of the geological formations in the area.

On Ella's claim: Carbon County court records show Ellen L. Watson filed a "squatter's claim"—Claim No. 2003—to one hundred sixty acres on Horse Creek on August 30, 1886.

Chapter Eight—The Man I Hate

On Robin Red Vest: Hufsmith notes this was the derisive nickname for A.J. Bothwell. He details Bothwell's family history and shenanigans, as does Daniel Y. Meschter, who devoted twenty-five years to researching the legal records of this affair. He self-published his findings in 1996 under the title *Sweetwater Sunset*. Bothwell was born February 18, 1854, in Iowa, where his well-off parents ran a "temperance" boardinghouse. He was the seventh of eight children and always idolized his older brothers, J.R., Frank, and George. He was an educated man, although tales that he was a Harvard graduate were fabrications. His oldest brother, J.R., was a Civil War quartermaster whose career ended in disgrace when he was court-martialed for stealing the army blind. But J.R. and his brothers went off into one financial scheme after another. Little brother Al decided to show his own mettle when, in about 1880, he tried cattle ranching in Colorado. But he was forced out as homesteaders moved in. By then, his brothers were in Wyoming Territory and lured him over to join their efforts: an oil well that had no oil; a railroad that had no rails. Every adventure brought in lots of investors, but no returns. Finally, Albert John Bothwell decided to try ranching one more time. He established his Broken Box Ranch in the Sweetwater Valley around 1883.

On John Fales: He was the handyman for Ella and Jim, whose mother made Ella a new bonnet. No physical description of him exists, so his look and personality are the author's imagination.

On joke Fales tells Ella: This is paraphrased from the joke "Horse Tale," found on the Only Funny Jokes website about Old West humor.

On James Averell: His background is recounted from the documentation of several historians, including Hufsmith and Meschter. Averell enlisted in the U.S. Army in 1871 in Wisconsin, but was soon assigned to Fort Fred Steele near Rawlins, Wyoming Territory. By a string of luck, he missed the major battles of the Indian Wars. His first five-year hitch was uneventful; he was discharged on May 22, 1876, but on June 20, reenlisted for another five years. He was sent to join General George Crook in Wyoming. Three days before Averell reenlisted, Chief Washakie saved General Crook and his men from an ambush by Crazy Horse and a large group of Ogallala Sioux in the Battle of the Rosebud. Had it not been for this battle, General Crook was slated to join George Armstrong Custer in searching out the Sioux in Montana. A month later, on July 25 and 26, 1876, Crazy Horse was among the Indian chiefs who annihilated Custer and his men at the Battle of the Little Bighorn.

On final Pickell divorce: Pickell refused to answer the notices of Ellen's claim for a divorce, but filed his own, claiming she had abandoned him. The divorce was finally official in early 1886, when Ella was already with Averell, Brumbaugh notes.

On Jim killing Charlie Johnson: This wasn't a clear-cut case of self-defense as Averell would always insist. There had been bad blood between the men for months and Averell had even alerted his fort commander that Johnson was out to get him for some slight that was never spelled out. On May 2, 1880, Johnson entered the bar in Buffalo and called Averell a "cowardly son of a bitch," demanding a fistfight. Johnson did not draw his revolver, but Averell had his out and shot at the advancing Johnson three times. While there was agreement on the first two shots, there was a conflict on the fatal third shot. Not everyone agreed Johnson had spun around when he was shot in the leg. Some say he was "rushing for the door" when he was shot in the back. The next day, Averell wrote to a prominent friend asking for help and declaring "I was compelled to do so or be shot myself." Before Johnson died several days later, he told a court official that he had no intention of killing Averell but, "My intentions were to settle the afare [sic] between us with a fistfight. I drew no weapon." After many delays over the next year, the court got weary of the case and used the excuse of it being a military matter to get rid of it. This information came from several sources, including Grand Jury testimony, May 5, 1880, Wyoming State Museum, Meschter and Hufsmith.

On handcarts: "Tongue nor pen can ever tell the sorrow," says a heartbreaking film on the tragic 1856 Mormon handcart disaster at the Handcart Historic Site operated by the Mormon Church on Tom Sun's original ranch. The site is open daily and proves a memorable visit. Mormons fled from Illinois to the Utah Territory after the murder of their founder, Joseph Smith, in 1844. Brigham Young became their new leader and founded Salt Lake City as their heaven on earth. He promised Mormons religious freedom, and an opportunity to build a wonderful new life. At first, converts came by wagon trains, but he realized many of his converts couldn't afford that expense. Brigham Young came up with the idea of handcarts—people would pull their own wooden carts almost a thousand miles from Iowa or Nebraska to Salt Lake City. As incredible as that sounds, it was embraced by many, including hundreds of foreign converts who'd immigrated to America so they could find their Zion in Salt Lake City. It actually worked, until disaster hit when two companies of handcarts started out from Nebraska in August of 1856—way too late to get through Wyoming before winter. The converts in the Martin and Willie Handcart Companies were converts from England and Scotland. The snows came early that year, and while some wanted to turn back until spring, others pressured to move forward. They got as far as Devil's Gate and couldn't make it any farther. The lucky ones froze to death. The unlucky ones starved to death. Children watched their parents die and parents watched their children perish. A thousand people started out and over two hundred died. Brigham Young wasn't aware these two units were still out there. Although he eventually tried to save them, it was too late. He canceled all future handcart travel.

On Big Nose George: Averell was in jail with Big Nose George at the time of his lynching, confirms Wyoming historian Rans Baker. A mob pulled George from jail, tied his hands behind his back, put him on an empty kerosene barrel with a rope tied around his neck and kicked out the barrel. But the rope broke, allowing George to fall to the ground "where he begged to be shot," according to "The Legend of Big Nose George" pamphlet published by the Carbon County Museum. As the lynch mob got a ladder and a heavier rope, George managed to untie his hands. When the ladder was pulled away, he was able to hold himself for a time but eventually, "gravity pulled him down, slowly choking him to death." The body was left hanging for several hours, and when it was inspected, it was found to have no ears, as the hanging rope had worn them off. His body was skinned; the flesh was tanned and made into a pair of shoes proudly worn by John Osborne, the first Democratic governor of the State of Wyoming, to his inaugural ball in 1893. The Carbon County Museum, 904 W. Walnut Street, Rawlins, displays Big Nose's death mask, lower skull, and the infamous shoes.

On Yellowstone: The idea of setting aside land for the public's benefit was revolutionary when President Ulysses S. Grant signed the bill creating the first national park in the world—Yellowstone National Park, on March 1, 1872. It covered two million acres in the northwest corner of Wyoming Territory and spilled into Idaho and Montana territories. The bill protected Yellowstone from private greed and ordered the area be "dedicated and set apart as a public park or pleasuring-ground for the benefit and enjoyment of the people," notes "The Place where Hell Bubbled Up" by David A. Clary, Office of Publications, National Park Service, 1972. But the idea of a national preserve continued to be controversial, and Yellowstone had none of the protections found today for the national park system. It was defenseless to "poachers, squatters, woodcutters, vandals and firebugs," Clary reports. In 1883 Congress debated the value of such publicly owned land, with some arguing that private enterprise should be in charge. In 1886, Congress stripped all money to protect

Yellowstone and the Secretary of the Interior called on the Secretary of War for help. After August 20, 1886, Yellowstone came under the protection of the U.S. Army.

On brush in front of teepee: According to Grace Raymond Hebard's *Washakie: Chief of the Shoshones*, brush in front of a teepee meant the occupants were away but returning, while graves were often adorned with a cherished item of the deceased.

On their wedding: Public records show that James Averell, thirty-five, and Ellen Liddy Andrews, twenty-four, applied for a marriage license in Lander, Fremont County, Wyoming, 105 miles west of the Sweetwater Valley. The license was issued on May 17, 1886. The application and the marriage license were signed by the county clerk and include the county's seal. A third document, a "certificate of marriage," was not filled out or signed. Hufsmith says it wasn't uncommon for this last document to be overlooked, since the marriage license was already signed and sealed. Historians are unanimous in agreeing that Ellen Liddy Andrews was Ellen Watson. They surmise she changed her name just enough to protect her homestead claim in case this license would be discovered before her land was "proved up." If the marriage had been discovered, she would have lost her own claim and it would become her husband's.

Chapter Nine—My Claim, No. 2003

On items stocked at the roadhouse: These were gleaned from a variety of sources, including *The White House Cookbook*; *The Boston Cooking-School Cook Book*, and *Mrs. Snow's Practical Cook Book*.

On Irish potato soup: Ella's recipe from a historic cookbook started with washing and peeling six large potatoes, cutting them thin, like she cut the four onions. Into a pot they went, with a couple chicken cubes, six pieces of chopped celery, dried parsley, garlic, salt, and pepper. She covered the pot and heated them to soften, then added four cups of milk and stirred it all until the soup thickened. To top it off, she stirred in three cups of grated cheese.

On Canzada and Boney Earnest: The true stories told of Canzada outwitting the highway men and the couple's friendship with famous western characters comes from Ruth Bebe's *Reminiscing Along the Sweetwater*. Bebe is the daughter of cowpuncher Joe Sharp, who was horrified by the hanging of Ella and Jim and confronted Bothwell about it the day after the hanging. Sharp later helped with Jim's estate and bought Jim's elaborate wall clock, that ended up in Ruth Beebe's home. Beebe's thorough and wonderful history of the Sweetwater Valley was an invaluable help to this author. But her *Reminiscing*, published in 1973, does not include any discussion of the hanging. It wasn't until a 1997 book by Mark Junge, *The Wind is my Witness: A Wyoming Album*, that the chapter on Ruth Beebe explained why: She said she went to see the descendants of Tom Sun "and told them that I was going to write a book, try to write a history of the Sweetwater Valley and its occupants, and how they came there and different things that happened. Oh, they just jumped on me and they said, 'You can't write a book!' I taught school for thirty years, but they said, 'You can't write a book. No, that's impossible.' And just shoved me off. I went home and I said to my sister, 'Why don't they think I can write a history of it?' She said, 'Because they think that you're going to expose that Cattle Kate thing again.' So I went back down and told them that I didn't intend to mention Cattle Kate, and I was gonna leave that part out. And they went to their museums, they got papers out, they got history of different things out that the first Mr. Sun had compiled, and they helped an awful lot with my book."

On Andrew Carnegie: One of the world's wealthiest men, Carnegie, 1835-1919, gave away over $350 million during his lifetime. One of his passions was free public libraries, and he's credited with founding 2,509 libraries in the English-speaking world. As the Columbia University Information Services reports: "Many persons of wealth have contributed to charity, but Carnegie was perhaps the first to state publicly that the rich have a moral obligation to give away their fortunes. In 1889, he wrote *The Gospel of Wealth*, in which he asserted that all personal wealth beyond that required to supply the needs of one's family should be regarded as a trust to be administered for the benefit of the community."

On the Statue of Liberty: There was much controversy about the American people paying for the pedestal to hold the female figure that was a gift from France in honor of America's independence of 1776. According to *Enlightening the World: The Creation of the Statue of Liberty*, by Yasmin Sabina Kahn, many felt the one hundred thousand dollar-plus expense was frivolous. The *New York Times* said, "No true patriot can countenance any such expenditures for bronze females in the present state of our finances." The Statue of Liberty was dedicated on October 28, 1886.

On Owen Wister: Author Owen Wister, who would pen the defining book on the American West, *The Virginian*, visited Wyoming several times in his youth, his journals note.

On Bothwell threatening Ella: Accounts of his threats and intimidations are detailed by Hufsmith and Meschter, including the skull left on her doorstep.

On maverick law: Fales correctly tells the legal basis of the hated Maverick Law, passed by the Territorial Legislature in 1884. The law is painstakingly spelled out by both Hufsmith and Meschter.

On the M brand for maverick: This was a "rolling M" that originally was owned by Eliza A. Kuykendall, wife of Judge W. L. Kuykendall of Cheyenne. "It is said to be the first brand registered inside the boundaries of this state. In 1884, the symbol was transferred to the Wyoming Stock Growers Association. For a long time, that group used it as the official mark to place on mavericks…during roundup seasons." This quote is from an article for the series, *Highlights in Wyoming History*, titled "A Backward Look at Early Branding Days" by Clarice Whittenburg on file at the American Heritage Center at the University of Wyoming in Laramie. This is an original manuscript with the author's handwritten editing and has no date or publication information.

On the milk cow story: Rawlins' *Carbon County Journal* created an uproar over the Larson cow incident and got the cow returned, Meschter notes.

On being pushed to becoming a thief: This is a paraphrase of a quote from Helena Huntington Smith in her "The War on Powder River."

On the value of cattle in Wyoming Territory: This was virtually the only industry in the territory and when the "golden days" came, they came fast. Wyoming historical records show that in 1870, there were only eleven thousand head roaming the open ranch lands. But by the 1880s, they counted cattle in the millions—sturdy Texas Longhorns and the broader, white-faced Herefords that could survive the harsh Wyoming winters. By the time Bothwell founded his ranch, a cattle investment could bring from twenty-five to sixty percent profit. Every single year. Plenty of gold mines didn't give that return.

On the "goose question": In her historical novel, *The All-True Travels and Adventures of Lidie Newton*, Jane Smiley wrote about this code used to discuss slavery in Kansas. The author wondered if there were a similar code to discuss homesteaders. Historian Rans Baker of the Carbon County Museum said the equivalent in Wyoming Territory was "the rustler problem." Baker assisted both Hufsmith and Meschler as they each spent decades researching the lynching. He says "the two books together tell the whole story."

On Rawlins School House: A new school was built in Rawlins, W.T., in 1886 and is described as it appears in photographs from that time.

On newspaper stories Ella reads to Jim: These were published in the August 14, 1886, edition of the *Carbon County Journal.*

On Geronimo: Perhaps the most famous Indian in American history, Geronimo was an Apache born in June of 1829, who lived most of his life in what is now Arizona. He became a famous guerilla warrior who fought against the white invasion of his ancestral lands. Historians debate whether he was a "murderous renegade or courageous warrior." At one point, one fourth of the entire U.S. Army was in Arizona Territory trying to find Geronimo and his band of thirty-six. He finally surrendered in 1886. On September 18, 1886, the *Cheyenne Mirror* noted in the "Wired Words" column: "Now that they have got Geronimo they don't know what to do with him. Turn him over to the cowboys and let them brand him and bury him." Geronimo lived many years as a prisoner of war, but became a celebrity—marching in the inauguration parade of President Theodore Roosevelt. He died on February 17, 1909, after falling from his horse. His nephew said his deathbed words were: "I should never have surrendered. I should have fought until I was the last man alive." To this day, the name Geronimo stands for bravery and daring. On May 2, 2011, when American forces found and killed Osama bin Laden, the mission was named "Operation Geronimo."

On the fair: The first Wyoming Territorial Fair was scheduled September 14 to 17, 1886, according to territorial newspapers.

Chapter Ten—I Wanted a Nice Christmas

On howling wolves: The Shoshone legend said a howling wolf was good luck, according to *Washakie* by Hebard.

On "Auld Lang Syne": On September 8, 1886, the Fourth Cavalry Regimental Band was on hand when Geronimo and the last free Apaches were marched from Fort Bowie to Bowie Station to be sent by train into exile in Florida. The band played "Auld Lang Syne" to mock Geronimo.

On winter losses: History calls the winter of 1886-87 "The Great Die-Up" or sometimes "The Great Die-Off." Eighty percent of the herds in Wyoming Territory died in the horrible storms.

On "The Raven": An original copy of this Edgar Allan Poe poem, as described, was found by the author in the Governor's Mansion in Cheyenne.

On "I may not see a hundred...": This poem is reproduced from Helena Huntington Smith's *The War on Powder River*. The poem was prophetic because after the winter of 1886-87, many of the large English, Scot, and Irish cattle barons left their Wyoming ranches.

On Durbin: Records suggest that Averell and Durbin indeed had old bad blood; probably from a fake land claim Durbin had Averell file years earlier, which Jim turned around and sold as his own. This conjecture is found in several sources, including Rea's *Devil's Gate* and Meschter's *Sweetwater Sunset*.

On defending her claim: Ellen L. Watson filed a complaint against Edgar P. Schoonmaker on January 4, 1887, contesting his timber claim on land she also claimed. She won the challenge. Meschter's *Sweetwater Sunset* sets out the entire details.

On the easement: Historical records show Bothwell was forced to buy an easement fifteen feet by 3,300 feet from Averell to get water from Horse Creek—a humiliation that invariably figured into the lynching.

On citizenship application: Ellen Watson applied for American citizenship on May 25, 1887, at the Carbon County Courthouse, described as it exists to this day. Jim Averell applied for citizenship on January 19, 1884, the public record shows.

Chapter Eleven—I Love Being a Homesteader

On cattle prices: In her award-winning magazine article, "Cattle Kate: Homesteader or Cattle Thief?" reprinted in *Wild Women of the Old West*, edited by Glenda Riley and Richard V. Etulain, Lori Van Pelt notes: "Cattle sold in the mid-1880s at an average of twenty-seven dollars per head."

On purchasing her cows: John Fales told territorial newspapers after the lynching that he had been with Ella when she purchased her twenty-eight head at one dollar apiece in the fall of 1888 from a Nebraska wrangler named Engerman. Fales said he drove the cattle from Independence Rock to Ella's homestead. Historical maps show that from Independence Rock, they'd be herded north, first past Jim's roadhouse, then Bothwell's ranch, and finally to Ella's claim. Bothwell lived about a mile from Ella and from his front porch, could see her place. He had to watch those cows in her corral all winter. Fales called Ella "not only a fine appearing woman, but a good woman." Hufsmith found a 1935 article on Marc Countryman, the son of a friendly cattle rancher at the time, who said he also witnessed the purchase of Ella's cows.

On throwing his John B. on the ground: Cowboys commonly referred to their hats as a "John B." in honor of John B. Stetson, who developed the beloved Stetson cowboy hat in 1865, according to *The Old West Quiz & Fact Book* and the Stetson website.

On brands: Information on brands—what they mean, how they're read—comes from *The Cowboy's Own Brand Book* by Duncan Emrich. The story of Judge Roy Bean comes from a pamphlet, "Levi's Stories of Western Brands and What They Mean," by Oren Arnold and John P. Hale.

On neighboring ranchers: The stories Fales tells Ella reflect the historical record from Hufsmith and Meschter.

- John Henry Durbin was born in 1842—Hufsmith says in Pennsylvania; Meschter says in Indiana—and his family indeed had the Midas Touch. He was the biggest rancher of the Sweetwater Valley and his family was revered throughout the territory. Hufsmith reports: "John Durbin was ruthlessly ambitious. He associated with the cattle thieves and rustlers in the Sweetwater country." He sold his Wyoming holdings in 1891 because, as Hufsmith says, "Durbin's enormous wealth wasn't able to buy him protection from relentless public humiliation." He moved to Denver, where his obituary in 1907 noted, "in comparison with his former tremendous financial power, he died a poor man. Millions, as he grew older, melted away like snow under a burning sun. The Midas gift to turn to gold all that he touched, was taken from him."

- Robert R. Conner was born in Pennsylvania in 1849. He became a ruthless cattleman, accumulating land and cattle illegally. But as Hufsmith notes, "There was just hardly any legal way to do it in a hurry, unless you had a fortune to purchase somebody's already-existing land and stock....Bob Conner was another example of a man playing the game." Quickly after the lynching, he sold his ranch and returned to Pennsylvania, where no one seemed aware of his involvement. The glowing 1921 obituary in the local paper lauded him as a man who "loved to do good for those in need and his charity was unbounded."

- Robert M. Galbraith was born in England in 1844. His Civil War experiences launched him into a railroad career, ending up in Wyoming Territory, where he quickly became a community leader and elected official. Hufsmith reports that he "suffered personal indignities and threats to himself and family and did not stay in the Sweetwater Valley very long after the lynching." And yet, almost four months after the lynching, he was elected to the territorial upper chamber, now known as the Senate. He eventually made a fortune selling his ranch and ended up as a banker in Little Rock, Arkansas. He died in 1939.

- Tom Sun was originally Thomas de Beau Soli, a French-Canadian born in the 1840s—historians disagree on the exact year. He created a thriving ranch in the shadow of Devil's Gate, a major geological formation in the Sweetwater Valley. He was widely respected, and a friend of Buffalo Bill. He died in Denver in 1909. His family still ranches in the Rawlins area.

On Thomas Edison: Thomas Edison and other scientists came to Wyoming in 1878 to see a total eclipse of the sun. While there, Cap'n Robert Galbraith—one of the lynchers—hosted a camping and fishing trip. Edison later credited the trip with his invention of the incandescent light bulb, according to several historical collection sources, including "In Old Wyoming," a newspaper column by John C. Thompson, printed in the Wyoming *State Tribune* on November 1, 1941.

On Ella's claim: On March 23, 1888, records show Ella Watson took the train from Rawlins to Cheyenne to formally file the claim on her land, explaining it had taken her this long for the formal filing because of the expense involved. Her claim number remained 2003, the same as when she had earlier filed the county claim.

On women voting: Kansas had two distinctions when it came to women's rights: in 1887, Susanna Salter of Argonia became the first woman mayor in the United States, and in 1888, the nation's first all-female municipal government—mayor and five councilwomen—was elected in Oskaloosa.

Wyoming's distinctions, besides being the first to give women full voting rights in 1869, came in 1870 when Esther Morris became the nation's first justice of the peace, and W.T. empanelled the nation's first all-female jury. The first woman elected to statewide office was Estelle Reel in 1894, who became Wyoming's superintendent of public instruction.

Chapter Twelve—I Became a Substitute Ma

On "nature's cure," home remedies and recipes: Taken from several collections, including *Potpourri of Yesteryear: Old Recipes, Cures, Remedies and Little Known Hints*, edited by E. Gretchen Vander-Meer; and *Grandma's Reliable Recipes and Remedies*, prepared by the staff of the Carbon County Museum from *A Book for a Cook*.

On rag doll Ella makes with girls: The instructions are based on a rag doll the author found at a historic museum in Jamestown, North Dakota, that was labeled as the type of doll used on the prairie.

On her brand: Carbon County records show the Brand Committee rejected Ella's request for a WT brand in December of 1888. On March 16, 1889, she bought the LU brand from John Crowder for ten dollars and duly registered it with Carbon County on Jimmy's birthday, March 20. There is no explanation for what either brand stood for. "Lucky Upstart" is the author's imagination. Historians, and the author, surmise that John Crowder was the father of Gene Crowder, who became Ella's ward.

On Jim's statement of either get along or shoot: This sentiment comes from Smith's book *The War on Powder River*.

Chapter Thirteen—I'm Sorry I Haven't Written Sooner

On Ella's birthday: Ella turned twenty-nine years of age on July 2, 1889—the birth date recorded in the family Bible, according to Brumbaugh. Other sources say she was a year younger, but Brumbaugh and the author believe the Bible. Tom Watson's birthday was August 6, while Frances Watson's birthday was August 17.

On Ella's barbed wire: According to Wyoming author and historian Tom Rea, Ella Watson was a pioneer in bringing barbed wire to Wyoming Territory. He spelled it out in his lecture on August 29, 2009, in Casper, Wyoming; Hufsmith notes she had a four-barbed-wire fence of three strands.

On James Averell's appointments: He was named postmaster by President Grover Cleveland on June 29, 1886; then a notary public by Territorial Governor Thomas Moonlight in January of 1887, and a justice of the peace by the Carbon County Board of Supervisors on March 6, 1889. In the election of 1886, when Averell had just moved into the Sweetwater area, he got two votes for Sand Creek Constable, even though he was a newcomer and a Democrat in a Republican precinct. The historical record of these appointments was recounted by several sources, including Hufsmith and Meschter.

On snakes: According to the American International Rattlesnake Museum in Albuquerque, New Mexico, snakes are virtually deaf, but use ground vibrations to sense things. This and other historical websites are the basis for Jim's correct story on the importance of thirteen on the original "Don't Tread on Me" flag and on the efforts to make the timber rattlesnake the nation's symbol.

On sidesaddles: The description of how these saddles worked comes from catalogs of the era and historical websites on Old West saddles. The price of a sidesaddle comes from advertisements in a Rawlins newspaper at the time.

On her gun: Hufsmith reports she had a twelve-gauge scattergun.

On the Montgomery Ward Catalog: The author used a reproduction of the 1875 catalog as the basis for these references.

On entering a sickroom: The advice to never enter a sickroom while perspiring is noted in *Potpourri of Yesteryear*.

On castor oil: Several references note that the original castor oil came in a green fish-shaped bottle.

On John DeCorey: Little is known about this fourteen-year-old boy who found work on Ella's homestead in early 1889. After the lynching, he fled to Springboat Springs, Colorado, where Hufsmith said he was under "heavy guard" as a surprise witness in the lynching hearing. But there was no hearing. What happened to DeCorey afterwards is unknown, historians agree.

On Crosse & Blackwell's Chow-Chow: This English-made mustard-pickle relish was popular in the Old West. As Billy Owen noted in his autobiography, restaurant tables included "the ever-present bottle of Crosse & Blackwell's Chow Chow." Owen also provided several colloquialisms of the Old West that are used in this book, including "tumbled to his talents," as reflecting the true picture of someone; and "scooped out of his boots" on besting someone.

On Belle Starr: The Women in History website notes Belle Starr was shot in the back outside her ranch near Eufaula, Oklahoma, on February 3, 1889, two days short of her forty-first birthday. One of the suspects was Edgar Watson, who was feuding with Starr over land he was renting from her. Starr had served time as a horse thief and was known as the "Bandit Queen." In her book *Wily Women of the West*, Grace Ernestine Ray notes Watson was released for insufficient evidence and the case went unsolved for many years, although several were suspected. But seventy-five years later, she reports, a man told a reporter he saw Belle's son, Ed, shoot her.

On Sarah and Able Cole: Sarah was James Averell's older sister; she and her husband, Able Cole, helped raise him. James was particularly close to this sister and was happy to help out her oldest son, Ralph Cole, who came to W.T. in April of 1889 from Wisconsin to get training from his uncle at the roadhouse, according to Hufsmith.

On Buffalo Bill: The famous Indian scout and showman, whose real name was William F. Cody, started his Wild West Show in 1882, and became a sensation throughout the United States and Europe until his death in 1917, thrilling crowds with shooting tricks, feats of daring and horsemanship. He brought the world Annie Oakley and took Sitting Bull to France. He is considered Wyoming's most famous showman, and was a friend to Tom Sun. A rifle he gave Sun still hangs over the fireplace of Sun's original ranch house near Devil's Gate, which is now the Mormon Handcart Historic Site.

On Independence Rock: Known as "The Register of the Desert," this is now a national Historic Site to honor the three hundred fifty to four hundred thousand immigrants who crossed Wyoming on the Oregon Trail in the early 1800s. The height of immigration was 1840-1860. The reference to "Hiram Meck, July, 50" is one of the authentic signatures on the rock; there are thousands. A display at the site notes: "Crowds of Emigrants got to the Rock to spend Independence Day, and the loud reports of firearms throughout the day, testifies that this is the birthday of American Freedom; and that although here in the wilds of the Rocky Mountains, a thousand miles from our home, we are yet *American citizens,* a part of a great family who have inherited Freedom from our ancestors. We do not forget this day, but every heart beats high with patriotic pride as it welcomes this Glorious Anniversary."

On buffalo: Millions of buffalo once roamed the plains of the Old West, and the story of their breath in the early morning forming a cloud to alert the Indians comes from *Washakie.*

On Chief Washakie: Hebard's excellent book tells how the Shoshone chief refused to blind the eye of his horse for buffalo hunts; how he resembled George Washington; and his role in saving General Crook in the Battle of the Rosebud. This is the same General Crook who originally got Geronimo to surrender in Arizona Territory on March 27, 1886, only to have his promises to the Apache medicine man broken, leading Geronimo to escape yet again, until his final surrender on September 3, 1886, to Brigadier Gen. Nelson A. Miles. The Washakie book begins with an introduction by Richard O. Clemmer: "Friend of emigrant, settler and soldier. Cooperator in the 'transition of the West from savagery to civilization'. Enemy of Blackfoot, Sioux, and Cheyenne. And 'benevolent despot'—'a czar in determination though a kindly ruler.' Thus does Grace Raymond Hebard describe Washakie." Hebard herself prefaced the book like this: "Had Chief Washakie been an enemy of our government and its people, battling with bow and arrow, spear, tomahawk and rifle to maintain a savage supremacy over the regions now peopled with industrious workers, he would be better known." Even given the prejudicial tone of that sentence, Hebard gives a remarkably insightful look at a chief who was so honored, that on December 30, 1878, a western Wyoming fort was named Fort Washakie.

On Tom Thumb: An eyewitness account of Tom Thumb's visit to Laramie around 1871 was recounted by William "Bill" Owen in his unpublished autobiography. While Barnum let the mistake stand that Queen Victoria had given the small carriage to Tom Thumb, it was Barnum who had the carriage built.

On "stampede for a penny": This is how Jim Averell was described in a letter by Dr. Frank O. Filbey, as quoted in Hufsmith's book.

On President Cleveland's investigation: The *Carbon County Journal* reported on June 25, 1887, that President Cleveland's interior secretary had canceled fifty-five desert land claims owned by Thomas Sturges, the longtime secretary of the Wyoming Stock Growers Association and a member of the Union Cattle Co. operating northeast of Cheyenne, Meschter notes.

On Averell's letter to the editor: The letter, quoted verbatim, was published by the *Casper Weekly Mail* on February 7, 1889. Both Hufsmith and Meschter agree this letter was the straw that broke the camel's back. Hufsmith says: "Jim had just tossed grenades, lobbed mortars, fired an entire artillery barrage, and mined the lakes and streams of the entire Wyoming cattle industry....He was absolutely correct in everything he wrote, of course, except for one major mistake. Contrary to what he wrote, he definitely should have 'disguised himself in the matter.' Jim unwittingly signed his own death warrant. He also unwittingly added his new bride's name to the same instrument of death." Meschter wrote: "Jim Averell was genuinely and widely well-regarded in his community. His only fault of which any Republican adversary—read 'cattleman'—could complain was his views on land settlement policies so much in contention just then and his willingness and ability to express them in writing!"

On Town of Bothwell: Bothwell and several investors were promoting the non-existent town to folks in the East, selling acre lots for up to four hundred dollars, according to Hufsmith and other sources. The *Sweetwater Chief* newspaper was the only structure in the town, although it regularly sent out stories claiming this was a town of homes, churches, and businesses. The *Cheyenne Sun* even quoted a dispatch from the *Chief* falsely claiming the town had a happy and boisterous celebration on July 4, 1889, where young women competed on horseback to the delight of young men.

On derisive headlines about the phony town: Meschter quotes these from various W.T. newspapers.

On Averell's prominence: The Rawlins *Journal* called James Averell "the gentlemanly Sweetwater postmaster," Hufsmith notes.

On petition to create County of Natrona: E.L. Watson signed the petition, along with at least one of her lynchers, John Durbin. Durbin later tried to rescind his signature, saying he had misunderstood the petition. Meschter notes this signature says a lot about how Ella was viewed *before* the lynching: "…she did come forward as a peer in the Natrona County controversy, which she would not have been allowed to do had she been a common prostitute."

On election at roadhouse: On July 8, 1889—twelve days before the lynching—Averell's roadhouse was the Sweetwater Polling Place for a special election to chose delegates to the Wyoming Constitutional Convention—a prelude to statehood. Averell was one of three election judges. Frank Buchanan and Ralph Cole were clerks. Historians universally have used this election, and Averell's position as an honored election judge, as evidence this was no "hog ranch" and he was running no house of prostitution here, as the Cheyenne papers would soon claim.

On Ella's branded cows: The spring branding roundup of 1889 ended on July 20. Fales used Ella's legally registered LU brand to brand the forty-one head in her corral.

On Ella trading cows: Hufsmith reports that John Burke, who drove a freight wagon, said "Ella Watson had received a few mavericks. These she had purchased from the cowboys and ranchmen." Carbon County historian Rans Baker told the author in a 2009 interview, "I don't think Ella ever stole a cow, but I don't know if she had stolen cows."

On Reverend Moore: In his autobiography, *Souls and Saddle-bags*, Rev. Frank Moore, National Secretary of Missions of the Congregational Home Missionary Society, recounts his visits to the roadhouse and how he knew almost everyone involved in the lynching. Hufsmith notes Rev. Moore visited the roadhouse on May 31, June 10, and 11 and perhaps even on July 19, the day before the lynching, when Rev. Moore writes that he spent the night at Bothwell's ranch. Rev. Moore wrote that he learned of the hanging from a newspaper clipping that said Jim and Ella were hanged for rustling. He comments: "A pretty severe way of dealing with a man and woman just for calf stealing. That seems to be the only value some people place on life out here. It seems terrible when I knew all the parties. Mr. Averill [sic] told me to come again and he would give me his house to hold a meeting in." Historians note that a man of the cloth like Dr. Moore would not even consider such an offer if Jim were running a "hog ranch," as the Cheyenne papers would claim.

On Ella's bonnet: John Fales, in telling his story to newspapers, noted that his mother had made Ella a new bonnet.

Chapter Fourteen—The Last Day of My Life

On her rising: *The Old Farmer's Almanac* of 1889 says that on Saturday, July 20, the sun rose at 4:25 a.m. and set at 7:15 p.m.

On magazine Ella was reading: *The Century Illustrated Monthly Magazine*, March, 1885, published in New York. This black-and-white magazine—with an elaborately illustrated paper cover—was a continuing series, with the first story in this issue listed as page 643. This edition, found in a bookstore in Prescott, Arizona, included "The New Astronomy: The Planets and the Moon," as well as a continuation of Henry James' "The Bostonians."

On the moccasins: History tells us Ella went to the Shoshone camp to buy beaded moccasins, but the author has discovered another twist to this story: the moccasins were very old and worn, signifying she wouldn't have "bought" them, but would have accepted them in trade as a face-saving gesture. This implies she knew this tribe and had dealt with them before. She wore the moccasins home and kicked them off as she was hanged. According to a letter to the editor to the *Casper Star-Tribune* on October 15, 1989, from Casper Historian Chuck Morrison, they were picked up a few days later by Nell Jameson, a young girl who went to the hanging site with her father and took a picture of the hanging tree. She eventually gave them to the Wyoming State Museum in Cheyenne, where they are sometimes displayed and where they were examined by this author.

On Averell being abducted: The eyewitness testimonies of Gene Crowder and John DeCorey, told to the inquest, outline Averell's abduction, and is told in several books, as is Bothwell's declaration that Averell was "under arrest" and that Bothwell's gun is all the "warrant" he needs.

On drowning them in the river: Frank Buchanan gave a detailed eyewitness account to officials at the original inquest and was expected to be the main witness against the lynchers at their trial. One of the specific things he heard was Ella making the joke about the shallow river.

On Ella's last outburst: Tom Rea reports in *Devil's Gate* a conversation he had with Dennis Sun, Tom Sun's great-grandson: "Way my great-grandfather told it, they went down there, they just wanted to scare them. But she got mouthy."

On the death scene: Frank Buchanan's eyewitness account of the hangings is detailed in several books and newspaper articles about this case. It is presented here as Buchanan described it— Bothwell putting the noose on Jim; McLean struggling to noose

Ella; Ella asking for a prayer; Bothwell telling her she can deliver it in person; Bothwell laughing that Jim should be "game" and jump; Buchanan shooting at the lynchers and hitting Durbin; the lynchers firing back; the couple strangling to death, writhing as they swung from the limb.

On "No! No!": Ella's last words were quoted by western history writer Dale T. Schoenberger, writing in *The National Tombstone Epitaph* in October, 1990, in an article titled "Notorious 'Cattle Kate' Not a Rustler. Wild Stories Spread to Excuse A Lynching."

On the immediate aftermath of the lynching: Hufsmith reports three telling stories from Sunday, July 21, 1889, that were told to him by historian Ruth Beebe:

- Her father, Stewart Joe Sharp, told her about "brave little Gene Crowder" confronting Bothwell.

- Charles Countryman of the BH6 Ranch was startled to find Ernie McLean on his doorstep "with swollen, red eyes, and then between wrenching sobs, he almost incoherently blathered out what had happened."

- John Crowder was camped with a new rig when someone told him what had happened. "Crowder promptly unhitched the horse, struggled up onto its back and galloped away leaving the wagon standing there in the sagebrush flats where it remained unmolested for three years before Crowder suddenly returned briefly and drove it off."

On the hanging tree: In *Devil's Gate*, Tom Rea records his recent visit to the hanging site: "Though dead, the tree is still there. The gulch is now called Spring Canyon; the rocks are called Sentinel Rocks. The tree is not large, twenty-five or thirty feet high, and even its largest limbs, blackened now from fire or lightning decades ago, would be too brittle to hold the weight of a pair of kicking, desperate people. There are two rocks at the base of the tree. Only one is big enough for two people to stand on before being pushed into space. Living, the biggest branch could have been limber enough to hold them without breaking, yet stiff enough to hold them off the ground. It was a short drop. Their toes, once the branch took their weight, would have been inches from the dead pine needles and dirt."

On the new prison in Rawlins: Wyoming Territory was building a prison in Rawlins to replace its original prison in Laramie. Construction began July 23, 1888, and it was named the Wyoming State Prison upon the Territory's admission to the Union on July 10, 1890. Today it is a museum open for public tours.

Part Two: Chapter Fifteen—"Cattle Kate" is Born

On Sunday events: Stories printed in the *Cheyenne Sun* on Sunday, July 21, 1889, depict the day.

On Esther Hobart (Slack) Morris: Her son, newspaper editor Ed Slack, labeled her "the mother of woman suffrage in Wyoming," upon her death in 1902. While stories have long persisted that in 1869, she invited influential Democrats and Republicans to a "tea party" at her home and wouldn't let them go until they'd pledged to vote for suffrage, that story is now in dispute. Some historians contend she had little, if anything, to do with the suffrage vote. But in 1870, she became the first woman in the nation to hold public office when she was appointed a judge. That same year, six Laramie women joined six men on a jury—the first women to ever serve on a jury in the nation. To this day Esther Hobart Morris is touted as the Mother of Wyoming Suffrage and in 1960, her statue was presented as Wyoming's representative in Statuary Hall in the Capitol Building in Washington, D.C.

On frontier newspaper philosophy: "Cattle Barons vs. Ink Slingers: The Decline and Fall of the Wyoming Stock Growers Association (1887-1894)"—a paper by Ross F. Collins, North Dakota State University, Fargo—notes: "Wyoming, more than any other state in the Old West era, was built and dominated by a single industry, cattle. Its association more than any other reserved power to enforce the law as it pertained to their business.

And their business was Wyoming's business." He also notes that in the heyday year of 1885—four years before the lynching—members of the association represented two million head of cattle worth $100 million. In the horrible winter of 1886, much of that was lost.

On Henderson: Stock detective George Henderson—a known murderer and enforcer for the stock growers—carried the news of the hanging to Cheyenne newspapers, as the papers themselves reported. How he did this or where he did it—at a home, in an office or at the Cheyenne Club—are the author's conjecture. In her book *The War on Powder River*, Smith reports: "So swiftly was the propaganda barrage laid down, within hours after Henderson reached Cheyenne, that the marks of advance planning are unmistakable....Everything in the stories, aside from their Cheyenne origin, stamps them as coming from a common source (a handout prepared by a party or parties who were interesting in stifling any questions concerning the Sweetwater murders): the similarity of tone, which was one of ranting diatribe, the repetition of details and even of identical phrases which were used over and over, and the misspelling of the name 'Averill,' a dead giveaway. All of this hints strongly of premeditation, involving how many individuals no one can say. It demolishes the convenient theory that a group of righteously outraged cattlemen, who had intended only to frighten the pair with threats, had somehow allowed the business to get out of hand and had hanged them by mistake, so to speak."

On "little Wall Street": The name appears in the papers of the Wyoming Stock Growers Association in the Archive of the American Heritage Center, University of Wyoming.

Chapter Sixteen—How to Stage a Hanging

On the spring roundup: Hufsmith notes that Bothwell, Sun and Durbin were the commissioners for the spring roundup of 1889 that began in mid-May and ended on July 20.

On "a thief or potential thief": This cattlemen's view of ranchers was well-known throughout the territory and variations on this theme are found in virtually every historical account of this case.

On the cattlemen's activities: Recounting of the morning's activities comes from multiple sources, including Hufsmith and Meschter. They note that Ernie McLean sobbed out the entire story the next morning to Charles Countryman, who owned the Bar H6 Ranch. Mrs. Countryman and her six children listened to the story, too. Hufsmith says Countryman ordered McLean off his property, saying he "didn't want to hear anything more about it."

On the ages of the lynchers: One of the mysteries of this story is how the youngest man in the mob was calling the shots, for indeed, Bothwell was far younger than the others. He was thirty-five, while Durbin was forty-seven, Sun was forty-five, Galbraith was forty-four, and Conner was forty. There is no biographical information on McLean. The day he died, Jim Averell was thirty-eight years old.

On Tom Sun: The Carbon County Museum in Rawlins includes recollections of pioneer families, including one attributed to the Harry L. Hays family. It says that at the time of the lynching, the oldest sons—Rob and Will—were riding for Bothwell. "They heard the cattlemen discussing the plans and knew that Tom Sun and one other rancher opposed the plans with vigor."

On Sam Johnson: He was the Durbin Precinct voting judge and foreman of the Bar II Ranch on Pete Creek. Historian Ruth Beebe shared with Hufsmith the story of him turning back when he found they were after Ella.

On the newspaper men knowing of the lynching: On November 2, 1889, the *Carbon County Journal* reported that Speer told the coroner that he and Fetz watched the entire thing. Furthermore, he admitted he told cowboys that afternoon that Jim and Ella had been lynched—because that's what he was told by the vigilantes before they left the newspaper office. "When pressed to tell where he got his information, [Speer] replied that there were some things connected with the case which he did not care to talk about," the paper reported. This information didn't emerge until it was too late—nobody realized these two men also were eyewitnesses to the abduction and well knew what the outcome would be.

Another eyewitness, although he never came forward at the time, Dan Fitger admitted to his family years later that he saw the abduction and lynching. Fitger, then a working cowboy, said he was plowing a hay meadow when he saw Tom Sun's white-topped tandem-seated buggy and watched all afternoon as the lynching party moved down the river bottom. He also watched Frank Buchanan skulking behind the caravan. This story came from his daughter, Helen, who shared it first with historian Ruth Beebe. Dan Fitger later became Natrone County assessor. "If this story is true, he could have changed history," Hufsmith notes.

On Buchanan: Frank Buchanan gave detailed interviews with the sheriff and newspapers on what happened that day. The death scene portrayed here follows his recollections. He reported Ella Watson laughing at her killers, "There's not enough water in this river to give a land hog a decent bath."

On Bothwell being sweet on Ella: Meschter notes an "elderly gentleman from the upper Platt River country" advanced this as a theory on the lynching. He says the man told him that Bothwell had proposed marriage to Ella and believed, "the hanging, then, was Bothwell's infantile reaction to destroy what he couldn't have and to erase the humiliation of rejection by someone clearly his inferior."

On Ralph Cole: At an inquest, Ralph Cole recounted how the boys ran in with news of the abduction and he ran to retrieve the horses left behind when Jim was kidnapped.

On the posse: All historical accounts note Deputy Sheriff Philip Watson deputized an acting coroner and brought the posse to the Sweetwater Valley. Historians differ if he took them out to the hanging site in the middle of the night, or if he waited for first light, but common sense says that after an exhausting day in the saddle, they waited.

On the inquest: A coroner's inquest was held after the burial, with eyewitness testimony given by Frank Buchanan, Gene Crowder, John DeCorey, and Ralph Cole. The coroner ruled that Ella and Jim had been hanged by the six men.

Chapter Seventeen—The Man with the Pen

On Ed Towse: Historians are united in their disgust at the stories written by this journalist, who had worked in Rawlins before he joined the *Leader* in Cheyenne. Some suggest he was on the payroll of the stock growers. His only real claim to fame is that he is the reporter who told the most fanciful lies about Ella Watson and James Averell.

On Ed Slack's article: This is quoted verbatim from the article printed in the *Cheyenne Daily Sun* of Tuesday, July 23, 1889.

On Ed Towse's original article: This is quoted verbatim from the article printed in the *Cheyenne Daily Leader*, July 23, 1889. In addition, the editor and part-owner of the *Leader*, John Carroll, offered an editorial the same day titled "Protecting Themselves." It read:

> "The lynching of a man and woman on the Sweetwater is but a natural outgrowth of the extraordinary conditions of affairs which have existed there and elsewhere in the territory for several years past. Notwithstanding that the large cattle companies contribute greatly to the taxable wealth of the various counties, that they add to the business of the counties by purchasing supplies and to its wealth by the sale of their cattle, things have come to such a pass that they cannot secure protection for their property.
>
> "In Rawlins recently several trials resulted in the most shameful travesty of justice. In Fremont County, out of sixteen cases, there was not a single conviction. In Johnson

County there were no convictions in forty cases and even in this county it has been up to the present almost impossible to secure the conviction of a single cattle thief. In many of those cases the evidence was overwhelming.

"The logical result of all this is that the cattlemen have been forced to organize for self protection. The rustlers and maverickers are carrying things with a high hand. Honest men are constantly in fear of their lives and are blind to much crookedness that is going on around them. Rewards aggregating $22,000 are offered by twenty-two different cattle companies for the arrest and conviction of anyone found altering the brands or killing their cattle. Nothing short of heroic treatment, however, seems to have any effect.

"Meanwhile everybody in the sections under the domination of the rustlers is going around armed to the teeth and red hot times may be expected at any moment."

On "The True Story": This is printed verbatim from the *Sun* on July 25, 1889, and comes from a telegram by rural newspaperman Bill Barlow, who is best remembered as the "sagebrush philosopher."

On Ella being a whore and Jim a pimp: Hufsmith says, "Not one shred of substantive evidence exists to show that those two settlers were anything but hard-working homesteaders, trying to eke out a living from a primitive and difficult environment. In fact, according to their neighbors and contemporaries, they were universally liked by nearly everyone who knew them, even including most of the valley cowmen, except Al Bothwell, of course, and his close friends whose free and legal use of rangeland Jim openly challenged."

Sharon Leigh wrote in "Ella Watson: Rustler or Homesteader," published in the *Annals of Wyoming* magazine: "On Wyoming's Sweetwater River in 1889, a homesteading woman and man were hanged by six cattlemen. She was reputed to be a prostitute, he supposedly her lover, and together they were considered cattle rustlers. In reality, they were merely homesteaders, legally settling on available government land which was open range claimed by one of the large cattlemen."

On the newspaper's smear campaign: The historical record is clear that *Sun* Editor Ed Slack mistakenly linked Ella Watson to someone called Cattle Kate. And then Ed Towse compounded the problem by giving her the mistaken identity of Kate Maxwell. Ella's father, Tom Watson, told the press that his daughter had spent June and July of 1888 in Kansas with her family, making it impossible for her to be the "Ellen Watson" who was arrested in Cheyenne for drunkenness and prostitution on June 23, 1888.

- Helena Huntington Smith decries the fanciful lies in *The War on Powder River*. She writes, "But while in the *Leader* and elsewhere she 'died with curses on her foul lips,' in the Chicago *Interocean* and *Omaha Bee* she remembered her mother and asked that her ill-gotten gains be used to found a home for wayward girls….Death itself offered no surcease for the poor wretch as the 'very best people' held a witches' sabbath over her remains and the press tore her to pieces in such an orgy of indecency and fakery as can seldom have been equaled even in the nineteenth century."

- Smith also notes that "The *Laramie Boomerang,* always cynical about the Cheyenne ring and all its works and ways, yawned mightily over the Cattle Kate yarn. 'Farewell, Cattle Queen Kate!' it perorated at the close of some editorial remarks, 'Thou didst never exist, but vale anyway.'"

- Smith on Averell writes, "If there is virtually no evidence to show that Averell was a thief, there is a formidable body of testimony to show that he quarreled with the biggest stockmen in the Sweetwater Valley, those accused in his lynching. Jack Flagg, who was well acquainted on the Sweetwater, wrote three years later: 'The reason for murdering him was the direct result of trouble he had with Bothwell over some fine meadow land that Bothwell was holding illegally…'"

- Smith on overall coverage of the story, claimed: "*The [New York] World* topped the record for silliness...with a remarkable editorial which proves that even as early as 1889 the myth of the pure cowboy who never kissed any-body but his horse had gained a firm foothold in the East. 'The cowboys of Wyoming did not like Kate Maxwell's style, so they lynched her...It wasn't a very gallant thing for "the boys" to do, but Kate's methods of getting cattle were not such as to popularize her on the plains. Her social life, too, was a trifle shady, and cowboys are particular.'"

- And it is Smith who is credited by other historians for "destroying" the myth that cattle thieves had free reign over W.T. and the courts looked the other way. "Statements regarding the number of acquittals in cattle-stealing cases were put out by the cattlemen's propaganda machine...with the most reckless defiance of truth," she wrote. Not only was this done with the Sweetwater lynching, but was repeated with vigor in 1892 in the most shameful and infamous moment of Wyoming history—the Johnson County War, when cattlemen imported Texan killers to wipe out homesteaders and destroy the town of Buffalo. Many believe Ella and Jim's murder planted the seed for that war, as cattlemen were emboldened by getting away with their murders. Smith notes the "machine" that claimed as many as four hundred thirty-five righteous rustler cases in Johnson County had resulted in no convictions, but she debunks that story by going to the county court record. In the ten years before the Johnson County War, "the total number of criminal cases in every category, including cattle-stealing, horse-stealing, assault, illegal cohabitation, fornication, murder and ordinary burglary, had barely passed the two hundred mark. So much for the tall tales."

- On August 16, 1889, the *Casper Weekly Mail* said on page one: "The victims of the late hanging party have not yet been proven to be thieves, but on the contrary, there is positive and convincing evidence that neither Averell or the woman ever stole or assisted in stealing any cattle."

On newspaper coverage in general: The Wyoming Newspaper Project is a computerized replication of newspapers in the territory, and is available online, so anyone can read all these stories as they were originally published.

On perpetrating the myth: For many years, the "authority" on the lynching was considered to be Alfred Mokler's 1923 book, *History of Natrona County Wyoming, 1888-1922*. But later texts found Mokler's version to parrot the Cheyenne newspaper view of things, and some historians took him on directly. Daniel Meschter is particularly perturbed by Mokler's "unreliable" reporting on this case, and takes several potshots at him in *Sweetwater Sunset*.

- Dozens of newspaper, magazine, and website articles also parrot the Cheyenne newspaper's views of the event.

- "Cattle Kate's Career: A Blaspheming Border Beauty Barbarously Boosted Branchward," was the headline in *The National Police Gazette* in New York on August 10, 1889.

- Currently on You Tube: "The Surprising Truth About Cattle Kate" by Dr. Franklin Ruehl. Although he has the wrong hanging date, his piece is close to accurate.

Chapter Eighteen—Pa Wept at Her Grave

On Pa Watson's activities: He had someone help him write a long letter about his trip to Wyoming, which was published in the *Lebanon, Kansas Criterion* on September 20, 1889. Part of his letter is quoted verbatim. He also told of going to Ella's home and the hanging site.

On the grave scene: Joe Sharp told his daughter, historian Ruth Beebe, that Ella's father cried at her gravesite, saying "I wish my little girl had listened to her mother. She told her not to leave home. If she had listened to her mother, she wouldn't be buried here today." Beebe shared the story with Hufsmith for his book on the lynching.

On Gene being fed to wolves: Hufsmith reports this horrible rumor comes from the journals of W.R. Hunt, a former reporter for the *Chicago Inter Ocean* who quit his job over this lynching. Hunt said he fought his editor over publishing the unsubstantiated stories from Ed Towse, believing Towse was "acting as the official writer—in pay of the Wyoming Stock Growers Association." Hunt came to Wyoming Territory on his own, finding "the people are reluctant to talk, seemed frightened." He found Buchanan, who was hiding out, discovering the man was waiting to testify and "whittles nearly all the time." His journal notes that on August 12, 1889, Hunt was in Rawlins. "This town, mostly favorable to Jim Averell and Ella Watson, abounds with bitterness about their fate….both are remembered fondly, even idealized, they have become martyrs of a sort to a cause of conflict brewing in the territory between big-time stockmen and homesteaders…."

On Ella's estate: Handwritten court records show the editors of the *Sweetwater Chief* went on a spending spree at her estate sale and their purchases are accurately reflected in the book.

On Jim's estate: Court records show the sale of Jim's estate included $18.50 for twelve chickens, nine ducks, three sacks of dried fruit, two saws, and one shovel plow.

On the Watson family being threatened: This was the conclusion of Ella's great-nephew Daniel Brumbaugh. He told the author that when he discovered his tie to "Cattle Kate," his cousins told him the family was ashamed that Ella Watson had become a bad woman. But as he researched, he found this conclusion impossible to believe, since the evidence kept growing that she wasn't any of the things the Cheyenne papers claimed. Considering how viciously the cattlemen slandered Ella, Brumbaugh believed they had threatened Tom Watson, and that accounted for his instructions to never speak of Ella.

Chapter Nineteen—A Man with Guts

On Durant's lawsuit: The records of this suit are contained in large, leather embossed books at the Carbon County Courthouse. Most writers have said the suit just disappeared, but this author found the entire record during a research trip to Wyoming in August, 2009. Durant was the coroner of Carbon County and his legal activities—from settling Ella and Jim's estates to the lawsuit—are recounted from the public record.

On John Lacey: The defense attorney for Bothwell and Durbin had been a justice of the territorial supreme court. His law partners included W.W. Corlett of Cheyenne, who had been a territorial delegate to Congress, and John A. Riner, a United States judge for Wyoming, according to "In Old Wyoming," a popular column by John C. Thompson, in the *Laramie State Journal* in the 1950s.

On the safe deposit box: There is no evidence that Ella Watson ever owned a safe deposit box, and her plea that she did could have been a ploy to get her kidnappers to take her to town, where she could get help. But the sale of the cows was witnessed by at least two people, so what became of the bill of sale is a mystery. If she had a safe deposit box in the Rawlins bank, nobody ever came forward to reveal that information.

On the men going free: Judge Samuel T. Corn presided over the grand jury hearings on October 14, 1889. Lacking any eyewitness testimony, and with the accused now claiming they were innocent, the grand jury could not issue a "true bill" that would have sent the men to trial. All five in attendance—Ernie McLean had long ago disappeared—walked out of the courtroom as free men.

Chapter Twenty—And in the End

On the lynchers: The summary of their lives comes from several sources, including Hufsmith and Mescher.

On Ernie McLean: Meschter found a pay ledger from the Durbin Land and Cattle Company showing John Durbin bought Ernie McLean a twenty-nine-dollar railroad ticket on July 21, 1889, and paid him two hundred forty dollars in advanced wages—"obviously a kind of severance pay to tide McLean over to his next job and to keep him out of Wyoming," says Meschter.

On Bothwell's lack of remorse: In a 1943 article for *Annals of Wyoming* magazine, A.C. Campbell wrote: "I knew all the lynchers. I was quite intimate with the leader during the later years of his life. If he had any regret for that atrocious deed or any remorse, he successful concealed the same."

On the Rawlins mural: The Rawlins Main Street Mural Project is a downtown educational walking tour of twelve murals highlighting the history and natural beauty of south central Wyoming. A brochure on the exhibit identifies Mural No. 8 as Cattle Kate. The brochure notes: "This surreal representation of the controversial Cattle Kate was painted by Dianne Johansson. Ella Watson, also known as Cattle Kate, and her husband, Jim Averell, were lynched on July 20, 1889. The left panel of the mural shows a map with significant places and events in their lives marked. Look carefully at the tree on the seam of the left panel to read more information about their story. The right panel portrays four of the men involved. In the center, Cattle Kate looks down from the rocks viewing the place of her death."

The mural itself, as viewed by the author, says Ella and Jim were "hanged by greedy land barons." It focuses its wrath on McLean, Durbin, Bothwell, and Conner, while exonerating Tom Sun, saying he "was against the affair." The handwritten story on the mural says "Ellen and Jim were married to each other, and their friends and neighbors mourned the tragic murder. Ellen and Jim fed the hungry, clothed the naked and took anyone in."

On the Johnson County War: It is almost impossible today to believe what cattlemen did in 1892 in the new State of Wyoming. Claiming widespread rustling, they imported hired Texas gunmen to kill homesteaders and wipe out the town of Buffalo. Worse yet, they were supported by the governor, their congressmen, and President Benjamin Harrison, to the horror of both citizens and history. *The War on Powder River* by Helena Huntington Smith, is just one of the dozens of excellent books that spell out this historical atrocity.

On the continuing legend of "Cattle Kate":

- "This Day in History, July 20, 1889" on www.History.com calls Ella a "former prostitute from Kansas" and Jim a "saloonkeeper." It describes Bothwell as "one of the most arrogant cattlemen in the region."

- In *Saga* magazine, November 1956, Jules Archer writes: "Kate was a blonde bombshell who could outcurse, outdrink and outfight any cowhand in the Sweetwater Valley, but she learned the hard way that sex and rustling don't mix."

- *Kansas Magazine* published E.B. Dykes Beachy's article "The Saga of Cattle Kate" in 1961. It says, "She was interested only in money, clothes, and a silver-tongued cattle rustler with whom she danced an airy jig."

- The 1965 poem "Cattle Kate" by Lillian T. Rendle, included these stanzas:

  "A devil in the saddle, she was handy with a gun.
  An expert with a branding iron, to the cowpoke she was fun!
  Jim set her up in business, he built a big corral. Where the cowpokes drove the mavericks, in pay for their low morale.
  Ella's place was called the hog ranch, by the cowmen of the State;

But the folks of ole Sweetwater had dubbed her Cattle Kate!"

- Movies about Cattle Kate include: *The Redhead from Wyoming*, with Maureen O'Hara, 1955; *Heaven's Gate* with Kris Kristofferson and Isabelle Huppert, 1982; and the 2001 Hallmark television movie *Johnson County War* with Tom Berrenger and Rachel Ward as "Queenie."

- *Stories of Century*, a 1950s syndicated television series, produced a most fanciful segment on Cattle Kate. "She and her partner in crime kept one of the last western frontiers in a state of terror." The piece claims she ordered the murder of a stock detective and controlled enormous herds. It says she was arrested and "delivered safely to jail," but a lynch mob broke her out and hanged her by slapping her horse out from under her. The segment is available on You Tube.

On uncovering the truth: Not until Dorothy Gray's 1976 *Women of the West*, was there a real attempt to correct the legend. Gray quotes an unnamed source (which was Wyoming Historian and State Librarian Agnes Wright Spring) calling Ella's hanging "the most revolting crime in the entire annals of the West." Gray went on: "No sooner was Ella Watson dead than the stockmen started a press campaign in which she was transformed into 'Cattle Kate,' characterized as having not only rustled more cattle than any man in the West but as having been a prostitute, husband-poisoner, and hold-up artist." But she goes on, recounting the hanging three years earlier of a woman named Elizabeth Taylor in Nebraska—she and her brother were hanged for supposedly killing a neighbor. Gray notes: "Like Ella Watson, without substantiation Elizabeth Taylor was subsequently accused of having poisoned her deceased husband and also of having paid off her ranch hands by 'entertaining' them. The technique of painting a woman as husband-killer and whore seemed to be a necessary ingredient in salving the image if not the conscience of men who committed the crime of lynching a woman."

- It was George W. Hufsmith who set everyone on their ear when his *The Wyoming Lynching of Cattle Kate 1889* was published in 1993. Hufsmith was a composer from Jackson, who was commissioned to write a musical for the nation's bicentennial. He chose the lynching of Cattle Kate as his subject. But as he researched, he found more and more questions. After finishing the opera, he spent the next twenty years researching the real story for his definitive book. He noted, "This story is so controversial that for over 100 years, it was a mistake to even ask what happened that hot July afternoon in 1889 when a gracious young woman and an innocent homesteader were hanged from a pine tree in the Sweetwater Valley."

- Daniel Y. Meschter also spent a lifetime on this story for his 1966 and 2005 book *Sweetwater Sunset*. After twenty-five years of research, he compiled an amazing array of original documents, many of which he reprints in their entirety. Among his conclusions: "Jim's and Ella's homesteads were unacceptable obstacles to the Bothwell Townsite promotion, and Jim's letter exposing it was a threat which the independent *Casper Weekly Mail* very well might use to warn away credulous investors."

- "This is not a story about cattle rustling, it's about who controls the land and water," Wyoming historian Tom Rea said in a lecture the author attended in Casper on August 29, 2009. "It's pretty hard not to conclude Ella and Jim were in the way—their neighbors wanted them gone and they wanted their land." His lecture was titled "Ella Watson's Fence: The Story behind the Lynching of Cattle Kate."

- "The bodies hung about thirty-six hours…." writes Tom Rea as he concludes his discussion of Cattle Kate in *Devil's Gate*. "But even though they were out of sight of the river and the road, even though the posse had to scramble and climb to find them, they hung long enough to make their point. And they hang there still, in the memory of the valley and the state, as a reminder of who was in charge, who owned what, and the lengths that power will go, to get its story told the way it chooses."

On the memorial erected on the hundredth anniversary: Ella's descendants honored her, according to news reports in the *Casper Journal,* published July 15 and October 7, 1989. The July 15 article by Jamie Ring noted the marker was made by Tim Monroe of the Bureau of Land Management, and the grave dedication was to be done by Reverend Ralph Nelson. The story concluded: "On this day, 100 years after the cold-blooded act of murder, it is fitting that the records will be corrected to reflect the truth."

Interesting footnotes: Owen Wister, the author of *The Virginian,* weighed in on the controversy in his diary entry for October 12, 1889: "Sat yesterday in smoking car with one of the gentlemen indicted for lynching the man and woman. He seemed a good solid citizen and I hope he'll get off. Sheriff Donell said, 'All the good folks say it was a good job; it's only the wayward classes that complain.'" Wister referred to the cattle barons as "the better classes." This was reported in many examinations of this case, including Hufsmith's and Smith's.

- "She had to be killed for the good of the country," was the excuse for the hangings by Dr. Charles Penrose, a surgeon who became part of the Johnson County War excursion, in his 1914 book, *The Rustler Business.* Historians say this was a prevailing attitude throughout the cattle industry in Wyoming Territory at the time.

- Former U.S. Senator Joseph C. O'Mahoney, a Democrat from Wyoming, in private correspondence to an author researching the lynching in the early sixties, wrote:"While at Lander, in the spring of 1921, I heard several old timers recount the hanging. The consensus was that it was a 'spite' hanging on the part of the cattlemen to gain control of more range, that the 'cattle theft' part was later to vindicate themselves, and to rationalize the matter....I believe the Averill's [sic] could be completely vindicated if a writer could completely research this matter." O'Mahoney also suggested the author might want to entitle his article: "The Homesteaders' Heroine, Cattle Kate, and the Land Grabbers in the West." The correspondence is in the William R. Kelly Collection at the American Heritage Center at the University of Wyoming in Laramie.

• In the Wyoming Bicentennial Commission publication of 1976, author Charles "Pat" Hall writes: "The most notorious example of 'justice' on the western frontier was the lynching of James Averell and a female companion by Wyoming cattlemen in 1889. Averell's so-called paramour—known variously as Cattle Kate, Kate Maxwell and Ella Watson—has never been fully identified."

Bibliography

Alderson, Nannie T. and Smith, Helena Huntington. *A Bride Goes West*. University of Nebraska Press, 1942.

Arnold, Oren, and Hale, John P. "Levi's Stories of Western Brands and What They Mean." Levi Strauss & Co. pamphlet. Text suggests 1950s.

Beachy, E. B. Dykes. "The Sage of Cattle Kate." *Kansas Magazine*, 1961.

Beebe, Ruth. *Reminiscing Along the Sweetwater*. Johnson Publishing, 1973.

Bloomingdale Brothers. "Bloomingdale's Illustrated 1886 Catalog: Fashions, Dry Goods and Housewares." Reproduced by Dover Publications, 1988.

Bommersbach, Jana. "So-called Cattle Kate Rises from Rubbish." *True West* magazine, *Women of the West* series. July, 2005.

Brown, Wynne. *More than Petticoats: Remarkable Arizona Women*. The Globe Pequot Press, 2003.

Brumbaugh, Daniel (Watson). "My Great Aunt's Lynching." A series of website reports reflecting his twenty years of research.

Campbell. A.C. "Fading Memories." *Annals of Wyoming* magazine. January, 1943.

Carbon County Museum. "The Legend of Big Nose George." Pamphlet.

Carley, Kenneth. *The Dakota War of 1862. Minnesota's Other Civil War.* Minnesota Historical Society Press, 1961, 1976.

Caughfield, Adrienne. *True Women & Westward Expansion.* Texas A&M University Press, 2005.

Clary, David A. "The Place Where Hell Bubbled Up." National Park Service Office of Publication, 1972.

Collins, Ross F. "Cattle Barons and Ink Slingers: How Cow Country Journalists Created a Great American Myth." *American Journalism 24.* 2007.

Emrich, Duncan. *The Cowboy's Own Brand Book.* Thomas Y. Crowell Co., New York, 1954.

Fuller, Margaret. *Women in the Nineteenth Century.* Originally published in 1855 by John P. Jewett & Co., this version is a 1971 reprint by W.W. Norton & Co.

Grace, Rod. *The Old West Quiz & Fact Book.* Harper & Row, 1986.

Gray, Dorothy. *Women of the West.* University of Nebraska Press, 1976.

Hall, Charles "Pat." "Wyoming Bicentennial Commission Publication." Limited edition of 1,000, 1976.

Hebard, Grace Raymond. *Washakie: Chief of the Shoshones.* University of Nebraska Press, 1995.

Hensley, Marcia Meredith. *Staking Her Claim: Women Homesteading the West.* High Plains Press, 2008.

Hufsmith, George W. *The Wyoming Lynching of Cattle Kate, 1889.* High Plains Press, 1993.

Joy, Betty E. Hammer. *Angela Hutchinson Hammer, Arizona's Pioneer Newspaperwoman.* University of Arizona Press, 2005.

Junge, Mark. *The Wind is My Witness: A Wyoming Album.* Roberts Rinehart, Pub., 1997.

Kelly, William R. "Homesteading. Ella Watson's (Cattle Kate) Capital Crime." *The Denver Westerners Monthly Roundup.* May, 1963.

Kahn, Yasmin Sabina. *Enlightening the World: The Creation of the Statue of Liberty.* Cornell University Press, 2010.

Leigh, Sharon. "Ella Watson, Rustler or Homesteader?" *Annals of Wyoming* magazine, Summer/Fall, 1992.

Luchetti, Cathy, in collaboration with Olwell, Carol. "Women of the West." W.W. Norton & Co., 1982.

McCutcheon, Marc. *The Writer's Guide to Everyday Life in the 1800s.* Writer's Digest Books, an imprint of F&W Publications, 1993.

Mercer, A.S. *The Banditti of the Plains, or The Cattlemen's Invasion of Wyoming in 1892.* Originally printed by author in Cheyenne in 1894; republished by University of Oklahoma Press, 1954.

Meschter, Daniel Y. *Sweetwater Sunset: A history of the lynching of JAMES AVERELL AND ELLA WATSON near Independence Rock, Wyoming on July 20, 1889.* Self-published from Albuquerque, New Mexico, 1966 and 2005.

Mokler, Alfred James. *History of Natrona County Wyoming, 1888-1922.* The Lakeside Press, 1923.

Moore, Frank. *Souls and Saddlebags: The Diaries and Correspondence of Frank Moore, Western Missionary, 1888-1896.* Big Mountain Press, 1962.

Myres, Sandra L. *Westering Women and the Frontier Experience 1800-1915*. University of New Mexico Press, 1982.

Niethammer, Carolyn. *Daughter of the Earth: The Lives and Legends of American Indian Women*. Simon & Schuster, 1977.

O'Neal, Bill. *The Johnson County War*. Eakin Press, 2004.

Old West Series of Time-Life Books, published in 1970s.

Owen, W.O. "Billy." Unpublished autobiography; typed eighty-four-page transcript. W. O. Owen Papers, Collection No. 94, Box 1, Folders 2 through 6, American Heritage Center, University of Wyoming. Undated, written about 1930.

Peavy, Linda, and Smith, Ursula. *Women in Waiting in the Westward Movement: Life on the Home Frontier*. University of Oklahoma Press, 1994.

Peavy, Linda and Smith, Ursula. *Frontier Women*. Barnes & Noble Books, 1996.

Peavy, Linda and Smith, Ursula. *Pioneer Women: The Lives of Women on the Frontier*. University of Oklahoma Press, 1996.

Pender, Rose. *A Lady's Experiences in the Wild West in 1883*. University of Nebraska Press, 1978.

Penrose, Charles B. *The Rustler Business. Douglas Budget*, Douglas, Wyoming, 1914 and later editions.

Ptacek, Kathryn, editor. *Women of the West: Short Stories by Contemporary Women Writers*, Doubleday, 1990.

Raison, Milton. "Stories of the Century," a film series. YouTube.

Ray, Grace Ernestine. *Wily Women of the West*. The Naylor Company, 1972.

Rea, Tom. *Devil's Gate: Owning The Land, Owning The Story*. University of Oklahoma Press, 2006.

Riley, Glenda and Etulain, Richard W., editors. *Wild Women of the Old West*. Fulcrum Publishing, 2003.

Robb, Gladys L., editor. "Cherished Memories: Dedicated to the memory of the stalwart pioneer men and women who brought civilization to the New World." Iowa Federation of Women's Clubs, 1992.

Ross, Nancy Wilson. *Westward the Woman*. North Point Press, San Francisco. Many reprints, first published 1944.

Rothschild, Mary Logan and Hronek, Pamela Claire. *Doing What the Day Brought: An Oral History of Arizona Women*. University of Arizona Press, 1992.

Rounds, Glen. *Sod Houses on the Great Plains*. Holiday House, 1995.

Ruehl, Dr. Franklin. "The Surprising Truth About Cattle Kate." YouTube.

Russell, Mary Doria. *Doc*. Ballantine Books, 2012.

Schoenberger, Dale T. "Notorious 'Cattle Kate' Not a Rustler. Wild Stories Spread to Excuse A Lynching." *The National Tombstone Epitaph*, October, 1990.

Seagraves, Anne. *Soiled Doves: Prostitution in the Early West*. Wesanne Publications, 1994.

Sears Roebuck & Co. Catalog, 1897, reproduction by Skyhorse Publishing, 2007.

Shirley, Gayle C. *More than Petticoats: Remarkable Montana Women*. The Globe Pequot Press, 1995.

Shirley, Gayle C. *More than Petticoats: Remarkable Colorado Women*. Morris Book Publishing, 2002.

Simar, Candace. *Abercrombie Trail*. North Star Press, 2009.

Smiley, Jane. *The All-True Travels and Adventures of Lidie Newton.* Alfred A. Knopf, 1998.

Smith, Helena Huntington. *The War on Powder River.* McGraw Hill Book Company, 1966.

Stratton, Joanna L. *Pioneer Women, Voices from the Kansas Frontier.* Simon & Schuster, 1981.

The Century Illustrated Monthly Magazine. Published in New York, March, 1885.

"This Day in History." www.History.com.

Thompson, John C. "In Old Wyoming." Newspaper column in the *Laramie State Journal,* 1950s.

True West magazine Editors. *True Tales and Amazing Legends of the Old West.* Clarkson Potter Publishers, 2005.

VanderMeer, E. Gretchen, editor. *Potpourri of Yesteryear: Old Recipes, Cures, Remedies and Little Known Hints.* Cambray Enterprises, 1974.

Ward, Geoffrey C. *The West.* Little Brown, 1996.

Whittenburg, Clarice. "A Backward Look at Early Branding Days." Original manuscript, no date or publication information.

To receive a free catalog of Poisoned Pen Press titles, please contact us in one of the following ways:

Phone: 1-800-421-3976
Facsimile: 1-480-949-1707
Email: info@poisonedpenpress.com
Website: www.poisonedpenpress.com

Poisoned Pen Press
6962 E. First Ave. Ste 103
Scottsdale, AZ 85251

To contact Jana Bommersbach, visit her website:
www.janabommersbach.com